To Barbo
A new fri
sister.

THE TRUTH SEEKERS, SECOND EDITION

R Glenn Brown

To Him who is Truth personified and to all Truth seekers.

CONTENTS

ACKNOWLEDGMENTS

I have written four non-fiction books, three of which have been published, and one should be published later in 2014. This is my first venture into fiction. It has been quite an adventure in an untried genre. I got a few ideas from three books I have in my limited library, all approximately thirty years old. Consequently, I owe a note of thanks to the respective authors, Claire Cook, Ethel Herr, and Janet Burroway. I hope you are still among the living after three decades and that you may note my appreciation. I'm a slow learner, so if I failed to practice what you preached, it is not your fault. Sometimes I even fail to practice what I preach.

Closer to home, to Sandy Frykholm, an author herself who read my manuscript and offered suggestions that helped significantly, I give sincere thanks. Also, I received and incorporated helpful suggestions from Daniel George and Emily Cotton, two author friends.

Since this novel is dealing with important theological issues, I deeply sensed the need for prayer support. Thanks to family members and friends across the nation who were praying. I particularly was buoyed by prayers from members of Dungeness Community Church where Donna and I attend. The Wordsmiths were especially faithful in undergirding me with regular prayer.

I want to thank the historic Pentecostal Vashchenko family, who are characters in this novel, for daring to challenge the communist tyranny in the USSR. They actually invaded the American embassy in Moscow in 1978 to find asylum from religious persecution. They were afforded refuge in the American embassy for five years until the USSR government finally gave approval for them to emigrate in 1983. I imaginatively describe some of what took place in connection with this embassy episode, but, except for excerpts from news articles, it is all a fictional account.

After the Vashchenkos emigrated in 1983, many settled in Washington State. Pyotr, the father, died years ago, but Augustina, the mother, is still living near Seattle, about two hours from Sequim. I have visited her and Vera, the daughter that cares for her. I told them about the novel I was writing and gave them the portion of the manuscript that contained the pertinent material relating to their family. I asked them to read the material, and if not pleased with my fictional account, to please call me. They apparently were happy with my account, as they should be. I depict them as the courageous heroes they were.

INTRODUCTORY MATERIAL

Major Characters

1. Viktor Gorgachuk: Russian immigrant pastor of Christians Together
2. Bill Ballard: Pastor of Sundale Community Church
3. Vasil Gorgachuk: Father of Viktor
4. Natasha Gorgachuk: Mother of Viktor
5. Pyotr Vashchenko: Father of twelve, leader of Siberian Seven
6. Augustina Vashchenko: Mother of twelve, wife of Pyotr, one of Siberian Seven
7. Professor Phillip King: Princeton Seminary professor, mentor of Viktor
8. George and Kathleen McGinnis: Sponsors of Viktor
9. Anna Melnik Gorgachuk: Minister of prayer, Viktor's wife

10. Jennifer Ballard: Bill's wife and close friend of Anna
11. Alexander: KGB agent who captured Vasil and Natasha
12. Vitali: KGB agent and partner of Alexander
13. Lida Vashchenko: Third daughter, one of Siberian Seven, fasted dangerously long

Some Minor Characters

1. Lila Vashchenko: Daughter of Pyotr and Natasha, one of Siberian Seven
2. Luba Vashchenko: Daughter of Pyotr and Natasha, one of Siberian Seven
3. Ambassador Malcolm Toon: American ambassador in Moscow
4. Gunnery Sgt. James Stevens: Commander of embassy marine guards
5. Vadim: Christian boss of Vasil at mine in Chernogorsk
6. Maria Chmykhalov: Pentecostal believer who was part of Siberian Seven
7. Vladymir Rasputin: KGB boss of Alexander and Vitali
8. Ivan Vostruk: Associate pastor of Christians Together trained by Viktor
9. Josef Kovarde: Associate pastor of Christians Together trained by Viktor
10. Vera Kovarde: Viktor's executive secretary and Josef's wife
11. Irina Vostruk: Church secretary and Ivan's wife
12. Andrew Melnik: Anna's son
13. Shana Melnik: Anna's daughter
14. Rabbi Cohen: Helped Viktor escape USSR

15. Josef: USSR official, secret Christian who helps Viktor escape USSR

Novel Theme

Pontius Pilate, in his arrogant, cynical, self-serving way, asked the question that has plagued humanity down through the ages, "What is truth?" That is the theme of this story told through the experience of two divergent pastors. Each is seeking an answer to Pilate's query as it relates to two Christian doctrines that are perversely opposed. Each is a devout follower of Jesus Christ, but each has a perspective that prevents them from having the unity they both desire. They honestly confess their differences and pledge to search scripture for reconciling truth. Somewhere along the way, you may find yourself intersecting one of these characters—if you dare pursue truth. Be forewarned: it is dangerous to pursue truth and follow where it leads. It may turn your world upside down, but it is wondrously liberating. Are you willing to take the risk?

Setting

Most of early chapters are set in Russia in the 1970s and early 1980s during the USSR regime. Later chapters are in the United States, primarily in one of the growing suburbs of Sacramento, California. They do things big in California. There are over five hundred churches in Sacramento and environs, from small missions to huge church complexes with congregations numbering in the thousands. Two pastors in this conglomerate are the primary characters, William (Bill) Ballard and Viktor Gorgachuk.

CHAPTER 1

THE GORGACHUKS

Viktor Gorgachuk was the son of Vasil and Natasha Gorgachuk, devout Russian Orthodox believers, from Leningrad. Most of their lives as young adults had been lived under the despotic rule of Nikita Khrushchev. One of Khrushchev's goals was to eliminate Christian believers from the USSR. His chief weapon was fear of death or torture or imprisonment if Christians did not submit to the demands of the atheistic, communist government. Many Orthodox leaders became minions of the KGB and were not trusted by true believers like Viktor's parents.

When his parents got married in 1963 they decided they would have no children. They did not want a child of theirs subjected to the brainwashing and ridicule that was the common lot of children of believers, particularly in the public school system. When Khrushchev was deposed in 1964, and Leonid Brezhnev succeeded him, his parents hoped that conditions might improve. They decided to risk having a child and Viktor was the result.

Conditions did improve somewhat. Since the number of devout believers did not decrease under Khrushchev's brutality, Brezhnev decided to take a different approach but a more insidious one. He determined to use the school system to influence children to reject religion, particularly Christianity. During Natasha's pregnancy Brezhnev announced his plan and began to flood the schools, from pre-school to university level, with attractive anti-religion and pro-atheism literature of all sorts and for all age groups. Therefore, before Viktor was born his parents decided try to keep his birth hidden from the government so he wouldn't be forced into the communist school system.

The mid-wife that assisted Natasha in Viktor's delivery was bribed to not report it. She promised to keep his birth secret and did. . . for twelve years. Her failure to keep her word led to the eventual discovery of Viktor's existence and tragic consequences for the Gorgachuk family.

Viktor was born on July 4, 1966 in a little cottage located on the outskirts of Leningrad. He had no friends to play with because his parents were very serious about keeping his existence a secret. The small back yard behind the cottage was enclosed in a high stone wall so no one inside could be seen.

Viktor was a particularly precocious child. When he was three years old his parents gave him a special edition of the New Testament written in Russian but with the English translation on the facing page. He had learned to read his native language several weeks previously. He didn't know it was highly unusual for a child to learn to read at such an early age since he had no one with which to compare himself. He supposed all children could read before they were three years old.

Not only was he able to read at an unusually early age but he had a prodigious memory. He could recall long biblical passages after having read them the day before. This gift of a photographic memory enabled him to develop a sizeable English vocabulary. Although he was totally unaware of his unusual giftedness, his parents fully recognized it. They knew that if his identity were discovered he would be forced to attend a state sponsored school which would be flooded with anti-Christian and pro-atheism literature of all sorts and for all age groups. The atheistic government would use his intellect for its own purposes. They were determined to prevent that.

In 1970 when Viktor was four years old Vasil and Natasha Gorgachuk accepted the offer of a monastic relative to shelter their son in his isolated monastery where learned monks could educate him.. He had already conquered the Cyrillic alphabet and learned to read and write Russian before coming to the monastery. One of the scholarly monks began to tutor him in the original biblical languages of Hebrew and Koine Greek. By the time he was ten years old, he was sight reading the ancient Greek and Hebrew manuscripts. Another monk took him under his wing and schooled him in Latin. Before long, he was reading the early church fathers in both Greek and Latin. Another monk taught him principles of mathematics. By the time he left the monastery in 1978, he had also learned English and Ukrainian. He essentially had the equivalent of advanced degrees in five languages plus theoretical mathematics at scarcely twelve years old.

CHAPTER 2
A TRUST RELATIONSHIP
FORMED

When Viktor returned home after eight years, his parents recognized they had a child prodigy in their care. How to further his education without arousing suspicion from the authorities was a troubling challenge. To get further away from the central government, his parents decided to move to Siberia. They didn't trust the Orthodox hierarchy since the patriarchate of Moscow had compromised his office with the KGB.

They traveled over three thousand kilometers east from Moscow all the way to Chernogorsk in south central Siberia in the republic of Khakassia. Vasil was able to find employment as a bookkeeper in the strip-mining coal industry. He soon became friends with another employee of the mine, a heavy-machine operator named Pyotr Vashchenko. In the course of several months, Natasha, Vasil's wife, and Augustina, Pyotr's wife, also became friends, and the families began socializing regularly. The Vashchenkos had twelve children, six girls and six boys, including a son near Viktor's age. Viktor was the Gorgachuks' only child.

As the Gorgachuks and Vashchenkos became better acquainted, they began to become more open and trusting. One evening, Vasil and Natasha were invited to the Vashchenkos to "get to know each other better, heart to heart." Pyotr revealed that he was a member of a religious group that was on the government's hit list. He was a non-registered Pentecostal, which meant that he had refused to join the government's approved All-Union Council of Evangelical Christians-Baptists. The Soviets had assigned registered Pentecostals and Baptists to the same administrative organization. Those registered received concessions that the unregistered were refused.

Pyotr explained: "For conscience sake I refused to register because I did not want to be officially associated with an atheistic government. It cost me dearly. I was sentenced to prison for two years doing forced labor. My children were taunted and ridiculed in school. Even the teachers mocked them and gave them lower grades though their work was superior. When I was released from labor camp, I applied for permission to immigrate to America. I knew I must get my family out of this godless land.

"I was arrested and sentenced to serve time in a psychiatric hospital. When I asked the attending doctor what my diagnosis was, he replied, 'Anyone who requests to leave the Soviet Union must be insane.' I was released from the hospital and then sentenced to another year in the labor camp. Those were difficult days for me and my family." Pyotr spoke slowly, pausing to gain control of his emotions.

Vasil and Natasha listened attentively. When Pyotr continued to pause, Vasil spoke up. "I know you and your family have endured outrageous abuse and maltreatment because of your religious convictions. However, Pentecostals are not the only ones who have been persecuted. Under Stalin, tens of thousands of Orthodox priests were murdered or sentenced to slave labor camps. Those that remained were intimidated, and many became agents of the NKVD and later the KGB. Stalin eased his persecution during WWII and revived the structure of the Orthodox Church to gain patriotic support for the war effort. He then presented Russia to the West as the defender of Christian civilization in order to gain support from western nations.

"This relaxation of terror continued for fourteen years after the war's end. I know thousands of churches were reopened in Russia during this period. However, this does not mean the war against Christianity was relaxed. It had only entered a different phase, targeting the mind instead of the body. Schools were ordered to intensify their efforts to instill atheism in the mind of every student. The public education system was ordered to reactivate atheistic propaganda at every level."

As Vasil paused for a moment, Pyotr said, "Vasil, why do you think our government is so determined to eliminate religion from our national life? What are the authorities afraid of?"

"Truth, Pyotr. They are afraid of truth. They deny God because they want the state to be supreme and all-powerful. It's ancient Rome all over again. Caesar is lord and is determined to destroy any competitor. This battle between would-be gods and the true and living God has gone on throughout human history. We are the heirs of ancient martyrs portrayed in the last portion of the holy apostolic letter to the Hebrews. I read it often, Pyotr, and it has become inscribed firmly in my memory. Listen. *Some were tortured and refused to be released, so that they may gain a better resurrection. Some faced jeers and flogging, while still others were chained and put in prison. They were stoned; they were sawed in two; they were put to death by the sword.* Is this not a description of our existence? Why do we endure the government's opposition? Why do we not surrender our faith and deny the reality of a living God? Answer me that, Pyotr."

"I can only answer for myself, Vasil, and I will in due course. However, I think it is time to bring our wives into our conversation. I want Augustina to reply to your question. She has a more difficult role to play than even I in our struggle against a godless government."

Augustina, a full-figured brunette with streaks of gray, retained vestiges of the physical charm that had attracted Pyotr. Running a household of twelve children had clothed her with a mantle of gentle authority. She smiled and then began to speak.

"I will share some of our journey, but Pyotr must help me. I was once part of the communist conspiracy to eliminate God from Soviet society and culture. I thought it exciting to be involved in a bold venture to build a classless society by human effort with no religious restrictions to hinder us. To have no God to which I must answer emboldened me to engage in a pleasure-seeking lifestyle, which I am now ashamed to describe. I joined several atheistic organizations dedicated to advancing our godless goals.

"Our world was hemmed in and defined by materialism. Human beings were a chance product of unknown materialistic forces and had no destiny beyond death. Any value for one's brief existence could only be determined by the yardstick of humanistic materialism. There was never an objective yardstick for 'value,' but it was always controlled by the subjective whim of those in power.

"I became disillusioned and recognized that I was now part of a system that cared nothing for me as an individual. I had value only if I contributed to the goals determined by those in authority. The idealism of my youth was being destroyed by the injustice, corruption, and depravity of communism. I began to question my commitment to a society that renounced God. What if there actually was a God to whom I must give an account?

"It was at this point in my life that I met Pyotr. He was a handsome young guy that seemed to have a mind of his own. We worked in the same factory, so I arranged with a friend to 'accidentally' sit near him during our lunch break. My friend introduced us, and we began meeting for lunch regularly. He recognized my turmoil and said something that surprised and confused me. Do you remember what you said, Pyotr?"

Pyotr nodded. "Yes, indeed I do. I said, 'Augustina, that's the Holy Spirit troubling your conscience.' And I remember you stared at me with eyes as big as saucers and whispered, 'Pyotr, what's the Holy Spirit?' Now, go on with your story."

"That day, Pyotr acknowledged that he was a Christian. I was intrigued but also frightened. He shared how his father had become a Christian during WWI and then led all his family to believe in Jesus Christ. He read from the gospel of John what Jesus said to his disciples about the Holy Spirit. I have long since memorized those verses. What a shock it must have been to his disciples to hear Jesus say he must leave them and return to heaven.

"Jesus understood their confusion and dismay. He said, *'Because I have said these things, you are filled with grief. But I tell you the truth: It is for your good that I am going away. Unless I go away, the Counselor will not come to you: but if I go, I will send him to you. When he comes, he will prove the world wrong about sin and righteousness and judgment.'* Pyotr explained that it was the Holy Spirit making me aware of my sin that caused me to feel empty inside. He also said it was the Holy Spirit that was challenging me to begin a new life of righteousness. And the terrifying portion that I had been trying to avoid was the part about judgment. He insisted it was the Holy Spirit that reminded me I would be judged as to whether I chose sin or righteousness. He urged me to repent of my sin and receive righteousness as a gift from God. But I wasn't ready to make such a decision yet.

"To complicate matters, we had fallen in love. I wanted to get married, but Pyotr said the Bible told believers not to marry unbelievers, and he refused to marry me. He wanted me to go to Chernogorsk in Siberia to meet his parents and siblings. I told him I wouldn't go unless we were married. Pyotr solved our dilemma by deciding we could be married in a civil ceremony but not live as a married couple until we could have a legitimate Christian ceremony.

"I was won to Jesus Christ by two irresistible influences. When I visited Pyotr's parents and their younger children, I was tremendously impressed by the love displayed in this Christian family. I had grown up in a household filled with drunken quarrels and hateful animosity. I was hungry for a home filled with love. The second influence was the Bible. Communism was responsible for destroying millions of Bibles. It was a crime to own one. And no wonder. In the light of the Bible, communism is seen for the heinous evil it is.

"As I read the Bible, I began to understand what Jesus meant when he said the Holy Spirit would lead us into truth. I was absolutely fascinated by the revelation that God invaded earth as a human baby. The love that compelled God to provide his son as the sacrificial offering that paid the penalty for my sin broke my resistance. I surrendered to his love and have never been sorry. We had a beautiful Christian wedding, and now, twelve children and five grandchildren later, our love continues to grow.

"Our life has not been easy. Pyotr has been sentenced to prison multiple times. I have been imprisoned, as well. Our children have been harassed and mocked at school, not only by other students but also by the teachers. We decided to home school them, but the authorities took them from us and placed them in juvenile homes for incorrigible criminals. For years we suffered in silence, patiently enduring every imaginable indignity. Vasil asked why we endure as we do. Why don't we throw away our faith and surrender to the government? For the same reason that Moses refused to surrender. *He chose to be mistreated along with the people of God rather than to enjoy the pleasures of sin for a short time.*

"We are part of a long line of people who have suffered rather than surrender to idolatrous tyranny. Just as Moses and his people were delivered from Egypt, we believe God will deliver us. We know God is able to deliver us, but if he chooses not to, we will never deny him. The blazing furnace could not destroy the three Hebrew captives, nor could the hungry lions devour Daniel. We admire their great faith, but their faith was not in deliverance, but rather in the God who could deliver if chose to do so. We value our everlasting destiny more than temporary material benefits. We will not throw away our eternal birthright for a mess of communism's creature comforts."

"Well said, Augustina. But what about your children? Are you willing to sacrifice them for the sake of an ideal, no matter how exalted or worthy?" Vasil probed.

Pyotr broke in, "Augustina and I would willingly die for our children. We love them more than we love ourselves. But they are not ours. They were dedicated back to God as infants. We are sure he loves them more than we do, and their future is secure in his hands. If we did not have that confidence, despair would overwhelm us. The Holy Spirit himself has planted that assurance in our hearts, and we marvel at it ourselves."

CHAPTER 3
THE SECRET

"I wish I had your confidence, particularly in regards to Viktor," Vasil responded. "I have never shared with anyone our son's secret. When it was near the time for him to be born, we bribed the midwife not to report his birth. When he was three years old, we were determined to protect him from entering the state-operated public schools, if we possibly could. We knew he was unusually bright even as a toddler. At nearly four, he was reading books assigned to high school students. His memory was phenomenal. He would read a poem and quote it back to us the next day. How could we protect his brilliant mind from being corrupted by communism? We prayed earnestly for divine guidance. I believe God answered our prayer, but I want Natasha to tell you about it."

Natasha, a slender, Slavic beauty with long, coal-black hair and the bearing and grace of a former gymnast, smiled and began, "I want to thank Pyotr and Augustina for sharing their story, although I am sure there is much more to be told. What I have heard has greatly encouraged me to trust God for our future. I have a close relative who is a monk in an isolated monastery, whom I try to visit once a year. Nine years ago when Viktor was just past three years old, I visited my relative, Slava. I told him about our gifted son, and he cautioned me to never reveal what I had shared with him.

"'Natasha,' he said, 'tell no one else about your little Viktor. You must protect him from being used by the pagan infidels.'

"'But how? What can I do?' I asked.

"'I have an idea, but I must speak to others before I share it with you. Visit me again in three months. By then I may have a plan that you can share with Vasil,' Slava said.

"Slava then blessed me, turned, and retreated into the interior of the monastery. I stood for a while, contemplating what I had just heard. As I stood quietly meditating, the silence was broken by Slava's voice chanting a prayer. I was suddenly surrounded by an awesome sense of God's presence, which conveyed a peace and love such as I had never experienced before. Reluctantly, I turned and began to slowly make my way down the mountain's winding path to the harsh world below."

As Natasha paused, reflecting on the scene she had just described, Vasil continued the narrative.

"Natasha joined me in the small room we occupied in a house maintained by Orthodox supporters of the monastery. We refrained from anything but small talk since we had heard the KGB may have installed listening devices. We spent the night, deposited a monetary gift for maintenance of the house, and caught the train that stopped briefly to receive or discharge passengers. We noticed that no one got off.

"After we returned home, Natasha told me of her experience at the monastery. We tried to guess what Slava had in
mind but gave it up as useless speculation. As Vasil has told
you, we had the crazy idea when Viktor was born to see that
his birth was never recorded in the official records. There was
so much corruption and rampant poverty that a few rubles to
the right person could accomplish wonders. As I said, it was a
crazy idea, but so far it has gone undetected. How long can we
keep him incognito? I fear what might happen if we are forced
to register him for mandatory public schooling. Persecution
of Orthodox Christians intensified under Khrushchev. We
hoped it would diminish under Brezhnev, but it continues
much as before. Will our idea to protect Viktor turn out to be
a horrible mistake?"

Augustina spoke out confidently, "God is in control, Vasil.
You and Natasha must trust God just as Moses's parents trusted him. They disobeyed Pharaoh's edict and hid their son as
long as possible. When it was no longer possible to conceal little Moses, God provided a powerful person to give him safety
and protection. Can he not also have a plan to provide Viktor
with safety and protection? I am sure he can, and I believe he
will."

"I wish I had your great faith," Vasil said.

"The amount of faith has nothing to do with it, Vasil,"
Augustina replied. "It is who one's faith is placed in that matters. A little faith placed in truth is far superior to great faith
placed in falsehood. Communism is a false god, as time will
tell. But, Vasil, you must tell us what happened. Did you return
to the monastery in three months?"

"We couldn't arrange the exact time, and it was almost
four months later when we returned," said Vasil. "Natasha's

training as a gymnast had left her with strong legs, and she enjoyed the winding walk up the mountain. I stayed behind in the same room we had occupied before. I'll let her tell what happened."

"I will try to recreate what happened as I remember it. It was eight years ago, you know. Slava, my half-brother, for that's who he is, greeted me at the entrance to the monastery and led me to a private alcove," said Natasha. "He asked me where Viktor was, and I told him we had left him with friends. He then asked if we had told anyone about his unregistered birth. I assured him we had not. He nodded approvingly and then spoke.

"'Good,' said Slava. 'That means no one will be looking for him. I have talked to the abbot and the elder monks, and all have agreed that we must prevent your gifted son from falling into the hands of the pagan infidels that have taken over our country. The monastery is prepared to receive your four-year-old son as a monk-in-training. We have many renowned scholars here who will challenge his mind with their great learning. We will keep him and educate him for eight years. In 1978 when he reaches twelve years of age, we will release him back to you. It will then be the responsibility of you and Vasil to counsel and advise him until he comes of age. None of us knows what will be taking place in the world at that time, but God does. We must not worry about things we can't control but leave all in the hands of our Lord.'"

Natasha continued, "My mind was relieved, but my heart was pained by what Slava shared. Viktor would be ably cared for and educated for the next eight years. This brought me great comfort and even joy. At the same time, my heart was filled with enormous grief at the thought of no longer having our son in our home. I steeled myself to press on to the matter at hand.

"'When should we bring Viktor to the monastery?' I asked.

"'We have thought much about that,' Slava said. 'The abbot is very concerned that no one knows that he has been delivered to us. Your boy is small enough that he can fit comfortably into a medium-size box or crate. He must be transported inside one of these small freight boxes. It is nearly twenty-five hours of travel time by train from your village to the monastery guesthouse at the foot of the mountain. You must travel at night. The train schedules are such that one train allows you to leaves your village at night and arrive nine hours later, shortly before daybreak at Lostevo, a small city with a rail yard. The Orthodox priest there will provide a safe house where you can remain inside during the day. That night, there is a train coming up from the north that will be switched to your tracks. You must board at ten that night with your boxed son. At six the next morning, you will arrive in the village of Rukov. There you will be met and accompanied to another safe house. The third night, you will catch the train from Rukov at eleven and arrive at the monastery guesthouse at six in the morning. Monks will be waiting to transport the box up the mountain trail.

"'You will be pleased to know arrangements have been made to have someone accompany you through each stage of the journey. A trusted monk will watch for anything suspicious and help transport your cargo. We have no reason to suspect any problems. The journey will begin one month from tonight on October 23. You must prepare Viktor carefully. Let him practice being in a box for hours at a time. Brief him thoroughly on what lies ahead. Any questions?'

"'Yes, one,' I said. 'How often will we be able to see our boy?'

"'Just once a year. For the sake of all concerned, visits must be kept to a minimum,' Slava said.

"'I understand, but it will be hard for Vasil and me,' I said. 'I am so grateful for all you have done for us. The monastery is taking a great risk, and I pledge that we will do everything we can to minimize the danger. We can never thank you enough for giving refuge to our son.'"

The month went by all too quickly for Vasil and Natasha. Viktor was a quick learner and loved to get in the wooden crate where he had to hide while traveling. He described it as his fort. The train trip to the monastery guesthouse went flawlessly. It was there they had the bittersweet experience of telling their boy good-bye. In the secure privacy of their room, they removed Viktor from his wooden "fort" and embraced him tenderly, showering his little face with kisses.

"You are such a brave little man," said Vasil. "Your papa is very proud of you."

"I never cried, not even once. And I used my pee-pee bottle and screwed the lid back on without spilling a drop, and I breathed in and out very slowly through the hollow tube," Viktor boasted proudly.

"Yes, yes. You did everything just right. Why did your mama ever worry that something might go wrong? You were marvelous, and I love you so much," said Natasha, taking her son into her arms for a final embrace and kiss.

Vasil glanced at his watch and said, "Son, it is time to get back in your hiding place one last time. The monks will carry you to your mountain home where you will go to school without fear. Remember, God is with you always, so be courageous, my son."

Viktor settled wordlessly into the wooden box. With clenched jaw, he stifled his sobs as if determined to make his parents proud of him. Vasil secured the lid to the crate and then knelt down beside it to pray as Natasha joined him.

"Holy Father, with confidence in your love, we commit our son into your care. Keep him from all harm and evil. In the name of your son, Jesus, we pray. Amen."

Vasil and Natasha arose together. As they looked into each other's tear-filled eyes. Vasil took his wife in his arms and whispered softly, "We have made the right choice, dearest. We will trust the heavenly Father to care for our son as he did his own. Now I must tell the monks their cargo is ready."

One of the two summoned monks grasped the crate's center handle and gingerly tested the weight. "It's not as heavy as I thought it might be. I can carry it myself," he said to his companion. "We'll take turns transporting it up the trail."

Vasil described the scene. "We watched silently as the monks began their trek up the winding trail with their precious cargo. All too quickly, they were swallowed by the darkness, and yet we tarried, listening intently to the muffled sound of departing footsteps. At last silence joined the darkness as a barrier to the location of our beloved son. Hand in hand, we retreated to the room to await the arrival of the train that would take us home.

"For seven years, we made an annual trip to visit Viktor at the monastery. His academic exploits filled us with pride and wonder. His knowledge and social skills made conversation a delightful experience, not only for us but also for the monks that tutored him. Careful plans had been made for his release after the completion of the eighth year. There would be no need of a wooden crate this trip. He would leave by train at night, accompanied by Natasha's half-brother, his Uncle Slava. They would await us at Argona where Viktor would join us for our trip to our new home. We had all agreed we must settle in a distant community far from any place we had previously lived. We chose Chernogorsk here in south central Siberia, where we arrived among you as total strangers a few months ago. Our biggest concern now is how and where we are to continue Viktor's education. That's our story. Now we would like to hear more of yours."

CHAPTER 4

MORE SECRETS AND A PLAN

Pyotr arose from his chair and began to pace about the room. After a bit, he stopped and addressed the Gorgachuks. "Vasil, you and Natasha have shared your secret from the past in which you chose to not register the birth of your son. As you may or may not know, in January 1963, my courageous Augustina, plus thirty other Pentecostals, stormed the American embassy in Moscow, rushing past the policeman that guarded the gate. They were desperate to leave the Soviet Union and hoped and prayed the Americans would help them emigrate. The Americans said they could help us only if the Soviet Union would grant exit visas, which they refused to do. Smooth-talking KGB officers promised that if they would leave the embassy and return to their homes, they would receive better treatment. The KGB claimed the higher authorities had no idea what had been going on and would prevent it happening in the future. They left the embassy, but it was all a conniving lie. Augustina was arrested and forced to spend time in prison.

"I learned much from our experience in 1963. I have been petitioning the American State Department to grant us emigration under the provisions of the Geneva Convention and US law. I recently received a letter in response, requesting I report to the American embassy in Moscow for consultation. I plan to go the Embassy the last week of June and present the letter. Augustina and four of our older children, plus Maria Chmykhalov and her son, Timothy, will all go with me. If the gate guard will not honor the letter, we will storm through as before, but we will not make the mistakes of 1963. The group will be smaller, only a fourth the former number. Once we gain admittance, we will not leave until the Americans force us to or we receive emigration status. I have reason to believe the embassy will provide us sanctuary for an extended period of time if necessary. I know you will keep this information as a sacred trust.

"Now I have something to share that is difficult for me to say and will be difficult for you to hear. As you know, Augustina and I are Pentecostal believers. What you may not know is what Pentecostals believe. We believe that the Holy Spirit is as active in the church today as he was in the apostolic church. We not only believe this, but we experience the same supernatural gifts that were common in the early church. During our worship service two weeks ago, one of our elders stated that he believed he had a prophetic word from the Holy Spirit concerning a family in Chernogorsk. He asked the congregation to pray that he would faithfully convey what the Holy Spirit wanted to communicate.

"After a moment of silence, the elder began to speak. Here is the gist of his message as I wrote it down: 'This is what I believe the Holy Spirit has revealed to me. A family has recently moved to Chernogorsk who has a secret they think will never be discovered. Very soon their secret will be revealed, and the powers of darkness will seek to take from them the one they wish to protect. Someone must warn this family and help protect the endangered one. Fear not, says the Lord, I am with you.'

"When you shared your story tonight and revealed the secret of Viktor's unregistered birth, the Spirit confirmed to me that you are the family spoken of. For some unknown reason, the midwife has betrayed your secret. You are in danger of being imprisoned again. If that happens, you will lose your gifted son to the government. But don't be afraid. The Lord has warned us in advance so that we can take steps to avert the enemy's designs.

"I have thought and prayed much during these past two weeks concerning what might be done. However, I will make no suggestions until you ask me to do so. Vasil, have you and Natasha made any contingency plans in case Viktor's unregistered birth became disclosed to the KGB?"

Vasil's face reflected his deep concern as he replied, "No, Pyotr, we have made no plans other than to home school Viktor as long as possible. Why should we? We have never told anyone our family secret except you and Augustina and Slava, Natasha's brother at the monastery. How could a member of your church possibly know anything of Viktor's unregistered birth? Surely he was referring to someone else."

"You misunderstand, my friend," said Pyotr. "Our elder had no knowledge of the matter. It is God, the Holy Spirit, who knows all things and revealed your secret to him. The same Holy Spirit encouraged us to have no fear because he is with us. The Spirit would not have given the warning unless he was going to provide an escape. Are you and Natasha willing to trust the Holy Spirit as we ask him to help us develop a contingency plan?"

While Vasil pondered, Natasha spoke up. "There is much I don't understand about what you have said. But one thing I know. While you were speaking, I sensed the same awesome peace and love that I experienced over eight years ago at the monastery. I trusted God then and found him trustworthy. I dare not doubt him now. As he lights my path, I pledge to walk in it."

Vasil listened attentively to his wife. As she concluded, he affirmed what his wife had said and then continued. "As a committed Orthodox believer, I have a deep reverence for our heavenly Father and for his blessed Son, our Lord Jesus Christ. But I know very little about the Holy Spirit. How will I know if I am receiving guidance from him or just my own imagination?"

"An excellent question," Pyotr said. "Some have been led astray by their vain imaginations. The Holy Spirit will never lead us in a way that is contrary to holyscripture. Maintain a close relationship with our Shepherd. Jesus assured us that his sheep know his voice and will follow him. The Holy Spirit brings the exact message Jesus would convey if he were present in a physical body. The Spirit will never lead us to do anything that is not in keeping with the character of Jesus, our great and good Shepherd. There is a remarkable description of this process in John 16:12–14 as Jesus instructs his disciples concerning the work of the Holy Spirit. Let me read it to you. *I have much more to say to you, more than you can now bear. But when he, the Spirit of truth comes, he will guide you into all truth. He will not speak on his own; he will speak only what he hears, and he will tell you what is yet to come. He will bring glory to me by taking what is mine and making it known to you."*

"Yes, yes," said Vasil. "I believe I understand. Jesus has forever taken a human body, and he resides in heaven. The Holy Spirit has no space limitations. He is everywhere at the same time and is always in the presence of Jesus and always with us as well. He can instantly share what Jesus wants to tell us. Is that right?"

Pyotr smiled and replied, "Our pastor may interpret it a little differently, but I like your explanation, Vasil. Yes, you have it right. Any more questions?"

"Since we have no contingency plan," Vasil said, "please share your thoughts."

Pyotr responded, "As you know, the goal of our atheist government from the beginning has been to eliminate all religion from our society and culture, particularly Christianity. We have had to devise means to protect ourselves. One means that we Pentecostals have used on rare occasions is false identification documents. Some of our members, before repentance and conversion, were heavily involved in smuggling. Their first line of defense was generous bribes to people in key places of authority. Their second line of defense was counterfeit documents. A few of the smugglers developed great skill in producing these false papers. One of them who repented and has been born again is now a member of our congregation.

"Here is what I propose for your consideration," said Pyotr. "Let's give Viktor a new identity with the help of my gifted friend. Augustina and I have twelve children. Why not make it thirteen?

Viktor is small for his age, so we can portray him as eleven years old since we had no children in 1967. He can live with our family. Our twelve-year-old Igor would love to have a brother his age. You have done well in keeping Viktor in seclusion, but you can't do that much longer. Nor is it good for your boy to be hidden away with his books. He needs physical activity out in the open air with other boys. I know this suggestion comes as a shocking surprise. You must consider it together and talk it over with your son. You will have questions that I must try to answer. We may not have much time to act, so let's meet here again in two days."

Vasil responded, "What you propose, Pyotr, is extremely shocking. We have to think much about this … and pray much. If we ever needed confirmation from the Holy Spirit, it is now. We will meet you again in two days. Will you pray for us before we go?"

Pyotr prayed a brief prayer for the Gorgachuks, committing them confidently into the Lord's hands. They then embraced and bid each other goodnight.

Vasil and Natasha walked somberly and silently hand in hand to their home where Ivan awaited them. Each was lost in private thoughts concerning the future of their family. What should they tell Viktor? How would he respond? Finally Vasil broke the silence.

"Natasha," said Vasil, "while I am at work tomorrow, please talk to Viktor and get his honest response to our friend's idea. Let him know the risks involved with either alternative we choose. After I return from work, we will deal with all the issues and make our decision."

Natasha replied, "Yes, dear, I certainly will talk to our son. In many ways, he is mature beyond his age; even so, he is still a child. It will be difficult for him no matter what we decide."

The next day, Natasha called Viktor to her side. "Listen, son," said Natasha, "your mother has some very important things to discuss with you. Do you remember why we placed you in the monastery with your Uncle Slava?"

"Yes, Mama. It was because my birth was not registered, and you and papa were afraid to enroll me in a public school. You were sure the monks would provide me a good education and not betray me to the government," said Viktor.

"That's right, son. And how did that work for you?"

"It worked very well, Mama. The monks made me study very hard, and I learned a lot. But it was really tough being separated from you and Papa for such a long time," said the boy.

"It was terribly difficult for your papa and me, too," Natasha said. "I hope we never have to experience anything like that again. That is what I want to talk to you about. We have learned it is possible that the police have been informed about your unregistered birth. If so, they will find us. When they do, we will likely be arrested, and only God knows what will follow. We are very concerned about what might happen to you."

"Mama, what shall we do?" Viktor asked. "Can we go away and hide somewhere?"

"That would be unrealistic. More than that, it would be impossible for very long. But there is a possible solution. It was suggested by Mr. Pyotr Vashchenko, your papa's new friend. Mr. and Mrs. Vashchenko have a large family of twelve children. He has suggested that you become their thirteenth child."

"No, Mama! You wouldn't give me away, would you?" cried Viktor.

"Never. Never. Never," Natasha assured her boy. "We would not give you away. Instead, we will hide you in plain sight. Mr. Vashchenko has a friend who can provide you a birth certificate that looks just like a real one. On the document, your name will be Viktor Vashchenko, and your birthdate will be listed as May 15, 1967. "

"But, Mama, I was born July 4, 1966," protested Viktor.

"I know, dear," said his mother. "We had to choose a date that allowed time for your birth between other children in the Vashchenko family. You are small and can easily pass for eleven years old. Now, tell me, what do you think of this idea?"

"Will you and Papa stay here so I can still see you?" asked Viktor.

"We certainly intend to," said his mother. "The important thing is that if something should happen to us, you will be in a godly home surrounded by people that care about you. The goal of the Vashchenko family is to immigrate to America where people are free to worship God as they please. Someday we pray that you will be able to immigrate to America where you can become all that God created you to be. When your papa returns from work this evening, we will talk about this some more. Save your questions till then. Your mama has to fix something for us to eat."

That evening around the dinner table, the Gorgachuk family agreed to tentatively accept the plan suggested by their friends. They would make their final decision when meeting with Vashchenkos the next night. It was agreed that Viktor should go with them to this meeting.

CHAPTER 5
PERSEVERING THROUGH TRIAL

Viktor was elated to be accompanying his parents for the night meeting with their friends. His future was at stake, and he was glad that he could sit in on the decision-making process. His knowledge of Hebrew lore had taught him that at his age Jewish boys celebrated the transition to manhood. He was grateful for the respect his parents had for his ability to think and express himself clearly, as the monks had taught him.

After a fifteen-minute walk down the unlighted street, they arrived at the Vashchenkos. Only Pyotr and Augustina met them, as the children had been sent to other rooms. They greeted one another warmly, and young Viktor got more than his share of attention. After everyone was greeted and seated, Pyotr got down to the business at hand.

"My friends," Pyotr began, "we have come together tonight to finalize our plans concerning action to be taken that will thwart our blasphemous government from gaining control of Viktor. The Holy Spirit has blessed you, Viktor, with unusual gifts and training, and we must be God's hands to help preserve you for our Lord's service. Before we begin any discussion, I want to read a bit of scripture I believe the Lord impressed upon me while I was praying today. It is James 1:2–4. *Consider it pure joy, my brothers, whenever you face trials of many kinds, because you know that the testing of your faith develops perseverance. Perseverance must finish its work so that you may be mature and complete, not lacking anything.* Does this describe our situation and can we use it as a guide to attain our goals? How do you see this scripture applying to us? Anyone want to comment?"

Natasha spoke first. "I understand about trials. We certainly face many kinds, as James says. What I don't understand is the 'pure joy' part. I find little to be joyful about."

"Mama, Mama," Viktor spoke up, "I was reading these very verses from my Greek New Testament just this morning. At first I felt the same as you. But after careful study, I noticed that the verb is in the imperative mood. Mama, we are commanded to have joy when we face trials. Joy doesn't come because of trials. We choose to have joy because we believe God is going to do something good in our character that is worth all the pain of the trials. We can choose joy because of who God is and what he will do if we persevere."

"Hear, hear," said Pyotr. "Now I know how the teachers must have felt after they encountered the boy Jesus in the temple. I am convinced more than ever that God desires that we be his agents to help preserve this gifted young man from the ravages of a perverted, blasphemous government. That's why we must talk about practical issues that will help us accomplish our goal. Where shall we begin?"

"We haven't resolved how Viktor is going to be enrolled in the public school as your son," Vasil replied. "The school officials know who your children are, so how can we do this?"

"I do not know," said Pyotr. "Scripture promises, *If any of you lacks wisdom, he should ask God, who gives generously to all without finding fault, and it will be given to him.* We must claim that promise and believe God will provide the answer at the appropriate time. It is now May, and the school year is almost over. Viktor will not have to register until September. God will provide an answer when it is needed."

"There's something else that troubles me," said Vasil. "You apparently expect to be given sanctuary at the American embassy. You may be there for an indefinite period. Who will care for your younger children while you are gone?"

"I truly thank you for your concern," said Pyotr. "Our children have had to learn to depend upon themselves since I and sometimes Augustina have been forcibly taken from them. There are Christian brothers and sisters in our church to whom they can turn for advice and help if needed. And Yuri, their older, married natural brother, lives in a nearby village. He will contact them from time to time."

"I have no doubt they have been well trained to care for themselves," said Natasha. "But they still need a mother's care. I will gladly prepare meals and spend time with them until you return home, Augustina."

"Would you?" said Augustina. "Oh, thank you, Natasha! You are an answer to prayer. Our children will love that."

"And it will allow me to keep an eye on Viktor during his adjustment to a large family," said Natasha. "He has not been taught to care for himself, although I am sure your children can train him. He does learn things quickly, and he was trained in self-discipline by the monks. Perhaps we should have had more children, but we took the cowardly way out and limited ourselves to one."

Viktor piped up, "I am glad you had me, Mama, regardless of what happens in the future."

A chuckle greeted Viktor's spontaneous remark. A spirit of warm comradeship enveloped the little group.

"We all thank God for you," said Pyotr, "and we will trust him to help us give you a good future. Now, I want to share more details about our visit to the American embassy. In addition to Augustina and me, our sixteen-year-old son, Ivan, plus our daughters, Lila, Luba, and Lida, will go from our family. Maria Chmykhalov and her sixteen-year-old son, Timothy, will also accompany us. We will depart here on June 24 by train and arrive in Moscow on June 26. On the morning of June 27, we will go to the American embassy and present the letter of invitation. If not permitted to enter, we will all rush in as planned. Only our Lord knows what comes next. In the intervening six weeks, we will give ourselves to prayer so as to be prepared spiritually and mentally for the ordeal ahead."

"And we will join you in praying daily for the success of your venture," said Vasil. "How long will it take for Viktor's documents to be completed? He is eager to escape house confinement, especially as the weather warms."

"Everything should be prepared in two more days," said Pyotr. "It is very intricate work, and Yuri takes great pride in the finished product. Except in dire emergencies, he refuses to rush."

"We owe him a great debt," said Natasha. "Sometime I hope we can meet him and thank him personally."

"He prefers to keep his identity unknown," said Augustina, "but we will express your thanks."

※⊰ ⊱※

In a few days, Viktor received his documents. They had been folded many times to give them an authentic, used appearance. He must not forget that his name was now Viktor Vashchenko, and he was eleven years old. He smiled as he thought to himself, *Most boys get older when they have a birthday. I just got younger.*

Viktor enjoyed the freedom provided by his identity papers. He and Igor quickly established a warm friendship. For the first time in his life, he was able to relate to peers his own age. When Viktor was introduced as the newest member of the Vashchenko household, twelve-year-old Igor approached him and threw his arm around his shoulder and whispered, "Viktor, I am glad you joined our family. My sisters are okay, but it will sure by great to have a boy to pal around with."

Viktor whispered back, "Thanks, Igor. I have never had a pal before, boy or girl. I had to stay hidden inside. It will be a lot of fun to go places with you."

Wherever they went and met new people, Igor would introduce him. "This is my brother, Viktor. He has been living with relatives who live a long ways away. With my parents and three sisters gone, there's plenty of room now in the house for him."

No further explanation was given, and no questions were asked. It was not wise or safe to know more than necessary. Viktor was readily accepted into the large, covert Pentecostal community that had settled in Chernogorsk.

"Natasha, how is Viktor responding to his newfound freedom with the Vashchenkos?" Vasil asked.

"The best answer I can give you is that Viktor is wonderfully happy. He is reveling in his new friends and opportunities to go places with them," said Natasha.

"That I am glad to hear," said Vasil. "He has been cooped up far too long. I pray he can regain his lost childhood. But is there risk that too much freedom may lead to carelessness?"

"There's always risk," said Natasha. "Remember, Viktor is with boys who have lived with risk all their lives. I really think it is a good environment for him. He will learn how to respond to risky situations in company with those who have likely faced them before."

"I have one more concern that I would like to discuss," said Vasil. "We have seen the godly character displayed by our Pentecostal friends. I truly trust them. But they are being more persecuted at this time than even we Orthodox. In addition, they have religious beliefs and practices that are strange to us, especially speaking in unknown languages that the Holy Spirit provides. Do you see danger in these things?"

"Vasil, you forget how gifted our boy is," said Natasha. "He is a student of Holy Scripture and reads Greek and Hebrew better than you and I speak Russian. He will study each teaching and let scripture be his guide. I believe God will preserve him safe from harmful heresy."

CHAPTER 6
THE SAGA OF THE SIBERIAN SEVEN BEGINS

O ther than family members, only a few Pentecostal leaders knew of the planned invasion of the American embassy. Sergei, an astute elder, had been designated to go to Moscow and surreptitiously observe what happened at the embassy and report back to family members and the congregation.

On the morning of June 24, 1978, the delegation chosen by Pyotr and Augustina to go with them to the American embassy met at the train station. Their oldest daughter, Lida, age twenty-seven, Luba, age twenty-five, Lila, age twenty, and son Ivan, age sixteen. In addition, Mrs. Maria Chmykhalov, age fifty-six, and her son, Timothy, age sixteen, were selected. The two boys were close friends.

Pyotr had purchased tickets for two sleeping compartments, each which accommodated four persons. There were two upper bunks and two lower, which also served as seats. The three Vashchenko daughters and Maria Chmykhalov were assigned one compartment. Pyotr and Augustina plus the two boys occupied the other. Pyotr encouraged them all to relax and enjoy the trip with thankful hearts.

A large group from the Pentecostal congregation met at the station to demonstrate their support. They knew nothing of any plan to possibly seek asylum, but they knew Pyotr had received a letter requesting he come to the American embassy for consultation. It was in response to numerous letters he had written requesting American help for persecuted Pentecostals desiring to emigrate. There was much singing mingled with scripture reading and a concluding prayer for God's purposes to be fulfilled. There were mingled shouts of "praise God" and "hallelujah" as the train left the station.

The train arrived on schedule the afternoon of June 26. The Vashchenko party quietly debarked and made their way to a nearby cheap hotel where reservations had been made. Sergei discreetly watched from a distance and then registered at a neighboring hotel. Later, the Vashchenkos purchased fresh bread and bottled water and then met to eat together the last of the salami, cheese, and fruit that had sustained them on the train. After eating, they softly sang a favorite hymn a cappella and then united in spontaneous prayer. Following prayer, they bid each other goodnight and retired to their rooms.

The following morning, they joined for an inexpensive breakfast of buckwheat, sausage, and chai. Following breakfast, they returned to the hotel to use the water closet and get their small bags of personal items. They met together in one room before checking out for one last briefing by Pyotr. His closing remark was a grim reminder of the danger they faced.

"Remember," he said, "if anyone is apprehended, the rest must continue into the embassy. Our only hope is the protection that publicity will afford us. If we leave the embassy, the KGB will imprison us, and our cause will be lost. As long as some of us are in the American embassy, the world will be watching." With these words ringing in their ears, they proceeded to the embassy as planned.

As usual, the entry gate was guarded by a small force of Soviet militia. Pyotr spoke to the leader and presented his letter. Sergei tried to edge closer in order to hear what was being said. One of the militia guards forced him back, but he had no trouble hearing Pyotr shout, "Let's go!" The eight rushed past the gate guard. Maria stumbled, and Ivan stopped to help her regain her feet. The guard pounced on the boy, allowing Maria to join the others fleeing into the embassy waiting room. Soon other militia nearby joined in subduing the struggling teen. Pyotr and the others watched helplessly as Ivan was kicked and beaten. They knew his best protection was for them to remain where they were.

For two months, the group occupied the waiting room of the embassy. They had to use the lavatories for washing up. They had sofas to sit on but not sufficient for sleeping, so several slept on the floor. Some of the embassy staff volunteered to bring them food.

Sergei had returned to Chernogorsk and reported his eyewitness account of what had taken place at the embassy. Family members there, including son Ivan who had been tortured by the KGB after his capture and then released, sent a message to the family members in the embassy. "Don't agree to come back home. If you do, they will kill or torture us all. Please stay in the embassy."

On August 27, 1978, matters came to a head. Embassy officials told the Vashchenkos and Chmykhalovs that they must leave. Apparently, the KGB had been notified that the group, dubbed by the press the "Siberian Seven," was being told to leave the embassy. Numerous KGB cars were lined up in front waiting to transport the seven wherever they had been ordered to take them.

Pyotr stubbornly refused to leave and said to the officials, "You are welcome to evict me, but you will have to carry me across the threshold. I will not walk out of here into the arms of the KGB."

When Pyotr refused to leave under his own power, the embassy officials were puzzled as to what to do. They decided to refer the crisis to Ambassador Toon. The ambassador had not wanted to get involved and had hoped the refugees would choose to go as they had in 1963. They refused to leave, and now he would be forced to make a decision. He was an experienced diplomat and had served effectively for years in the Soviet bloc of Eastern Europe. He knew the Russian language and was able to converse effectively without a translator.

He gamely donned his diplomatic smile, and approaching Pyotr, he said, "Mr. Vashchenko, I am Ambassador Malcolm Toon. I understand you are reluctant to accept our offer to provide you free transportation home in the cars waiting below." Pyotr did not smile at the ambassador's attempt to inject some humor. Ambassador Toon continued. "Our government is sympathetic to you but fears if we allow you asylum, our embassies around the world will be flooded by refugees. Do you understand our concern?"

"No, sir, I do not," Pyotr said boldly. "We did not come as refugees planning to invade the American embassy. We came with a letter of invitation from the American State Department to visit the embassy to consult about our request to immigrate to the United States. We were told the USSR approved the consultation. Our government reneged and refused to honor the invitation. We are determined to keep it, sir. Mr. Ambassador, we have suffered intense persecution for years because of our Christian faith. When my wife came to your embassy in 1963 with a larger group to seek emigrant status, the KGB promised if we left and returned home the government would no longer mistreat us and would help us achieve our goal. It was a lie, and my wife and others were imprisoned. We do not trust our government, nor should you."

"Mr. Vashchenko," said Ambassador Toon, "I heartily agree with you, but I had to relay an opinion voiced by high officials in our government. I have the authority to make an onsite decision. I am going to grant you permission to remain in our embassy until your situation is properly resolved by the two governments concerned."

"Thank you, Mr. Ambassador, not only for myself but for all those I represent," said Pyotr.

"You are welcome, Mr. Vashchenko. However, I have been ordered to inform you of the following limitations regarding your time in the embassy. There will be no frills or conveniences provided beyond the ordinary necessities. This is not a hotel, nor will we operate as one. Today marks the second month you have been temporarily housed in our waiting room, where you must depend on the lavatories for toilet facilities. This afternoon, you will be moved to two rooms in the basement where there are toilet facilities with showers. There is a shortage of beds, but foam mats for sleeping on the floor will be provided."

"We are deeply grateful, sir," said Pyotr. "We are used to living under hardship conditions. We are not interested in frills or conveniences. Our concerns are liberty and freedom of conscience. That's why we are fighting for permission to immigrate to the United States."

"I pray you make it," said Ambassador Toon. "Our country needs courageous, honorable people like you. I hope someday I can welcome you all as fellow citizens."

As the ambassador made his way back to his office, a marine gunnery sergeant stepped forward and introduced himself, with the aid of a translator.

"I'm Gunnery Sergeant Stevens, commander of the embassy marine detachment. We are going to relocate you down below. Please follow me," he said.

"We will follow gladly," Augustina said. "It will be good to have some privacy after all these weeks."

"You will be crowded, but you will have privacy down here," Gunny Stevens said. "This larger room will be shared by the five women. The two single beds are for Mrs. Vashchenko and Mrs. Chmykhalov. I'm sorry that is all the beds we have."

"Do you have any cots we could use?" Pyotr asked.

"No, sir, we don't, but we do have foam mats for sleeping on the floor."

"I'll be happy to sleep in the hall," said Luba. "That will provide more sleeping space in the room."

Pyotr and Timothy had the smaller room all to themselves. They, too, slept on the floor.

As Gunny Stevens prepared to leave, Pyotr asked if he might speak to him.

"Yes, Mr. Vashchenko, how can I help you?" Gunny Stevens inquired.

"As you may know, in addition to our three daughters here, we have nine more children remaining in Chernogorsk. We also have boy there named Viktor Gorgachuk whom we have taken under our wing because his parents had to flee the KGB. Would it be possible to arrange weekly telephone visits with these children to hear how they are doing? In addition to the children, I am particularly concerned about Viktor's parents."

"I'm not authorized to make that decision, but I will speak to the communications officer and make your request to him. My guess is that he will authorize periodic telephone calls to your children," Gunny Stevens said.

After the gunny departed, the Siberian Seven considered their situation. The basement quarters were austere but livable. They were used to crowded living conditions. At least in the embassy they could go to the toilets without trudging through snow and bitter cold. They looked at one another and smiled appreciatively. They sought freedom, not material comfort.

CHAPTER 7
THE WARNING

Natasha enjoyed her relationship with the Vashchenko children, and they enjoyed the meals she prepared. She was careful not to display any favoritism toward Viktor, and he was careful to call her Mrs. Gorgachuk. Once he forgot momentarily, and his greeting came out as ma … ss Gorgachuk. He must not let himself call her Mama. At home with Vasil at night, she shared how their boy was adjusting. They were pleased and grateful that he had opportunity to be part of a close-knit family and that they could watch him continue to develop.

But Vasil was worried. "Natasha, why hasn't the KGB contacted us about the information fed them by the midwife? Have they lost track of us? Have they stopped looking? Maybe they have bigger fish to catch. Maybe we should move far away so that we will not be in the vicinity of Viktor. I have talked to a couple of Pentecostal friends about moving for fear of the KGB. They asked no questions, nor did I give them any information. They have both been in our shoes. They recommended we consider Nakhodka if we think we should leave Chernogorsk. There is a large unregistered Pentecostal congregation there that will welcome us because of our relationship with the Vashchenkos. Elder Sergei said he would write a letter describing our help, your help really, to the Vashchenko children. Because of the close bond between these congregations, they will be eager to help us find work and housing."

"Oh, Vasil," said Natasha, "that would mean we must leave Viktor behind. I find that very hard to accept. Can't you think of some other way to elude the police?"

"Natasha," said Vasil, "we must leave Viktor behind for his own protection. Don't you see, the KGB will reason that if we actually know where our boy is that we will choose to be close by. If we leave here and go far away, should that not lessen their suspicion that he is here? I really believe the Holy Spirit is directing us to go to Nakhodka."

"You may be right," said Natasha. "I have no idea what goes on in the minds of KGB agents. I just know I enjoy being close to our son so I can watch him grow up. We have been separated for so many years. I would give my life to preserve his if need be. If you think our move to a distant location will make him safer, then we must do it. Love always acts in the best interest of the loved one. That's what my brother Slava used to tell me before he entered the monastery."

"Your brother is a wise and good man," said Vasil. "If we decide to leave, we must not tell Viktor where we are going. That is in his best interest. The less he knows, the safer he will be. Before making a definite decision, we must pray our Lord will help us make the right one. My overseer at the strip mine is a secret believer. It is only right that I confer with him. Perhaps he will agree to fire me so we have a legitimate reason for leaving Chernogorsk. That is a thought that just occurred to me this very minute. Why didn't I think of it before? Do you think God puts thoughts in our mind to help fulfill his will? If so, maybe he does want us to move. Perhaps the Holy Spirit is truly directing me to Nakhodka."

"But why Nakhodka?" asked Natasha. "I know there are Pentecostals there that will welcome us because of our link with friends here. But are there other reasons for choosing that location? After all, we are Orthodox, not Pentecostal. Why don't we seek closer association with our own kind of people? I admire bravery and devotion to God, such as the Pentecostals have demonstrated numerous times. And I appreciate all they have done for Viktor and us. But frankly, some of their beliefs and practices seem a little weird to me."

"Weird or not, it is better that we associate with Pentecostals rather than Orthodox," said Vasil. "Following the massive persecution of Orthodox priests and lay believers we endured under Stalin and later under Khrushchev, our surviving priests are so filled with fear they are easily intimidated by the KGB. Many have become paid lackeys of the police state, and now our Orthodox Church is riddled with these faithless turncoats. The Pentecostals have refused to sell out to the government. They would rather die than betray a brother or sister. The short answer to your question is that I don't know who I can trust among our own kind of people. But Nakhodka is a good choice for other reasons. It is a Pacific seaport city with a relatively mild climate moderated by the Sea of Japan. I think you would like that, Natasha. The population of 160,000 is big enough to provide excellent shopping facilities. I know you will like that. There are many businesses located there, so job opportunities for my bookkeeping profession should be available. An added bonus is numerous tourists visit this region. We may have opportunity to meet some from America and become friends. You know you have always been intrigued by America."

"I see you are convinced we should move," said Natasha. "Perhaps you are right. But I want some indication that it is more than your will. Shouldn't we have some indication that it is also God's will? I know our Lord has kept Viktor and us safe thus far. That gives me hope for the future. Surely he will not forsake us now. We must pray earnestly for our boy and commit him to God's protection. Can we do it now, Vasil, before we sleep?"

Vasil nodded and knelt beside the bed as Natasha knelt beside him. They began to repeat in Orthodox tradition a prayer they had recited for years as they entreated God in behalf of their son; "*O God, our heavenly father, who loves mankind, and are most merciful and compassionate, have mercy upon our child, your servant Viktor, for whom we humbly pray and commend him to your gracious protection. Be, O God, his guide and guardian in all his endeavors; lead him in your path of truth, and draw him near to you, that he may lead a godly and righteous life in your love and fear, doing your will in all matters. Give him grace that he may be temperate, industrious, diligent, devout, and charitable. Defend him against the assaults of the enemy, and grant him wisdom and strength to resist all temptation and corruption of this life, and direct him in the way of salvation, for the merits of your son, our savior Jesus Christ, and the intercessions of his holy mother and your blessed saints. Amen.*"

Assured in their hearts that God had heard their petition, they arose and retired in peace. After awaking the next morning, they decided to forego breakfast and spend more time in prayer. They both sensed the importance of making the right decision concerning whether to leave or stay in Chernogorsk. Natasha asked Vasil to lead in the morning prayer of the Optina Elders, a favorite of hers. Optina was an influential monastery founded in obscurity but going back at least until the sixteenth century. After the Bolshevik revolution, Stalin forced the monastery to cease operations. The writings of past leaders, some martyred, continued to provide guidance and inspiration for the Orthodox faithful, especially among those themselves facing persecution.

Vasil began to pray, finding the familiar words especially meaningful on this morning. *"Grant unto me, O Lord, that with peace of mind I may face all that this new day is to bring. Grant unto me to dedicate myself to your holy will. For every hour of this day, instruct and support me in all things. Whatsoever tidings I may receive during the day, do teach me to accept tranquilly, in the firm conviction that all eventualities fulfill your holy will. Govern my thoughts and feelings in all I do and say. When things unforeseen occur, let me not forget that all comes down from you. Teach me to behave sincerely and rationally toward every member of my family, that I may bring confusion and sorrow to none. Bestow upon me, my Lord, strength to endure the fatigue of the day, and to bear my part in all its passing events. Guide my will and teach me to pray, to believe, to hope, to suffer, to forgive, and to love. Amen."*

After praying, Vasil paused in thought and then spoke slowly. "Natasha, I love the prayers that we have inherited from our Orthodox faith. Our tradition has passed on to us a great treasure. But after observing the Pentecostals in prayer, there are times I would like to express myself informally as they do. When Pyotr was still with us, I once asked him how they dare address God so boldly in an informal manner. His reply surprised me. He said, 'That's the way God wants us to pray.' He then showed me these verses in Hebrews 4:14–16. Let me read them to you.

"Therefore, since we have a great high priest who has gone into heaven, Jesus the Son of God, let us hold firmly to the faith we profess. For we do not have a high priest who is unable to sympathize with our weaknesses, but we have one who has been tempted in every way just as we are—yet without sin. Let us then approach the throne of grace with confidence, so that we may receive mercy and find grace to help us in our time of need. Hebrews 4:14–16.

"Isn't that amazing? We are actually invited to come right into God's throne room and petition him for help. I have never dared be so bold, but I would like to do that this morning. Do you mind?"

"I have read that passage many times," said Natasha, "but I never thought it applied to individuals like you and me. I thought it was only for the priests and religious leaders. I think I was wrong. I believe Pyotr is correct. This is an invitation for all God's children to come confidently before him. Yes! Pray, Vasil, pray."

With some trepidation, Vasil began, "Heavenly Father, I would not dare speak to you this way if I did not believe you have invited me to. Natasha and I have an important decision to make, and we need your guidance. I know I don't need to inform you of all the details. Here is my request. If we should depart Chernogorsk and move to Nakhodka, may my supervisor encourage me in this and choose to fire me so we have an excuse for leaving. Thank you for inviting me to talk to you this way. And thank you, Jesus, for being our high priest. Amen."

Natasha smiled as Vasil concluded his short prayer. "Well, dear," she said, "you didn't mince any words or waste God's time. I think God may have liked that. The scripture tells us he looks on the heart and not the outward appearance. I believe he liked what he saw. Now you had better go to work or your supervisor won't have to invent a reason for firing you. Since you didn't have breakfast, I added an extra sandwich to your lunch."

Vasil smiled appreciatively and gave her a quick kiss.

"I'll be praying for you," she promised as he departed.

It was lunchtime before Vasil found a suitable time to privately talk to Vadim, his boss. "Sir," he began, "I have circumstances that lead me to think that it may be better if I depart Chernogorsk and move elsewhere. It will be better if I do not share any more details in case some unpleasant people make inquiries. You have been very kind, and I do not want to depart and leave you in a difficult situation without a bookkeeper. I value greatly your wisdom and experience and would appreciate any recommendations or advice you could offer to someone who wants to keep a low profile."

"Vasil, you have been a good employee," said Vadim. "You have done a first-rate job getting our books and records back in order. I'll be sorry to see you go. I commend you for leaving the area if you have any indication that the KGB might have reason for wanting to question you. They have ways of getting information that are not pleasant.

"I have had some experience with the KGB. For what it's worth, here's what I have learned. Most are cruel bordering on psychopathic, the majority are lazy, and only a minority are intelligent. The most dangerous is an intelligent, hardworking psychopath. This combination is scarce, and they are not likely to be involved in minor issues. The least dangerous is a softhearted, lazy dunce. This combination is quite small, perhaps as many as 10 percent. You will be fortunate to have an agent from this category assigned. The bulk of agents are self-centered slobs of average intelligence who like to throw their weight around and will not hesitate to break a few bones.

"As far as advice is concerned, if you depart Chernogorsk, I recommend you get as far away as possible. Find a support group in the new area but be slow about revealing anything you don't want the KGB to know. They have eyes in many places and ears where you would least expect. One more thing. You need to have a legitimate reason for leaving your old home and seeking a new place to live. Have you thought about that?" asked Vadim.

"As a matter of fact, I have," said Vasil. "I was hoping you might help provide one."

"There is something that I could do," said Vadim, "that would provide a reason for you going away. However, I am reluctant to mention it since it would cause me to lose a valuable employee. I could fire you. Is that what you were hoping I might do?"

"I was thinking of that. Yes, sir, I was," said Vasil.

"You are a clever man," said Vadim. "I should have thought of that immediately. But firing you is the last thing I want to do. Perhaps that is the reason it never entered my mind until just now. But since you have forced me to consider it, let's provide the Lord a chance to help me make the right decision. Here's what I propose. I will write a letter dated today saying you are dismissed from my employment effective in seven days. Let us pray that God will supply a replacement for you in this time period if it is his will that I do indeed dismiss you. Will you agree to that?"

"I will," said Vasil. "But what should I do if there is no replacement within a week?"

"Just believe that God has a better plan and it doesn't include you departing at this time," said Vadim. "Your safety doesn't depend on your locale but being where God wants you to be. Do you trust him enough to accept that?"

"Sometimes my faith is weak, and I become fearful," confessed Vasil. "But I do know that he has protected us many times in the past. When I recall those times, my faith becomes stronger. I must trust him, sir. I must. There is no one else to turn to. "

"God led you here, and he will guide your departure," assured Vadim. "But in the interval, there is much you can do to prepare for a move just in case. Decide what you wish to take with you and what you want to sell or leave with friends. I recommend you travel as lightly as possible. Check the train schedule to your destination. See if there is one leaving at night that has private sleeping compartments. If so, secure one just for you and Natasha. The less attention you draw to yourselves the better. Tell your friends good-bye in advance so there is no group bidding you farewell at the station. Now, are you ready to commit all this to the Lord in prayer as we agreed?"

"With great gratitude, I am, sir," said Vasil. "Would you please lead in prayer? I know no Orthodox prayer that fits this occasion, and I am not well practiced in spontaneous prayers."

Vadim nodded and stood to pray. "Lord Jesus," he began, "my friend and I have agreed to ask you to provide a replacement for him in seven days if it is your will that he depart this city and locate elsewhere. He realizes there is no safer place than being right where you want him to be. We confidently entrust this situation into your hands. Thank you, Jesus, for being such a powerful and loving savior. Amen."

Vasil turned to go. "I'd better get back to work," he said. "Thank you again for your understanding and support. I'll be here until God directs otherwise."

Natasha greeted Vasil's return from work with a quick kiss followed by a question. "Was our prayer answered?"

"Only partially," said Vasil. "Vadim wrote a letter today terminating my employment in seven days, but it is conditional."

"Conditional? What does that mean?" said Natasha.

"It means that my termination is effective only if Vadim gets a replacement bookkeeper before the week is up. He said he needed confirmation that God is really directing us to leave."

"What happens if no bookkeeper is obtained?"

"Vadim said it just means that God has a better plan in mind, and we must wait for Him to reveal it. This is where we have to persevere and demonstrate trust and faith in God. This is the hard part. However, he did suggest we be prepared to move in case a bookkeeper shows up. It's important that you brief Viktor about our plans. Make sure he understands we are doing this to guarantee more safety for him. Explain that the greater distance between us the safer he will be. Assure him that we do this only because we love him so much," said Vasil.

"Viktor will be just fine," said Natasha. "He is surrounded by adults who will keep an eye on him. Maybe more important, he is forming close relationships with boys his age and having real boyhood fun. I love to hear him laugh and joke around. Most important, he has a genuine love relationship with God. We are blessed, Vasil. It's us I am concerned about, not Viktor."

Vasil furrowed his brow. "Why are you concerned about us?" he asked.

"Oh, Vasil," she said. "That's part of the problem. I am not sure of the source of my uneasiness. I have a sense in my spirit that something or someone is plotting evil against us. Maybe it is a woman's intuition. Or maybe ... Do you think God may be trying to warn us?"

"Warn us about what?" asked Vasil.

"I'm not sure," said Natasha. "I know scripture tells of St. Paul being warned by the Holy Spirit through a prophet about a terrible thing awaiting him in Jerusalem. Paul was convinced God wanted him to go anyway and insisted he was willing to suffer and die for Jesus if need be. Do you think the Holy Spirit may be warning me that serious danger awaits us in Nakhodka?"

Vasil pursed his lips as he considered the question. "Perhaps. Why not? That means we may have the same choice Paul did when warned by the prophet."

Natasha wasn't sure she understood. "What do you mean, Vasil? In what way is our choice like the great apostle's?" she asked.

"It's pretty simple," said Vasil. "Paul was convinced the Lord had directed him to go to Jerusalem. A prophet from the Lord warned him not to go. He refused to back down from what he believed the Lord had told him to do. He went and suffered the painful consequences the prophet predicted. I believe the Lord has directed me to take us to Nakhodka. We have asked the Lord to confirm this by providing Vadim with a replacement bookkeeper before seven days pass. If what I sense in my heart is confirmed to be true, then we must choose to go and accept the danger or choose another option."

"Yes, put like that, it is simple," said Natasha. "But there is more included that is not so simple. I do believe that God is really giving me a warning about something bad that shall happen to us. The bad event of which we are warned is not from God. He is warning us about an evil attack from Satan. Why does God want us to go to Nakhodka and experience this evil? He has given us an option. Should we consider it?"

"What option do we have? To disobey God? That is not an option for me," said Vasil. "Think about it, Natasha. If we choose not to go to Nakhodka, we can either stay here or choose some other destination. We will escape the evil Satan has planned for Nakhodka, but he will have other plans for us in other places. If God calls us to go someplace, even though evil may await us, it's because obedience will produce a far greater good. Pyotr taught me that before he went to the embassy. He said it is the principle of the cross. No cross, no resurrection."

"Thank you, dear husband. I wanted to be sure you were fully committed to obey God, regardless of circumstances," said Natasha. "You have removed all doubt. We are in this together whatever the future holds because we know God holds the future. Tomorrow I will prepare Viktor for our likely departure."

CHAPTER 8
THE FLIGHT

July 1978

When Vasil reported to work, Vadim met him as he was taking off his coat.

"Vasil, a man came by my house last night and asked if he might talk to me about a job. I asked him to come by the office at nine o'clock this morning. I don't know if this is an answer to our prayer, but we should know soon. If it is, please be prepared to spend the next three days briefing your replacement on standard operating procedures of your office. Make sure he understands why you changed the SOP you inherited and how the efficiencies you introduced have increased production. You have saved us a lot of money."

"Natasha and I talked a long time last night," said Vasil. "If God confirms it is his will for us to move, we are prepared to go whatever the cost. She is informing Viktor today of our impending departure. She will not tell him our destination, just as I have not told you. It's better that way since one can't reveal what he doesn't know."

Vasil was engrossed in making notes for briefing his successor when there was a rap on his closed office door. Before he could say, "Come in," the door was half open, and Vadim stepped inside, closing the door again. "The man showed up promptly at 0900. His name is Yuri Leskovich. He is forty-two years old, and he is seeking a job as bookkeeper," Vadim reported. "I got his job history for the past twenty years and the telephone number of his most recent employer, whom I will call when I go back to my office. This is either an amazing coincidence or it is God's response to our prayer. I'm assuming it is God's doing."

"I agree," said Vasil. "I am amazed that the creator of the universe would get involved in the little details of our lives. Isn't that marvelous beyond imagination? Why do I have so much difficulty trusting him with my brief, fragmentary life on earth? Why do I struggle so much with my faith? Can you tell me, Vadim?"

"For the same reason I struggle with mine," Vadim replied. "Because our life here is so short we want immediate answers to our desires. God is building citizens to inhabit his everlasting kingdom. It is the Holy Spirit that provides our link to eternity. It is God's Spirit within us that witnesses to our spirit that we are children of God and joint heirs with Jesus Christ of an eternal kingdom. It is the Holy Spirit that enables us to have anticipatory joy in the midst of trials because he bears witness to who we are and where we are going. And when the Holy Spirit makes heaven real to us, faith rises, and we persevere in joy."

"Vadim, you may find this hard to believe, but my own son has told me much of this before," said Vasil. "God is not only encouraging me to trust him through every trial, but to joyfully anticipate the eternal good that will result."

"God has reinforced his truth to your heart," said Vadim. "It will sustain you through difficult days when they come. And they do come to all of us."

Vasil was greeted by Natasha with a warm hug and lingering kiss when he returned from work.

"Oh, Vasil," she said, "I wish you could have been with Viktor and me today as I told him we may leave Chernogorsk soon. He asked why, and I explained that it was to decrease the danger to him. He wrapped his arms around me and cried that you and I meant more to him than life itself.

"He looked at me and said, 'Mama, you and Papa stay, and we will face danger together.'

"I explained that we believed God was directing us to go, and it all had something to do with God's purpose for his future. I told him, 'You are special, Viktor. God has gifted you with something more than a brilliant mind. You have spiritual insight into holy scripture that will provide light for those in darkness. Somehow, in a way I don't understand, our going away is tied to what God has planned for you.'"

"How did Viktor respond to that?" Vasil asked.

"He said something I will never forget. 'Mama, I will dedicate my life to serve Jesus Christ and love him with all my heart, all my soul, and all my strength. I pledge that I will invest everything I am or have to advance the kingdom of God.' God has his hand upon our boy, Vasil. He will be all right."

"I am glad you talked to Viktor," Vasil interjected, "because today God has confirmed it is his will that we leave.

A bookkeeper came looking for a job as if God sent him to confirm our prayer. I can scarcely believe that the Holy Spirit is guiding us in such a direct way. It's as if we were characters out of the Bible. Oh, Natasha, for some reason I don't understand, we are important to God. We are part of a plan that is bigger than we are. Why? Who are we that the creator would take a personal interest in our insignificant lives? Natasha, what does your heart tell you about all these things? Tell me what you think."

"My heart tells me to rejoice because God loves me and you," answered Natasha. "Nothing can separate us from his love, not trouble or hardship, not persecution or danger, not the KGB or demons from hell. He proved his love beyond doubt when he gave his own son to die to pay the penalty for our sin. My mind is at rest. I know we have a future beyond the here and now, guaranteed by the resurrection of Jesus Christ. Our godless society offers no future except a burial plot one meter wide by two meters long … straight down. We Christians have real hope, Vasil, based on real acts of God. Man can't live without hope, and that's why we Christians will win."

"That is a powerful reinforcement of what Vadim told me earlier today," said Vasil. It also complements the affirmation of Paul, my favorite apostle. *I consider that our present sufferings are not worth comparing with the glory that will be revealed in us.* How empty and vain the promises of humanistic materialism compared to God's promises confirmed by the Holy Spirit. But the temptation to succumb to the lure of temporal things is real and strong. I confess I am not exempt from times when I question my faith. I don't doubt the reality of God. I doubt myself. I fear that in a time of severe trial I will fail the test.

Natasha, my dear Natasha, will I persevere in the face of torture or will I betray a sacred trust? I am filled with resolve
now, but what will I do if my fingernails are being pulled out
with bloody pliers? I know myself. My spirit is willing, but my
flesh is weak."

"Vasil, what are you talking about? Who is going to torture you? What sacred trust will be betrayed? Are there things
going on that you have not shared with me?" The questions
poured from Natasha.

"I have shared everything with you," said Vasil. "Except
one thing that may not be important at all. In 1976 while
Viktor was at the monastery and we lived near Leningrad,
I was approached by a junior KGB officer named Vladymir
Rasputin. His assignment was recruiting agents who could recruit spies from among visitors from the West. He knew I was
an Orthodox believer, and he knew that Orthodox officials
from America often come to USSR. He wanted me to try to
recruit an Orthodox bishop from Washington, DC to be a spy.
'Just to let us know about the coming and going of certain
people. Nothing classified,' he said.

"I refused, but Rasputin did not want to take no for an answer. I explained it would be immoral for an Orthodox believer to tempt another Orthodox. Rasputin became angry and
demanded if I would put my faith ahead of my country. I told
him that nothing could come between me and my loyalty to
God. He snarled and said, 'That's near treason, Gorgachuk.
Let me tell you a secret. My mother had me secretly baptized as
an Orthodox Christian when I was born. The Christian God
is weak and powerless. He allowed himself to be mocked and
spit upon before dying a shameful death. I will never serve
him. I serve the omnipotent power of human government in

the hands of strong men. Never get in our way or we will crush you.'

"It's just possible that when the midwife reported Viktor's unregistered birth to the KGB that she may have talked to Rasputin. We went under a false name, so that can't help identify us, but the woman knows our physical description, and that may have tipped Rasputin to me. It was only two years ago he saw me in Leningrad. He impressed me as the kind of man that likes to push people around. He would love to have an opportunity to show off his power against me.

"The sacred trust that I fear torture may tempt me to reveal is Viktor's whereabouts. I would gladly die rather than reveal it, and I think Rasputin will quickly realize that. If he is serious about getting information, he will resort to torture. That's what worries me,' said Vasil.

"Remember the promise God has given through Saint Paul, who was tested grievously many times," Natasha said. *"God is faithful; he will not let you be tempted beyond what you can bear. But when you are tempted, he will also provide a way out so that you can stand up under it.* You are a mighty man of God, dear husband. Don't let the evil one intimidate you. *Greater is he that is in you than he that is in the world."*

"Thank you, dearest. You are God's gift to me. I have much to do to prepare for our departure in three days. After we eat, I must visit Elder Sergei. He has had the artist make false identity papers for us to present when our train tickets are purchased. The false papers will then be destroyed. It's very dangerous to be caught with two sets. Tomorrow night, I want to slip over to the Vashchenko house and spend some private time with Viktor. Please arrange that with the Vashchenko children. Will the children be able to handle things after you are gone?"

"I will make arrangements for you to have private time with Viktor tomorrow night. As for the children, they are sorry to see me go, but they will be all right. They are amazingly resilient. Let me set the table. Then I will ladle the soup, and we can eat after you give thanks."

⇒+ +⇐

The night session for Vasil and Viktor was an emotionally trying time for both.

"My dear son, I have things on my heart I must share with you," Vasil began. "From your birth, your mother and I dedicated you to God. We vowed we would do everything in our power to prevent you from being corrupted by our pagan government. Your birth was never registered in order that you could not be forced to attend public schools. You were educated by monk specialists at the monastery who were astounded by your mental ability. You have capabilities that our godless government would exploit if they knew you existed. You have been born into God's family, and His Holy Spirit lives within you. You may now have to enroll in godless institutions, but you have a spirit of discernment that will enable you to see truth and error. Do not reveal your knowledge and education to the infidels. You must not cast your pearls before swine. They will destroy you in order to gain your gifts. In God's good time, they will be manifested. Your mother has explained why we must depart. I leave you in God's hands, which are far safer than mine."

"Dear Papa, I promised myself I would not cry. What an evil system that forces a child to be separated from his parents. But we will not be separated. Your love and strength will always be part of me. Do not fear. I will be on guard against the antichrist regime. I remember what the true Christ said, *'I am sending you out like sheep among wolves. So be shrewd as serpents but innocent as doves.'* I will pray for you and Mama every day. No matter what happens, I will never forget you. Your sacrificial love has made me aware of how great must be the love of my heavenly father. Your example gives me courage to face life unafraid." With this, Viktor buried his face in his father's chest.

They wrapped their arms around each other and held each other close. Finally, Viktor whispered, "Father, bless me before you go."

Vasil reverently laid his right hand upon Viktor's head and blessed him with these ancient words: "*I bless you in the name and power of him who is able to keep you from falling and to present you before his glorious presence without fault and with great joy— to the only God our Savior be glory, majesty, power and authority, through Jesus Christ our Lord, before all ages, now and forevermore!* Amen." After the traditional holy kiss, Vasil returned home, rejoicing in what he had experienced.

"You are right, Natasha. Our boy is going to be all right. The Holy Spirit confirmed that to me tonight. We can leave with the assurance that God will keep him safe until he has fulfilled God's purpose for him," Vasil said.

CHAPTER 9
THE FLIGHT FOILED

July 1978

T he next day, Vasil found the new bookkeeper very competent and quick to comprehend his system. By the end of the second day, there was nothing left to explain. The third day, he stayed home and helped Natasha pack their luggage. At 10:30 p.m., they made their way alone to the rail station and sat quietly in a darkened corner. There were a half-dozen others awaiting the arrival of the eleven o'clock train to Vladivostok. Gorgachuks recognized none of them.

As the train arrived, Vasil and Natasha made their way to the designated car. A female conductor looked briefly at their ticket and mumbled, "Third compartment forward."

Stashing their luggage on the top bunks, they relaxed on the seats below. Natasha remarked, "I'm glad we decided to pay a little extra and get a compartment all to ourselves. I'm exhausted. Let's have our evening prayer and get some sleep."

It was nine thousand kilometers from Chernogorsk to Vladivostok. They would have another four nights on the train before reaching their destination. They spent the days relaxing, reading, and enjoying brief walks at the station stops along the way. Most passengers were going to these intermediate stops. Only a few passengers were going all the way to Vladivostok. They arrived there in the early morning of the fifth day.

"Natasha, will you keep an eye on our luggage while I go to the Information Center and inquire about telephone service?" said Vasil. "Elder Sergei gave me the name and phone number of a contact in Nakhodka that I must call."

Vasil returned in a few minutes, smiling broadly. "We can catch a bus directly to the main telephone exchange, but we will have to walk nearly a kilometer to the bus stop. Are you up to walking that far?"

"You ask if I can walk a kilometer? You must be joking. Who is the champion walker in this family?" challenged Natasha.

"I know. I know. I was just trying to be polite, showing consideration for the weaker sex," teased Vasil.

Natasha was pleased to see Vasil in good spirits. It was as if the long emotional siege was over, and he could at last relax. "Let's go find that bus stop," she said, gripping her luggage and striding away. Vasil joined her, and in ten minutes they arrived at the bus stop.

The bus wound its way into the heart of Vladivostok, making stops along the way. Arriving at the Telephone Exchange, they gathered their belongings and exited to a wide sidewalk. An empty bench sat near the entrance.

"Now you watch the luggage while I go inside and call our Nakhodka contact," said Vasil.

He returned twenty minutes later. "Good news, dear. Elder Sergei had called his friend Tibor three days ago and alerted him to our likely arrival today. He has procured a small apartment for us, ready to occupy. Busses depart every forty minutes, and it is a 180-kilometer trip. Takes four hours. I told him we would take the next available bus and should be there about two thirty this afternoon."

"So long?" Natasha asked. "We will need to eat on the bus. You watch the luggage while I take a few minutes and get some bread, salami, and cheese for snacks and a bottle of water."

Natasha returned in a few minutes, stowing the water bottle in Vasil's bag and the food in hers. "Do you have any idea how far it is to the bus station?" she asked.

"No, but there is a taxi parked at the curb. I'll ask the driver," said Vasil. Returning, he reported, "The driver said it is a long walk, at least two kilometers, but he will take us there for half a ruble. He thinks the next bus will leave in about fifteen minutes. We had better take the taxi."

Vasil called to the driver, "We are going to accept your offer. Can you help us put the luggage in the trunk?"

The driver emerged from the cab with an odd smile. He was a husky man, perhaps near forty, with long, straggly hair loosely framing the course features of a face wreathed in three-day stubble. Opening the trunk, he helped stow the luggage without saying a word but continuing to smile. He then opened the rear door. "Please get in," he said softly.

"Thank you," said Vasil, stepping back as Natasha entered and then following her.

The driver exited the shopping center and made his way to a main thoroughfare. He then half turned his head and spoke in a barely audible voice, "I am pleased to see you up close. I have been following you from a distance ever since you arrived at the train station." The fixed smile was still in place.

Alarm bells went off simultaneously for Vasil and Natasha, and they each breathed a silent prayer. "Who are you?" asked Vasil. "We were not expecting anyone to meet us."

"You can call me Alexander, Alexander the great. But who I am is not important. It is who I represent that should concern you," he said softly.

"Alexander, where are you going? Where are you taking us? Who do you represent? Tell us what is going on," Natasha demanded.

"All in good time, my dear," Alexander said quietly. "All in good time. But first I must give Comrade Vasil greetings from an old friend. It is my pleasure to bring you special greetings from Comrade Rasputin." His smile broadened as he continued, "Comrade Rasputin requests that you reconsider the request he made when you were last together. Demonstrate your patriotism in a practical way and prove your love for Mother Russia."

Vasil's mind raced. How had his efforts to hide his identity failed? How could he persuade his captor to reveal where his subterfuge had been inadequate? Perhaps that knowledge would be helpful at some future time … if there was to be a future. He decided he would not beg; he would try another tack.

"So you are an almighty KGB agent. Why did it take you so long to discover our identity?" Vasil taunted.

"You were very clever, Comrade Vasil, but not clever enough. You hid your true identity from the midwife so we had no name. You should have hidden your face as well. When she was arrested for thievery a few weeks ago, she attempted to win favor by reporting an illegal unregistered birth from her past. Her report was referred to the KGB. Although it was a relatively minor issue, Comrade Rasputin's curiosity was aroused, and he interviewed the woman at length. She described you and your wife in great detail even though the incident happened a dozen years ago.

"As you may know, Comrade Rasputin is very sharp and has a photographic memory. Her description reminded him of you as he recalled attempting to recruit you in 1976. He is not so concerned about an unregistered birth, as those are usually detected by schools or other government agencies. Your boy is still unregistered. Acting on his educated hunch, he sent your photo and name to agents across Russia. He is very concerned about an unregistered citizen of the USSR roaming about the country, even if he is only twelve years old. He is determined to learn his whereabouts. You will tell him." His voice could barely be heard as a smile spread slowly across his face.

"When will we see Comrade Rasputin?" Vasil inquired.

"Comrade Rasputin does not get involved in the fun stuff," Alexander said, smirking. "That's my domain."

CHAPTER 10
THE SAGA OF THE SIBERIAN SEVEN CONTINUES

June 1978–June 1979

G unnery Sergeant James Stevens, commander of the twelve-man marine detachment assigned to the American embassy in Moscow, knocked on the office door of the State Department officer who was designated as the RSO (Regional Security Officer).

"Come in, Gunny. What's up?" said RSO Bill Hailes. Mr. Hailes was the principle security attaché and chief advisor to the ambassador on security matters. The marine detachment commander came under his authority.

"Sir, I have an idea I want to run by you," said Gunny Stevens. "We have these seven religious refugees marking time in the embassy. I have heard that one of the ladies wants very much to improve her English. She's convinced she will be able to immigrate to the United States and wants to be prepared. As you know, I want very much to improve my grasp of Russian. What if I made a deal to teach her English if she would teach me Russian? An hour session for a couple days a week would probably be sufficient."

"Now let me see if I have this right," said RSO Hailes. "You want permission to fraternize a couple of times a week with a young female guest. Is that about right?" A mocking smile revealed his attempt at humor.

"No, sir. Not at all, sir," responded the gunny. "I was thinking more in terms of an academic endeavor to advance my value to the marine corps and our State Department. For our guest, it would entail an opportunity to master English well enough to serve as a translator for her family. This would greatly enhance her value as a new citizen of the United States."

"All jesting aside, Commander," responded RSO Hailes (he always called him by his official title when he was serious), "your idea does have merit. Let's kick it around some more before I present it to Ambassador Toon. I see immediately that we must have a third person present. I suggest the young lady you have in mind invite one of her sisters to join the class. I absolutely trust you, but I want to nip any gossip in the bud. Where do you suggest you meet?"

"Why not in my office annex? I can make sure it is available a couple of hours a week," said the gunny. "One more thing occurs to me," he added. "Since my Russian is atrocious, and the Vashchenko ladies are beginners in English, it could be helpful to have one of our translators available for consultation."

"I'll put that in the mix when I talk to the ambassador, and if he approves, it's a go," said Mr. Hailes.

"Thank you, sir," said Gunny Stevens. "I'll wait until I hear from you before proceeding further."

The phone rang in Gunny Stevens's office at midmorning the next day. "Good morning. Gunnery Sergeant Stevens speaking."

"Good morning to you, Commander. I talked to the ambassador after the morning briefing. He approved of your idea in general but vetoed the translator. He said, and I quote him, 'Start simple and have two good Russian/English dictionaries available. You will learn faster and remember more.' He speaks Russian fluently, so he should know what he is talking about. And even if not, the ambassador is the ultimate authority here. So go for it, but with no translator other than a couple of good dictionaries," Mr. Hailes said.

With permission granted to pursue his idea, Gunny Stevens went to the basement where the Vashchenkos were housed. Spotting Lila, he called to her.

"Hello, Miss Lila," Stevens spoke in fractured Russian. "The ambassador and the regional security officer approved my request. I will help you develop your English, and you can assist me with Russian. We will make a lot of mistakes and will need to correct each other often. I will provide a couple of good English/Russian dictionaries. It should be a lot of fun and a lot of laughs. You shall choose one of your sisters to also attend the class. We will meet Monday and Thursday from 1400 to 1500 hours in my office annex. How does that sound?"

"I am much happy," said Lila. "I like speak English more good. *Bolshoi spasibo.* I thank you very big. First, before class, I have big question."

"What is this important question, Lila?" said Stevens.

"What your name? I don't know what I call you," said Lila.

"My name is James Stevens," he said.

"Why no one call your name?" said Lila. "Sometimes you called Gunny, sometimes Commander, and sometimes Gunnery Sergeant. You never called James."

"Yeah, you are right. I bet you are confused. Let me see if I can explain it. I am in the Marine Corps, a military organization. In military organizations, the level of authority is designated by rank. My rank is gunnery sergeant. This is usually shortened to gunny in everyday informal situations. In addition to my rank, I also have a title. Because I command the twelve-man marine detachment at the embassy, my title is commander. This is a unique title for marine non-commissioned officers who command embassy detachments. Embassy personnel call me Commander when doing official business. But to end the confusion, why don't you just call me James? Okay?"

"Okay. I like James," said Lila. "Now I must go tell Mama and Papa about English class. They will like very much."

Pyotr remarked to Augustina, "The Lord is preparing us for America. We will have children who can serve as translators and help teach us English."

"Pyotr, you speak as if our asylum in the embassy was all part of God's big plan for us to learn English," Augustina said, smiling. "I can think of better ways to do that."

"As a matter of fact," said Pyotr, "you are absolutely right. I do believe that all that has happened to us is part of God's big plan. Once we freely surrender our lives to him, he is in control. That is why we can have peace amidst the uncertainties we face. There are no unknowns to our Lord."

"I know you are right," said Augustina. "I only wish the embassy officials were more aware that we are here because this is where God wants us. I am convinced that if Ambassador Toon had not permitted asylum, we would have been returned to the KGB. Commander Stevens told Lila that some high-ranking State Department officials believe that offering asylum to us will incite other abused people around the world to flood American embassies."

"Yes, I know," said Pyotr. "Ambassador Toon made that point when we first entered the embassy. I refuted it and pointed out that we did not come seeking asylum. We came as a result of a letter of invitation from the American State Department. The ambassador agreed, and that's why he has permitted us to stay."

"Lila shared something else that Commander Stevens told her," said Augustina. "He said that the churches in America showed little concern about our situation, even the Pentecostal churches. He said if the Christians in America would contact congressmen and speak out against Soviet oppression and persecution, the American congress would pass a bill condemning the USSR. Why don't our Christian brothers and sisters in America get involved, Pyotr?"

"I know why, and it hurts me to say it," said Pyotr. "Our Soviet government has adopted a plan of Divide and Conquer. Those churches that have registered with the government have agreed not to criticize government policies and to conduct their church activities in conformity to government demands. The leaders of these churches, and many are Pentecostal and Baptist, are provided special privileges. They are even permitted to go to large denominational meetings in America at government expense. There they testify how benign our government is and persuade them not to believe the propaganda of non-registered zealots. The government has bribed registered Pentecostals to persuade their Pentecostal American hosts that there is no reason to fear what is taking place over here."

"Why has the embassy staff made it so difficult for us to be interviewed by the media? Can you think of a reason, Pyotr?" asked Augustina.

"I can," said Pyotr. "It is all tied to American politics. President Carter doesn't want our plight broadcast to the American people because of his high hope for an arms treaty with the USSR. He has no concept of how our leaders think or what influences them. But there is an American presidential election later this year. If a new president is elected, he may view our government more realistically … and our situation more sympathetically."

Pyotr's assessment of the situation was accurate. Because of the delicate arms treaty President Carter was negotiating with the Soviets he likely would have ordered the "Siberian Seven' removed were it not for the immense publicity they were generating nationally and internationally.

When President Reagon was elected he quietly, behind the scenes, negotiated their release so they could immigrate to the United States via Israel. By the end of June, 1983, all the Vashenko family, including Viktor, plus the Chmykhalov family, were safely in Israel, preparing to process to America. Their courage and endurance, while bottled up in the confines of our embassy, won the admiration of freedom lovers everywhere.

CHAPTER 11
THE WRECK

July 1978

A few weeks after the Siberian Seven had found refuge in the American embassy in Moscow, Viktor's parents had been captured in Vladivostok by a KGB agent named Alexander, posing as a taxi driver. Vasil and Natasha are seated in the back seat of the taxi as the agent departs the city.

Alexander lapsed into silence. Vasil and Natasha clasped hands and looked at each other in bewilderment. Vasil silently mouthed the words, "Don't be afraid. Whatever happens, God is with us." Alexander continued driving through the maze of downtown Vladivostok until he reached the main thoroughfare going north out of the city. His backseat passengers were silently praying but had their eyes wide open watching for passing landmarks. Alexander followed the main highway for an estimated twenty kilometers and then turned right on a secondary, two-lane paved road. There was a narrow shoulder between the edge of the road and the embankment that sloped down to the edge of the forest.

Vasil once again decided to try to engage their captor in conversation. "Alexander, is Comrade Rasputin still stationed in Leningrad?" he asked.

"Where Comrade Rasputin is located is none of your business, but where you are located is Comrade Rasputin's business. What's important is that you are located in the backseat of my vehicle. That pleases Comrade Rasputin very much," said Alexander with a giggle.

Suddenly a scripture verse emerged from Vasil's memory bank. *Consider it pure joy, my brothers, whenever you face trials of many kinds.*

Why this verse? he asked himself. And then he remembered where he had last heard these words. It was in the home of Pyotr and Augustina Vashchenko when he and Natasha had taken their son with them to discuss the plan for Viktor to become a member of the Vashchenko family. Pyotr had read this verse to encourage them. Natasha expressed that it was impossible for her to feel joy in trials. Vasil clearly remembered Viktor's response. As a result of his knowledge of New Testament Greek, he had pointed out to his mother that joy didn't come automatically. The Greek imperative verb demanded joy be a deliberate choice. Did he dare to consider this trial with joy? Yes, yes he dared!

"It pleases me very much, also," said Vasil. "I am really very thankful to be here."

"Idiot! Damnable idiot!" shouted Alexander. "If you knew what lies ahead, you wouldn't be pleased or thankful."

"You're wrong, Comrade Alexander," said Vasil. "It's because I know what lies ahead that makes it possible to choose joy and give thanks. My God is in control. He permitted you to capture us. That is part of his plan."

"What insane gibberish," responded Alexander. "You think God is in control? I have news for you: there is no God. And if there were, he sure as hell is not in control." Pulling a revolver from an inside pocket holster, he waved it about in front of him. "This Nagant revolver and I, that's who's in control. One click of this trigger, and it is all over for you," snarled Alexander.

"You are wrong, Comrade Alexander. One click of that trigger, and real life for me would just begin. I would be welcomed into my eternal home that Jesus Christ has prepared for me," said Vasil. "Where would you be, Alexander, if your life on earth suddenly ended?"

"Shut your mouth, you traitor," shouted Alexander. "I only live for the present. I have no time for pie-in-the-sky by and by, so don't throw that religious garbage at me."

"I am not talking about religion, Alexander. I'm talking about reality," said Vasil. "The reason we don't fear death is because we have good reason to believe God has a marvelous future planned for those who love and serve him."

"Reason? Good reason to believe?" Alexander mocked. "You have nothing but ancient myths and fables peopled by ghosts, spirits, demons, and strange people with supernatural power."

Natasha suddenly broke into the conversation. "Alexander, you think our hope is built on religious nonsense. Not so. It is built on the solid truth of history. Jesus was killed by evil men, like you may kill us. But he came back from the grave gloriously alive and for forty days appeared to hundreds of people. These people told others and—"

Alexander interrupted, "Be quiet, bitch. You are nothing but a powerless, ignorant woman repeating old babushka tales."

"I will not be silent," said Natasha boldly. "As long as I have breath, I will declare the truth about Jesus Christ. After rising from the dead, he ascended to heaven and sent the Holy Spirit to give us power to do what we are doing. I am not brave. I would be terrified speaking as I am if the Holy Spirit were not with us."

"Natasha, my dear Natasha," cried Vasil. "I have never been so proud of you as I am now. You are as bold as St. Stephen. May the Lord welcome you as he did the blessed saint. Let us follow his example and pray for Alexander, our persecutor." Vasil then began to pray the ancient Orthodox prayer for enemies, Natasha quickly joining him. *"Lord Jesus Christ, who commanded us to love our enemies and those who defame and injure us, and to pray for them and forgive them as you yourself did pray for your enemies who crucified you. Grant—"*

In the midst of the prayer, Alexander uttered a loud, shrieking curse. Keeping his eyes on the road, he half turned in his seat with his right arm raised as if to strike a backward blow. In his hand, he gripped the Nagant revolver. Surprised, Natasha uttered a piercing scream, thinking Alexander was going to shoot Vasil. Alexander, momentarily distracted, shifted his gaze to the rearview mirror. As he did so, the speeding vehicle drifted just over the center line as it neared a blind curve. An approaching driver, speeding around the curve from the other direction, blinked his lights and sounded his horn. Recognizing the danger, in his maddened rage Alexander overcorrected. The vehicle veered sharply, causing the right front wheel to go off the hard surface and engage the mushy gravel and dirt shoulder. Cursing in anger and fear, Alexander attempted to return to the pavement. As the front wheels tried to gain traction, the rear of the car continued drifting right until both right wheels engaged the soft shoulder, resulting in a violent overturn of the vehicle. It continued to cascade down the grassy embankment until it landed upside down at the bottom. Alexander lay moaning in the front roof section, his left leg twisted at an awkward angle and his body contorted by the roof indentation. He was obviously unconscious. A nasty gash in his scalp bled profusely.

Vasil, knocked temporarily unconscious by a blow to his head, soon recovered. Surveying the situation, he saw Natasha, half conscious, attempting to say something. "Lie still, Natasha," he cautioned, "until we can determine your injuries. Except for a few bruises and minor cuts from broken glass, I think I am all right. Can you tell if you have broken bones or any serious injuries?"

"Oh, Vasil, I really don't think I have any serious injuries," said Natasha. "My right shoulder hurts and may be sprained. I am sure there are multiple bruises I'll feel tomorrow. God has surely protected us from the hand of the adversary. When you spoke to Alexander so courageously, it gave me courage. I'm sure the Holy Spirit used our words to enrage him, which caused him to act as he did."

"It looks like our KGB friend may be seriously injured. We must get out of this crumpled vehicle and try to help him," said Vasil. "The bleeding from his scalp has started to coagulate very nicely. A good sign that it is not too deep."

"How are we going to get out with glass shards protruding from the windows and the roof all crumpled and impeding the doors?" inquired Natasha.

"I think if I knock out all the glass from one of the rear windows, the opening will be big enough that I can squirm through, and you can easily crawl through. Now if I just had something to knock those glass shards out of the way," said Vasil.

"I see something that may work," said Natasha. "From where I am, I can see the revolver Alexander was waving just before the crash. I believe I can reach it with my left hand. Yes, here it is, Vasil. It's ugly. Please take it."

"Good work, Natasha. Before I go using this as a hammer, I want to eject all the bullets. Remind me to throw them away when we get out," said Vasil.

After removing all seven rounds from the Nagant revolver, Vasil began to methodically remove every sliver of glass that might cut or impede their egress. He then wormed himself carefully through the constricted opening, pausing occasionally to regain his breath and strength. Finally, kicking himself free, he arose gingerly and pronounced himself all in one piece.

"Your turn, Natasha," Vasil said, kneeling to help her through the window.

Natasha emerged with minimal exertion and stood triumphantly in the bruised arms of her husband. "We are still alive," she whispered. "Where do you think God will take us now?"

"I have no idea," said Vasil. "A short time ago, I thought heaven was our next destination. Now we must figure a way to extricate Alexander from the vehicle. I'm surprised we have not seen or heard other vehicles pass by. Surely someone will drive by soon and offer to help. You pray, Natasha, that the Lord will give us wisdom and help me to figure a way to get our enemy friend out of this wreck."

"St. James said if anyone needs wisdom to deal successfully with trials, just ask God, and he will provide it," said Natasha. "Now I'll pray, and you think."

"If Alexander were just slightly smaller, we could get him through the window we exited. Too bad the doors will need a cutting torch to free them. If there were only some way we could enlarge that window opening a few centimeters. Wait a minute," said Vasil. "Why didn't I think of this before? I'll extract the key ring from the ignition and unlock the trunk. It suffered very little damage. There may be something useful inside."

"See," said Natasha, "you have already acquired more wisdom."

Pulling the upside-down trunk lid to the ground, Vasil produced an opening of eight or ten inches. He found a tool box containing an assortment of small wrenches, including a pair of water pump pliers and a machinist hammer. There was also a pack of safety flares.

"Anything look promising?" asked Natasha.

"Pray for more wisdom," said Vasil. "Hey, you forgot to re-mind me to throw those revolver rounds away. I just had an idea. I'll use them to blast through the metal frame that con-tains the window mechanism. Fortunately for this job, these appear to be hollow points. If I weaken a section, we may be able to bend it out of the way so as to enlarge the window suf-ficiently to get Alexander through. It's worth a try, so here goes."

Vasil reloaded the revolver with the seven high-powered, hollow-point bullets. Estimating a distance of forty-five cen-timeters on the window frame, he fired three bullets, one below the other at each end of the approximate eighteen inches. The first bullets shattered the rim edge of the frame where the glass emerged. The next two bullets penetrated the thinner double walls that housed the glass and the winding mechanism. There was now a six-centimeter vertical wall held together by narrow fragments of metal between the bullet holes. With the pliers, he quickly completed severing the forty-five-centimeter section from the body of the door.

"Now the hard work begins," said Vasil.

Gripping the sheet metal that formed the exterior of the door below the window frame (now above with the car overturned), Vasil began bending the metal so as to enlarge the opening. Slowly, a small bite at a time, he worked his way across the forty-five-centimeter space.

"Well, that's half of it," said Vasil. "Now I'll do the interior half. This should go a little faster because I can take bigger bites."

"Why can you take bigger bites?" asked Natasha.

"I think now I can use the machinist's hammer effectively to smooth down the rough protrusions left from bending larger sections," Vasil explained.

"You should have been a mechanic instead of a bookkeeper," said Natasha.

"Not really," Vasil demurred. "Necessity is the mother of invention."

"Owww." A guttural cry of pain came from inside the car. "Help me, somebody," pleaded Alexander.

CHAPTER 12

LOVE YOUR ENEMY

"Alexander, thank God you have regained consciousness. Listen carefully, and I will explain our situation," said Vasil. "The car is demolished, and you are pinned inside. Natasha and I were able to squeeze out the side window in the rear door, but the opening is too small for you. I am in the process of enlarging the opening so we can get you out. Do you understand?"

"Yes, I understand the situation, but I don't understand why you are trying to help me," said Alexander. "You know who I am and what I have been ordered to do. Why are you protecting me and helping to preserve my life? Explain that to me."

"It is very simple, Alexander," said Vasil. "Like you, we also have orders that we must obey. Our master has commanded us to love our enemies and to do good to those who mistreat us. He cares about you, so we must care about you. We want to help preserve your natural life so you will have further opportunity to accept eternal life. You may deny him, but God still loves you and wants you to be part of his family."

"That sounds too good to be true," said Alexander. "You know that if you help me to survive, I will have to report to Comrade Rasputin what has happened. You will once again be hounded until captured, and the KGB will get the information it wants. It always does."

"Yes, we know," said Natasha. "The KGB may capture us, but we will never be under their control. Our Lord is always in charge. You see how he has delivered us from you."

"This hammering is going to make a lot of racket," said Vasil. "You may have to wait a while to talk ... or maybe I should say *to hear*."

Vasil pounded away until the horizontal projections were hammered even. He then worked on the two short vertical walls formed by the bullets.

"These have some jagged edges and may snag Alexander's clothing," said Vasil. "I'll ding the bead about six centimeters back from the vertical edge with the hammer and then bend it back at a forty-five-degree angle. That will leave a smooth metal surface."

"Alexander, we are ready to get you out of there," Vasil announced. "Are you able to maneuver at all?"

"Whenever I try to move my left leg, there is excruciating pain in the upper thigh. I first believed it was broken, but now I think the femur head has been wrenched out of its socket. If it were possible to get the head of the femur relocated in the socket, I think I could crawl."

"I saw an injury like this on one of the miners where I worked," said Vasil. "Without anesthesia and traction, it may be impossible to manipulate the head back into the socket. Regardless, the effort will be unbelievably painful."

"I know," said Alexander. "I have a torture machine that inflicts this injury on intractable prisoners. I wear earplugs to block out the screams of victims. Maybe there is a God and he is repaying me for years of cruelty. Is that what you think?"

"God didn't cause the accident that produced your injury. You did," said Vasil. "God knew it was going to happen, and he permitted it. But even bad things can turn to good things if you trust God with your life."

"My life would be over if I became a Christian," said Alexander. "The KGB would see to that."

"Your life would just begin if you became a Christian," said Natasha. "Jesus Christ would see to that."

"I am going to join you inside," said Vasil. "I can get back in much easier than I got out."

Vasil pushed his upper body through the opening and had room to spare. He supported his weight with his lowered arms and hands while he wiggled his hips and legs through.

"I'm sure the opening is plenty big enough, Alexander," said Vasil. "Our challenge is to get you to it and then through it. I can try to manually put the femur head back into the socket. Or you can put your body weight on your right leg and do a one-leg crawl. It's your choice. What do you think?"

"I prefer to do the one-leg crawl. That way I can monitor my own pain and stop moving if necessary. Maybe you can try the manual fix when I'm out of the wreck," said Alexander.

"All right, let's do it," said Vasil. "Easy now, Alexander, as you get into position for the crawl. Can I help?"

"No thanks," grunted Alexander. "I've practiced a one-leg crawl many times in infantry training before joining the KGB."

Slowly, torturously, Alexander inched himself the short distance to the rear opening.

"Alexander, relax for a couple of minutes," said Vasil. "This is where it gets very tricky. You will have to do a quarter turn so your hips are parallel with the bottom of the opening. Then insert your arms and head through the opening as you support your weight on your bent right leg. I will position myself on your right side away from your injury. On a signal from me, you will use your bent right leg to lift your torso up and forward. I will lift up and forward on your belt while Natasha pulls on your arms. It may take a couple of times, but if you can stand the pain, we will get you through."

"Wait one more moment," said Natasha. "I would feel much better if we prayed, asking Jesus to help us. Do you mind, Alexander?"

"I'm beginning to think I would be a fool to protest," responded the contrite KGB agent. "Please pray, and if you don't mind, please ask your God to alleviate my pain."

"Jesus, we love you and know you are with us. We pray that you will help us get Alexander to safety and heal him, body, mind, and spirit. And please do alleviate his terrible pain. In the name of the Father, Son, and Holy Spirit. Amen. Now give us your signal when ready, Vasil."

"We're ready inside. I'll count to three and then shout *go*. One, two three, go!"

They were able to get Alexander's body through to where the displaced hip impeded movement. Vasil carefully pondered the situation and then reached a decision.

"Alexander, your dislocated left femur has dropped lower than the right one and is impeding our progress. I am going to come around on your left side and apply upward pressure to raise the head of the femur with my left hand and right knee. With my right hand and arm, I will push against your rear. Like before, I will count to three and give the 'go' signal. Any questions? Okay, I am now in position, so let's do it. One, two, three, go!"

The concerted effort produced the desired result. Alexander's hips and then his legs passed through the opening. Suddenly Alexander erupted in a loud shout.

"He did it! Your God did it! Is there really a God? There must be. He answered your prayer. It can't be, but it must be true!"

"What are you saying, Alexander? What happened? What did God do? Take some deep breaths and explain yourself," said Vasil.

"I don't think I can explain it, but I can tell what happened," said Alexander. "When you raised the head of the femur and then pushed on my rear end, I felt the ball slip into the socket. I didn't really believe it. I waited until I was all the way through the opening before I said anything. When I was lying on the grass, I made sure both hips were actually level. I knew the pain had subsided. I was astounded and could not remain silent any longer. Now I understand why you were not afraid of me. God is not a myth. You told me the truth. He is real and powerfully alive. There is a God. There is a God," Alexander repeated.

"Alexander, you have experienced the power and the love of Jesus Christ, whom we serve. You are important to him. He cares about you. There is so much I want to share with you. But first we need to get you to a medical facility for an examination and follow-up care," said Vasil. "God has done his part, and now we must do ours. Alexander, is there any communication device inside the wreck that can be used to summon help?"

"I'm afraid not," said Alexander. "A sending and receiving shortwave radio was installed in the vehicle. I checked it while you were struggling out of the wreck. It was crushed in the rollovers."

"Tell us, Alexander, where does this road lead? Where were you taking us?" asked Vasil.

"This road takes us to a KGB mission station. About five kilometers ahead, public access to this road is no longer possible. There is a maximum-security rail gate across the road, bordered on either side by a maximum-security fence three meters high, topped with razor wire. A large sign reads: **Do Not Enter. KGB Mission Station # 12.** The gate is not actually needed. The sign is enough to deter all but the insane. This is where the KGB interrogates its victims."

"Does someone stay there?" asked Natasha.

"Occasionally, but not regularly unless there are prisoners to be interrogated," Alexander replied. "The Interrogation Module contains four holding cells, a lounge for KGB agents, a kitchen, three bedrooms with toilets and showers, and an interrogation room with adjoining closets holding various devices to expedite the interrogation process. I am ashamed to describe them. I am even more ashamed to admit that I have enjoyed using them. I see now there is no limit to beastly action when God is denied. Oh God, I'm so scared. I need help. I desperately need help."

"What is it, Alexander? Has the intense pain returned?" asked Vasil.

"No, not physical pain," replied Alexander. "It's worse. My mind is so messed up. I get these urges to inflict pain.

I have obeyed the urges so often the action has become part of me. I get a physical thrill of pleasure from watching people suffer and hearing them cry for mercy. What's wrong with me?"

"Have you ever had a psychiatric exam?" asked Vasil.

"Oh yes. I've been categorized as borderline psychopathic. The KGB likes men in that category."

"What does that mean to you?" asked Vasil.

"It means I don't like people, and I like to make them suffer. But I don't want to hurt you or Natasha. I want to help you. I haven't felt like this since I was a boy with my babushka. What's happening?"

"It's Jesus Christ doing his work, Alexander," said Vasil. "He wants to make you well, mind and body and spirit. The devil has had you long enough. It's time to let Jesus make you a new person."

"Do you think that devils actually exist?"

"Absolutely," said Vasil. "There are mysterious, dark, evil powers at work in the world. The Bible calls them devils or demons. They are ruled by the prince of darkness named Satan. Satan and his hordes of devils have one aim, to corrupt and destroy men whom God loves. You have been influenced by these evil beings. But there is hope. Jesus came to destroy the works of the devil. He can change you and make you a new person. He wants you to be with him forever."

"I wish I could believe that. There's no place in God's family for the likes of me. Even my own family has rejected me."

"So, you are a sinner," Vasil said. "So am I. Even Natasha, my lovely wife, is a sinner. That means none of us measures up to God's standard required to become part of his family."

"And just what is the standard?" asked Alexander.

"Perfection. One must be morally perfect before God will accept him as a son or daughter."

CHAPTER 13
THE TRANSFORMATION

"Just like I thought," said Alexander. "I don't stand the chance of a snowball in hell."

"Exactly. Neither do I," Vasil said. "Think of it this way, Alexander. Imagine perfection is represented as a steel pole rising straight up toward heaven a thousand meters high. Say you measure three meters on the perfection scale. Say I measure five meters, and Natasha measures eight meters. What do we all have in common?"

"We all fall way short of perfection. Looks like you and Natasha are in the same boat I am," answered Alexander.

"You are absolutely right," said Vasil. "Tell me, Alexander, have you ever read the Bible?"

"It's against the law," Alexander replied "What makes you ask?"

"You just quoted part of a Bible verse in response to my question, *What do we all have in common?* Here is the verse. *All have sinned and fallen short of the glory of God.* The 'glory of God' is his perfection. We all have a serious problem, don't we?"

"We sure as hell do if we want to be part of God's family. That's why I quit trying a long time ago," said Alexander.

"You toss the word hell around quite a bit. Is there any particular reason?" Vasil asked.

"Probably," Alexander said. "My babushka kept a Bible hidden in her house. Sometimes she would read to me from the last book, I forget what it's called. It told of a burning pit called hell where the devil was assigned and everyone who wasn't listed in God's ledger. She said I had better be good or that's where God would send me. Then I learned in school that God didn't exist. What a relief that was. I began to use 'hell' carelessly since I had no fear of it any longer. I figured I could be as bad as I wanted as long as I could get away with it. And I've gotten away with a lot."

"There's a far better way of overcoming your fear of hell," said Vasil.

"What do you mean?" asked Alexander.

"I mean that someone else has already suffered hell in your place. He paid your penalty, and you can be pardoned."

"I don't understand," said Alexander. "What are you talking about?"

"Alexander, this is the central theme of the Bible. God invaded earth as a real man in the person of Jesus. As a man, Jesus did God's will perfectly. He had no sin and scored at the very top of the thousand-meter standard."

"I still don't understand," said Alexander. "What does Jesus's perfection have to do with me? It just makes my failure all the more glaring."

"True, if he were only man," said Vasil. "But he was also God. He laid aside his glory but retained his divinity. As God, his life had infinite more value than all humanity combined. He suffered an agonizing death and descended into hell on your behalf. That's how much he loves you."

"You have no idea the terrible things I have done," said Alexander. "He could never love me."

"It's not what you have done or haven't done," said Vasil. "It's what Jesus has done on your behalf. He not only died for you, but three days later he arose from the dead and appeared to hundreds of people for forty days, proving he was who he claimed to be. He then ascended into heaven and sent the Holy Spirit to take his place on earth. His Spirit is here right now."

Natasha could remain silent no longer. "Alexander, right now the Holy Spirit is urging you to accept Jesus Christ as Lord by faith. The Spirit will give you spiritual life and equip you for the kingdom of God. Jesus never lies. Will you trust him?"

"Yes, yes I will," said Alexander. "Something is happening. I feel a strange warmth throughout my body like when babushka held me when I was a little boy. It feels like … it feels like love. It has been so long, I had forgotten what love feels like. God … really … loves … me," he said as sobs wracked his unkempt frame. "Jesus, thank you for paying the penalty for my wretched life. Forgive me for messing it up so badly. I do trust you. I will follow you."

Natasha and Vasil were awestruck as they watched the Holy Spirit do his cleansing, transforming work. "What a great savior we serve," said Natasha. "Let's welcome Alexander into God's family."

"Not too heartily," Vasil warned. "Remember, he's injured."

Gently but warmly, they embraced the KGB agent and welcomed him as a new brother in Christ. There was so much to talk about, so much to be thankful for.

Alexander was still trying to comprehend what had happened to him. The beastly urge to cause harm was gone. The hip joint pain was receding. These were tangible demonstrations of God's power at work and immensely reassuring to the KGB agent. It wasn't his imagination playing tricks on him. He was experiencing reality. Nevertheless, he was still a KGB agent, and he must take that reality into consideration.

Looking at her watch and seeing it was after two in the afternoon, Natasha realized that in the excitement she had forgotten all about food. Now her stomach was sending signals she couldn't ignore. "Are either of you interested in food?" she asked. "I just remembered there are snacks and a bottle of water in our luggage. Vasil, will you please get them out of the trunk?"

"I could barely get the door down enough to get the tool box out," Vasil said. "I may have to go through the back of the rear seat to get the luggage. One way or another, I'll get it."

Natasha and Alexander watched as Vasil crawled back into the wreck. Inside, he soon pulled the cushioning material away to provide entry into the trunk. "I can reach the luggage," he grunted. "Come, Natasha, let me hand the bags to you. When you extract the food and water, please get my Bible as well."

Natasha soon had a large towel on the grass spread with fragrant salami, cheese, and bread. "Smells good," said Alexander. "I didn't realize how hungry I was until the smell of salami reached my nose."

"Alexander, before we eat I am going to ask you to do something you likely have never done before," Vasil said. "In your own words, please thank God for this food and for all the blessings we have enjoyed today. Will you do that please?"

Alexander hesitated as if he might refuse. After a moment, he nodded in assent and began to pray. "God, my friend asked me to give thanks for the food, and I really do thank you. I've never talked to God before, so while I am at it, there are a few other things I'd like to say. I never knew you existed and hoped you didn't. But in my pain and despair today, you touched me with your love and healing power. I knew I could never measure up to your standard, and then I learned that your son, Jesus, took my punishment and paid my penalty. He died for me. Now I want to live for him. Send your Holy Spirit to help me. That's all for now, God. Amen."

"God heard your prayer," said Vasil.

"Are you sure?" Alexander asked. "It wasn't much of a prayer, but I meant every word."

"If he heard the prayers of a murderous terrorist like Saul of Tarsus and the rough soldiers enforcing Roman law in Caesarea, we can be sure he heard yours," Vasil assured him. "God looks on the heart, not outward appearances."

"Tell me more about that terrorist guy," said Alexander. "I think I can relate to him."

"After we eat, I'll tell you all about Saul. You will love his story and how God changed his life. First, let's enjoy the food that Natasha had the foresight to bring. Thank you, dear."

As they ate and relaxed in the warm sunshine, a deep peace filled Alexander's heart. He could not explain why or how. Would his friends have an explanation? He would ask.

"I have this wonderful release from fear and a sense of peace and even joy," Alexander said. "It's something vodka and heroin have never provided. Was there something special in the food or water you served?"

"Just God's love," Natasha said with a smile. "That is the Holy Spirit confirming you have been accepted into God's family. Here is the way the Bible describes it. Let me read it to you. *Those who are led by the Spirit of God are sons of God. For you did not receive a spirit that makes you a slave again to fear, but you received the Spirit who makes you sons. And by him we cry, Abba, Father. The Spirit himself testifies with our spirit that we are God's children. Now if we are children, then we are heirs—heirs of God and co-heirs with Christ, if indeed we share in his sufferings in order that we may also share in his glory."*

"I have many more questions to ask about my new life with Jesus, but first I must share some things with you," Alexander said. "KGB officers often work in pairs. I have a partner who is to meet me tomorrow morning for the second phase of the interrogation. My job is to soften up the prisoners with rough, painful questioning. If that doesn't get results, Vitali comes in as the nice guy and professes to want to help the victims. He promises to work for their release if they will provide the information or confession he wants."

"What happens if the prisoners still don't cooperate?" asked Natasha.

"Vitali expresses great regret at the lack of cooperation and indicates there is nothing more he can do. He states he will have to turn the prisoners back to the bad guy. If that threat doesn't produce results, he releases them back to me for more persuasion."

"What happens if they continue to resist?" Natasha persisted.

Alexander hung his head and whispered, "You don't want to know."

"Jesus knows all about it, Alexander, and he has forgiven you," Natasha replied. "Nevertheless, confession is important for Christians. The Bible says, *Confess your sins to each other and pray for each other so that you may be healed.* I don't know why confession of sin is connected to healing, but it is. And I don't want anything to hinder the complete healing of your hip."

"Confession is also essential because sin must be acknowledged in order to be forgiven," Vasil said. "Let me read another verse from the Bible. It is one of my favorites because I have had to apply it so often. *If we claim to be without sin, we deceive ourselves and the truth is not in us. If we confess our sins, he is faithful and just and will forgive us our sins and purify us from all unrighteousness.* That is a promise from God that will give us hope all through our lives. Do you see the importance of confession?"

"Yes, I really do," said Alexander. "It illustrates the contrast between God and the KGB."

"How's that?" Natasha asked.

"Don't you see? God wants us to confess so he can forgive us. The KGB wants prisoners to confess so they can be imprisoned or killed," Alexander explained. "Now I see more clearly what Jesus has done. God can forgive me because his son has already paid my penalty. I heard you say it before, but now I really get it. What a deal God has given me! I'm ready to come clean before you and God."

"Just talk directly to God and confess to him because he is the one you have sinned against. We will just listen quietly as you make your confession," Vasil said.

"God, I want you to know I offer this confession freely with no coercion," Alexander began as if he were in a courtroom. "I have been a liar, a murderer, an adulterer, a thief, a perjurer, a rapist, and betrayer of good people. I have taken your name in vain countless times. I have dishonored my parents and my saintly babushka. I have brought pain and anguish to many innocent people. Oh God, my guilt overwhelms me. Your word promises that if I confess my sin you will forgive. I don't deserve to be forgiven, but I claim your promise and thank you with all my heart. Thank you, Jesus, for shedding your blood and paying the penalty for my sins against you and humanity. I will do my best to serve you, so help me God, amen."

"Alexander, you are absolutely right," Vasil said. "God is trustworthy. He heard your confession, and you are forgiven and clean in his sight. He is pleased that you know this is all made possible by what Jesus has done in your behalf. He honors those who honor his son."

CHAPTER 14
GETTING READY FOR THE KGB SHOWDOWN

"I would like to know more about the interrogation process," Natasha said. "I asked, Alexander, what happened if prisoners refused to cooperate with Vitali."

"Yes, I remember," Alexander said. "Your question stirred memories of heinous things I did to get information or confessions. I sensed an overwhelming need to confess my wicked acts. Now that I know God has forgiven and cleansed me, I can continue. However, I am sure the usual routine will not be followed tomorrow. We must pray that the Holy Spirit will guide us."

"What time in the morning do you expect Vitali?" Vasil asked.

"Our appointment is 0900," said Alexander. "He is usually very punctual but seldom early. I don't expect him to come by here before 0830. If we climb up the embankment after awaking in the morning, he will see us as he approaches, that is, if he comes by car."

"How else would he come?" Natasha asked.

"Sometimes he is flown in by helicopter if he has been pursuing an out of area assignment. It doesn't happen often, but it is a possibility," Alexander said.

"So we must wait and see what develops," Vasil said. "Natasha, can we wait until this evening to talk about tomorrow? It is so warm and pleasant this afternoon. I would like to gather some soft pine branch tips and stack them for bed-making material tonight. May as well make ourselves as comfortable as we can. We have another eighteen hours to wait."

"Alexander, how does your hip feel?" Natasha asked.

"Much better, thanks. There is a dull ache in the whole hip area but nothing like the excruciating pain before. I think I will walk around slowly with a support stick and see how the hip responds. I agree with Vasil. Let's put tomorrow out of our minds for a few hours and enjoy this beautiful day. How could I ever have denied there is a creator?"

The threesome enjoyed a relaxing afternoon. The cool shelter of the dense pine forest offered relief from the beaming July sun. Vasil's pile of bough tips kept growing larger by the hour, augmented by armfuls from Natasha and Alexander. By 1800, there was sufficient to make three cushioned sleeping billets. They surveyed their handiwork with satisfaction and congratulated themselves on a job well done.

"A worker is worthy of his reward," Natasha said. "We have enough food left for another meal. We can have a small portion tonight and reserve some for tomorrow morning, or we can eat it all tonight. What would you rather do? If there's a tie, I'll cast my vote. You first, Alexander."

"That's an easy choice for me. I'll take it all tonight."

"That's my vote, too," said Vasil. "I worked up an appetite, and I don't mind missing breakfast."

"I'll make it unanimous," said Natasha. "Vasil, please give thanks before I lay out the food."

Vasil prayed a fervent prayer of praise and thanksgiving for all God's blessings. It was as if he were an ancient psalmist borne along by the Holy Spirit to express an ode of adoration and worship to the creator. As he concluded, an awesome, holy hush settled over them for a moment before Alexander broke the silence.

"Jesus is here. I know he is here. He spoke to me and called me by name."

"What did Jesus say to you?" asked Vasil.

"He said, 'Sasha, I love you. I have been waiting a long time to answer your babushka's prayers. Welcome home.' He called me Sasha. Only Babushka called me that. My Babushka is with Jesus where I will join her someday. Surely this is the happiest day of my life. Think of it. Jesus loves me, and he called me by my nickname."

"This is a supremely happy day for us too," said Vasil. "God has surprised us beyond our wildest expectations. Whatever happens from now on, it has been worth it to see what God has done in your life. Come on. Let's share a joyful meal together."

"Have you decided what you are going to tell Vitali when we meet?" Vasil asked.

"Not yet," Alexander answered. "I've been thinking hard and praying for wisdom. Sometime in the process, I will have to inform Vitali about what has happened. It's unpredictable what his response will be. In order to prevent him from hurting you, I need to be armed. There are no bullets in the revolver. Did you recover any from the wreck?"

"The only bullets I've seen are the rounds I fired to help enlarge the opening," said Vasil. "Did you bring more with you?"

"Yes. There were fourteen in a small cardboard box stored in the map pocket of the front left door," said Alexander. "When the car flipped and rolled down the embankment, the box must have been thrown out."

"If so, they may be on the embankment somewhere above us," said Natasha. "There's still lots of light for another hour. Let's look in the grass."

"I've found one," Vasil said. "Look! Here's two more. The box must have broken open. There should be others scattered in the grass."

"Yes, here's another," Natasha cried. "And one more over there."

"Here are two way down here," said Alexander. "That's enough to load the revolver, so stop looking."

"Would you shoot Vitali?" asked Natasha.

"Only in defense of you and Vasil. I would not defend myself unless you two would be at the mercy of Vitali if I were not around."

"Use your experience and your imagination, Alexander, and describe what we may face tomorrow," Vasil said. "Can you do that for us?"

"I'll try," Alexander replied. "There are not that many scenarios to depict. First, I will tell him about the wreck. He will ask me to proceed with the rough interrogation as we have done in the past. I'll refuse, telling him you saved my life and even I can't be so devilish. Chances are he will volunteer to do my routine. I won't permit that. Then he will become angry and demand to know what's going on. I will tell him of my new life and announce my loyalty to Jesus Christ. Only God knows what will happen after that."

"I'm happy to leave it in God's hands," said Vasil. "I believe that whatever happens will be what is best for all concerned in the long run."

"Oh, Vasil and Alexander, I am so grateful we have heaven to look forward to when this life is over," said Natasha. "Whatever pain we endure here will seem as nothing in comparison to what we gain over there."

"Since we don't know what will happen tomorrow, I would like to take a moment now and tell both of you how thankful I am that God caused our paths to cross," Alexander said. "You saved my life, first physically and then spiritually. I pledge to you I will protect your lives with my own if need be. I have no fear of death or of life. My whole perspective changed when Jesus called me Sasha and told me he loved me. If Jesus is for me, what does it matter who is against me?"

"Alexander, you are a miracle of God's grace," Vasil said. "We knew God was in control when you took us into custody, but we, at least I, never dreamed of what God had in store for us. Not only does Jesus love you, but Natasha and I have learned to love you in these hours we have had together. We marvel at the transformation God has made in your mind and spirit. We are privileged to be with you regardless of what lies ahead."

"There is one more critical issue that needs to be discussed before we face tomorrow," Natasha said. "It involves our son, Viktor, and his whereabouts."

"I didn't dare mention that lest you think I was trying to coerce information," said Alexander. "I would die before betraying your trust."

"Natasha is right," Vasil said. "We trust you not only with our own lives but with our son's future. I'll summarize his life, some of which you know. The KGB vendetta against Christians that accelerated under Khrushchev and continued under Brezhnev prompted us to not register Viktor's birth. He was secretly educated in a secluded monastery for eight years and released back to us earlier this year when he was twelve. We settled in Siberia in the mining town of Chernogorsk and were there when we heard that the attending midwife at our son's birth had revealed our secret to the KGB. We knew we must relocate ourselves far from Viktor since the KGB could discover him only through us. We left Viktor with Pyotr and Augustina Vashchenko and their twelve children. Our son has documents identifying him as Viktor Vashchenko, and he will be registered in school under that name. The Vashchenkos are Pentecostals desperately trying to immigrate to America, and our hope and prayer is that Viktor will be able to escape with them. There is a lot I have left unexplained, but this provides the essential information."

"I may be able to help when I have access to our communication equipment at the Interrogation Station. There is a powerful man in the emigration department who owes me a huge favor. I will suggest what he might do sometime in the future to repay his debt in full. Don't tell me anymore. I have enough information to start wheels turning at the proper time. Are there any other loose ends we need to talk over?"

"I'm exhausted," Natasha said. "If there is nothing urgent, I suggest we pray together and then test Vasil's skill as a bed maker. Those cushy pine boughs look very tempting."

Natasha's suggestion was readily accepted, and soon earnest prayers ascended into the Siberian sky. The sound of praying was soon followed by steady snoring, interrupted occasionally by a slap at preying mosquitoes.

Natasha awakened shortly after dawn. She quickly arose while the men pretended to continue sleeping. She slipped into the dark recesses of the dense pine forest to attend to her toilette routine as best she could without water. She had rescued a comb from her luggage and vigorously applied it to her tangled hair. When she returned, the men were sitting up, rubbing sleep from their eyes.

"Your turn," she announced cheerfully. "Be careful and don't burn your hands. The hot water will scald you."

"You must have slept well," Vasil commented. "I'm not sure I'm ready for gallows humor this early in the morning."

"The Bible says, 'Rejoice always.' Humor is my rejoicing language."

"Since there is no food left, we will fast physically, but we can feast spiritually," Vasil said. "We have an hour before we need to think about assembling on the road."

"How do we feast spiritually?" Alexander inquired.

"Scripture is our basic spiritual ration," Vasil explained. "Sacred music can feed us spiritually. An inspired sermon or testimony may nourish our spirits. This morning, we must limit ourselves to a basic ration from the Bible. Natasha and I will read a favorite passage of scripture. Alexander, somewhere in your memory is a recollection of something your babushka read to you. Does anything come to mind?"

"Yes, there certainly does," Alexander replied. "I told you about Babushka reading passages about hell and warning me to be good. In that same last book of the Bible between two warnings about hell was a beautiful description of heaven. If you know where that is found, I want to read it."

"I do know where that is," Vasil said. "I would like Natasha to feed us first with her passage. I will read after her. Then I will show Alexander the verses he recalls his babushka reading."

"Scripture is filled with rich spiritual food, and it is difficult to select just one. My choice is Romans 8:28–39," Natasha said. *"And we know that in all things God works for the good of those that love him, who have been called according to his purpose. For those God foreknew he predestined to be conformed to the likeness of his son, that he might be the firstborn among many brothers. And those he predestined he also called; those he called, he also justified; those he justified, he also glorified.*

"What, then, shall we say in response to this? If God is for us, who can be against us? He who did not spare his own son, but gave him up for us all—how shall he not also, along with him, graciously give us all things? Who will bring any charge against those whom God has chosen? It is God who justifies. Who is he that condemns? Christ Jesus who died—more than that, who was raised to life—is at the right hand of God and is interceding for us. Who shall separate us from the love of Christ? Shall trouble or hardship or persecution or famine or nakedness or danger or sword? As it is written: For your sake we face death all day long; we are considered as sheep to be slaughtered. No, in all these things we are more than conquerors through him that loved us. For I am convinced that neither death nor life, neither angels nor demons, neither the present nor the future, nor any powers, neither height nor depth, nor anything else in all creation, will be able

to separate us from the love of God that is in Christ Jesus our Lord. Amen."

"My selection is short but extremely nourishing considering our situation," Vasil began. "It is the first five verses of second Corinthians five. *Now we know that if the earthly tent we live in is destroyed, we have a building from God, an eternal house in heaven, not built by human hands. Meanwhile we groan, longing to be clothed with our heavenly dwelling, since when we are clothed we shall not be found naked. For while we are in this tent, we groan and are burdened, because we do not wish to be unclothed but clothed with our heavenly dwelling, so that what is mortal may be swallowed up by life. Now it is God who has made us for this very purpose and has given us the Spirit as a deposit, guaranteeing what is to come.* Hallelujah!

"The portion Alexander is going to share is more like dessert. It's Revelation 21:1–7."

"When babushka would bring out her hidden Bible and read, I loved this section. *Then I saw a new heaven and a new earth, for the first heaven and the first earth had passed away and there was no longer any sea. I saw the Holy City, the new Jerusalem, coming down out of heaven from God, prepared as a bride beautifully dressed for her husband. And I heard a loud voice from the throne saying, 'Now the dwelling of God is with men, and he will live with them. They will be his people, and God himself will be with them and be their God. He will wipe every tear from their eyes. There will be no more death or mourning or crying or pain, for the old order of things has passed away.'*

"*He who was seated on the throne said, 'I am making everything new!' Then he said, 'Write these things down, for these words are trustworthy and true.'*

"He said to me: 'It is done. I am the Alpha and the Omega, the Beginning and the End. To him who is thirsty, I will give to drink without cost from the spring of the water of life. He who overcomes will inherit all this, and I will be his God and he will be my son.'"

"Yes, yes! I was thirsty, and I did drink. My babushka, I will see you again in the Holy City."

CHAPTER 15
MY PARTNER, VITALI

Vasil looked at his watch and then spoke. "We have had spiritual food. Now we'll take time for spiritual exercise. Spiritual health demands a balance of food and exercise. Each of us will take a few minutes to exercise ourselves by praying. Natasha will begin, Alexander will follow, and I will close. I have called this an exercise, and so it is. But it is far more. It is a glorious privilege to talk to our heavenly father as his son or daughter. So come boldly and gratefully, giving thanks as well as presenting needs. Natasha will begin."

Each of the threesome offered fervent prayers filled with thanksgiving and earnest petitions. Alexander reminded them of what lay just ahead in his closing request.

"Dear God, you have changed my life and destiny. Somehow, someway get through to my partner, Vitali, and do for him what you have done for me. Help him to see that Jesus has paid his penalty and he can go free. In Jesus's authority, Amen.

"I think it is time to assemble by the road," said Alexander. "We don't want to miss Vitali should he come earlier than expected. I think I will work my way up the slope on my back. That way I can do most of the pushing with my right leg and thigh and not risk damage to the injury."

"Good idea," said Vasil. "If that doesn't work, I can help you walk up."

Reaching the top, they surveyed their surroundings. All they could see on either side of the road was seemingly an endless mass of verdant green pines. The bright sun glistened as it was reflected off the shining needles. They stood silently, each immersed in his or her own thoughts. It passed 0830, and they heard nothing but birds chirping in the pines. At 0845, there was the sound of a distant engine. Where was the sound coming from? They could see no vehicle approaching.

"There it is," Alexander shouted. "Vitali is coming in by helicopter. The pilot is circling the helipad, I'm sure. Chances are he will let Vitali debark without stopping the rotors and then take off immediately. Quick, light a safety flare."

They watched the chopper disappear below the treetops but could hear the engine and revolving blades in the distance. The level of noise remained constant for a few minutes, and then suddenly it increased. In a moment, the chopper arose in view above the treetops, headed in the direction from which it arrived.

"Oh, no," Natasha said. "It's going away from us. Now what?"

"Don't panic," Alexander said. "Likely, as soon as Vitali discovers no one is at the site, he will radio the pilot and ask him to make an aerial reconnaissance of the road. He should be over this area soon. Better ignite another flare."

"He's disappearing to the west," Vasil said. "No, wait. He's circling back and coming our way."

"He should have plenty of clearance to set down on the road," Alexander said. "I think he can carry four passengers. We will find out in a moment. As soon as it is obvious he has spotted us, extinguish the flares or hold them tightly. The rotor wash will blow them into the trees and could start a fire. Okay, I'm sure he has seen us."

"Hey, he's climbing instead of landing. What's going on?" Vasil asked.

"Just a safety precaution, I think," Alexander said. "He is making sure there is no approaching vehicle before he lands. All right, he's coming down. Looks like he is going to park just forward of where we are. I think he will stop the rotors, but make sure they have fully stopped before approaching the helicopter."

The three watched as the pilot skillfully sat his bird down in the middle of the road. He killed the engine, and the rotor blades soon stopped. The pilot climbed out of the cockpit and assayed the three awaiting him. In contrast to Alexander, he was well groomed with neatly cut, black hair atop a broad Slavic face. His well-muscled, medium frame was decked out in black slacks and a black turtle neck pullover. A maroon scarf was loosely draped about his neck. After eyeing them to his satisfaction, he finally spoke.

"What happened, Alexander? How did you survive that mangled mess down below?"

"I was distracted momentarily and drifted across the center line as a speeding car approached," Alexander explained. "I overcorrected, and the right wheels caught the soft shoulder, flipping us over. The car rolled down the embankment, ending up as you can see."

"That answers my first question. What about the second? Why are you not dead?"

"As for my survival, I owe that to my two passengers. They managed to extricate me, or my body would still be trapped in the wreckage below. Let me introduce you to each other. Igor, meet Vasil and Natasha. And this is Igor, who knows more about flying helicopters than Igor Sikorsky."

Igor acknowledged Vasil and Natasha with a nod but made no further overtures, so they nodded in return.

"I'm running a little behind schedule, so let's get you on board and over to the IS," Igor said. "I talked to Vitali on the radio before landing and suggested he make arrangements to have a vehicle delivered. He was pleased to know that you all survived the accident. Fasten your seatbelts, and I'll see if I can get this bird in the air."

Vasil helped Alexander navigate the step into the small passenger area with four seats, two on either side, one behind the other. Vasil and Natasha were assigned one side, and Alexander the other. As soon as they were safely seated with belts fastened, Alexander announced, "Seatbelts secured. Passengers ready for takeoff." Obviously he was familiar with the routine.

Igor started the engine and engaged the rotor blades. Ascending swiftly, they were soon high enough to view Vladivostok and the harbor area clearly. In the other directions, seemingly endless pine forests stretched over the Siberian landscape. The Interrogation Station sat like an ugly wound in the middle of pristine beauty. On the roof, unseen from below but clearly visible above, were the sinister initials, KGB.

Igor descended as quickly as he had risen. This time he left the engine idling and the rotors turning. Alexander explained, "Igor is anxious to leave. He doesn't want to be here for the interrogation procedure. The only danger after we debark is the tail rotor. One prisoner I was escorting ran head-first into it after debarking and was killed instantly."

"On purpose?" Natasha asked.

"Oh, yes. He was an indiscreet political opponent of KGB Chief Andropov. He chose a quick death rather than a painful, lingering one. If I wasn't assured of God's forgiveness and cleansing, I would be tempted to do the same. All right, let's go. Be careful as you step down," Alexander cautioned.

Once they were clear of the rotor wash, Igor took off quickly, heading in an easterly direction. As they were watching him disappear, a voice called from the Interrogation Station.

"Come quickly, Alexander. You have a job to do. I want to see what our prisoners look like before you have your session with them."

Vasil and Natasha glanced toward the sound and saw an imposing figure standing in the doorway. He was nearly two meters tall with a bloated waistline and a blotchy face, signaling his excessive consumption of vodka. His head was bald and blotchy as well. He wore faded, dingy slacks that may have been blue at one time. His half-open sport shirt revealed a thick growth of chest hair that would have looked better on his bare pate.

"We'd better go but slowly," Alexander said softly. "I don't know how this is going to play out, but I will not let Vitali torture you. While Vitali is playing his role of 'nice guy,' I am going to send a coded message about your son, Viktor, to my friend of whom I spoke earlier. Someday he may help your son get to America. Whatever happens, know that I love you. Because of you, Jesus has changed me forever. Yesterday morning, I wanted to hurt you. Now I am willing to die for you, if need be. That's a miracle I can't explain but know it's true."

"Hey, speed it up," Vitali called. "Why are you going at a snail's pace when there is important work to be done?"

"Vitali, I was seriously hurt in the accident, and if it were not for these two, I would likely be dead," Alexander responded. "Let me introduce you to the couple who gave me a new lease on life. You have read the KGB file we have on them. Now you can meet them personally. This is Vasil and Natasha Gorgachuk. This is my work partner, Vitali."

"That accident must have addled your brain, Alexander. I prefer not to fraternize with enemies of the state. And how you can do so, knowing what is ahead a little later, is beyond me."

"Must we do our work today?" Alexander asked. "I would much prefer to wait until tomorrow. I'm hungry and tired, as are Vasil and Natasha. They shared their food with me, and I will not let them go hungry. We have holding cells where they can spend the night."

"I cannot agree to a postponement until tomorrow," Vitali asserted. "This meeting is scheduled for today, and we should adhere to the schedule. I will delay until this afternoon. You will have time to eat and relax for a few hours. If you insist on feeding our prisoners, then that is your choice, but I will not share in the meal or help prepare it. While you fix the food, I will secure our prisoners in the holding cell."

"No," Alexander countered. "If you won't help with the food preparation, I will use them as kitchen help."

"I won't argue, but I warn you. I am going to make a note about your fraternizing with enemies of the state when I submit our report."

They were left in the kitchen area alone, although there was a monitoring camera in the ceiling and sound sensors as well. The refrigerator was well stocked, and soon they had a meal prepared that most Russians could only dream about. Eggs fried in butter mixed with mushrooms and onions, sliced ham and salami, an assortment of cheeses, a salad of sliced tomatoes, cucumbers, and cabbage with a savory Russian dressing. There were various fruits, including cherries and peaches. There was a variety of drinks, soft and hard, but they limited themselves to chai and coffee.

"Thank you, Alexander, for pleading our case," Natasha whispered. "I'm glad Vitali insisted on getting this over with today. God will either miraculously deliver us, or our next meal will be in heaven. We will be winners either way."

At 1300, Vitali spoke over the intercom. "It is time to adjourn to the interrogation room. I'll conduct the prisoners there and secure them while you prepare your equipment. You will have one hour with the prisoners to persuade them to answer each question completely and truthfully. You will give each of them a sample of what is in store for them if they do not cooperate."

"I know the routine, Vitali," Alexander said. "I suggest we change our normal procedure in this case. I need to be mentally prepared to do what I must do."

"What do you mean?" Vitali demanded.

"Think about it, Vitali. I have spent most of two days with this couple. They saved my life. We have eaten meals together. I can't just practice my trade like nothing has happened. I have to prepare mentally to do what I must do. You do your routine first. If you can persuade them to cooperate, then it won't be necessary for my routine to follow. And if it is necessary, I will be mentally prepared to do it effectively. Can you understand why I'm asking this?"

"I can't understand what's going on with you," Vitali said. "You are not turning soft on me, are you? But as a practical matter, I see no reason why we can't reverse the order of our interrogation. It certainly is an unusual situation we haven't confronted before. You take the prisoners and secure them for interrogation, and I will assemble my notes and their file and be along shortly."

CHAPTER 16
THE INTERROGATION ROOM

Alexander escorted the Gorgachuks to the interrogation room. "I will place Vasil in the adjoining holding cell. Natasha, you will be questioned first," he explained. "As you can see, there is a dividing partition about a meter high. You will sit on one side, and Vitali on the other. Vitali prides himself on his ability to convince the prisoner he truly wants to help them and save them from further suffering. The longer he talks to you and Vasil, the more time I will have alone to make coded contact with persons who may be able to help your son escape to America. The arm of the KGB reaches deep and wide, and I am privy to information that may be useful in the future."

"Alexander, you have become a precious brother," Natasha said. "I know God is working things out according to his will.

I trust him, and I trust you. Whatever happens, we are secure in his love for all eternity."

"While you are contacting persons to assist Viktor, I will be praying earnestly," Vasil said as he entered the cell. "I can say with the psalmist, 'The Lord is my helper; I will not fear what man may do to me.' May the Lord guide you in all you say and do."

"Thank you, Vasil. I'm leaning heavily on Jesus. Now I must notify Vitali that the prisoners are securely in place. It's part of our operating procedure.

"Alexander to Vitali, prisoners are in designated areas. Security doors all closed and locked."

"Vitali to Alexander, I am proceeding to interrogation room. Will provide visual confirmation at entry door."

Vitali entered the interrogation room and sat opposite Natasha with the half partition between. He lost no time beginning his "good guy" routine.

"Natasha, it is my privilege to be part of a segment within the KGB that believes more flies are caught by honey than by vinegar. There is another segment, and the prevailing one, I am sorry to say, that insists that painful and coercive grilling is necessary to arrive at the truth. Even now, the man whose life you and your husband saved is actually devising how he may break your will, your spirit, and your body. He enjoys seeing you suffer and beg for mercy. I truly want to spare you the pain and indignities that Alexander wants to inflict. All I want are complete and truthful answers to a few questions I must ask. Can I count on your cooperation?"

"If my life only were involved, I might be persuaded. But the life and future of my son is involved, and his is more precious to me than my own."

"I can appreciate a mother's love," Vitali said. "But have you ever considered what your son might think of himself if he became aware that he was the cause of needless suffering and humiliation to his mother? Do you think he could be proud of that? Do you think he would be able to bear that burden on his young shoulders?"

"My son would know that he was not the cause of my suffering. He would know that it was caused by an evil, atheistic government that is attempting to eliminate God from our culture through fear and intimidation. The threat of death does not terrify me because for me to die will be everlasting gain. I do not enjoy suffering. I do not want it or seek it. But if it comes, I will endure it because of the joy that lies ahead. I am free. It is you that is imprisoned."

"You dare lecture me," Vitali growled. "It is I who am free. You are bound by religious myths and superstitious nonsense. You will risk your life and future on a fairytale. Yes, I live for the present, assured that death will end my existence. I like it that way. I can do as I want, with no fear of future retribution. I set my own rules and determine my own destiny. I am here only for a brief moment, but for that moment I am god."

"Vitali, it is you that is delusional, not I," Natasha responded. "You are controlled by powerful men with the same philosophy you have. Because they have more power than you, they will use you to fulfill their will. You are the lackey; they are the gods you toady to. They would squash you like a roach if you dared cross them. You are not free. You are in servile bondage to evil men. Look at the history of our government. Stalin destroyed his competitors and assumed the role of god over a vast kingdom. His reign was based on intimidation, fear, corruption, violence, lies, and betrayal of associates. And you know how Lavrenty Beria, Stalin's close associate and head of the NKVD, was treated after Stalin's death. Why did Stalin's successors falsely accuse Beria of treason and then execute him? Those that formerly feared him turned and destroyed him. The executor of millions of innocents reaped what he had sown. And you are free?"

"Yes, you describe the reality of my existence," Vitali confessed. "I cannot deny it. But I prefer my reality to your dream world."

"It is not a dream world," Natasha countered. "God has created a spiritual world characterized by spiritual realities, such as peace, joy, kindness, love, self-control, and kindness. These realities are not determined by external, physical realities. They are determined by God's Holy Spirit dwelling within the core of one's being. You cannot see the Spirit, but you can see the result of his presence."

"Why should I continue this conversation?" Vitali asked. "You have made my point. For you, reality is the result of some mystical spirit being, who we can't see, invading our personalities and imparting some weird character traits that don't exist in the world I inhabit. If I can't see it, touch it, taste it, hear it, or smell it, then it is not real as far as I'm concerned."

"Vitali, you don't really believe that. Have you ever seen electricity? Have you ever seen gravity? Tell me what electricity looks like. Describe the appearance of gravity."

"I see where you are going with that. There are some things our five senses can't identify, but we can clearly detect their presence by how they affect reality that we can identify. Is that your point?"

"It is, and I congratulate you on seeing it so quickly," Natasha said. "The same principle is operative in the spiritual realm. The Holy Spirit can change a vicious, self-centered man or woman into a caring, compassionate human being. You can't see the Holy Spirit, but you can see results the Spirit produces. I have observed this reality many times."

"Perhaps if I see this reality on my turf, I will give it some further thought. As it is, I must now test my persuasive powers on your husband. But first, there is the formality of placing you in the holding cell before I release him. Then I must inform Alexander of what has happened. Operating procedures, you know."

After placing Natasha in her holding cell and releasing Vasil to his place in the interrogation room, the required call was made. "Vitali to Alexander, interrogation of first prisoner completed. She is now in holding cell. Second prisoner is awaiting my interrogation."

"Alexander to Vitali, message received. Proceed with interrogation."

"Vasil, I have the privilege of being part of a minority in the KGB that believes friendly persuasion can be more effective in gaining required information than more forceful methods. Your wife was very adept at sidestepping reality. I trust you will be more realistic."

"Vitali, I appreciate your dedication to friendly persuasion. Just what is the information that you want to persuade me to give you? I have not heard you mention that. I must know that before any decision is made."

"You and your wife have been apprehended because you failed to register the birth of your son more than twelve years ago. His location and status still have not been determined. The internal security agency of the USSR is very concerned about citizens of any age roaming about unidentified. All I want to know is the location of your son and by what name he is identified. Is that not a reasonable request?"

"No, it is not a reasonable request. We will not release information about our boy that will cause him to be subjected to persecution and godless and intimidating propaganda in the public schools. Be assured that I agree totally with my wife concerning the nature of reality. There is a creator who came among us as God incarnate in Jesus Christ to whom our son has been dedicated to serve."

"You leave me no choice," Vitali said. "Further conversation will be useless. I must release you to the tender mercies of my partner. I am sure he is eager to demonstrate how much more effective is his approach to arriving at truth. I must call him and report my failure. If there is a God, may he have mercy on you."

"Oh, he has. He already has," Vasil replied as Vitali returned him to his cell.

"Vitali to Alexander, interrogation completed. Prisoners remain recalcitrant. I am ready to release them into your care. Acknowledge."

"Alexander to Vitali, message received. I will meet you at the entrance to the interrogation room."

Alexander was stone-faced as he met Vitali at the entrance. They nodded, and Vitali continued walking toward the lounge. Alexander watched him for a moment before entering and locking the door. He then opened the cell doors and released Vasil and Natasha.

"I have been thinking much about our course of action when we leave this room and rejoin Vitali. I want my conscience to be free so I can respond as I believe the Holy Spirit wants me to. I understand that the promptings of the Holy

Spirit will always be in accord with scripture. Isn't that what you taught me last night?"

"Yes, yes it is," Vasil said.

"While you were being interrogated, I placed an important phone call and sent a coded message to someone who can help your son in the future. Afterward, I was reading your Bible. I came across something that has troubled my conscience. Here is what I understood Paul to say: *God has instituted human government, and we are to submit to it.* But I, and you, are rebelling against an agency of the government. Are we disobeying God?"

"Alexander, I am so happy that you are investigating your Christian faith. In two days, you have gone farther than many Christians ever go. Natasha and I have had to wrestle with this very question. To interpret scripture, you need to apply the total context of biblical truth. As Natasha and I examined the context of the New Testament, we saw more clearly what Paul is saying. Answer me this question: what are the two primary functions God has assigned to the government he has ordained?"

"If I understand correctly, it is to reward those doing good and to punish those doing evil."

"What if a government completely reverses these functions and promotes those doing evil and punishes those doing good? Is this a government ordained of God that we should submit to?"

"I think it would depend on who defines good and evil."

"Yes. That's it exactly. And earlier in his letter to the Romans, that is what the apostle has been doing. Much of the New Testament is God's commentary on the Ten Commandments of the Old Testament. And the first and chief commandment is to love the Lord God with all your total being."

"I think I see what you are saying," Alexander said. "To submit to and obey a government that demands we reject the very God we are to love with all our mind and heart and strength is clearly not what Paul means. Scripture defines the good that is to be commended as well as the evil that is to be suppressed and punished."

"Absolutely. Twice in the New Testament is a record of the governing powers demanding the Christian leaders no longer proclaim the gospel publically. Their response was, 'We must obey God rather than man.' And they continued to defy the government despite imprisonment and lashings."

"I believe my conscience is clear on this issue," said Alexander. "But there is one more thing that I need to have clarified. I have heard it said that Jesus told his followers not to retaliate against evildoers. *If someone strikes you on the right cheek don't resist, but give him a chance to hit the left one.* That's the way I understand it. Is that correct?"

"Jesus did teach his followers not to retaliate when personally attacked," Vasil replied. "He was the supreme example of practicing what he preached. He was reviled, struck, spit upon, and worse but bore it all even though he could have called thousands of angels to defend him. However, scripture also teaches that the strong have a responsibility to protect and defend the weak and powerless. He personally practiced this when he saw the merchants and temple authorities fleecing the poor who came to worship and offer sacrifices in keeping with Jewish law. Jesus got physical and overturned tables and scattered money and with a whip drove out the greedy money-changers. So the principle of scripture seems to be this: Don't retaliate or seek revenge when you are mistreated, but leave vengeance to God. If you see the weak and powerless being misused or taken advantage of, then you are expected to help them, with physical force if need be. Does that clarify this issue?"

"Yes, it helps a lot. I can now resolve what to do with a good conscience if certain situations develop," Alexander said.

"It's good you understand the biblical principles, but the Holy Spirit must guide you as to when and how to apply them," Natasha said.

"I understand," Alexander said. "The time has arrived for us to confront Vitali. Let us each pray that we will be guided by the Holy Spirit in all we do and say."

Each of the three led in a short prayer. After prayer, Alexander made voice contact with his partner. "Alexander to Vitali: interrogation completed. I am returning to the lounge, accompanied by the Gorgachuks. Acknowledge."

"Vitali to Alexander: message received. I am awaiting you."

CHAPTER 17
MARTYRS

"This certainly is an unprecedented turn of events," Vitali said as they entered. "Please explain what is going on. Why are the prisoners not in holding cells?"

"It is all my doing," Alexander said. "I could not torture and abuse those who had saved my life. More than that, they introduced me to a reality that I didn't think existed."

"And what reality is that, may I ask?" Vitali enquired. "Has that clever bitch beguiled you with her God talk?"

"You don't understand, Vitali," Alexander said. "It wasn't what Natasha or Vasil said. It is what God did. When my body was broken and I was suffering unbearable pain, God healed me in answer to prayer. When I confessed what a miserable wretch I was and repented and asked forgiveness, I was suddenly enveloped by this awesome sense of loving acceptance. I don't understand how God works, but he suddenly changed the whole direction of my life."

"I do understand," Vitali said. "I understand that you are a traitor and a betrayer of your oath. I must ask you to hand over your weapon, your KGB ID, and all classified material you may possess."

"Were I the only one concerned, I would consider doing as you demand. But I will not leave the Gorgachuks in your care. I know and you know your soft talk is an act. As long as I live, I will not permit you to molest and torture this man and woman whom God has used to lead me from death into life eternal."

"Then I may have to kill you, for I cannot permit the prisoners to escape," Vitali said coldly.

"Do what you must do," Alexander replied. "But remember, I too have a weapon and will use whatever means necessary to protect my friends."

Vitali half turned away from Alexander, making his right side unseen by Alexander. Reaching furtively into his holstered pocket, he withdrew his revolver, unseen by Alexander but clearly detected by Natasha. Seeing the weapon emerge as Vitali turned to face her defender, Natasha leapt from her chair, shouting, "Watch out!" Distracted momentarily, Vitali glanced toward Natasha, who was moving rapidly toward Alexander. Vitali saw Alexander was also distracted by Natasha's action and raised his revolver for a shot at Alexander's chest. Just as he pulled the trigger, Natasha leapt in front of Alexander and took the bullet in the upper back between her shoulder blades.

"Jesus, help us!" Vasil cried, as he raced to his wife's side.

Foaming blood was exiting her mouth and nose. Her lungs had been savaged by the hollow-point bullet, and her heart was in the final throes of attempting to maintain life. Miraculously, with her last gasp, Natasha cried out: "Jesus, forgive and save Vitali. I'm coming ho ..."

Vasil cradled her dying body in his arms, his own body wracked by sobs.

Vitali was startled to hear his name called by the dying woman. "What did she say? Why did she call my name?" he asked wildly.

"She asked Jesus to forgive and save you," Vasil choked out. "Now she can ask him face to face."

"The woman was crazy," said Vitali. "She deliberately placed herself in my line of fire. I was shooting at the traitor behind her. It looks like a stand-off. I am going to call our KGB headquarters in Vladivostok and request another agent be flown in."

"No, I can't permit that," Alexander said. "My friend has no weapon and would be defenseless. It is my Christian duty to defend the weak. With God's help, that is what I am going to do."

"It may be a long night," Vitali said. "I suggest we adjourn to the kitchen, and Vasil can fix snacks."

"I have no appetite," Vasil said. "But I am familiar with the kitchen after helping Alexander prepare our meal this morning. I will fix some cold cuts from the meat and cheese in the refrigerator."

As Vasil passed near Vitali to reach the refrigerator, the KGB agent, standing in the doorway, struck like a cobra. In an instant, he wrapped his left arm around Vasil's neck in a hammer lock and pulled him close to his front.

"Drop your weapon, Alexander, or I will kill your friend."

Vasil, desperate to protect Alexander, began to flail his hands and arms, striking Vitali in the face. Furious and raging out of control, the KGB agent went on auto pilot and did what he had been programmed to do when attacked by a prisoner. He shot him again and again and, yet more, until the hammer clicked on an empty chamber, all the while cursing and spewing invective against Christians and the God whom they served. At last, exhausted by rage, he collapsed in a chair, looking up at Alexander.

"Go ahead and shoot me. You know my revolver is empty."

"You murdered my friend before I could take aim to avoid hitting him," Alexander responded. "He's with Jesus and Natasha now, the two persons he most loves and wants to be with forever. I don't need to protect him any longer."

"Tell me, Alexander, what really happened to you? I don't buy this supernatural stuff about God and all that garbage."

"Nor did I. Science, materialism, and raw physical power was my unholy trinity. Science taught me to never accept an important theorem without experimenting to see if it proved to be true or false. I decided to use my time with this Christian couple as an opportunity to field test their theorem about God. They insist he exists, and he honors sincere attempts to communicate with him."

"How did you expect to test that theorem?"

"I wasn't sure. I decided to devise my own tests as situations arose that suggested an experiment," Alexander said. "My first experiment was to see if they truly trusted this God they claim existed. I attempted to terrorize them with threats of torture. I wanted to intimidate them and hear them beg for mercy or offer a bribe. They did nothing of the sort. Vasil was bold as a lion and said he was glad I had captured them because that was part of God's plan. Even his wife spoke up boldly and tried to convince me history validated the truth of Christianity."

"So? How does that prove God exists?"

"It doesn't, of course," Alexander agreed. "But it proved that they were convinced he existed and that they trusted him with their future. Also, their response to my threats demonstrated some source of courage that I could not explain in terms of humanistic materialism. I was enraged by their lack of intimidation and fear and was considering shooting them while driving. It was this rage that led to the accident."

"What other experiments came to your crazed mind?" Vitali asked.

"When I became conscious in the front area of the wrecked vehicle my passengers had already exited. When I tried to move, I was overcome with excruciating pain. The head of the femur joint connected to the ilium inside the acetabulum had been forced out of its slot by the force of the tumbling vehicle. Isn't it ironic that I learned these terms when I was being taught methods of torture for effective interrogation at the KGB Academy? The ligaments that held the head in place were stretched and mangled into a tangled mass of torture. When it was time to attempt to exit the wreck, every movement was wracked with torment. It was then I decided to experiment by asking God to alleviate my intense pain."

"And what was the result?"

"The pain not only decreased, but *the head of the femur slipped back into the joint slot.* God answered prayer and threw in a bonus miracle as well. My scientific testing of Vasil's and Natasha's theorem was seriously influencing me to rethink my denial of God."

"What did you do next?"

"Vasil and Natasha explained what Christianity is all about. It is not so much a religion as a relationship with God made possible by Jesus Christ paying the penalty for our sin by his death on the cross. Because he was God as well as man, his life had infinite worth, so he paid the penalty for all humanity. All I had to do was accept what Jesus had done for me and trust my life into his hands. I decided to do that, and Jesus flooded me with a sense of his love and acceptance. I felt clean and forgiven of my detestable past. It was as if I had been reborn, and God was holding me in his arms, assuring me of his love. God does exist, Vitali. Whatever else he may be, his symbol is the cross, a symbol of holy love."

"Very interesting. Were there any further experiments to confirm your conclusion?"

"Not of my making, but of yours," Alexander replied.

"Whoa! I never set up any experiments. What are you talking about?" Vitali demanded.

"When you turned away from facing me, so you could deceptively pull your revolver and kill me, Natasha saw what you planned and deliberately took the bullet that was intended for me. She gave her life for me. That was God's love within her that drove her to give her life for her new Christian brother. Tell me, Vitali, what is the first law of nature?"

"Everyone knows that. It's self-preservation. That's the law I live by."

"And that's the law I lived by ... until yesterday. There is a higher law built into the very heart of the universe. It's the law of self-giving love."

"And just what does that mean?" Vitali asked.

"That was my question. Vasil and Natasha explained it like this. God in his Divine Being is one God comprised of three distinct persons, Father, Son, and Holy Spirit. Before creation came into being, they existed in timeless intimacy and infinite, harmonious love. At some point, this Triune God made a decision to share his love with creatures that could respond freely to it."

"Wait. Don't go any further. How can there be one God but three persons?" Vitali asked. "I completely fail to understand the Christian view of God. It sounds incomprehensible. No wonder our psychiatrists categorize them as suffering a form of insanity."

"I am glad to hear you say that," Alexander said. "I would feel very threatened to serve a God you could understand. Of course you don't understand God's personhood. Neither do I or any other human. God is absolutely unique. There is no way we can describe him because there is nothing in creation to compare him with. If he had not revealed himself in scripture as a trinity, we would never have figured it out on our own. Because God is infinite in his being, we will continue discovering more about him forever and ever. We will never stop growing in the knowledge and understanding of God or exhaust his unlimited potential of active love."

"You are right. I don't understand all this, and it is still nonsense to me," said Vitali. "But go on and continue the fairy story."

"It's a wonderful story, and it reflects reality. I can't tell it as Vasil did, so I'll summarize. God created a universe immense beyond our imagination. On one small planet, he eventually created a man and woman to begin the human race and gave them a perfect environment to live in. God loved them and communicated with them, and they loved God in return. But eventually, since God had given them free will, they rebelled and chose to go their way instead of God's. Man, living apart from God, accounts for all the evil in the world today."

CHAPTER 18
ALEXANDER'S EXPERIMENT CONCLUDES

"Hold on just a minute," said Vitali. "I'm trying to relate to this fantastic fable, so bear with my questions. Why didn't this all-powerful, loving creator just form these creatures so they would always choose to do what he wanted them to do? Why allow the possibility of bad choices and evil acts?"

"That's what I asked my friends. As best I understand—remember, I'm new at this—it has to do with God's purpose for creation. He wanted creatures who could genuinely respond to his love and love him in return. True love must allow for genuine exercise of free will. A response to love stigmatized by coercion, force, or bribe can never qualify as genuine. Nor can a response that is robotic, instinctive, involuntary, or determined by another. So God, because he is love personified, must seek a free response to his expressions of love. And real freedom must include freedom to make bad choices."

"You have finally said something that makes sense. So God is the rejected lover, and his purpose for creation has been thwarted. The almighty one has created quite a can of worms to untangle, hasn't he?"

"It's worse than you describe it, Vitali," Alexander said. "Not only is God absolutely loving, he is also infinitely holy. He is free of the slightest taint of sin or moral imperfection. No one can be in his presence or share in his kingdom that is not also morally perfect. And who measures up to that standard?"

"One thing for sure, that disqualifies all the people I know, including you," Vitali said. "So the great plan of the all-wise God backfired. Did he have a plan B?"

"God was not taken by surprise," Alexander affirmed. "God had a plan in place before he created that took into account his absolute holiness, his infinite love, and man's sin. The plan was for God the Son to invade humanity as Jesus of Nazareth. The heart of the plan, conceived in eternity, was for Jesus to suffer and die on the cross, paying the penalty for the sins of all mankind."

"Now I'm confused again," Vitali said. "How could one man pay the penalty for the sins of all humanity? I suppose that includes past, present, and future."

"Jesus is an absolutely unique human being. He never relinquished his divinity although he laid aside his divine attributes. His miracles were all performed by the power of the Holy Spirit that indwelt him as he does all Christians. Because he was God as well as man, his life had infinite worth, so the sacrifice of his life redeemed all humanity."

"Does that mean that the penalty for my sin has been paid for by Jesus? If there is a judgment day, am I off the hook?"

"Yes, Jesus paid your penalty. But that only becomes effective if you freely respond to his love in trust and commitment to him. Remember, all this took place to pave the way to a love relationship between God and man. Are you ready to freely respond to his love?"

"Never. I'm still not convinced there is actually a God. And if there is, this God who asks his followers to sacrifice themselves on behalf of others does not appeal to me. I don't expect help from others, nor do I intend to offer any. It's dog-eat-dog in the world I live in."

"You provided one more experimental opportunity for me, Vitali," Alexander said. "When you grabbed Vasil to serve as your human shield, I was terrified, not for my life, but for what might happen to Vasil if I were killed. When Vasil risked his life and eventually gave his life to save mine, that was the coup de grace to my doubt. Two wonderful people, full of God's love, had freely given their lives to save mine. Every vestige of doubt disappeared when I watched Vasil's blood drain away as he died on my behalf. Why did you keep shooting him again and again until you had no bullets?"

"Why? Because I despised him and his kind. He was a Christian, therefore an enemy of my country. How can we build our atheistic paradise when scum like him pollute our culture?"

"You are describing me, Vitali, because I am now a Christian. I should hate you for killing two innocent friends, but, strangely, I don't. I hate what you did and am horrified and incensed by it. Nevertheless, I care deeply about you. If God had not truly changed me, I would gladly have killed you in turn. I know you don't understand, even as I didn't before my experiments led me to faith in Jesus. I dare say you don't know one person who would willingly give his life to save yours? I know one, and you have just murdered two of his followers. As surely as Natasha and Vasil died in my place, Jesus died for you. You killed two beautiful people because they were committed to Jesus Christ. And Jesus still loves you despite what you've done. He wants you to be part of God's eternal family, his family. There is a place for people like me and you in God's kingdom. Surrender to his love, and he will change you as surely as he changed me. Give him that chance."

"You are contemptible, Alexander," Vitali hissed. "You are living in a religious fantasy bubble. You have betrayed your country and consorted with her enemies. You have dishonored the KGB. You are worthless garbage, and it is people like you who prevent the noble experiment of communism from succeeding. I am going to notify KGB Headquarters in Vladivostok and request they send agents to take you into custody. But first things first, I need a glass of vodka. Listening to you would drive any sane man to drink. You can oppose me if you choose."

"I will not oppose you, but I will warn you," Alexander said. "It is a dangerous thing to know the truth and ignore or deny it. You know what I was before, and you can see the change that has taken place. I have not changed myself. God has transformed me and made me a new person. I am the miracle that God has sent to you to demonstrate that he exists. The choice is yours. God will make himself real to you if you want to know him and serve him. To the scientist, you are an accident of nature, an insignificant speck of protoplasm without purpose or meaning. But to your creator, you are worth the life of his son, Jesus."

"That's enough. I will hear no more. I don't want his love. I don't need his favor. Quit pushing me. If there is a God, let him damn me. Come, share this vodka and let us drink to my damnation."

"Put down the bottle, Vitali. You know there is to be no drinking when working an assignment. You know how it effects your judgment and self-control."

"I'll drink when I choose. No religious nut will tell me what to do," Vitali shouted.

"What reality are you going to turn to, Vitali, when vodka no longer anesthetizes you? What reality is going to sustain you when the only inheritance you have to look forward to is two meters of real estate in some crowded cemetery?"

"Stop! Stop!" screamed Vitali. "You damnable traitor, I will hear no more of your God talk. I am going to close your mouth if it's the last thing I do. Don't say I didn't warn you," Vitali cried as he rushed toward the seated Alexander, vodka bottle in hand.

Alexander offered no resistance as Vitali raised the bottle high over his head. The bottle struck with a sickening thud, and immediately blood spurted from Alexander's skull and mixed with vodka from the shattered bottle.

Stunned and barely conscious, Alexander looked up into the eyes of Vitali, who had seized his revolver. "May God forgive you." He gasped. Wild eyed and cursing, the murderer pulled the trigger again and again in maniacal fury. Bullet after bullet shattered the body until the hammer clicked on empty.

Still angry, he turned from the shattered body of his loathed partner and retrieved another bottle of vodka. Half choking on a fiery gulp, he shook his fist at God and raged, "I hate you. I hate you."

CHAPTER 19
BORIS

Vitali, exhausted by his raging fury, had sunk into a drunken stupor. He awakened the next morning with a fuzzy tongue, bleary eyes and a throbbing drum beating incessantly against his pain-filled temples. Blinking his eyes and shaking his head he attempted to clear his addled brain. Grabbing the edge of a nearby door he dragged himself to his feet. Steadying himself he surveyed the bloody havoc spread out before him.

Rage welled up as he began to walk from corpse to corpse, kicking each one contemptuously. He began to curse the bullet-riddled bodies.

"Damn you, damn you, damn you everyone," he shouted. "You religious idiots. Look what you caused me to do."

Filled with self-pity he sank into a chair and began to moan, "What am I going to do? How am I going to explain these three dead bodies? Is there anyone I dare trust ?"

As Vitali mulled over these questions he realized he knew no one he could trust with the truth. He must invent a story that would substitute for what actually happened. As he continued to contemplate his situation a plot begin to form in his twisted mind. Satanic glee erupted in a hideous chuckle as he wrote furiously on a note pad the things he must say that would fit the physical evidence: (1) describe the prisoners as conniving con artists that agreed to save Alexander's life if he would help them escape and provide them with his weapon. (2) Tell how Alexander related to him that his revolver had been thrown out of the car as it rolled down the embankment and apparently ended up under the overturned vehicle. Actually, Vasil had the weapon hidden under his clothing and intended to use it to kill him. (3) Vasil hurriedly drew the revolver from his clothing and fired a hasty shot that barely missed. I returned fire and killed the male prisoner. Alexander grabbed the female prisoner and used her as a shield as he retrieved his weapon from the floor. I was forced to kill the woman in order to have a shot at the traitor. Handicapped by his injuries, Alexander had difficulty handling and aiming the revolver and none of his shots came close. I soon killed him as well. Fortunately, I escaped unscathed.

When he had his script firmly in mind he telephoned Rasputin at the KGB headquarters in Leningrad. "Comrade Rasputin, this is Comrade Vitali at KGB Interrogation Station 12 reporting in."

"Comrade Vitali, you are late. I anticipated a report yesterday after the interrogation was completed," Rasputin replied.

"Comrade, wait until you hear what happened and you will understand how lucky I am to be calling at all," said Vitali.

"Do you have time to hear an oral report now or should I prepare a written report and dispatch that to you?"

"Give me the condensed version now and send me the written 'after action report' later," Rasputin said.

"Two days ago KGB agent Comrade Alexander spotted the suspects you ordered us to apprehend as they were debarking from the early morning train in Vladivostok. He followed them and took them into custody after they entered his taxi. They were on their way to catch a bus to Nokhodka," Vitali began.

"I'm a busy man," Vasputin interjected. "Cut the fluff and just give me the bare –bone facts."

"Yes, sir, Comrade Rasputin. Fact one is that Comrade Alexander lost control of his vehicle on the sharp curve near the entrance to KGB Interrogation Station twelve. The car tumbled down the steep embankment and landed upside down on its top. Fact two is Alexander was severely injured while the prisoners escaped serious injury. Fact three, the prisoners retrieved Alexander's weapon and threatened to shoot him unless he would help them escape. Fact four, Alexander agreed to help them if they would stay and extricate him from the wreck."

"I get the picture, Comrade Vitali," said Rasputin. " Cut to the chase."

"When Alexander didn't show up as scheduled with the prisoners in tow, I notified our helicopter station," said Vitali. "The pilot followed the road from Vladivostok to where the accident occurred near the main gate to KGB Interrogation Station 12. He radioed a report saying Alexander had been painfully injured but was mobile. The prisoners appeared to

have escaped injury. At my request the accident victims were
flown to Station 12 where I met them."

"Did you release the helicopter to depart?" asked Rasputin.

"Not really, Comrade. We have an agreement. Unless I ask
him to stick around for some purpose he is free to go immediately," said Vitali. "That glamour boy pilot is always eager to
get back to the city. He leaves the blades engaged and takes
off the moment the passengers debark."

"You didn't anticipate any trouble even though you knew
Alexander had been seriously injured and the prisoners may
have taken his weapon?" Rasputin asked.

"Alexander assured me that his revolver was never found
and it must have ended up under the overturned taxi," said
Vitali. "Nevertheless, I ordered Alexander to search the prisoners for weapons of any kind."

"You asked an injured, unarmed Agent to frisk two healthy,
unfettered prisoners? What were you thinking, Comrade?"
barked Rasputin.

"I had my weapon, Comrade, and was prepared for any
eventuality,' said Vitali. "But, frankly, I never expected any resistance at all from these religious fanatics."

Vitali paused as if trying to recall what happened next.
Finally Rasputin prodded him.

"Go on. What was the result of the search?" Rasputin
asked.

"After Alexander searched the woman, finding nothing,
he approached the male prisoner from the side and said something in his ear which I couldn't hear," said Vitali. "Suddenly
the man drew a revolver from somewhere, his back pocket I
think, under his shirt. I immediately dropped to the floor.

The prisoner fired a hasty shot but missed me. I returned fire and Killed him."

"What was agent Alexander doing while this was all happening?" asked Rasputin.

"He grabbed the female prisoner for a shield as he retrieved the fallen weapon.

"I demanded that he surrender. When he refused I shot the female shielding him. He fired his revolver in my direction but missed. I think his serious injuries prevented proper aim. I then shot the traitor. I retrieved his revolver and emptied the remaining rounds into the bodies to assure they were dead."

"Then what?"

"I must confess, Comrade Rasputin, I was physically and emotionally drained. I drank myself into a vodka produced stupor and fell into a deep sleep, not awakening until this morning," admitted Vitali. "That was scarcely an hour ago. At which time I called you."

"Are the bodies still there at Station twelve?" asked Rasputin.

"Yes, Comrade," Vitali responded meekly.

"Don't touch them. Leave them as they fell," ordered Rasputin. "There is an investigating team already dispatched which should arrive soon. "

Vitali had hoped to avoid any further official inquiry on the basis of his concocted explanation of the killings. Why the investigation? Were there holes in his story that aroused suspicion? Apparently the shooting of two prisoners prior to interrogation and the killing of the arresting KGB agent demanded further scrutiny. He must be very careful and not say too much in his written report.

Two KGB agents, unknown to Vitali, comprised the investigating team. They arrived shortly after 1000 on a helicopter piloted by the dapper Igor. He greeted Vitali casually with a nod of his head. "Understand you had some excitement yesterday after I departed. Everything under control?" Igor asked.

"Yeah, I think so. The prisoners turned Alexander and I had to shoot the traitor and the two prisoners. Your passengers are here to investigate the shooting," said Vitali as he nodded in the direction of the two debarking agents. "I guess I had better introduce myself and escort them to the Interrogation Station. See you around."

Igor was already back in the cockpit. He waved languidly as the rotors gained speed and then he was up and away.

"Welcome to Interrogation Station 12. My name is Vitali and I am the landlord here, so to speak. I like to use capitalist language occasionally," he chuckled as he reached out to shake hands. "Have you had breakfast?" he interjected as an afterthought. "I'd be glad to fix you something."

"No, thanks. We grabbed a bite in the city. I'm Boris and this is my partner, Ivan," said the grizzled older but smaller man. He was obviously the agent in charge and had an aura of authority that radiated from his eyes and voice. They each responded with perfunctory handshakes to Vitali's outstretched hand.

"We work in KGB's Internal Security Department," Boris explained. "We are here primarily for two purposes. First, to help determine how an agent of Alexander's experience and stellar record could have been turned so quickly and completely. Second, to oversee the disposal of these three bodies."

"And while we are at it, we want to see if he may have influenced you to turn in the same direction," said Ivan.

"Wait one minute," Vitali responded angrily. "Have you forgotten or did you not know that it was I who killed the traitor?"

"We know," said Boris. "But in our line of work we have discovered many motives that can lead to the killing of both friends and enemies. But in no way is this a trial so why don't we all sit down and be comfortable."

"Comrade Vitali, we want you to describe exactly what happened that led to this triple killing," said Ivan."We will listen, take a few notes for our report, and may ask a question now and then. So just relax and tell us what you know."

Vitali nervously licked his dry lips and began to repeat the story he had told Rasputin just hours before. He stuck to his mental script without embellishents. The ISD agents took numerous notes and occasionally asked for clarification at some point in the narrative. In an hour the oral testimony was completed. The agents then took photos of the corpses, noting the position of the bodies in death and recording particularly where bullets entered and exited. Altogether less than two hours had passed since the agents arrived.

"Now what?" Vitali asked his guests.

"Comrade Vitali, as you know, this is a unique situation. We have had KGB agents turned before but usually it happens slowly over a period of time and the motivation is money or some other materialistic reward. You have given us no clues why Alexander suddenly had a dramatic transformation of character and direction of his life," said Boris.

"Frankly, Comrade, we have discovered some inconsistencies in your account and believe there are things you have not revealed," said Ivan. "However, our task is simply to gather information, not make judgments."

"Because two of its veteran agents are involved in this situation the KGB has decided to prevent what has happened here from becoming known to the general public or even throughout the KGB family," said Boris. "This means you are never to speak to anyone outside the KGB about what has happened or what will happen shortly."

"Comrades, don't tell me something else is about to happen that I can't talk about," Vitali said.

Boris glanced at his watch as he began to speak. "I told you our second mission is to oversee the disposal of these three bodies. Very soon, a large, enclosed van will arrive at the entrance gate. Chained and cuffed inside are two prisoners who have been sentenced to be executed today. Before their sentence is carried out they are going to perform one final patriotic duty. They are going to secretly help us dispose of these bodies then they will be shot. Nobody will know about the disposition of the bodies except KGB agents."

In a short time the driver of the van arrived at the gate and pushed the signal button. Vitali hit the switch that released the electric locking mechanism and the gate opened on its track. In five minutes the van was parked at the Station.

"Let's go meet our disposal team," said Boris as he led the way outside. "We must guard them carefully for these are desperate men. But four men with weapons ought to be enough to discourage any heroics."

The agents assembled near the van where Boris introduced them to KGB agent Andre, the van driver. He then turned to Ivan and said, "Comrade Ivan, the show is all yours now until we get the bodies disposed of. Proceed to carry out your instructions."

Ivan nodded his head and barked out an order. "Comrade Andre, unlock the rear of the van and present the work detail."

The prisoners were released from the truck and unmanacled. Ivan addressed them. "Prisoners, you are under sentence of death and are scheduled to be executed today. You have been given one last opportunity to serve mother Russia before you die. If you do your task well your death will be painless and instant. If not, you will reap an unpleasant penalty. Your task will be dirty and grisly, but it could be worse. They were killed only yesterday and have been in an air-conditioned house since death. I have no idea why the manner of disposal for the bodies was chosen. We are here to follow orders as are you. Let's get to it."

The work detail was escorted inside where the victims lay as they had fallen when shot. Pools of coagulated and dried blood were pooled around the gaping wounds where the bullets had exited. Little emotion appeared on the prisoners' faces as if such scenes may have been commonplace.

"One of you grab the shoulders and the other the feet and place the body in the van," Ivan ordered. This was repeated until all the bodies were removed and stashed in the vehicle. The prisoners were then secured in the rear of the van where the bodies lay.

The KGB agents settled in the two front seats and the van driver was given instructions by agent Boris. "Comrade Andre, proceed through the gate and follow the road for approximately five kilometers until you get to the site of the accident that occurred two days ago that involved the dead people on the floor behind us. We will stop there."

"I saw the site as I drove out here today," said Andre. "I know just where it is.

Vitali was puzzled. "Why stop there?" he asked.

"In a few minutes I'll do more than tell you. I'll show you," Boris said. "Just wait."

"There it is on the left, down the embankment," Andre called out a few minutes later as he slowed to a stop.

"Everyone out. Here is where we dispose of the bodies," said agent Boris. Comrade Ivan, proceed with the disposal of the bodies."

"Prisoners, listen carefully to your instructions," said agent Ivan, " You will carry each corpse down the embankment to the overturned vehicle. When you reach the wreck one of you must enter through the broken rear window to help position the bodies in the designated locations. Agent Alexander's body will first be placed in the front seat area. Next, the woman's body will be placed in the rear seat section followed by the man's body next to hers. Any questions?"

The prisoners remained silent. Agent Ivan continued: "Proceed with your orders as instructed."

The prisoners seized the first body and began the descent, keeping the body horizontally parallel to the embankment. They took, small, deliberate steps down the steep incline as if they were treasuring every additional moment of life this procured. With difficulty but measured persistence they wrestled the first body into place. This process was repeated for the other two bodies. The KGB agents watched the macabre procedure in silence.

When the ordeal was concluded the prisoners were again manacled and secured in the rear of the van. The KGB agents took their seats, looking to Boris for further direction. He then issued a brief order.

"Andre, return us to IS twelve where the prisoners will have an opportunity to extend their lives another hour. They must clean the bloody floor and remove all signs of last night's violence. Let's go."

The van returned quickly. The prisoners were released and briefed on their task. Vitali provided them with equipment and supplies to expedite their work. Within an hour all evidence of the recent gore had been removed. The prisoners were again manacled and placed in the back of the van.

"Comrade Andre, you will proceed with the prisoners to the designated place where the execution squad awaits. Stay until the sentence has been carried out," Boris said. "Allow them to talk to no one. I need not remind you that your lips are to remain sealed concerning what you observed this afternoon."

The three KGB agents walked slowly back into the Station house, each lost in his own thoughts. Finally Boris broke the silence. "Comrade Vitali, how long did you know your partner Alexander?"

"Not that long, Comrade Boris. Why do you ask?

"I've known him for many years. We grew up in the same neighborhood," said Boris. "I knew his family, especially his sainted babushka. Alexander loved his grandmother and he and I spent a lot of time in her little house when we were youngsters. She always had a secret cache of cookies which she doled out sparingly. She was very poor. But it was more than the cookies that attracted us. She had an unending supply of fascinating stories about ancient heroes who believed in a

Creator God and were determined to serve him whatever the consequences."

Vitali interrupted. "Did you actually believe her fairy tales?"

"I'm not sure. But we had no doubt that she did. Of course, we learned in school that the Bible, the source of her stories, was nothing but a collection of ancient fables and myths. Outwardly, we accepted that because we knew there weresevere penalties for those who did not. But a seed of doubt was planted somewhere deep in my mind...and, I'm sure, in Alexander's as well."

"But I don't understand," Vitali continued. "How could you even entertain the thought that it's possible there might be a God?"

"Comrade Vitali, look at me. Can you truthfully say that you have never considered that possibility? Now look me in the eyes and answer my question," Boris demanded.

There was a long silence as Vitali looked at Boris and struggled with his reply. At last he glanced away and slowly answered.

"Yes, of course, I have considered the possibility that there is a Creator God but I have chosen to reject that possibility. I have deliberately chosen to cast my lot with communism and its godless ideology," said Vitali. "I am interested only in what seems best for me here and now."

"I believe you have answered me truthfully," Boris said. "I give you credit for that. Now I'll be equally honest with you. I do not believe you have been truthful about the death of agent Alexander and his prisoners."

"Why do you doubt me, Comrade Boris? Doesn't my report line up with the physical evidence?"

"Not entirely, Comrade, but don't be alarmed. I am neither judge nor jury and I am not here to put you on trial. Comrade Ivan and I are here simply to gather some initial evidence and report back to senior agent Rasputin," said Boris. "But there is another reason I don't believe you and it is tied to your honest answer to my question."

"Now you are talking nonsense," said Vitali. "How could my honest answer lead you to suspect I was lying about my report?"

"Let me quote a portion of your answer," said Boris. " 'I am interested only in what seems best for me here and now.' Remember that?"

"Of course I do. But what has that to do with my report?"

"I believe you are convinced that it is not in your best interest to share all the facts relating to your execution of the three victims. I think you concocted a story to protect yourself from any disciplinary action," Boris said.

Vitali, pale and trembling, glanced at the floor. Finally he asked, "What leads you to that conclusion?"

"Because that's exactly what I would have done if I were in your shoes, Comrade Vitali. That's what Ivan would have done. That's what all the committed communists in the USSR would have done whether politicians, lawyers, judges, police, merchants and bureaucrats of every stripe. Twenty years in my investigating profession has not led me to a single exception... except one that I am ashamed to talk about," Boris added softly.

"What can I say? I can't argue with your experience," said Vitali. "But you have aroused my curiosity. Can I possibly persuade you to reveal the one exception you referred to?"

"It's been locked up in my memory bank for nearly twenty years. Maybe if I bring it out to light of day it will no longer torment me," Boris reflected. "Comrade Ivan, do you want to listen to a tale prompted by a troubled conscience?"

"By all means, Comrade Boris, if you choose to share it," replied Ivan.

"Alexander and I were young agents together twenty years ago," Boris began. "He was an idealistic young man as I was. We believed the rhetoric of our leaders and we were eager to serve our country and promote communism around the world. Alexander was even more idealistic than I was with a trace of altruism thrown in. We applied together for acceptance into the elite KGB Academy and were both selected. Alexander's grandmother was appalled that we had even considered entering the KGB. When we told her that we had been accepted into their training program at the Academy she was disappointed and deeply troubled. She didn't hesitate letting us know how she felt. I'll never forget her words."

"Alexander and Boris I want to talk to you," she began. "I know you are big boys and you don't need an old, shriveled grandmother to tell you what to do. But I am going to tell you anyway because I love you. You are part of a big organization with lots of power. They promise you a materialistic paradise but they'll create hell on earth. Family members will spy upon and betray one another in order to advance themselves within this monstrous beast."

"My babushka, you exaggerate," Alexander protested. "We are going to help produce a new society where everyone works for each other. There will be no rich or poor but all will share equally."

"Even if that were true about material things, which it isn't, there is no equality of power," said the old babushka. "Those who assume a position of power will fight desperately to retain it and advance in the power structure. This is the way Jesus, the Lord who I am forbidden to serve, describes how far one will go to protect his power position: "Brother will betray brother to death, and a father his child; children will rebel against their parents and have them put to death." These old eyes have seen that very thing come to pass in your paradise. Brute power is god and it will destroy you if you do not surrender to it. And if you do surrender to it, your destruction will be far worse. You will forfeit your humanity."

"With these words babushka buried her face in her rough hands and began to sob," Boris recalled. "Alexander went to her and put his arms around her in an attempt to console her. I watched with mixed feelings of pity and contempt.

"Gaining control of her emotions, Babushka grasped Alexander's hands in her own and looked into his face. 'I have said what I believe God wanted me to say. I will never stop loving you or praying for you,' she said. 'Do not feel sorry for me. I have a glorious future awaiting when this life is over. Go now and do what you must do as I will continue doing what I must do.'

"Alexander and I turned and slowly walked away. I remarked, 'Your babushka is a gutsy old gal.' 'Yes. She has far more courage than I. That's what frightens me. Eventually she will get into trouble with the power structure she warned us about,' Alexander said.

"I didn't realize how prophetic Alexander's words were. A neighbor reported to the KGB that Alexander's babushka had a Bible hidden in her house. I was the agent dispatched to investigate. I questioned her about the charge and she readily admitted her guilt. I tried to reason with her about defying the law. She said to me, 'Boris, I told you a few days ago to do what you must do and that I would continue doing what I must do. I will continue reading my Bible because its truths are my source of hope and strength.'

"I had no choice. I confiscated the old book and submitted my report. Fortunately, another agent was selected to arrest her. She was given a short hearing and sent to prison to await an official trial.

"When Alexander found out that his beloved babushka had been imprisoned he called me. He was beside himself. 'I was afraid this would happen,' he moaned. I didn't dare tell Alexander that I had been the agent sent to investigate. 'What shall I do, Boris?' he asked me.

"You must visit her in prison and try to persuade her to be reasonable and compromise with the authorities. If she promises not to conceal or read a Bible again I think you can get her released. He agreed to try and he did but with no success. He refused to talk about what took place between him and his babushka. I think she may have told him I was the investigative agent. But whatever happened between him and her produced a change in Alexander. He became moody and didn't want to talk about it. A short time later she was tried in secret and sentenced to a women's labor camp in Siberia where she died within the year. Alexander was notified of her death and was given a few days to retrieve her body if he wished to do so. For whatever reason, he didn't choose to do so but sent an influential friend empowered to receive her remains and provide a Christian burial in an Orthodox cemetery.

"Following the death of his grandmother, Alexander's personality began to change even more radically. He developed a hatred for Christians and a morbid desire to inflict pain upon them. I think he may have blamed Christians for creating the rift between him and his babushka. That, coupled with the torment of a guilty conscience, twisted his mind.

"So there you have it," Boris concluded. "In my twenty years as a KGB agent that little insignificant babushka was the only exception I ran across who had a higher loyalty than her own immediate self-interest. And that's why I don't believe you Vitali. Your highest loyalty is to what you consider is best for you here and now. In this matter under investigation, I don't think you consider telling the truth to be in your best interest."

"I'm sorry you feel that way," Said Vitali. "I don't suppose you want to tell me where I erred. I am convinced I told a believable story."

"You are right. I prefer not to do someone elses work for him," Boris said. "What I do want to do is inform you about our schedule for tomorrow. A helicopter will arrive at 10 a.m. to convey us to the Vladivostok airport where we will board a flight to Vnukovo airport in Moscow. Ivan and I will say in Moscow on assignment. Vitali will catch a flight to Leningrad after a short layover and report to Comrade Rasputin, senior KGB agent."

"In all your scheduling have you included plans for dinner tonight, Comrade Boris?" Agent Ivan asked. "It has been a long time since we ate a light lunch in Vladivostok and my stomach is protesting."

"While Andre and you two were guarding the prisoners when they were cleaning I was inspecting the food supplies in the refrigerator, pantry and freezer," Boris said. "Comrades, we are going to have a dinner fit for a king tonight. My hobby is cooking and once a week I prepare a special meal, usually dinner, and invite selected friends over to share it. Tonight you are my guests."

"Hurrah for Comrade Boris." said agent Vitali. "What's on the menu for tonight?"

"I discovered a treasure in the meat drawer of the refrigerator…three choice tenderloin steaks. I will prepare a special marinade in which to soak them briefly. That will impart a delectable aroma and flavor that will excite even your most listless taste buds. I also found a few carrots and beets in the vegetable bin and in the pantry were some onions, potatoes and a head of cabbage."

"I predict a flavorful bowl of borscht will be on the menu," said Ivan. "What is a Russian meal without borscht?"

"Borscht has preserved the life of many Russian peasants in years past and is imbedded in our diet and history. However, it will not grace our table tonight. The USSR is an international confederation and tonight you will partake of a way vegetables are prepared in one of the French provinces; I forget which. A Comrade visiting from Paris shared this," Boris said. "All the veggies, except cabbage, will be sliced into medium size chunks, brushed with olive oil and then a tasty salt seasoning applied. They will be placed on a flat pan and roasted in the oven until tender. The cabbage will be shredded for our salad and topped with a sour cream and wine dressing. We won't have borscht but we will have beets, cabbage, potatoes and sour cream, all major ingredients in many borscht recipes. After dinner we will sit around and pretend we are part of the bourgeoisie. We will enjoy a scoop of Italian gelato, sip a small glass of cognac and tell some of our favorite stories. I hope it will be a pleasant break from our usual routine."

"Hear, hear," said agent Ivan. "Comrade Boris, tonight I am seeing a side of you I didn't know existed."

"In our society few indeed dare reveal all of themselves," Boris said. "The only transparent citizen I ever knew was agent Alexander's babushka. Now, get out of my kitchen, comrades, and give me an hour and a half. I will call you when dinner is prepared."

Boris was in high spirits as he got involved in his favorite pastime. Ivan found a book that interested him and began to peruse the chapter headings. Vitali found a quiet corner and began to scribble on a note pad as he worked to improve his 'after action report'.

At 1930 agent Boris announced, "Dinner is about to be served. Comrade Vitali, you know where the china and utensils are stored. Would you please set the table. Comrade Ivan, would you please place the chairs at their proper places."

In a few minutes they were all seated and prepared to sample Comrade Boris's skill as chef. Vitali and Ivan waited for a signal from their host to begin. Instead, he made a short announcement. "Since we have no father god to thank for his bounty let us express appreciation to mother nature for providing these delicious accidents of her creative genius and for placing us in a position to enjoy them richly as multitudes suffer from hunger while they languish in prison. In the names of comrades Lenin, Stalin and Kruschev. Amen"

Surprised, Vitali and Ivan sat for a moment in awkward silence before Boris broke in, "Comrades, forgive my inept attempt at satirical humor. Don't let it spoil your appetites. Dig in and let's eat heartily."

The food was exceptionally delicious. The select beef cut was fork tender so that a knife was superfluous had the steak not been so thick. Grilled to medium rare perfection, the savory flavors infused from the exotic marinade were even more flavorful than Boris had promised. The roasted vegetables and the salad with the unusual dressing proved to be an ideal accompaniment to the rich-flavored meat. The good food restored the comradery of the KGB agents. Boris basked in the sincere compliments of his associates. Finally he broached a subject he was sure was on all their minds.

"Comrades, what did you think about the manner in which the bodies were disposed ?" he asked.

There was silence as Vitali and Ivan looked at each other.

"I thought it was really weird," said Ivan finally.

"My sentiments exactly," replied Vitali. "I figured it must have some meaning to someone but I had no idea what it was."

"The story behind the disposal is more weird than the reality of the disposal," said Boris. "Vitali's report to Colonel Rasputin following his killing of agent Alexander and the prisoners was forwarded immediately that morning to Viktor Chebrikov, head of the KGB. Chebrikov had planned a midday luncheon party with some of his senior officers from the national office. He had heard of my reputation and asked me to serve as chef. I agreed to plan and oversee the preparation of the menu for the affair. Later in the afternoon he read Vitali's report to his guests, which I happened to hear. He asked for suggestions as to how he should order the bodies to be disposed. By this time they had drunk liberally from vodka and other spirits and their tongues were loosened.

"Chebrikov prefaced his request for suggestions with brief remarks about the victims. 'Agent Alexander apparently was a traitor. The prisoners were devoted Christians and therefore enemies of the State. Now let me hear your suggestions. Comrade Boris, would you please take notes.'"

"Whatever is done we must do nothing that would reflect honor on these despicable people," said one.

"I suggest something humiliating and degrading," said another

"Order something mysterious and grotesque. It doesn't have to have any purpose other than to keep people guessing as to what the purpose was."

"Each suggestion was greeted with drunken laughter and ribald comments. When suggestions ceased I handed my notes to Chairman Chebrikov. He read them and then, to my surprise, spoke directly to me.

"Comrade Boris, in addition to your talent for preparing delicious food I understand you are a skilled investigator. This evening I want you to board an overnight flight to Vladivostok. With the seven time zones you cross it will be tomorrow morning when you arrive at your destination. A helicopter will be ready to transport you to Interrogation Station 12. Agent Vitali, who shot each of the victims, has been ordered to leave the bodies as they fell.

"Investigate the scene thoroughly. If you find nothing that would make it improper to incorporate my friends suggestion for the disposal of the bodies then use your imagination and devise such a plan. I will issue an order to the local KGB office to assist you in every way possible."

"I devised the plan that we carried out today. Did it fulfill the suggestions of our esteemed leaders?" Boris asked.

"That and more, Comrade Boris. Your talents amaze me," said agent Ivan. "Thank you for selecting me to accompany you."

"I would never have guessed you concocted a plan suggested by drunk KGB leaders," said Vitali. "Thanks for sharing how it all came about. It was certainly mysterious and grotesque."

"Comrades, tomorrow will soon be here and it will be a busy day," said Boris at last. "I must go to bed and suggest you do likewise."

"Before we retire I would like to express my appreciation to you, comrade Boris, for an evening I will never forget," said Vitali. "It was more than the great meal you prepared, as delicious as that was. It was the spirit of togetherness that you helped develop among us. How did you do that?"

"Thank you for your encouraging words," said Boris. "As to your question, the answer is simple. I tried to do something that was in the best interest of you and Ivan even though it cost me some time and effort. I made a deliberate decision to serve my comrades. When I use my gifts to serve others rather than serve myself something magical happens. I cannot explain it. It is as if it were written into the very nature of the universe. Maybe it was. Good night, comrades."

The next morning the KGB agents were all packed and prepared to leave when the helicopter arrived a few minutes before 1000. In twenty minutes they arrived at the airport and picked up the tickets to Moscow that were awaiting. Vitali noticed that he had a thirty minute layover before continuing to Leningrad. By eleven a.m. they were airborne. Boris was seated in first class. Vitali and Ivan had choice seats in the first row behind the first class section.

"We have eight hours to get better acquainted, comrade Vitali," said Ivan. "Tell me, how long had you worked with agent Alexander?"

"Comrade Ivan, I would rather not discuss anything about my former partner," said Vitali icily. "I slept poorly last night. If you don't mind I'm going to try to catch some shut-eye."

"I meant no offense, Comrade," said Ivan. "Sleep well."

CHAPTER 20
THE VOICE

Due to seven time changes the Vladivostok Avia jet landed at Vnukovo airport in Moscow at 1200 noon. Despite eight hours of flight time they were only one hour behind the sun. The three KGB agents exited the plane together and paused briefly to bid each other farewell before each went his separate way.

Vitali double checked his ticket to make sure of the boarding schedule for his Leningrad flight. His connecting flight departed at 1230 and arrived at 1320. "Good," he said to himself. "I'll go right to the gate where they must be boarding at this time."

They were boarding when he arrived. The flight attendant met him at the open hatch. "Welcome aboard, Comrade. You seat is forward, second row on the aisle."

Vitali conferred with himself as he sat with head bowed as if asleep. "Do I dare tell Rasputin the full story about what happened at Interrogation Station 12? Just what was in the report submitted by agents Boris and Ivan? I think I am in too deep now to change my report. I'll go with it and see what happens."

With his decision made to stick to his story, Vitali began to think about more mundane matters like lunch. "Should I report to Rasputin immediately or should I fortify myself with a hearty lunch and then call him?" As he weighed the advantages and disadvantages of each he decided he should call first. He hoped it would send a message to Rasputin that indicated he had nothing to hide and was eager to come in and tell him the truth about what had happened.

Vitali followed through with a phone call to Rasputin's office immediately after debarking.

` "Leningrad KGB headquarters, duty officer Petyr speaking."

"Comrade Petyr, this is agent Vitali and I just arrived from Vladivostok. My orders are to report to Lt.Col Rasputin upon arrival. Is Colonel Rasputin available?"

"Comrade Vitali, Colonel Rasputin is in conference but he should be available in an hour. Is there a phone number where I can reach you when he is available?"

"I have a better idea, Comrade. This will give me time to eat lunch and I will call him from my favorite restaurant in about an hour," said Vitali. "Please tell him if you have an opportunity."

"I will inform the Colonel. Enjoy your meal, Comrade."

Vitali did enjoy his meal immensely. He then called KGB headquarters again and the same duty officer answered as before.

"Comrade Petyr, this is KGB agent Vitali. I talked to you an hour or so ago. Is Colonel Rasputin now available?"

"Comrade Vitali, I informed the Colonel of your call. He was pleased that you had called but he is unable to see you this afternoon. He scribbled a brief note and asked that I read it to you. 'Comrade Vitali, welcome back to Leningrad. I regret I cannot meet with you today. You have had a long flight and are no doubt tired. Enjoy a relaxing evening and report to my office at 0900 tomorrow morning.' He authenticated it with his initials. Any questions?"

"None," replied Vital. "I will report to Colonel Rasputin tomorrow at 0900. Thank you, Comrade and good afternoon."

Rising early the next morning, Vitali ate a leisurely breakfast as he read PRAVDA. "The same old garbage," he said to himself. "Whoever tells the truth anymore?"

He arrived at the local KGB headquarters a few minutes before 0900 and signed in with agent Petyr, apparently the day time duty officer. At exactly 0900 he was ushered in to Lt. Col. Rasputin's office.

"Good morning, comrade Vitali. Please be seated," said Colonel Rasputin. "I have been going through your record and I have noticed some troubling insertions regarding reports you have submitted. I am sorry to say, you do not have a stellar reputation for honesty."

"There was an incident in past years that I saw things a little differently than other agents did," Vitali responded. "Unfortunately, the only person who could verify my report was dead."

"It was suspiciously unfortunate that the man killed happened to be an undercover agent from KGB national headquarters," said Rasputin. "His written report was never recovered which just happened to contain his report on your participation in his "sting"."

"We were investigating some international criminal scum," said Vitali. "They had no compulsion about eliminating anyone who threatened them. Apparently, they discovered the identity of the undercover agent and arranged an unfortunate accident."

"We are not here to review ancient history," said Rasputin. "Yesterday I carefully went through the report submitted by comrade Boris in regards to the recent affair that took place at Interrogation Station 12."

"I had no idea comrade Boris was a master chef," said Vitali.

"Please, Vitali, don't try to shift the subject to something more pleasant," Rasputin said. "Comrade Boris is a great cook, as I well know. More to the subject, his is a skilled investigator. He and his assistant, agent Ivan, are both convinced you have not given an honest report of what took place in IS 12 which resulted in you killing three people, agent Alexander and two prisoners."

"I am most interested in hearing how he came to such an absurd conclusion," Vitali said.

"Your story line is totally unsuitable to the characters depicted," said Rasputin. "Agent Alexander has a long history of loyal service to the motherland. He would betray his own grandmother before he would betray his country."

"No one could have been more surprised than I to see the treachery displayed by my trusted partner," said Vitali. "I was so surprised that I may have acted hastily, but when you are being shot at you act by instinct, with little thought involved."

R Glenn Brown

"Furthermore, I knew Vasil Gorgachuk," Rasputin said. "He was a deeply religious Orthodox believer. I tried to recruit him years ago to keep an eye on visiting Orthodox dignitaries from the United States and report to me who they contacted in the USSR. He refused, saying it wouldn't be morally right for one Orthodox believer to spy on another. He would never have considered killing another human being under the conditions you describe."

"I had heard he and his wife were religious fanatics," Vitali said.

"No, not fanatics but very devout and sincere," said Rasputin. "I tried to recruit him a couple of other times but his answer never varied. Secretly, I admired his moral perseverance. Finally, he left the area and I never heard of him again for several years. Recently an alcoholic mid-wife was arrested for shoplifting and she tried to get a reduced sentence by squealing on the Gorgachuks. She had assisted in the delivery of their son twelve years ago but had been bribed not to report the birth."

"And that was when you assigned agent Alexander and me to find the Gorgachuks," said Vitali. "If I may ask, comrade Rasputin, why were you so eager to take this couple into custody?"

"I am tempted to say, 'That's none of your business,'" answered Rasputin. "But maybe I owe you that much. There were two reasons. First, I held a grudge for being refused what I considered a simple, patriotic request. I thought if Gorgachuks were apprehended I could gain access to the boy. I planned to use him as leverage to get Vasil Gorgachuk to agree to observe and report on activities of visiting Orthodox dignitaries. Second, I didn't like the idea of a young Soviet

162

citizen wandering around unregistered. I was determined to find him. You destroyed my plans when you destroyed the Gorgachuks."

"I responded as the situation demanded," said Vitali. "It was kill or be killed."

"You lie, Vitali," accused Rasputin. "Not only is your story unsuitable to the characters depicted. The physical evidence at the scene proves you are lying."

"How can that be, comrade Rasputin? I can't understand how you can say that," said Vitali.

"I will illustrate how I can say that. Listen to this recording of your telephone report to me:

"After I shot the male prisoner, Alexander grabbed the woman from behind and used her as a shield while he attempted to retrieve his revolver from the floor. I didn't hesitate to shoot the woman and then demanded that Alexander surrender."

"If Alexander grabbed the woman from behind she would have been facing you as you shot her, would she not, comrade Vitali?"

"Yes, she was facing me, comrade Rasputin," answered Vitali.

"Now listen as I quote an extract from agent Boris's report," said Rasputin.

"As a matter of fact, the bullet that killed Natasha Gorgachuk was fired into her back and went out through her chest as the massive exit wound clearly depicts. The blood that formed below the wound was the initial eruption that flowed from her body in the final moments her heart was still beating."

"The evidence clearly reveals your report of the killings is false through and through," Rasputin said scornfully. "Are you going to tell me the truth or must I resort to a procedure you are very familiar with?"

"I will tell you exactly what happened," promised Vitali. "Although I must warn you, the truth is harder to believe than the story I concocted."

"Proceed," Rasputin ordered. "The recorder is on."

"When Alexander did not show up with his prisoners at the appointed time, and I received no radio transmission, I suspected there may have been an accident," Vitali said. "I called Igor and asked him to check the road from Vladivostok to the turn off to Interrogation Station 12. It didn't take him long to discover the wreck at the foot of the embankment. Alexander and his prisoners were up above on the roadside signaling him. Igor landed, picked up his passengers and de- livered them to me."

"I want you to walk me through everything that took place after Alexander and the prisoners joined you," said Rasputin.

"I wanted to begin the interrogation immediately after they arrived but Alexander requested we wait until the next day. He said they had saved his life and shared their food and he wasn't mentally prepared to apply torture. I refused, insist- ing we do it on the day scheduled, but agreed to wait until the afternoon. I also agreed to do my "good cop" routine first to give him more time to prepare mentally for his "tough cop" procedure."

"Was there any indication at this point that Alexander was conspiring with the prisoners?" Rasputin asked.

"None that couldn't be explained by the unusual circum- stances," said Vitali. "I thought it out of character for him to insist on preparing lunch for the prisoners and then eating with them but rationalized it was an expression of thanks for saving his life."

"So you changed the usual order of interrogation and applied your charm attack to the female prisoner," said Rasputin. "Was it effective?"

"No, it was not. That woman was not the least intimidated," said Vitali. "She attacked me with truths about our government and its history that set me back on my heels. She threw the story of our former boss, Lavrenty Beria, in my face and I was shamed into silence. She bombarded me with "God talk" and I was forced to consider things I'd rather not think about. I was seething inside. It was all I could do to retain my good guy image."

"Did your approach work any better with her husband?"

"Not at all," Vitali admitted. "I quickly saw he was of the same mind as his wife. I was not in the mood for another sermon so I terminated the interrogation. I notified Alexander and he met me and took control of the prisoners."

"So you had no further contact with the prisoners until they were returned from the Interrogation room," Rasputin remarked. "Isn't that unusual?"

"Yes it is," acknowledged Vitali. "Usually the prisoners are left in holding cells in the IR for security reasons."

"And why wasn't that procedure followed in this case?"

"Alexander explained that he could not abuse those who had saved his life," said Vitali. "He further confessed that he had repented and was now a follower of Jesus Christ. He was determined to protect his prisoners from any harm on my part. Since we both had loaded weapons we were at a stand-off."

"How did you gain the advantage so that Alexander and his new friend were both killed after you had shot the woman?"

"I was able to suddenly seize the prisoner as he walked near me and use him as a shield. He began to struggle and flail his arms so that I was forced to shoot him. I admit I was so enraged I lost control. I kept firing into his body until my hammer clicked on empty."

"So now only Alexander had a loaded weapon. Is that correct?" asked Rasputin.

"That's true, Comrade. I collapsed into a chair and told him to go ahead and kill me but the fool refused to pull the trigger. He just stood across the room and looked at me."

"Did he offer any reason for not shooting you?"

"He did. He said he had only retained the revolver in order to protect his friends. Now that they were dead they no longer needed his protection."

"Then what happened?"

"He just sat down across the room from me and I said to him, 'Alexander, I don't buy that supernatural stuff about God and all that other crap. Tell me, what really happened to you?'" Vitali lapsed into silence.

"So? What did he say?" prodded Rasputin.

"Comrade, we talked for two hours. How can I summarize that conversation? I want to eliminate it from my mind but I can't. I keep hearing Alexander's voice as he answers my questions. It's not the arrogant, critical, harsh, belligerent voice that I knew for so long. His transformed voice…I can't explain it. I can't erase it. I can't forget it. It revealed such patience, such kindness, such concern for me and my future. I was in danger of being trapped into believing his depiction of reality. I was becoming entranced by his picture of God's timeless plan for humanity. It made our corrupt, temporary, materialistic paradise founded on force and fear seem so tawdry. I had to silence him before he enchanted me into becoming as crazy as he was."

"Vitali, snap out of it," demanded Rasputin. "You are talking gibberish. What was it he said that has so impacted you?"

"I knew Alexander well. I know he was an ardent communist and atheist," said Vitali. " When he faced death, as the result of the wreck and the terrible injury he suffered, he saw a demonstration of God's power that created doubt about his commitment to atheism. When his displaced hip ball slipped into its socket and his excruciating pain subsided in answer to prayer he actually began to consider that God may really exist."

"I can understand how that might happen," said Rasputin, "Alexander had a babushka who was a devout believer. I think she had a profound influence on him even though he chose to ally himself with communism."

"I'll never forget our final moments together," said Vitali. "He said something that I would like to forget but can't. 'You know what I was before and you can see the change that has taken place. I did not change myself. God has transformed me…I am the miracle that God has sent to you to demonstrate that he exists. The choice is yours. God will become real to you if you want to know him and serve him.' When he said this, Comrade Rasputin, I couldn't take it any longer. He was driving me mad. I had to destroy him or I might yield and become like him."

"And just how did you destroy him?" asked Rasputin.

"I flew into a violent rage and grabbed a heavy bottle of vodka," said Vitali. "I rushed toward where he was sitting with the revolver on his lap. I was sure he would revert to his old form and shoot me. I anticipated that self-preservation, the first law of nature, would take control. I didn't care. I had to stop his God talk if it was the last thing I did.

"I raised the bottle high and paused for a moment, hoping he would shoot and stop the voice pounding in my head. When he offered no resistance I brought the bottle down with all the force I could muster. With blood and vodka streaming from his head he looked at me and said, 'May God forgive you.' Enraged, I seized his revolver and emptied the rounds into his body.

"I killed the only man who cared more about me than himself. He said he had discovered a higher law that annulled the law of self-preservation. He called it 'the law of self-giving love'. He lived and died because of his commitment to that law. I destroyed his body but I can't silence his voice. I hear it even now. What can I do? Where can I go to escape it?"

"Comrade Vitali, I am going to help you escape the influence of Alexander's life and death. Our Psychological Services Division has a nine month program that will reorient you to the truths of communism and atheism. The brute force of our godless State will crush the likes of the traitor Alexander and the Gorgachuks."

Vitali received orders to the next PSD class that began in September. On January 7, Orthodox Christmas, his body was found near an emptied bottle of vodka. In one hand his cold fingers clutched a revolver; in the other a note that said simply; "I could not silence his voice".

CHAPTER 21
VIKTOR

August 1978

The bond that Viktor Gorgachuk had made with his parents following his release from the monastery made his separation from them all the more painful. He loved the Vashchenko family and relished the friends they had brought into his life from the Pentecostal community. He appreciated the freedom that his new identity provided. Nevertheless, he longed for the loving intimacy he had known with his mother and father when he was confined to the home. He was deeply troubled after a week passed since they left for Nakhodka and he had heard nothing. He shared his concern with his Vashchenko friend.

"Igor, how long does it take to go from Chernogorsk to Vladivostok by rail?" Viktor asked that evening.

"Unless you are on a special high-speed train, it takes five days. It is a very long trip. Why do you ask?" Igor said.

"My parents have been gone for seven days, and I haven't heard if they arrived safely," Viktor replied.

"You must talk to Elder Sergei. He is the one who is entrusted with information about your parents," Igor said. "If you want, I will go with you."

The two boys walked to Elder Sergei's house. "Hello, boys," the elder greeted them at the door. "I am glad you came by, especially Viktor. Come inside, please. I have some troubling news to share with Viktor."

"Is it about my parents? Are they all right?" Viktor asked.

"I was going to wait until tomorrow to tell you, Viktor, just in case the mystery was resolved," Elder Sergei said. "Since I've heard nothing and you are here, I will tell you what I know. Your parents arrived safely in Vladivostok two days ago. Your father called my friend in Nakhodka, and Tibor told him he had an apartment rented and waiting for them. Your father told Tibor they were catching the next bus and should see him about midafternoon. They did not arrive, and he has heard nothing since."

"Has anyone tried to find them?" Viktor asked.

"Some of the brothers from Nakhodka traveled to Vladivostok and made inquiries at the train station and shopping center about two kilometers away. Someone had noticed them walking from the station toward the shopping center carrying their luggage. An employee at the food market said the blonde lady bought some food items. The clerk distinctly remembered because she remarked, 'It looks like you're going on a picnic.' Your mother responded, 'No. It's for the bus ride to Nakhodka.' She thinks they boarded a taxi to take them to the bus station."

"Has anyone checked with the taxi drivers?" Igor asked.

"One driver said there is a KGB agent working out of Interrogation Station number 12 who is known around the city. He uses a taxi as a means of stifling any resistance when he wants to apprehend suspects without a street scene. The driver refused to give a name or any other information. No one wants to get on the wrong side of the KGB."

"What more can we do?" Viktor asked.

"We must pray, Viktor, and wait upon the Lord," Elder Sergei replied. "There is one thing we can be sure of. Your father and mother never revealed any information concerning where you are, or you would have been apprehended by now."

"It's my fault they are in trouble. Why do they take such extraordinary measures to hide my identity from the government?" Viktor asked.

"I think you know why," Elder Sergei chided. "Your parents believe they must hide you just as Moses's parents concealed their son from Pharaoh. God provided a high-ranking Egyptian to protect Moses. They believe God will provide someone with authority to protect you and enable you to get to the promised land of America. In freedom, you can continue preparing for the special task for which God has gifted and called you."

"Yes, I know. We talked about it many times. They sacrificed much to assure my protection from communist control of my education. The scholars at the monastery excited me about searching for biblical truth. I am developing a greater appreciation for how great our God is as I read the Hebrew and Greek texts. After additional training, I would like to dedicate my life to finding and sharing the truth God has revealed in scripture."

"Your parents earnestly prayed that would be your lifelong vocation," Elder Sergei said. "Viktor, my heart is grieved that they're not here for you. I would not minimize your grief and emotional pain with your parents gone. No one can take their place. But I want you to know that I will be a substitute dad to you to the best of my ability. Feel free to visit me any time you wish. Use me as a sounding board for your ideas or questions. I am here for you."

"Thank you, Elder Sergei. Igor is without his parents as well. May he come with me?"

"You have a caring heart, my boy. I already made my offer to Igor as soon as I heard what his parents planned to do. Of course he can come. This home is your home until you both get your parents back," Elder Sergei said heartily.

Throughout the summer, the Chernogorsk Pentecostals were riveted by the twin dramas that impacted their community. Sixteen-year-old Ivan Shevchenko, after being captured by the KGB at the American embassy and savagely beaten, had been released to return home. Everyone wanted to hear details about what had transpired at the embassy as well as his experience with the KGB. He enjoyed his role as hero, including an interview by a local Pravda reporter. The other drama being played out was the mysterious disappearance of Vasil and Natasha Gorgachuk.

Months went by with no further clues regarding the Gorgachuks whereabouts. In October 1978, a short article appeared in a locally printed Vladivostok newspaper.

Mysterious Accident Discovered

Three badly decomposed bodies were discovered inside an up-side-down wrecked vehicle at the foot of an embankment bordering seldom-used road. One male, apparently the driver, was in front. One male and one female were passengers in the rear. An unidentified person reports that authorities are puzzled by signs of multiple gunshot wounds on all three victims. Whether death resulted from the accident or from bullets fired after the accident is unknown. Adding to the confusion, the same unidentified source reported that bullets had been fired from outside the vehicle into the window frame of the rear left door to enable enlarging the opening. An unconfirmed rumor among residents is that the driver is a local KGB agent who called himself Alexander. The two in the rear may be an unknown couple he was seen apprehending on July 4. Authorities have refused to provide any clarification or answer our questions.

Members of the Pentecostal community in Nakhodka saw the article, including Brother Tibor. He immediately placed a telephone call.

"Hello, this is Brother Tibor in Nakhodka. Is this Elder Sergei?"

"Brother Tibor, so good to hear your voice. What prompts your call?"

"I believe I have a lead on what happened to Vasil and Natasha Gorgachuk," Tibor said. "It is not the kind of report I had hoped to give."

"We have reconciled ourselves to the worst, my brother. Young Viktor has entrusted them into God's care and knows that if they are not to be with us they are safe with the Lord. What is the information you have?"

"Briefly, it is this. Three badly decomposed bodies were found in an upside-down demolished vehicle at the foot of an embankment bordering a seldom-used road. The article didn't say, but I think that is the road leading to KGB Interrogation Station 12. I believe the driver is a locally known KGB agent called Alexander. I'm convinced the bodies in the rear are the Gorgachuks. I'll send you a copy of the article, and you can draw your own conclusions."

"I thank you, Brother Tibor, on behalf of myself as well as Viktor. At last he can be sure the Lord has called them home. Greetings to all our friends at Nakhodka," Sergei said.

Elder Sergei shared the telephone conversation with Viktor and later the newspaper article. It assured the boy that his beloved parents had moved their home address beyond the reach of the KGB. Viktor sensed a deep need for God's comfort and presence now that there was no hope of seeing his father and mother again on earth. He walked to the Orthodox Church where he had worshipped with his parents. Retreating to one of the side chapels, he began to bare the pain in his heart.

"Lord Jesus, I miss my mama and papa so very much. My heart is heavy, and I desperately need to be comforted. You promised to send the Holy Spirit to be my comforter and counselor. I know Mama and Papa are with you, and because of that, I rejoice even in my sorrow. I thank you, Jesus, for what you mean to me. I have hope. I have a future because of you. I praise you and worship you."

As Viktor poured out his heart in praise and worship to Jesus, he began to speak in a language he didn't recognize as he was borne along by the Holy Spirit. He was suddenly filled with the joyful, comforting presence of Almighty God in the Person of his Spirit. It was a sacred moment, and he was glad there was no one there but him and Jesus. He wondered if this was the gift of a language spoken by the enablement of the Holy Spirit for communication with God, spirit to Spirit. He would have to search scripture carefully.

The public school provided no intellectual challenge at all, and he required little time to prepare for his classes. He was much more educated than his teachers and had to deliberately conceal the extent of his knowledge so as not to arouse suspicion or embarrass his instructors. Consequently, he had a great deal of time to immerse himself in the language studies he loved. Viktor had resolved to particularly master the nuances and grammar of American English as he looked forward to immigrating to the United States. He had been able to keep some of his grammar texts from the monastery, which he had practically memorized. He also retained the Hebrew and Greek texts of the Old and New Testaments. He was never bored because the variety of languages continually challenged him. He was intrigued by the earthy, picturesque Hebrew language, which the great Hebrew prophets and poets employed so well. He was equally impressed by the precise, logical Greek of the New Testament that philosophers loved.

Thanks to the intervention of American embassy personnel, the Vashchenko parents were able to make periodic telephone calls to their children from the embassy to the Chernogorsk telephone exchange. Viktor was fascinated by the saga unfolding within the family he was now associated with. He shared their frustration as the USSR refused to give permission for the family to emigrate. He admired the tenacity of the Pentecostals who refused to surrender their dream of immigrating to America. He shared that dream. Would he be able to accompany them?

As the years passed, Viktor could tell the ordeal was wearing on all members of the Vashchenko and Chmykhalovs families. When mother Augustina and daughter Lida decided to add fasting to their prayers, this caught the attention of international media. When Lida had to be admitted to a Soviet hospital because of severe weight loss and malnourishment, this applied more pressure on the Soviets to grant emigration. When released from the hospital, she was ordered to go back to Chernogorsk and rejoin her siblings. Almost five years had passed since her parents and sisters had invaded the United States embassy. Would they ever be permitted to emigrate?

CHAPTER 22

JOSEF

One morning on February 6, 1983, an unexpected telephone call was received at the Vashchenko home. Lida answered, thinking it was for her, as most were. An unfamiliar, deep voice greeted her.

"Hello. Is this the Vashchenko household?"

"Yes, it is. Who is speaking?" Lida asked.

"That is not important," the man said. "What is important is that I speak to Viktor Vashchenko. Is he available, please?"

"Yes he is. One moment, please," Lida said, then calling Viktor.

"Hello. This is Viktor."

"Viktor, you must pay close attention to what I say, and you will have to trust me," a deep voice said.

"Who is this and why should I trust you?" Viktor asked.

"My name is not important, but you can call me Josef. I am a senior official in the Soviet Emigration Service. I will tell you a little of what I know to help establish trust between us.

"As I'm sure you know, your birth was never registered with the Vital Statistics Agency. For years, the government never knew you existed. The midwife who helped in your birth revealed your secret to KGB agent Vladymir Rasputin when she was arrested twelve years later. Rasputin decided to have KGB agents arrest your parents in order to get you under control of the government and to pressure your father to be his source of information about activities of the Orthodox hierarchy. Your true name is Viktor Gorgachuk. You will soon be seventeen years old. Your parents are Vasil and Natasha."

"Are they alive?" Viktor interjected.

"Not on this planet, I'm sorry to say," Josef said. "They were killed more than four years ago by a mad KGB agent. They both died protecting the life of another KGB agent called Alexander, the man responsible for this call. While his partner was interrogating your parents, Alexander sent me a message, using a code we had devised years ago. You were the chief subject of his message."

"How did he know about me?" Viktor asked. "My parents would never have revealed anything. I am sure of that."

"That is true," Josef said, "unless they revealed information to someone they trusted fully. Which is what happened in this case."

"What did Alexander tell you that motivated you to call me four years later?" Viktor asked.

"I do not want to discuss it on the telephone," Josef said. "I must meet you privately, face to face."

"Where do you live?" Viktor asked.

"I live far from Chernogorsk, but I arrived here last night on the 2300 train, and I am staying in room 182 at the Miners Hotel. I realize it is the day before Christmas, and no doubt there will be festivities tonight. Can you meet me in one hour at my room?"

"It is only two kilometers to the hotel," Viktor said. "Yes, I will meet you at ten o'clock. I don't know you, but you are right; I must trust you. If my parents trusted Alexander, and he trusted you, then I dare not break this chain of trust. I will see you soon, Mr. Josef. Good-bye."

"What was that all about?" Lida asked.

"I'm not sure," Viktor said. "Some official in the Emigration Service wants to talk to me. He knows a lot about me and my parents. I believe he can be trusted, so I agreed to meet him at the Miners Hotel at ten o'clock. Tell Igor where I am when he comes home. You guys pray for me."

After a brisk fifteen-minute walk to the Miners Hotel, Viktor saw by the lobby clock that he was nearly ten minutes early. The extensive coal mining nearby brought in observing engineers from China, Nigeria, both Germanys, Canada, and, occasionally, the United States. It was largely for this clientele that the hotel was built, and it was the pride of Chernogorsk. By western standards, it would have rated two stars at best.

Viktor looked at the pictures displayed on a wall in the lobby. There was one photo of the administrative offices of the mine where his father was employed as bookkeeper. At two minutes until ten, he began walking down the hall toward room 182. Pausing briefly at the door before knocking, he breathed a silent prayer. Taking a deep breath, he rapped firmly three times.

He recognized the deep, sonorous voice that called out as the one on the phone, "The door's unlatched. Please come in."

Entering the room, Viktor was greeted by a man much smaller than he had envisioned him. He judged him to be about one meter and sixty-five centimeters tall (5'6"). He surely weighed no more than seventy kilograms. He wondered how such a powerful voice could be produced by a man this small. He guessed his age to be near sixty. His close-cropped, steel-gray hair and smooth-shaven face plus his Napoleon-like stance gave him a military appearance.

"Viktor, thank you for coming to see me so promptly. I realize I gave you little notice, but there are things on the horizon that demanded quick action. Please take a seat and let me explain," Josef said. "I have waited a long time before I felt the time was appropriate to meet with you. It's a long story, but I'll make it as brief as possible. First, let me tell you what remarkable parents you had."

"Did you know my parents, Mr. Josef?" Viktor asked eagerly.

"No, I did not know them personally," said Josef. "But let me tell you what I do know. Your parents were apprehended by a KGB agent that I have known for many years called Alexander. He was a heartless, borderline psychopath who loved to bring emotional and physical pain to those he arrested. He more than met his match in your parents. They were not intimidated by him or fearful of him. This infuriated him and led to his losing control of the car he was driving. The car overturned, rolling down the bordering embankment."

"Were my parents injured?"

"Not seriously," Josef replied. "But Alexander was badly injured and unconscious in the front area of the overturned car. Your parents were able to exit the demolished vehicle through a broken window of a rear door. When Alexander came to, your father reentered the vehicle and helped extricate the injured KGB agent. Then the unimaginable happened. Alexander decided to become a Christian."

"Out of the blue, this KGB agent just suddenly decided to give his allegiance to Jesus Christ?"

"It does sound unbelievable, doesn't it?" Josef said. "Actually, it wasn't quite that immediate. When your parents were not intimidated or made fearful by his threats, Alexander was tremendously impressed. When they dared to boldly refute his atheism and confront him with facts about their Christian faith, he himself became intimidated and responded with raging anger."

"And that's when he lost control of the car, and it rolled down the embankment?"

"That's right," Josef replied. "When Alexander became conscious and found his revolver missing, he was fearful his prisoners might shoot him. When he tried to move and learned the seriousness of his injury, he really panicked. Would they leave him to suffer a tortuous death? When your parents demonstrated compassion and attempted to rescue him, he began to reevaluate his heartless atheism."

"But he was still trapped inside the wreck, wasn't he?"

"Yes. And his injury was so serious and the pain so severe when he moved that there was some question if they could extricate him. It was at this point that Alexander agreed for your parents to pray for God's help."

"What happened then?" Viktor asked.

"God alleviated the pain and gave your father an idea that resulted in the dislocated hip being restored," Josef answered.

"And then the KGB agent became a Christian?" Viktor asked.

"No, not quite," Josef said. "But now he was ready to consider the possibility of becoming a Christian. That was a huge change of attitude for a man firmly entrenched in godless communism."

"So how did he get from considering the possibility to actually becoming a Christian?" Viktor asked.

"It was a process of events," Josef replied. "It began when Alexander saw the boldness your parents displayed in the face of threats. It continued when he experienced the compassion and tender love of your parents when his injury rendered him helpless. When he experienced a miracle in his own body in answer to prayer, he was prepared to listen to the gospel. Your parents proceeded to explain God's plan of salvation through Jesus Christ in a credible way to Alexander, and he made the decision that transformed his life."

"Wow!" exclaimed Viktor. "That is an amazing story. As a result of my parents' fearlessness, their compassion for their captor, and a supernatural demonstration of God's power and love, a man I would have considered hopelessly beyond redemption was saved. Thank you, Mr. Josef, for sharing that with me. My parents' example will be an inspiration that I will treasure all my life. I have never been more proud of them than now. How did you come to know all this?"

"Alexander talked to me on a secure sputnik telephone at KGB Interrogation Station number 12 and told me," Josef replied. "Your parents were being interrogated by Vitali, his partner, so Alexander had access to the communication center. He also sent me a coded message concerning you, which I will discuss soon."

CHAPTER 23
JOSEF AND ALEXANDER

"One thing is a mystery to me. What is the tie between you and Alexander? Why did he call you with all this information?" Viktor asked Josef.

"That is a perceptive question and one I will attempt to answer, although some details are classified. Alexander was not always the creep that apprehended your parents in Vladivostok. He became an agent with the KGB about 1963, a year before Khrushchev was deposed. He was intelligent, dedicated to communism and the role of the USSR in the world. His career proceeded well. He was liked by his superiors and respected by his contemporaries. In 1967, Yuri Andropov became head of the KGB. Leonid Brezhnev had succeeded Khrushchev in 1964. Andropov and Brezhnev were two of a kind."

"What does this political history have to do with my question?" Viktor asked.

"Young men are too much in a hurry," Josef chided. "Just be patient. I'm getting there. Khrushchev had initiated some reforms that Brezhnev opposed. He was a Stalinist and took a hard line against opponents of communism. Andropov shared his sentiments and vigorously searched for enemies of the state. Christianity was considered the most threatening internal enemy, and Brezhnev tasked the KGB with eliminating Christianity from the culture. In case you haven't guessed, I am a secret believer. I have not declared my faith publically because I believe I can help the cause more by being imbedded with the enemy. I am like Joseph of Arimathea who remained in the Sanhedrin until the right time to reveal himself."

"I'm sorry, Josef. I still don't see the connection," Viktor said.

"Patience, son. I'm trying to give you the background material. Alexander became one of the best investigative agents in the organization. He had a nose for clues and pursued them wherever they led. His pursuit of clues led him to me and to an underground organization that I had founded within the Emigration Service to expedite the escape of Christians imprisoned because of their faith. He threatened to expose me unless I promised to use my connections to help a Christian designated by him to immigrate to America. I gave him my word, and he deposited the sealed evidence with someone he trusted. I know not who or where."

"Why and how would Alexander have knowledge of someone that would need help to immigrate to America at some time in the future?" Viktor asked. "It makes no sense to me."

"Nor did it to me," said Josef. "I asked Alexander what prompted such a strange request. To the best of my memory, what follows is the gist of his answer:

"'Josef, I know you know my babushka. She is a secret believer as you are. She spends much time in prayer and says that God communicates with her by his Spirit to her spirit. One day she was praying and sensed the presence of God in an unusually awesome way. She had a dream or vision, and an angel told her God had heard her prayers. The angel assured her that her grandson would become a Christian and he would be instrumental in helping a chosen young man immigrate to America. When the time was right, he would know who the man was.'

"He went on to tell me he didn't ever envision becoming a Christian, but he had promised his babushka that if he ever became a Christian, he would remember her words," Josef said.

"How long ago did this take place?" Viktor inquired.

"It was shortly after Yuri Andropov became head of the KGB, probably 1968 or '69," Josef said.

"What happened in the fourteen or fifteen years since then that produced the degeneration in Alexander's character?" Viktor inquired.

"Andropov pursued Christians with extreme zeal and recruited citizens to report any believers they knew of. Someone, probably a neighbor, had reported to the KGB that Alexander's babushka had a Bible hidden in her house. An agent was sent to investigate, and the old lady admitted her guilt. Her beloved Bible was confiscated, and she was arrested and imprisoned."

"That must have made Alexander furious. What did he do?" Viktor asked.

"He visited his grandmother in prison and told her he thought he could get her released if she would repent and promise never to harbor or read a Bible again," Josef said.

"And what was her response to that?" Viktor asked.

"She bristled and scolded, 'Sasha, shame on you. You are asking me not to read God's word or harbor it in my house. I will die in this filthy jail before I make such a pledge. I have God's word concealed right now where they will never find it.'

"'Babushka, please don't antagonize the authorities,' Alexander pled.

"'Your babushka is an old woman, my dear Sasha. I don't have long for this earth. Let them keep the words on paper that they took. I have them hidden away in my heart where they will be safe until I go see God face to face. I hope it is soon. Come, kiss your babushka good-bye. I will never stop praying for you.'

"That was the last time he saw his grandmother alive," Josef said. "She was tried in secret and sentenced to a women's labor camp in Siberia. She survived less than a year. Alexander got in touch with me and asked if I would go to the camp and retrieve his grandmother's body. I agreed to do so and went with a letter authorizing me to receive the corpse. I bought an inexpensive burial box made in the camp in which her emaciated body was placed. Some of the inmates spoke to me and described how blessed they had been by her. 'We would gather about her in the evening, and she would quote sacred scripture to us. We loved her and miss her greatly.'

"I accompanied her simple coffin on the train ride to the cemetery where she was interred. I paid for the professional grave diggers and grave site and found a state-approved Russian priest to conduct a short Orthodox committal ritual. Her death marked the point where a radical downhill change began in Alexander's personality."

"Why should her death induce such a radical change?"

"I am not a psychiatrist or a priest or minister, but I have some insight into human behavior. For what it's worth, here is what I think. He was dealing with a lot of guilt because he virtually neglected his grandmother after her arrest. That guilt was never resolved before she died. After her death, he made a conscious decision to devote himself to advancing the agenda of the communist regime. Having chosen commitment to godlessness, he was tormented with guilt every time he saw someone that reminded him of his Christian babushka, and he lashed out savagely."

"Alexander knew you were a Christian," said Viktor. "Why did he not turn on you but rather protected you?"

"Strange, isn't it? Who but God knows what goes on in troubled minds?" Josef replied. "I think it had something to do with my connection with his babushka. Protecting me was an attempt to atone for his failure to protect her. But despite this, the torment of a guilty conscience was never stilled."

"There must have been quite a celebration when Alexander was reunited with his beloved babushka," Viktor said. "Someday my parents and I will have a joyous family reunion. I hope I don't disappoint them."

"Viktor, it is time we talk about the plan to get you safely to America," Josef said. "I examined your identification document carefully. The forger is quite skilled, and his product will deceive most inspectors. But he is not as skilled as my employees in the Emigration Service. One of the most skilled is a secret believer who prepares many of the documents that enable me to successfully get carefully selected people out of the USSR."

"But how can you do that when emigration is so tightly restricted and controlled?" Viktor asked.

"Most don't go labeled as emigrants," Josef explained. "There are hundreds of Soviet airplanes and ships departing weekly. We manage to create an identity that can fit a passenger or crew member or some other legitimate category that can be aboard one of these departing craft. Sometimes we have to resort to monetary persuasion. The Soviet Union is riddled with corruption. With few exceptions, every person with a position of power has his or her price."

"Where do most of these people go?" Viktor asked.

"America, of course, is a popular destination but not always the best choice," Josef said. "I'm speaking from my point of view as the one planning the escape."

"Why do you say that?"

"Because the KGB and other police agencies scrutinize more carefully all those boarding a plane or ship bound for the United States. I have done it successfully, but it is more costly and hazardous."

"What about me? Have you determined where I should go?" Viktor asked.

"For you, it was an easy choice," Joseph said.

"I don't understand why choosing my destination was easy," Viktor said.

"Don't you now? The choice was practically made for us when you mastered the Hebrew language in the monastery. We sponsor more Jewish emigrants now than any other group. Most are going to Israel, as are you. For your exit adventure, you will have a new name fitting your assigned ethnic origin. How does Dan ben Chagai sound?"

"Any name that will assist me to emigrate is welcome," Viktor said. "But please, don't overestimate my mastery of Hebrew. I read it fluently, but I have had little opportunity to practice speaking since I departed the monastery. Is there a time line for all this to happen?"

"I cannot give you exact dates and times," Josef replied. "There has been much negotiation going on behind the scenes for the release of the Pentecostal families taking sanctuary in the American embassy. I can tell you this. A decision has been made to soften the hard position the Soviet government has taken. Soon Lida will be asked to apply for an emigration visa to West Germany or Israel. I'm sure she will specify Israel."

"Why will only Lida be asked to apply?" Viktor asked.

"It's a way for our Foreign Office to save face. Soviet emigration law states that if there is a family member already lawfully living in a foreign country, other members of the family may apply for emigration visas to join them. They break this law for one family member in order to legitimize all the others who will request permission to join her. Those in power can bend rules any way they choose to fit their agenda."

"Will I be departing with the Vashchenko family?"

"No. They have been receiving far too much international media attention to risk having an additional family member become part of their entourage. An investigation would be triggered and your identity revealed. They are going by air. You will travel by sea departing from the Ukrainian port of Odessa.

"What's your plan to get me from landlocked Chernogorsk to Odessa?"

"I can give you a rough outline, but nothing definite will be decided until the Vashchenko exit date has been decided," replied Josef. "You will travel by train to Moscow. It is a slow train making many short stops, so allow at least four days. You will continue from Moscow to Odessa. The train is faster, and the distance is less, so it will only take about twenty-seven hours."

"So I will be traveling by train overland at least five days. How about aboard ship?"

"As soon as I can pinpoint dates, I will inform you of details about the ship, the captain's name, and so on. I will give you the name and phone number of your contact in Odessa, and he can help you. You will sail through the Black Sea, then via the Bosporus Strait into the Sea of Marmara, which separates Europe from Asia. You will exit the Sea of Marmara through the long, narrow Dardanelles Strait into the Aegean Sea, which is an arm of the Mediterranean Sea separating Greece and Turkey. The ship will cross the Mediterranean to the Israeli port of Haifa where you will debark. It is a beautiful voyage. You will love it."

"I can scarcely believe that after five long years in the wilderness, I see the promised land in the distance," Viktor mused. "Josef, I can never thank you enough for keeping your promise to Alexander."

"Each has his part to play in God's drama," Josef responded.

CHAPTER 24

RABBI COHEN

Events moved rapidly following Josef's visit. In February, the Soviet authorities asked Lida to initiate a request to immigrate to either West Germany or Israel. She chose Israel, and on April 6, 1983, she arrived triumphantly at the Tel Aviv airport. Officials at the American embassy saw this as a sure sign the Soviets had softened their stance, and Pyotr was easily persuaded to leave the embassy and return to Chernogorsk on April 12. One evening seven weeks later, Pyotr received a phone call from an unidentified caller asking to speak to Viktor.

"Hello, this is Viktor."

"Viktor, this is a friend of your friend Josef. He has sent me to convey to you some important information. Can you meet me at the Miners Hotel, room 176?" an unfamiliar voice asked.

"Yes, sir. What time should I be there?" Viktor inquired.

"How about in half an hour at 1900 hours. Is that too soon?"

"No, sir. I'll be at your door in half an hour," Viktor promised.

As soon as he hung up the phone, Viktor explained the call to Pyotr.

"I don't know who that is, but he brings information from Josef," Viktor said. "I am to meet him at the hotel in half an hour. Josef promised he would contact me again shortly before I was to begin my journey. He said the timing of my departure was tied to you and the rest of your family's emigration."

"Yes, I am sure with Lida already in Israel we will hear soon as to when we may join her. Your overland and sea travel will likely require a two-week head start if we are to arrive approximately the same time."

"I must go and meet this man. It's hard to believe that the long wait may soon be over. I'll share with you later," Viktor said.

Viktor strolled leisurely toward the Miners Hotel. He talked silently to Jesus as he walked along, expressing his gratitude for the hope that filled his heart.

With only two minutes to spare, he walked directly to room 176 and knocked. Someone within called out, "The door's unlocked. Come in."

Viktor stepped inside the room and was greeted by a tall, distinguished-looking man with a full head of iron-gray hair. A neatly trimmed beard and mustache of the same hue adorned his face. His brown eyes sparkled as he flashed a warm smile and greeted Viktor with a handshake and embrace. "Viktor, my son, my name is Rabbi Cohen. I am a close friend of Josef who has helped many of my people emigrate. He has told me much about you and your heroic parents.

"I am delighted to meet you personally and to have some small part in your emigration process."

"Thank you, Rabbi. I am humbled that you have taken time to meet with me. I understand that my new identity papers will cast me as one of you," Viktor said.

"That's true," said Rabbi Cohen. "I am pleased to know that you read and speak Hebrew. Do you speak Yiddish as well?"

"No, I'm sorry I don't speak Yiddish, although I understand a little," Viktor said. "I read Hebrew very well and love the Semitic manner of describing reality. However, I have had little practice speaking Hebrew and don't converse very fluently."

"Let me give you some practice," said Rabbi Cohen in Hebrew. "From here on, we will carry on our conversation in Hebrew. Are you game for that?"

"Yes indeed. That would be very helpful," Viktor replied.

"Your Hebrew name is Dan ben Chagai, as I think Josef suggested," said the Rabbi. Here in this envelope are the train schedules with ticket prices, time tables, the name and sailing date of your ship out of Odessa, etc. Your departure date from Chernogorsk is June 15. As you can see, you have just two weeks to get ready to depart on your grand adventure."

"I am very excited and so grateful for all who have been involved in my life. My parents have given me a heritage at a price I can never repay. The Vashchenko family has given me a home full of loving brothers and sisters. You and Josef have risked much to enable me to look forward with hope and anticipation to the future," Viktor said.

"Your spoken Hebrew is not so bad," said the rabbi. "A few weeks in Israel will have you speaking like a native. The God of Abraham, Isaak, and Jacob has gifted you and set you apart for a special mission to prepare the way for the Messiah. I know you anticipate his second coming, and we look forward to his first. I would gladly pray that you are right if we had not endured so much suffering at the hands of your people."

"I grieve with you," said Viktor. "I am grateful that your people are now able to return to their ancient homeland. I am looking forward to my visit there before proceeding to America. I hope you will not judge Jesus by the despicable acts of some who have professed to be Christians."

"Thank you for daring to chide me, Viktor," Rabbi Cohen said. "We Jews are not without our shameful betrayal of God's laws. Jewish leaders in godless communism have been responsible for the murder of millions of Orthodox Christians and other believers. I grieve with you also, my young friend. Now I must bid you good-bye. My train departs soon. Before you go, let me quote the conclusion of Psalm 111. *The fear of the Lord is the beginning of wisdom; all who follow his precepts have good understanding. To him belongs eternal praise.* Wisdom and understanding will characterize your life, and God will be praised. Farewell, my son."

Viktor left the hotel deep in thought. His right hand securely grasped the worn briefcase into which he had thrust the priceless packet delivered by Rabbi Cohen. The series of events that had brought him to this hour were rapidly reviewed in his mind. How reassuring to know that God was in control of these events. As he often did, he began to use his walk as a private time to converse with Jesus.

"Lord Jesus," Viktor began tentatively, "I'm not sure if I have interposed my desires for my life and interpreted that as your will. Sometimes I am not sure of my own motives. But there is one thing I am sure of. I truly want you to be Lord of my life. If you want me to stay in Russia, I will be content to do so. But unless you direct otherwise, I shall confidently continue my journey to America. Thank you for calling me to follow you. I have no other desire."

After his talk with Jesus, an inner peace swept through his being. Without reservation, he was committed to being God's man, wherever that led.

The next two weeks sped by. The Vashchenko family had been notified that their application to join Lida had been approved. Their flight date to Tel Aviv was June 29. Viktor was now assured he would have two weeks to reach Israel by their arrival date. On the evening of June 15, Dan ben Chagai began his long train ride to Odessa. He had to keep reminding himself of his new identity.

The trip from Chernogorsk to Moscow took nearly five days. The train made many stops as it wound its way across the steppes of Siberia. Dan came prepared for a long trip with plenty of salami, dried fruit, cheese, and crackers. He would augment this with fresh bread, yogurt, and chai from venders in the train stations. He read much from his Hebrew Bible, lending credibility to his Jewish identity.

After arriving in Moscow, he decided to investigate a youth hostel for the night. The raucous crowd of inebriated teens caused him to reconsider. He decided to get a sleeping compartment on an overnight train. This would give him more security for his baggage as well as a place to stretch out. He was eager to get to Odessa and meet his contact.

Dan ben Chagai arrived in Odessa on the sixth day after leaving Chernogorsk. Gathering his luggage, he debarked from the train and looked around. He was amazed by the baroque grandeur of the train station. He took in the impressive building for a few minutes before reminding himself he had business to attend to. He must find a public phone and call his contact. After a few inquiries, he got directions to the Central Phone Exchange and placed a call to his contact. The operator placed his call and assigned him a booth to carry on his conversation. He put the receiver to his ear and addressed the speaker.

"Hello. This is Dan ben Chagai. I was told I should contact you when I arrived in Odessa."

"Dan, this is Juda ben Israel. I welcome you to Odessa. Where are you as we speak?"

"I am at the phone exchange next to the post office."

"Wait at the entrance. I'll be there in about twenty minutes, driving a red Lada sedan. See you then," Juda said as he hung up.

Dan was entranced by the beautiful buildings displayed in the city center. Mediterranean architecture, particularly Greek, French, and Italian varieties, predominated. He was still engrossed in absorbing the beauty of the city when the beep of an auto horn interrupted his reverie.

"Dan, jump in, and I'll show you more of our distinguished seaport."

Recognizing his name but not the voice, Dan turned to see who had addressed him. A young man driving a black Volga smiled and beckoned for him to get in the car. Dan sensed there was something amiss. Juda had clearly said he would arrive in a red Lada. And the timing was off. Surely it had not been more than ten minutes since he had talked to his contact. He couldn't explain how his name was known by this stranger, but he sensed that he should not get in the car.

"I'm sorry, but I'm waiting for a friend who will be here soon," Dan said.

"Your friend has been delayed, and he asked me to meet you instead," the stranger replied.

"Is that right? What is my friend's name?" Dan asked.

"I know him as Ivan. I think he goes by other names as well, but that's what I call him. What do you know him as?" the stranger prodded.

Uncertain as to what was going on, Dan decided to play along for more time. "That's a nice car you're driving. How can a young man like you afford such an automobile?" Dan asked.

"You like it? It belongs to my father. He's the commissar for this region," the driver explained.

"What's your father's name?" Dan asked.

"Awful nosey, aren't you, Jew boy? Hope your friend shows up soon. I have another appointment, so I must go. Shalom."

Puzzled, Dan hoped Juda would have an explanation for his unsettling, bizarre experience with a stranger. "If he knew my name, what else did he know about me?" Dan asked himself.

After waiting a few more minutes, his deep thought was broken by two short beeps followed by one long. He looked up to see a red Lada pulling to the curb in a no-parking zone.

"Dan, put your luggage in the backseat and hop in. I can't stay in this red zone." A fiftyish looking, rotund, baldheaded man with a red beard was speaking from behind the steering wheel.

"What's your name?" Dan called out.

"What do you mean? My name hasn't changed since I talked to you on the phone. I am still Juda ben Israel. Now get in before a militia comes and I have to pay him off."

"I am really glad to see you, Juda," Dan said. "Incidentally, do you know the commissar of this region?"

"I know who he is, but I don't normally run in his circle. Why do you ask?" Juda said.

"While I was waiting for you, I met someone who claimed to be his son. He drove up about ten minutes before you came. He called my name and told me to jump into his car. I'm glad you told me you were driving a red Lada because he was driving a black Volga. When I told him I was waiting for a friend, he said my friend had been delayed and he was asked to come instead. When he couldn't tell me your name, I knew something was fishy. But he knew my name. That's what puzzled me. Do you have any idea how he knew my name?" Dan asked.

"As a matter of fact, I do," Juda said. "That man in the black Volga is a member of the local mafia. One of their rackets is to prey on young men, particularly Jews, who arrive here alone. The mafia here partners with the Moscow mafia. One of the ticket agents at the railway station in Moscow screens the passenger list looking for single men who have through tickets from Moscow to Odessa. The names of these passengers are phoned to their mafia contact in Odessa."

"But how does the mafia agent link a name to the right passenger?"

"There is an accomplice working as a conductor on the train. She checks the names against the compartment or seat assignments and provides a physical description," Juda said. "There are seldom more than two or three passengers on a train who are suitable candidates for this scam, so it doesn't require a lot of talent or time."

"What would have happened to me if I had fallen victim to the mafia?"

"The mafia equates young Jews traveling alone with money," Juda said. "They would have attempted to get names and phone numbers of close relatives, your parents or grandparents, from whom they could extort money. Failing that, they would have taken your money and other valuables, roughed you up a bit, warned you to keep your mouth shut, and then released you."

"Thank God I didn't take the bait and get caught," Dan said.

"Not only would it have been painful for you, but it would have created problems for our planned liaison with the captain of the ship you will sail to Haifa on," said Juda. "Let's go to a kosher restaurant near here, and I will brief you regarding the planned schedule."

The exotic food fragrances wafting from the kosher kitchen whetted Dan's appetite. "I didn't think I was hungry until we came in and I smelled the food," Dan said.

"Order up. The food's on me," Juda said. "If you don't know what to order, just ask for the daily special. It's always good."

As the server waited to take their orders, Dan scanned the menu.

"Explain why the menu is in separate columns," Dan said. "One column is headed by Ashkenazi, the other by Sephardic."

"The headings indicate traditional cuisine of Jews from a certain region," the server explained. "Ashkenazi cuisine was developed by Jews in Central and Eastern Europe and features a hearty 'meat and potatoes' kind of meal. Sephardic food is the fare of Mediterranean Jews. It is lighter and features more salads, fish, and fruit. Both are served here."

"Both sound equally tempting, so I'll let the chef decide and order the special for the day," said Dan.

"I'll have the snapper, a Greek salad, and a cup of chicken soup," Juda said. "Now, Dan, let me share what I have planned for you in Odessa. I know you are tired after six days of rail travel. I have a room reserved for you in a small hotel near the waterfront. After we eat, I can take you there if you like or I can show you a little more of Odessa. Your ship, *Rose of Sharon*, is scheduled to dock at 1900 this evening. Tomorrow morning at 1000, we meet the captain and have coffee with him in his cabin. I hope he will be able to place you in the small cabin you will berth in during the voyage. Here comes the food. Let's enjoy our lunch."

After lunch, Dan's eyes were drooping, and he elected to go straight to the hotel. He treated himself to a hot shower before he crashed. He quickly fell into a deep sleep and didn't awaken until rays of the rising sun struck his eyes. He arose refreshed and eager to face the day. After a shower and shave, he stretched out on the bed and read portions from his Hebrew Bible and Greek New Testament. Fortified by spiritual nourishment, he decided to get dressed and take an early-morning prayer walk.

Prayer walks had long been part of his devotional life in Chernogorsk. The walks provided him privacy with his Lord away from the loving but hectic Vashchenko household. He began his silent prayer with thanksgiving. His spirit rejoiced in God's goodness and provision for all his needs. He gave thanks for the nudge by the Holy Spirit that protected him

from the double-tongued deception of the mafia. He concluded his prayer time with a fresh dedication of his life to Jesus
Christ for this day. "Jesus, I love you and want to serve you with
all my heart, mind, and strength. Use me as you choose this
day to advance your kingdom. Amen."

CHAPTER 25
ANCHORS AWEIGH

ooking at the sun's position on the horizon, Dan estimated it must be nearing 0700. He began to look for a Jewish deli where he could get a light breakfast. Seeing a bagel shop, he decided a bagel with cream cheese and chai would suffice him until coffee with Juda and the captain at 1000. Sitting outside with the sun on his back, he munched leisurely and watched the pedestrians and motor traffic go by. He enjoyed it so much he decided to splurge on another bagel and cheese.

After sitting for nearly an hour, he decided he would walk around more of the city before returning to the hotel. The beautiful buildings, public and private, were in sharp contrast to the drab scenery he was used to in the mining center of Chernogorsk. After feasting his eyes for another hour of walking, he made his way back to the hotel. The clock in the lobby pointed to 0915. He had half an hour to relax before Juda arrived. He told the clerk at the desk he didn't know yet whether he would be staying another night but would know by check-out time at noon. Dan was waiting outside the hotel when Juda drove up promptly at 0945.

"Good morning, Dan," Juda greeted. "Did you have a good night?"

"Good morning to you, sir," Dan responded. "I had a wonderful night … I think. I don't remember a thing about it. I slept through all afternoon and night until just after dawn this morning." Dan went on to tell Juda of his morning activities.

"Sounds like you had a good night and a wonderful morning so far," Juda said as he pulled into a parking space. "Well, there's the *Rose of Sharon*, your home for the next five or six days. Let's go aboard and meet your landlord, Captain Bernstein. I think you will like each other. He has a son about your age."

At the top of the gangplank, they were met by the officer of the deck who asked to see their identification papers. After a perfunctory check, he called a seaman and told him to escort the two men to the captain's cabin. They followed the sailor to the cabin amidships bearing the captain's name and title.

The sailor's knock on the door was followed by a call from inside, "Who's there?"

"Seaman Raddis, sir, with guests Juda ben Israel and Dan ben Chagai."

"Send them in please, Raddis," called the captain.

Captain Bernstein arose as they entered and greeted them cordially. "Good to see you again, Juda. So this is the apprentice seaman you brought aboard to augment our crew back to Haifa," Captain Bernstein said, laughing. "Welcome aboard, Dan. You must have friends in high places to be granted immigration authority to Israel."

"Yes, sir, the highest," Dan said, pointing a hand heavenward.

"You're right, son. No one outranks the almighty, even those who say he doesn't exist. Let's see, I think this get-together was advertised as coffee with the captain. I'd best have the coffee brought in or I'll be sued for false advertising. Pardon me while I call the galley. This is the captain. Please have someone bring the coffee and whatever else you have prepared for my guests."

"Captain, Dan must let the hotel know by noon whether he is checking out or staying another night. Will there be a berth available aboard ship tonight?" Juda inquired.

"That's what I like about you, Juda. Business before pleasure is your motto. Yes, there is a berth available. But I must warn you, Dan, it will be noisy at times. Some of the cargo needs to be shifted. There will be cargo being unloaded from the forward compartments and incoming cargo loaded in the aft compartments. It's your choice," the captain concluded.

"Even with the noise, I think I prefer the ship. But if I could see the berth before we depart, that will help me make up my mind," Dan said.

A knock on the door followed by the captain's "Come in" produced a mess man with a tray of coffee and assorted fruit.

"The fruits on the tray are samples of our cargo from Israel," the captain explained. "They are the tastiest in the world. Do you know there are over thirty fruits grown in Israel exported to this region? In our cargo, we have a dozen varieties, including bananas, pomegranates, grapes, apples, pears, cherries, loquats, and oranges. Later we will ship other varieties. I'm sorry to say our coffee is not grown in Israel. It is brewed from a special blend we get from Yemen. It will require a little more sugar than some milder varieties."

"Is fruit your only cargo?" Dan asked.

"It is our primary cargo. Sometimes we ship containers of other commodities if it doesn't conflict with our contract for fruit delivery."

"What do you ship back to Israel?" Dan asked.

"Cement, fertilizer, agricultural implements, things like that mostly," the captain replied.

"While you sample the fruit and sip your coffee, I'll brief Dan on our return voyage to Haifa," said the captain. "We'll hoist anchor the day after tomorrow and transit the Black Sea to Istanbul and pass through the Bosporus Strait into the Sea of Marmara. We exit into the Dardanelles Strait, the long narrow channel that leads into the Aegean Sea. This is one of the most picturesque voyages on our planet."

"How long does it take to steam from Odessa to the Aegean Sea?" Dan asked.

"It takes about forty-four hours, nearly two days," Captain Bernstein said. "We have to reduce speed through the constricted straits because of heavy traffic. Once we get into the open sea, we can steam at a steady nine knots. To Haifa, it's another six hundred nautical miles or about three days sailing time. We should get there by midmorning on June 28."

"Perfect timing," said Dan.

"Juda, I have another appointment soon, and you must get Dan back to his hotel," Captain Bernstein said. "I'll have the officer on deck show Dan the berthing space as you leave. You can tell him your decision."

Dan checked the berth and decided he would rather be aboard a noisy ship than risk another visit by the mafia. He informed the OOD of his decision as he and Juda debarked.

"I'm glad you decided to sleep aboard the ship. I am uneasy until the contact I am responsible for is safely out to sea.

Very seldom is there an unmanageable difficulty, but I like to keep our operation under the radar as much as possible. After you check out of the hotel, I will spend this afternoon with you," said Juda as he parked.

"I'll get my gear and be right back," Dan said.

Dan retrieved his luggage, paid his bill, and checked out. He spent an enjoyable afternoon with Juda visiting more of the sights of Odessa. After an early dinner together, Juda returned him to the ship and saw him safely on board. They embraced warmly and bid each other good-bye.

After stowing his gear in the berthing space, Dan found a secluded spot away from the hectic activity of loading and removing cargo. His heart was overflowing with joy and gratitude to God for bringing him safely through the most perilous and vulnerable stage of his escape. He thanked God for his beloved parents and his Uncle Slava; for his teachers in the monastery; for the Vashchenko family and the Pentecostal community at Chernogorsk; finally, he gave thanks for Josef and Rabbi Cohen and Juda and prayed for their protection. He concluded with a reaffirmation of his commitment to serve Jesus Christ with all his being.

"Jesus, I am yours, body, soul, and spirit. I desire nothing but the priceless honor of serving you. I surrender my will, my hopes, and ambitions to your will and plan for my life through time and eternity. I love and trust you, my Lord and Savior. Amen."

Following prayer, Dan was reenergized by the Holy Spirit. He found the officer of the deck and hailed him.

"Sir, if you need someone to run errands, sweep the decks, or any other chore, I'll be glad to lend a hand."

"Thank you, young man. I don't know if our insurance will permit that, but I'll pass it on to the skipper," the officer replied.

As darkness closed in, Dan decided to retire to his small cabin. It was designed for a junior officer, barely two meters wide and three meters long. At one end, there was a small sink and toilet stool. At the other was a hinged writing surface secured against the bulkhead when not in use. Chains attached to the two forward corners and anchored to the bulkhead allowed it to be lowered and serve as a writing surface. His new sleeping berth was hinged and folded down with each outer end corner supported by a sturdy chain secured to the bulkhead. The three-inch foam mattress inside a cotton tick proved to be reasonably comfortable. So comfortable, in fact, Dan decided he would turn in for the night.

Dan slept soundly despite the activity on deck. After breakfast, he wandered about the ship talking to the crew when it didn't interfere with work. There was much activity on deck as the sailors and longshoremen rushed to complete loading and unloading cargo. He was intrigued by the crane that hoisted shipping containers from the dock to the deck. He admired the skill of the operator as he placed containers in the designated areas. Dan began walking away to another area of the ship when he heard an urgent warning shout. He turned to see that one of the cables cradling the suspended container had broken or come loose. The huge metal box was in danger of slipping out of its harness and falling to the deck, crushing whatever was in its path.

Dan turned to rush away from the danger area. As he did so, he tripped over a loose hawser and fell heavily, crashing his head against the steel deck. The crane operator, seeing what had happened, was able to steer the container away from the inert body that lay unconscious on the deck. A sailor rushed to Dan's side and, seeing no movement, called for someone to fetch the captain. Placing his finger on the carotid artery, he was reassured by feeling a steady pulse.

Captain Bernstein soon arrived and took in the situation as the sailor explained what had happened. It was not the first time a serious concussion had occurred on his ship. He was glad they were still in port. He knew just who to call for help. He addressed the sailor standing by.

"I am going to call Dr. Oxana Bigun at the nearby Port Dispensary. She has assisted us before and will be glad to do so again for a generous portion of fruit. I want you to go meet her and escort her aboard the ship. I'll call her on the deck phone connection and wait with this young man until you return."

The vast majority of medical doctors and nurses in the Soviet medical system were women. Soviet propaganda would lead one to believe this was because of the high value the Soviet Union placed upon its female citizens. The truth of the matter was something less virtuous. Women were largely selected for professional training, both doctors and nurses, primarily because the government's socialized medicine could get away with paying females a mere pittance. Men would have rebelled against the less than living wages paid to the more compliant women.

Many of the doctors and nurses had clients who paid extra under the table for professional medical care administered outside the government system. Because of her excellent reputation, Dr. Bigun had many patients outside the system that provided her with a good living. Often she was rewarded with various farm products and bartered labor. She would welcome the tasty Israeli fruit Captain Bernstein offered.

"Hello, my dear Oxana," Captain Bernstein greeted the doctor as she arrived. "Thank you for your prompt response to our medical emergency. You have helped us before with concussions resulting from accidents, so I know you are experienced in this area."

"How long has he been unconscious?" the doctor asked.

"Nearly a half hour now," the captain replied.

"If he doesn't regain consciousness within an hour, we may have to take him to a hospital for an X-ray."

"That would be most unfortunate," the captain said. "Is there nothing you can do to speed the process?"

"Nothing that I would recommend," the doctor answered. "Wait. I think I may have seen an eyelid flutter. Yes, I do believe he is coming to."

"Watcsh shappens," Dan asked in slurred speech. "Woar am I?"

"Dan, I am Captain Bernstein. You fell and struck your head on the deck, resulting in a severe concussion. Dr. Oxana Bigun is here and wants to talk to you. Do you understand?"

"Yesh. Watcsh shappens? Woar am I?"

"Dan, this is Dr. Bigun. You have had a severe concussion, so your brain is a little rattled temporarily. I am going to ask you some questions that will help me diagnose the severity of your injury. Are you ready?"

"Yesh. Watcsh shappens? Woar am I?"

"Concussion victims sometimes have slurred speech and repeat themselves. You are just acting normal for someone who has had his brain severely shaken. You will be back to normal soon. Now, my first question: What is your name?"

"I am Victorsh Gorgeschuk," Dan said.

"He was adopted. That was his original family name," the captain explained.

"How do you feel?" the doctor continued.

"Ver, ver bad headasche," said Dan.

"Any other pain?"

"Ver, ver upseth stomasch," Dan said. "I may upschuk."

"That's normal also, Dan. You just do what you have to do. Someone please fetch a container in case he must vomit. Now look this way. How many fingers am I holding up?"

"Your fingers are very blurred," said Dan more plainly as his speech became near normal. "I think I see four."

"There are two, which means your eyesight is still quite blurred. Now, Dan, I think it is time to see if you can stand up. Captain, if we can have a sailor on each side to steady Dan. It is not unusual for a concussion to result in dizziness to the victim," the doctor said.

"I think I am going to throw up. Please help me kneel. Now, the bucket," Dan said. "Wow. I feel better already," Dan said after upchucking his breakfast in the pail before him. "I apologize, guys. Thank you for all your help."

"How do you feel now?" asked Dr. Bigun.

"My head feels much better, and my stomachache is gone. I'm just very weak and tired. I feel like I could sleep for a week," Dan replied.

"Once again, let's try to get Dan up on his feet," said Dr. Bigun. "Can you stand by yourself?" asked the doctor.

"I'll try," said Dan as the two sailors backed away slightly. "Woops. Everything is topsy-turvy. I feel like I may get sick again," Dan said.

"Give him support, please, and let's get him into his cabin," Dr. Bigun said. Dan's berth was lowered, and he was carefully eased into it.

"I'm really grateful to you guys," Dan said. "I never thought a berth would feel so good."

"I must leave you now," said Dr. Bigun. "It may take you a week or more to fully recover from the concussion. You will likely be quite weak and tired for several days. That's not uncommon. Your dizziness should subside within a week. You may or may not recover your short-term memory relating to the accident events. Stay in bed when you don't have someone to assist you. Don't get overly adventuresome. Another fall before you are healed could be extremely serious, maybe fatal. I will write a report when I return to my dispensary office and send it to the captain later this afternoon. Good-bye and good luck."

"Thank you, Dr. Oxana Bigun. God bless you for your kindness," Dan said sleepily.

As far as Dan was concerned, the next five days were mostly a sleepy blur. The ship was through the Black Sea, the Bosporus, the Sea of Marmara, the Strait of Dardanelles, and the Aegean Sea before he was stable enough to walk by himself. A day out from Haifa, he was able to enjoy some sun on the fo'c'sle. The sun, the fresh sea breeze, and exercise coupled with good food from the galley did wonders to restore his youthful vitality. At one point, he feared he might not be able to join his friends, the Vashchenkos, who were arriving in Tel Aviv in two days. Now he was filled with hope and optimism.

At 0930 on the morning of June, 28, 1983, the *Rose of Sharon* was met by a tugboat that eased the ship into its assigned berth. By 1030, the hawsers were secured and the gangway was in place. Dan ben Chagai stood looking over the deck rail at the faces looking up from the dock. Who among them was the contact that was to meet him here? As he scanned faces, he was startled to see a large banner held up in the back row that read: "Dan ben Chagai, Welcome to Israel, Welcome to Freedom." He began to weep with joy and give praise to God.

CHAPTER 26
PROFESSOR PHILLIP KING

Dan wasn't sure how much longer he would be required to use his Jewish alias. Certainly his Israeli contact was still using it. He was eager to meet his contact or contacts. It looked like there may be at least two. He had to wait until an Israeli customs agent came on board and cleared him. He had already thanked the captain and told him good-bye, as well as the sailors who had helped him recover.

"Attention on deck," the ship's PA system blared. "Dan ben Chagai, please report to the quarterdeck with ID papers and luggage prepared to clear ship. Best wishes for smooth seas and prevailing tailwinds in your new life, Dan."

The Israeli customs agent glanced at Dan's passport. Dan suspected he knew it was counterfeited. He scarcely looked at his meager supply of clothes in his battered suitcase.

"Welcome to Israel, son," the agent said warmly. "There's a couple waiting to greet you on the dock. I expect you saw their sign already."

"Thank you, sir. Yes, I saw them and am eager to meet them. Good-bye, sir." He strode eagerly off the ship to meet his new friends.

"Welcome, Dan. I'm Benjamin Cohen, and this is my wife, Anna. We have been looking forward to your arrival and are pleased that we can converse in Hebrew. We are volunteers associated with a group that meets new arrivals escaping from the Soviet Union. We have talked to Lida Vashchenko and know a little of your history. Should we continue to call you Dan or do you want to revert to your actual name of Viktor?"

"Dan has served me well for two weeks, but now I prefer Viktor."

"Viktor it is, and you can call me Ben. You will spend today and tonight with us, and tomorrow we will take you to the Tel Aviv airport to meet the Vashchenko family arriving from Moscow."

"How kind of you," Viktor said. "I don't want to be a burden. Everyone has been so good to me. I'm beginning to feel guilty for all the extra work and time that has been expended on my behalf."

"Nonsense, Viktor," said Ben. "We love doing this. We are volunteers, remember. We can opt out of this program anytime we want to. You can repay us many times over by sharing some of your unique experiences in the Soviet Union. The Vashchenko family made headlines all over the world as the result of their five-year sit-in at the American embassy in

Moscow. We would love to get your perspective on that whole slice of history."

"You have erased my fears," said Viktor. "We will have a great time together now that I am no longer conflicted by guilt. Thank you very much."

And Viktor did have a relaxing, enjoyable time with Ben and Anna. He luxuriated in the atmosphere of freedom. Being able to speak freely without fear was therapeutic and exhilarating to his spirit. He awakened on the morning of June 29, 1983, eager to rejoin his adopted family flying in from Moscow. Along with Lida, he rushed to embrace them as they debarked from the Aeroflot plane.

The next three weeks in Israel were a dream come true. They were guests of the Israeli Tourist Bureau, who provided bus tours and professional guides. They visited the traditional holy sites and other tourist attractions the length and breadth of the land. Viktor's knowledge of the Hebrew language and history made him a popular companion when they had free time to shop or just walk about.

On a hot day in July, Viktor was window shopping in the city of Ashdod with several of the Vashchenkos, including Lila and Luba, who were insisting that Viktor help them with conversational English. Viktor was trying to practice conversational Hebrew with some of the shop owners and clerks. As a result, he was speaking English and Hebrew intermittently, with Russian thrown in when talking to his friend Igor and other family members.

There was a small knot of middle-age English-speaking tourists strolling along behind the Vashchenkos. One man was listening intently to the conversations going on within the

Vashchenko group. He turned to his neighbor and said, "Do you hear what's going on in the group just ahead of us?"

"I heard a few sentences in English and then some foreign languages that I didn't understand. But I wasn't really paying that much attention. Why? What's going on?"

"Do you see that young man in the middle of the group a couple paces ahead? He's been engaging in three different conversations in three different languages, English, Hebrew, and Russian. Can you imagine an American teen being able to do that? I want to talk to him and find out where he went to school."

"There's a bus stop ahead. What if they get on the bus and you lose contact?"

"If they board the bus, I will too. That may be my chance to have a conversation with him. You can go on with the others, and I'll catch you at the hotel," said the intrigued tourist.

As they neared the bus stop, the Vashchenko group was discussing whether to go back to the hotel or continue their stroll. When they decided to continue, Viktor spoke up.

"The concussion I suffered three weeks ago still affects my endurance. I think I will take the bus back to the hotel. I'll see you later."

"Here comes the bus," the interested observer said. "This is going to work out better than I expected. Tell the others what I'm up to, and I'll fill you in later."

As Viktor waited for the passengers to debark, he noticed an older gentleman had moved beside him. The man smiled and then spoke, "Pardon me. I hope you don't think me rude, but do you mind if I ask you a few questions when we get aboard?"

"Not at all," Viktor responded. "But we had better get on while seats are available."

"My name is Phillip King, and I am a professor of Semitic languages at Princeton Seminary in the United States. I couldn't help overhearing your conversation, or should I say *conversations*, with your group just ahead of us. I want to congratulate you on the grammatical excellence of your Hebrew, although your Russian accent was unmistakable. May I ask where you studied and who your professor was?"

"My name is Viktor Gorgachuk, although for the past five years I was unofficially adopted by the Vashchenko family and took their last name. I studied at the Holy Mount Monastery. My professor was a monk named Stefan Almschek. I believe he had been professor of Hebrew at one of the Orthodox seminaries. He never discussed it with me. Under Khrushchev's murderous onslaught against Orthodox priests and educators, he fled the seminary and took refuge in the monastery. He taught me Hebrew from 1970 until 1978."

"How old are you now, Viktor?" Professor King asked.

"I was seventeen on the fourth of July."

"You mean to tell me you were studying Hebrew when you were four years old?"

"Yes, sir, and Greek and mathematics and English," replied Viktor. "There wasn't much else for a four-year-old to do. I had great professors, and they made the classes fun."

"Remarkable. The Vashchenko family has been in the news a great deal over the past five years. I have followed their bold efforts to obtain religious freedom with much interest. Your release to emigrate by the Soviet government has brought great rejoicing to many people. However, I don't remember seeing your name among the list of family members. There must be a story behind that."

"There certainly is," Viktor said. "Someday I expect to share it. I escaped aboard a cargo ship thanks to some wonderful, daring people God provided. I arrived in Haifa the day before the Vashchenkos flew to Tel Aviv."

"What are your plans for the future? I understand the group's ultimate goal is to immigrate to the United States," said the professor.

"The Vashchenkos and I have been granted three-month Israeli visas. I will immigrate to America with them and then trust the Lord for guidance as far as the next step is concerned. I've learned to take one step at a time when walking with God," Viktor said.

"I take it from your conversation that you're a dedicated Christian. Can you share a bit of your spiritual journey with me? I'm always fascinated at the way God has directed different people," Professor King said.

"I was baptized into the body of Christ in accordance with Orthodox tradition when I was five years old at the monastery. I made a very personal commitment to serve Jesus Christ when I was twelve. I have been trying to live out that commitment for the past five years."

"From press reports, I understand the Vashchenkos are fervent Pentecostals," said Professor King. "I have two questions relating to the five years you spent with the Chernogorsk Pentecostals as a member of the Vashchenko family. Did they alter your theological perspective? What do you see as the major difference between Orthodox and Pentecostal approaches to Christianity?"

"The answer to your first question is yes. Five years with the Pentecostals did change my theological perspective," Viktor said. "I will elaborate on that a little as I attempt to answer your second question. The Orthodox take a sacramental approach to Christianity. The Pentecostals take an experiential approach. For the Orthodox, you become a member of the body of Christ as a result of baptism, normally as an infant. Pentecostals believe you become a member of the body of Christ as result of confession of sin, repentance, and exercising faith in Jesus as Lord and Savior. Baptism then becomes an act of obedience, symbolizing your participation by faith in the death and resurrection of Jesus."

"Have you rejected the Orthodox view as a result of Pentecostal influence?"

"Not entirely," said Viktor. "Salvation by baptism is not magical. The rite of baptism is accompanied by vows taken by parents and godparents to train the child in the truth of Christian faith and life. Actually, the Orthodox guidelines for living out the Christian life are largely based on scripture and Greek Church fathers. The goal is to bring believers into participation of the divine life of the Trinity through participation in the sacramental ministry of the Church. What I am beginning to understand is that the Orthodox Church tries to retain control of all that God does through the dispensing of sacraments. "

"Perhaps someday we will have an opportunity to discuss these things in more depth," said the professor. "Have you thought of continuing your education in an American university?"

"That's something I would like to investigate when I reach America," Viktor said. "I very much hope to plumb the minds of great theological thinkers, past and present, that have challenged and motivated the Church to be all the Church can and should be. I find the search for truth to be the most exciting and demanding pursuit possible."

"I must get off the next stop. Viktor, when you begin the process leading to a decision about a school, I invite you to contact me," Professor King said. "I have some influence in the Christian academic world, and I may be able to help you obtain a scholarship. Here's my card. It has all the data you need to get in touch. Thank you for permitting me to barge in like I did. I hope our paths cross again in America. God bless you, son, in your pursuit of truth."

When Viktor returned to the hotel, he paused before taking a nap and quietly gave thanks for the meeting with Professor King. He prayed that the Holy Spirit would oversee any results that would come about from this apparent chance encounter. He was convinced it had been providential.

The opportunity to fulfill his dream of going to America materialized sooner than he expected. On July 14, the Vashchenkos were notified that a flight had been arranged to fly them to Washington, DC on July 18. Questions flooded his mind. Where should he settle? What school should he attend? What church should he become part of? Who would be his sponsor in America? Should he let Professor King know of his arrival date? He knew he must seek God earnestly for the Spirit's guidance. After earnest prayer and quiet meditation, Viktor sensed he should contact Professor King. He composed and sent a telegram.

Professor King, depart 18 July. Arrive Washington National 1230 p.m. New address ASAP. Will phone in USA about Univ. possibilities. V. Gorgachuk

CHAPTER 27

SPONSORS GEORGE AND KATHLEEN MCGINNIS

The plane with the Vashchenkos and Viktor departed the Tel Aviv airport at 0900 a.m. The six-hour time differential provided plenty of flight time for an early arrival at 10:00 a.m. They joined the other passengers as they departed the plane and entered the lines to clear customs. Viktor's knowledge of English was in great demand as he helped his Russian-speaking friends through the process. The press was waiting as they emerged from customs. Viktor stayed in the background as reporters interviewed Luba and Lila, the two English-speaking members of the family. An announcement over the PA system got his attention. "Attention all Russian immigrants just arrived from Tel Aviv. Your sponsoring contacts await you at the El Al lounge area near the ticketing counter."

"Did you hear that announcement, Igor? I must go meet my contact." Viktor gathered his luggage and took the escalator to the designated section.

He spotted the group of sponsors, one of whom held a sign with his name inscribed in large letters. He paused some distance away and watched the man holding the sign as he engaged in conversation with another waiting sponsor. He looked to be about sixty years old. His trimly built, six-foot frame was topped by a mop of unruly red hair tinged with gray. He liked the sound of his hearty laughter as he responded to some comment. At last he had a living link to America waiting for him. He hastened to meet him. "I am Viktor Gorgachuk," he said, extending his hand. It was grasped and shaken firmly by the man who greeted him.

"And I am George McGinnis. Welcome to America, young man. Welcome to freedom."

"Thank you, sir. I have prayed for and dreamed of this moment for a long time. I can hardly believe it is happening. If only my parents were still living. They died to help make this happen."

"Someday you must tell me about them," said George. "But now my lovely Irish colleen is impatiently waiting to meet you. Why don't you tell your friends good-bye. Here are a few of my cards that you can give to those you want to call you when everyone is relocated."

Viktor told the Vashchenkos good-bye, pausing for a special moment with his friend Igor as they promised to keep in touch. "Here's my contact's address and phone number. Call me when you get relocated," said Viktor.

George took Viktor in tow and led the way to his parked car. "Jump in, Viktor. We are going to a small town called

Manchester, Maryland. It's seventy miles north of here, so it will take us about an hour and a half. We will have a chance to get better acquainted before I introduce you to Kathleen."

"Sir, how many people live in Manchester?" Viktor asked.

"I would feel more comfortable if you would call me George. But to answer your question, somewhere near four thousand. It's what we call a 'bedroom community.' Most of our employed commute to jobs either in Baltimore or Washington," George said.

"Where do you work?"

"I am one of the favored few that don't have to make this commute," George replied. "I own and operate an independent grocery store in town. I had a high-salaried government job in Washington but got tired of spending three hours a day fighting traffic. When the previous owner of the local market wanted to retire, he put it up for sale. Kathleen and I decided to make an offer, which was accepted. That was ten years ago. We are still in business and beginning to think we may know what we are doing. But that's enough about me. Tell me about your life in Russia, particularly about your parents and how their death opened the door for you to come here."

For the rest of the trip, Viktor shared his story. George, spellbound, listened without interruption, except for an occasional question. When they parked the car in his driveway, he turned to Viktor and said, "Young man, God has had his hand upon your life from birth. I am thankful he has given Kathleen and me a bit part to play in this drama. When we get together with her, we will share the responsibilities we have assumed as your contact sponsor."

"You have a beautiful home," said Viktor. He stood admiring the split-level brick veneer house with the manicured lawn and decorative shrubbery and flowers.

"Thank you. It's larger than we need, but we had it especially designed with a small suite for visiting missionaries and others the Lord leads our way. Right now he has led you our way. Now, come on in, and I will show you what I mean. My wife is at the store and will be home in a couple of hours. Feel free to shower and take a nap if you like. You have been on the go for over twenty hours."

"Thank you, George. A nap sounds like a good idea. My energy level is still recovering from the concussion. But first, if I may, I would like to call Professor King and give him your phone number and postal address," said Viktor.

"By all means. This is your home now, so treat it like yours," George said as he showed Viktor his new quarters. "There's a wall phone in the lounge next to your bedroom."

Viktor called Professor King and left a message on his answering machine. After showering, he knelt beside his bed and began to talk to his Lord. "Jesus, I have done nothing to deserve all the blessings you have showered upon me. It is the result of your grace. I feel so unworthy of all the people who have invested themselves in helping me. Grant that I will never take people or their gifts for granted. Guard my heart, Lord Jesus, so that I remain humble and ever grateful for everything you provide. Protect and guide my fellow immigrants as they establish their new lives in this great land. I love you, my Lord, and again pledge my life to serve you. Amen." He stretched out on the bed, clad in his shorts. The murmur from the air-conditioner and the soft, cool breeze it produced soon lulled him into a deep sleep.

He awoke refreshed and alert with renewed energy. He glanced at the bedside clock. It was six in the evening. He had slept nearly four hours. He arose and put on his last clean sport shirt and pair of cotton slacks. He heard activity downstairs so headed in that direction. George met him at the foot of the stairs.

"Viktor, do come in the family room and meet Kathleen, who has been impatiently awaiting you. She actually tried to convince me I should awaken you lest you not be able to sleep later tonight. She has forgotten what it was like when our son was seventeen. He could sleep around the clock if we let him.

"Kathleen, I didn't have to wake him up. Here he is. Viktor, meet Kathleen, the love of my life for thirty-six years."

"It's a privilege to meet you and be in your home, Mrs. McGinnis," Viktor said. "Pardon me if I stare, but you remind me very much of my mother. She had lovely jet-black hair like yours. She was so beautiful, like you, and I miss ..." Viktor's voice broke as he sought to gain control of his emotions. "I'm so sorry. I thought I had moved beyond mourning the loss of my mother. I know she is with the Lord, and that is far better for her. Your remarkable resemblance to her must have triggered emotions I thought time had healed. The immensity of my loss suddenly overwhelmed me when I saw you. I do apologize."

"My dear boy, never apologize for mourning the death of your wonderful mother. I feel greatly honored to have reminded you of her. You have released emotion that was bottled up. That is healthy, and now further healing can continue. I am not a psychiatrist or psychologist. That is just 'Dr. Mom' giving her opinion. And please call me Kathleen. Mrs. McGinnis sounds much too formal. Besides, it reminds me of my advancing years. I don't want George to think he's married to an old woman.

"To celebrate your arrival, George is going to take us out to dinner this evening. You get to choose the restaurant, which is not difficult since we only have three worth considering. There is a Chinese restaurant, an Italian/American restaurant, and a Mexican restaurant. Which will it be?"

"Since this is my first day in America, I choose the Italian/American. After all, America was named after an Italian, so what could be more fitting?" Viktor said.

"Bravo. An excellent choice for the reasons you mention and one other incidental reason: the food is superb," George said. "So let's go celebrate the start of this new chapter in Viktor's life."

They found a corner booth in the rear of the dining area that provided privacy and quiet. After they were seated and placed their orders, George spoke.

"Viktor, Kathleen and I are so pleased that we can help launch you into your American experience. We have prayed much about our involvement and believe that God has led us to take this step. Let us explain what our relationship will be. We have pledged to provide for your livelihood for one year. This includes food, clothing, and shelter. We will provide counsel and assistance in your decisions regarding further education and will help you get started in the process that leads to citizenship. We will be available to answer questions about any number of things that may arise. We won't have all the answers, but we can direct you to someone that should be able to help. That's pretty much it. Do you have any questions?"

"I hardly know what to say. How can I possibly express how thankful I am to you and to God? It goes without saying that I must find employment until I am enrolled in a school so that I contribute to my living expenses. I could not be happy doing otherwise," Viktor said.

"George and I were sure you would want to do that. Until you choose a university and are accepted, we can certainly use your help in our supermarket. Regular employees will be taking summer vacations, and you can replace them temporarily. Does that sound like something you would like to do?" Kathleen asked.

"That excites me. I have read about your American supermarkets. Just to be around that much food in one place at one time will be a wonderful new experience," Viktor said.

"Well, those details are taken care of. There will be no business while we enjoy our dinner together. I think it is coming now," George said.

After arriving home shortly after eight o'clock, the phone rang. "Hello, this is Kathleen. Yes, yes. He is right here, Professor. Just hold a moment. It's a Professor King. He wants to speak to you, Viktor."

"Hello, Professor King."

"Hello, Viktor. Thanks for keeping me informed of your whereabouts. I did not forget my promise I made you in Israel concerning a university and scholarship possibilities. I think I have struck oil on my first attempt. I have talked to friends at Princeton University and explained your unique situation. The scholarship committee is very interested in meeting you. I am going to send some forms requesting information the committee requires. When completed, send to me, and I will have them delivered. With your permission, I will peruse them first in case I need to recommend a little fine tuning. Any questions so far?" the professor asked.

"No, sir. I am stunned that you have taken this time on my behalf. I told you I thought our meeting in Israel was providential. I am more convinced than ever that is true," Viktor said.

"I agree. Incidentally, I have checked Manchester, Maryland, on the map. It looks close to two hundred miles from Princeton. I may drive there someday and see you and meet your host family."

"Please do. My hosts are wonderful people, and I am greatly blessed. I thank you again with all my heart. Good-bye, sir."

Viktor shared the good news with George and Kathleen. They were both ecstatic. "Viktor, I'm sure you don't know this, but Princeton University is one of the best, if not the best, private university in the United States. It will be wonderful if you can get a scholarship to that institution. It will stretch you and make you think outside the cultural box in which you were reared," said Kathleen.

"Some Christians will criticize you for enrolling at Princeton. They point to well-known Princeton professors who oppose Christianity or even belief in God. And that is true. But there are also committed Christian professors there who live out their faith in a secular environment with grace and perseverance.

"Some point out that Christian youth have gone into universities like Princeton and have had their faith undermined. Cultural faith is undermined and should be. Living faith connected to the risen Christ will be strengthened because opposition will drive one to prayer and to investigate and think more deeply about critical issues. That produces the atmosphere in which the Holy Spirit illuminates truth to the honest seeker," George affirmed.

"I am not afraid of atheistic philosophy under any guise," Viktor said. "I grew up in a country in which the government was obsessed with eliminating belief in God. Every teacher in grammar school and every professor in a university had to profess belief in atheism. Christians were demeaned, ridiculed, imprisoned, many killed and tortured, but their faith triumphed through it all. I seek truth wherever it may lead, but one foundational truth I have already discovered: God is."

"We have no fear of you losing your faith, but it will be tried," said Kathleen. "Now, let me introduce another subject. While George is at the store tomorrow, I am going to take you on a shopping tour to replenish your wardrobe. There's a shopping mall on the north side of Baltimore that has some men's shops plus several big box stores that are having summer sales. We will go explore what young men are wearing these days."

Soon after, Professor Phillip King did drive to Manchester to see Viktor and to meet George and Kathleen McGinnis. The four of them sat down and discussed the process of an international student gaining admittance to Princeton's undergraduate program. They decided to focus on getting Viktor approved for the 1984–85 academic year rather than 1983–84. Dr. King went over the rigorous admission requirements. The intervening year would enable Viktor to prepare for the required tests.

"You can obtain tests similar to the ones you must take. The questions and problems change each year, but the subjects are the same," the professor explained. "With your disciplined study habits and near photographic memory, I am confident the tests will be no problem for you, Viktor. But I must say the competition is stiff, so be well prepared. In addition to the academic tests, there is an interview by a member of the Alumni School Committee. I am a member of that committee and have already submitted a report recommending acceptance with full scholarship. Viktor's status as a member of a persecuted minority will also be a factor. While acceptance is never automatic, I am confident that Viktor is the kind of student Princeton would like to have."

"There is one other important issue we need to discuss while you are with us, Phillip," George said. "As Viktor's sponsor, I must get him legally registered as a refugee. Because of his age and no relatives, he must file form I-360, which is a special form for immigrants in his juvenile status. After that is approved, there is another form to register for permanent residence in the US. Some input from you can be helpful when we submit that application."

"I'll help wherever and whenever I can in the process for Viktor to obtain his green card. I know he wants to apply for US citizenship as soon as he is eligible," said the professor.

"This has been most helpful, Phillip," George said. "Viktor will be able to establish a routine here that will be productive academically. He can work fifteen to twenty hours a week in the market and have plenty of time to devote to study and research. He must not neglect his social development with other youth his age. We have a fine group of young collegians in our church that will welcome him."

Viktor pursued the regimen George suggested with enthusiasm. He read voraciously, studied difficult subjects with determined discipline, and reveled in the atmosphere of freedom that he had never previously known. He made friends quickly and enjoyed recreational time with a small group of collegians and other young adults from Grace Bible Church.

229

His vibrant Christian life was exercised with regular prayer walks and fed by daily intake of scripture from the original languages.

When it was time to take the entrance exams, he did so confidently, knowing that he had prepared diligently. He had no fear of failure because he was sure God was in control. If not Princeton, then God had something better for him somewhere else. Professor King first thought Viktor was approaching the exams cavalierly. He came to realize his positive attitude was the result of wholehearted surrender to Jesus Christ. He trusted Jesus completely to order his life as he saw fit. He was determined to accept what came with thanksgiving.

As it turned out, God must have wanted Viktor in Princeton. He passed all entrance tests with record or near-record scores. His notification of acceptance with full scholarship produced several congratulatory dinners. The last weekend of August, George and Kathleen drove him to Princeton and stayed through parents' orientation. They helped him move into his dorm room, met his roommate, had a quiet moment of prayer together, gave him a bear hug, and departed. Later, they shed a few tears. He had become like a son to them.

Viktor survived frosh week and the snoring of his roomie. The first soon passed, and he became accustomed to the latter. The word quickly circulated through the campus that he was a Russian immigrant. This endeared him to students taking Russian as a foreign language. When it also became known he was a Hebrew scholar, this widened his circle of friends. He could have made a small fortune as a tutor if he had chosen.

When it was time to declare his major, Viktor decided to call Professor King. "Hello, sir. This is Viktor. Do you have a minute?"

"Just barely. What's up?"

"I need to declare a major. I have one in mind but want to get your ideas," Viktor said.

"Let's review. Tell me again the ministry God has laid on your heart."

"I feel called to exercise ministry gifts of preaching and teaching as a pastor," Viktor replied.

"It won't take me a minute to tell you my idea for a major. I recommend oral communication and rhetoric. Princeton has a great department of spoken communication that will help you become an able proclaimer of God's truth. The gospel is exciting, and we have too many boring preachers. I'm not talking about being bombastic. I'm talking about developing a speaking style that enhances the truth you proclaim. It gives the Holy Spirit a better tool with which to get his job done," Professor King explained. "Does this jibe with your idea?"

"Thank you. You have absolutely confirmed what I have been thinking. Good-bye, sir."

CHAPTER 28
THE GRADUATION PRESENT

Viktor's years at Princeton provided an atmosphere in which to explore concepts he had never considered before. He was surprised to discover that American freedom allowed the expression of ideas that would nullify freedom if widely adopted. He wondered about students who had no solid foundation of revealed scriptural truth reinforced by a personal relationship with him who is truth personified. How could they escape falling victim to philosophies that appealed to their physical appetites and demanded immediate gratification? His appreciation of his Christian faith was immensely strengthened as he compared it to the competition. He graduated summa cum laude, which brought immense satisfaction to George, Kathleen, and Phillip, his American friends who had entwined their lives with his.

Following graduation in 1988, these three close friends and champions of Viktor got together and planned a graduation present. Gorbachev had introduced *perestroika* (restructuring) and *glasnost* (openness) to the USSR. Hope of radical change was beginning to ferment beyond what had been anticipated or expected by even the most liberal leaders in the Communist party. Even negotiations were developing for opening the first McDonald's in the USSR. Professor Phillip King saw this as a good time for Viktor to visit the Soviet empire after an absence of five years.

"I propose the three of us offer Viktor a trip back to his homeland as our graduation present," said Phillip. "What do you think?"

"Why don't we go with him?" Kathleen asked. "I would love to see the places where he lived, meet some of his friends who helped him escape, and visit where his parents lost their lives. What better tour guide than Viktor himself?"

"Why didn't I think of that?" Phillip and George exclaimed in unison.

"Great idea," George continued. "We had better check with Viktor before we pursue it further, but I think he will be delighted."

Viktor was thrilled beyond words and helped plan the itinerary. They decided to fly from JFK to Vladivostok to begin their two-week tour. This was the area where Vasil and Natasha Gorgachuk had lost their lives. Viktor wanted very much to trace his parents' final days and hours. They would then fly to Abakan, near Chernogorsk, the mining city where Viktor had last seen his parents and spent the next five years after their death. Then to the monastery where he was reared and educated by the monks. Next to Leningrad where he was born and lived until four. From there to Moscow for a flight to Odessa and then to Tel Aviv and back to JFK.

The expectation of seeing once again people who were dear to him and had contributed so much to his life produced a euphoric spirit in Viktor. He confessed to his friends, "If the reality of this trip brings me more joy and excitement than the anticipation, then I don't know if I can contain it."

In the intervening month before the start of their trip, Viktor was busy notifying friends in all the places they planned to visit, with the exception of Leningrad, his home from infancy to four.

The foursome departed JFK the first of July and arrived in Vladivostok the afternoon of the next day. They checked into their hotel and then made arrangements for a taxi to meet them the next morning. The taxi driver knew immediately the location of the wrecked vehicle that marked where three bodies had been found.

"I knew Alexander, the driver," said the taxi owner. "He was a KGB agent who masqueraded as a taxi driver sometimes when he was working a case. He was a bad one."

The taxi arrived at 0900 as scheduled. He explained where they were going. "There used to be a KGB Interrogation Station near where the wreck occurred. It is no longer in operation. There are much fewer arrests now under Gorbachev. The road dead-ends at the locked gate that allowed entry to the facility, so it never has much traffic. It gets more recreational bicycle traffic than anything else, especially on weekends with picnickers."

In half an hour, they arrived at the scene of the accident. They stood on the road shoulder and looked at the twisted, rusted, ten-year-old remains of the vehicle carcass half hidden by weeds. Viktor carefully made his way down the embankment to the wreck. He stood silently with head bowed, picturing his parents still inside the crushed, inverted metal. After a few moments of silent prayer, he called to his friends, "How anyone survived this tangled scrap heap is a miracle. According to Josef, my parents were relatively unscathed. Only Alexander, the driver, was seriously injured."

The taxi driver called down to Viktor, "Look at the left rear door window opening. See how the opening has been enlarged. The police theorized that was done by the uninjured man in order to extricate the injured driver. Later all three were found back inside the vehicle with multiple bullet wounds in each body. How they got there and who did it is still a mystery, but many believe it was by the KGB partner of Alexander."

"I thank you for sharing this moment with me," Viktor said to his friends. "After seeing this, I am all the more impressed by what God did through my parents in winning Alexander to Christ. It's like the conversion of Saul of Tarsus all over again."

"Viktor, I feel like this is hallowed ground," Professor King said. "I would like to offer a prayer of thanks to God for your parents and all they did to preserve your life so that we could share it with you today."

Viktor smiled and said, "I would like that very much."

Having fulfilled his dream of seeing the locale where his parents were killed, he was now ready to conduct his friends to locations connected with his own life. The next twelve days were a virtual kaleidoscope of people and places. From Vladivostok to Chernogorsk for a joyous potluck dinner celebration with the Pentecostals. Viktor laughed and sometimes wept as they reminisced together.

Next, by air and rail they made the lengthy trip to the Holy Mount Monastery. Several of the monks spoke English, much to the delight of Phillip, Kathleen, and George. The three Americans were regaled with stories of Viktor's eight years among them. Peals of laughter erupted frequently. Even the monks had difficulty restraining themselves. With reluctance, Viktor and his American friends tore themselves away so as not to miss their train. Viktor's Uncle Slava remembered July fourth was his nephew's birthday. All heartily congratulated him. Everyone agreed this visit alone was worth the price of the trip. Even Viktor learned things about himself that he didn't know or had forgotten.

From the monastery, they went by rail to Novosibirsk and flew on to Moscow and then to Leningrad where Viktor lived with his parents before he went to the monastery. The beauty and grandeur of this "Venice of the North," founded by Peter the Great, had been badly scarred by the German army in World War Two. Now, forty four years later, the city glittered magnificently once again. Viktor was surprised that he still remembered much about the area where he lived when he was four years old.

After two days in Leningrad, they returned to Moscow. A partial day sufficed for a city that had no connections with Viktor. That afternoon, they caught a nonstop flight to Odessa. They registered at the hotel where Viktor previously stayed. Later, Juda ben Israel and Dr. Oxana Bigun were honored guests at a dinner party in Odessa's premier kosher restaurant. When asked if there were any side effects from his severe concussion, Viktor assured the doctor that her diagnosis and treatment had resulted in his complete recovery.

The *Rose of Sharon* was docking the next day. Viktor was able to go aboard and show his friends the little cabin assigned him and where he had suffered the concussion. Captain Bernstein greeted him and friends with obvious delight and then excused himself because of responsibilities connected with unloading cargo. On departing the ship, they were presented with a beautiful assortment of choice Israeli fruit, courtesy of Captain Bernstein.

The remaining three days were spent in Israel. It was decided that each person could choose one destination. Viktor hosted a dinner for Benjamin and Anna Cohen in Haifa and thanked them again for their gracious hospitality on his first arrival to Israel. Professor King insisted they visit Ashdod where he had first seen Viktor and heard his multi-language conversations that grabbed his attention.

"It was right here in this row of shops where I first saw and heard him," said the professor. "Just ahead is the bus stop where we boarded the bus together."

"And you have paid for that bus ride ever since," Viktor said, laughing.

George chose a trip to Masada, having already researched much of its history. Kathleen wanted a shopping trip in Jerusalem, augmented by a visit to the Wailing Wall. They returned to JFK, satiated with traveling and grateful to be home. Nevertheless, they had treasured memories that would warm each of their hearts for a lifetime. Viktor acknowledged the reality greatly exceeded the anticipation. He would be forever indebted to Phillip, George, and Kathleen ... and to the Lord whom they served.

CHAPTER 29
THE SEMINARIAN

When Viktor returned, he realized he had now fulfilled the prerequisites to apply for US citizenship. He decided to wait until he was enrolled in seminary somewhere before initiating the application. He narrowed his choice of seminaries to four: Princeton Seminary, Duke Divinity School, Harvard Divinity School, and Fuller Theological Seminary. When he showed his list to his mentor, Professor King discouraged him from selecting Princeton.

"Princeton is an outstanding seminary, one of the best. As much as I would like you close by, I think it best if you establish your own identity apart from me. You are going to excel wherever you go. Do your research, bare your soul to the Lord, and listen for his still, small voice," counseled the professor.

George and Kathleen questioned if he would thrive at Harvard or Duke. "These schools are predominantly liberal in their theology, and many professors will propose a theological position contrary to both the Orthodox or Pentecostal convictions. Does it seem wise to get training in either?"

"I can understand your concern and have considered it. But be assured, my faith is not in its formative stage. It is firmly rooted in Jesus Christ. I have encountered him. He has communicated his love to me. I trust him with my past, present, and future. I am not fearful about engaging in honest dialogue about theological truth. Truth, whatever its source, has nothing to fear. How can I engage other positions if I don't know what they are? I am dedicated to following truth wherever it may lead," Viktor declared.

"But what is the criterion by which you ascertain truth?" Kathleen asked gently.

"For me, it will always be holy scripture prayerfully and carefully examined and diligently exegeted in the original languages."

"But many Christian leaders, even scholars, don't have your understanding of Greek and Hebrew. Are they disqualified from knowing truth?" George asked.

"Not at all. There are good translations of the Bible as well as good texts explaining nuances of the original languages. But they are disqualified from basing a doctrine on their ignorance of scripture or on a religious experience that is not thoroughly grounded in the broad context of scripture. Heresies are founded on texts taken out of context or on religious experiences supported by a text taken out of context," Viktor concluded.

"You have calmed my fears. I believe you can 'contend for the faith that God has once for all delivered to the saints' in any setting," Kathleen said.

"Amen and amen," George murmured.

Viktor struggled with the decision concerning a seminary as long as he dared without a waiver on the date required. He was tempted to choose Harvard or Duke so he could stay on the East Coast but knew that was a selfish and invalid basis. He obeyed the gentle nudge of the Spirit and chose Fuller. He shared his decision with Dr. King.

"Any of these schools would have been a good choice," Professor King said. "I congratulate you on being guided by the Holy Spirit and choosing a school that is on the cutting edge of making Christ and Christianity relevant to the global community. I'll be interested in your assessment after the first quarter is concluded."

After returning from Europe, Viktor had a month to complete the admissions application process. In addition to his signed application, he had to submit his religious autobiography, an official transcript of college work, and three reference forms, one from a pastor or church leader. Within two weeks, he had his package all prepared to submit with his non-refundable application fee. His acceptance followed soon after, and he scheduled a meeting with his academic advisor. With her targeted questions, the advisor helped Viktor clarify his long-range goals and the classes that would help attain them. He was eager to get started.

To Viktor's surprise, various theological positions were permitted to have a hearing in classes. Fuller Seminary was a strong citadel of evangelical theology but did not fear to have its students wrestle with opposing viewpoints. Convinced of the truth and strength of its position, students were allowed to discover the truth and power of scripture for themselves. Vigorous dialogue was not only permitted but encouraged. Viktor's own presuppositions were challenged, and he was driven to rigorous and careful investigation of scripture and history.

In July, 1989 Viktor's dream of becoming an American citizen was fulfilled. He had requested that he be part of a group being sworn in at Washington, DC on July 4. Friends in the area from church and university, plus his inner circle of George, Kathleen, and Professor King, were there to share in the moving ceremony. Afterward there was another celebration of his twenty-third birthday. On Monday morning, he flew back to rejoin his Seminary classmates in the summer session he was enrolled in.

His passion for the pursuit of truth had led him to request permission to attend summer quarter sessions without interruption. His request initially was denied because it was against Fuller's policy. He requested he be granted a waiver to the seminary position. After careful consideration, they recognized the uniqueness of this immigrant student and granted his request. As a result, he completed the required hours for his master of divinity degree at the end of the fall session in 1990. He pursued a master of theology degree during the winter, spring, and summer quarters of 1991. He graduated with high honors in August 1991 and was awarded twin degrees of MDiv and ThM.

Although three thousand miles distant, Viktor had retained close emotional contact with his trilogy of close friends via telephone and correspondence. They had flown out to be with him at his graduation in Pasadena and applauded the academic honors and twin degrees he had earned. They spent three days together, just hanging out and talking, talking, talking. Could Gorbachev contain the rising unrest in USSR? Where should Viktor invest his gifts and time? Should he continue academic pursuits and attain a PhD? Was there a romantic "other" that he is interested in? Nothing was solved, nothing resolved, but after three days, Viktor was free of stress and ready to tackle a new challenge. Would that he knew what it was.

After his friends returned home, he knew he must spend time with his closest Friend. He determined to fast and pray until he had insight as to where God desired him to be and what he should do. It wasn't that he lacked opportunities. Even without a PhD, he could have taught biblical languages in his choice of multiple institutions. There were mega Pentecostal churches that desired to interview him for staff positions. He had vowed to himself, to his friends, and to God that he would make no decision without direction from the Holy Spirit. The only direction he received was simply to wait.

At the same time that Viktor was completing his years of intensive study, the USSR was unraveling. In December 1991, Gorbachev would "throw in the towel." The mighty Soviet Union, under the weight of its own corruption and inept, god-less leadership, had collapsed. In a cataclysmic moment, na-tions were unchained from political, economic, and spiritual bondage. New democracies were birthed overnight. The im-prisoning wall of tyranny was struck down. Viktor watched the international drama with intense interest. Surely God had something he could and should do at this critical time in the history of his own people. But what and where?

New emigrant policies initiated by Gorbachev when he came to power had made it possible for large numbers of Pentecostals in Russia and Ukraine to request and be grant-ed emigrant status. Legislation passed by the United States Congress permitted members of persecuted religions to settle in America beyond the normal quota assigned. This resulted in an influx of Pentecostals from Russia and Ukraine settling in California.

As Viktor continued waiting for direction from the Lord, he sensed the Holy Spirit nudging him to begin a ministry to the Slavic immigrants in Sacramento. He had sensed such nudges before and recognized the gentle voice of the Shepherd. He went to Sacramento first to conduct a strategic reconnaissance. He discovered that most of the new arrivals had settled in one of the outlying suburbs with less expensive housing. He visited several immigrant churches and found that they ministered only in the Russian language. He talked to pastors about job skills among the immigrants and learned there were skilled craftsmen and skilled women in various professions, including nurses and physicians, carpenters, masons, mechanics, tile layers, truck drivers, and more.

He returned home and used his reconnaissance data to plan his strategy. It was simple: *(1) plant myself in the heart of the Slavic community; (2) become a servant to the immigrants, assisting them with my language gifts and experience in America; (3) be an ombudsman and spokesman when requested; (4) demonstrate respect and honor to leaders in the community; (5) undergird all activity with prayer; (6) be ready for the next step when God nudges.* He gave the required thirty-day notice to terminate his current rental agreement effective the end of November.

CHAPTER 30
A SERVANT TO
IMMIGRANTS

On December 1, 1991, he moved into a furnished studio apartment as a base for his activities. He discovered that many of the new arrivals had come to Sacramento because of a Russian language religious program beamed to the USSR from Sacramento. He visited the preacher who was the speaker and established a friendly relationship with him. He mentioned he was willing to assist immigrants who needed the help of a translator getting settled in their new land. The preacher said he would share this with his local radio audience.

Viktor visited the pastors and offered to use his language skills and experience in America to help the newcomers. His name and phone number were placed in church bulletins. A few calls began to come in. Viktor met them and often was able to help resolve the problems with a simple phone call. He helped some find jobs. Word spread throughout the community. Soon he was flooded with more calls than he could handle. He sensed the Spirit nudging him to take the next step.

He talked to the pastors and other leaders in the immigrant community and explained the situation. He needed to rent a small office where a secretary would handle and classify incoming calls for help. To cover expenses, there would be no set fee, but there would be an opportunity for volunteer contributions. Viktor wrote and made available an explanatory statement. To his surprise, donations flooded in from those who had been helped and from those who wanted help available if needed. Viktor was reassured the nudge had been from God.

He found a small office that was suitable for his needs with space for a secretary, telephone, and computer. He hired an experienced Russian-speaking secretary who grasped the essentials of her work quickly. She listened to call-ins and categorized them as trite, important, urgent, immediate/emergency or one, two, three, four. Most calls were categories one and two. Occasionally category three calls were fielded. Only once had Viktor responded to a category four. A frantic mother had called in because her toddler had ingested poison. He calmed her, got the name of the poison, home address, and then dialed 911. He called her back, told her medical help was on the way. He told her to have the child drink as much water as she could. Paramedics arrived with an antidote in fifteen minutes and took over. The three-year-old suffered no ill effects, and Viktor's stock rose.

Thousands more Slavic immigrants had arrived in the Sacramento area, many of them Pentecostals. Young couples from among the earlier arrivals were dissatisfied with retaining Russian-language church services. Thousands of school children had learned to speak English and were lobbying parents for services in English. Some couples had integrated with English-speaking Evangelical and Pentecostal churches in the wider community. Others were considering doing so. Others withdrew from organized churches altogether and met in home groups with friends. Many of these families shared their frustrations with Viktor.

As the years passed, Viktor wondered if God had forgotten him. What about the call to preach the gospel he had so clearly heard years previously? What about the years of study and preparation? What about the time and money investments his Russian and American friends had made on his behalf? He thought of his parents and the high hopes and expectations they had for him. Surely they would be disappointed that he had accomplished so little.

His frustration and deep discouragement drew him to his knees. He vowed to take no phone calls or answer any requests for assistance until he heard from heaven. He determined to seek God with all his heart and wait upon him until the Holy Spirit responded to his questions: "Why have you placed me here? Did I misunderstand your call?" After hours of pouring out his frustration, his discouragement, and confessing his doubt and fear, he was drained physically and emotionally. He prostrated himself quietly before the Lord and waited. At two in the morning on July 4, 2000, the Lord clearly spoke to him, Spirit to spirit. He would never forget the message.

"My son, you must learn to be a servant before you can be a shepherd. All whom I want to bless must spend time in disciplined preparation. Saul of Tarsus required fourteen years of preparation, three alone in the desert, before he was ready to be Paul, the apostle. You did not misunderstand your call. Your days of servant training are almost over. Continue steadfast in my love and be assured I will never leave you."

Expressions of praise spontaneously burst forth from Viktor, interspersed with tears of shame and repentance for his lack of trust. God had not forgotten him. He was right where God wanted him at this point in his life. Joy indescribable sprang up from the depth of his being. He was mature and realistic enough to know there would be times of frustration and discouragement in the future. But never again would he doubt the Lord's love or presence or call.

Later that morning, he received birthday greetings from George and Kathleen McGinnis. He had actually forgotten it was his birthday until they called. They laughed and cried as he shared with them the struggle he had been going through. A short time later, his mentor and friend, Professor King, called and congratulated him. Viktor shared with him his story of agony leading to ecstasy.

"Viktor, I extend further congratulations for your endurance in a situation where most young men of your brilliance and training would have thrown in the towel a long time ago. I am more convinced than ever that God is going to bless your ministry beyond your expectations. No matter what success or accolades you eventually receive, I am convinced before heaven's tribunal your highest commendation will be for your servant years among the immigrants. I am tremendously proud of you, my boy," Professor King concluded.

Buoyed by his fresh encounter with God and the encouragement of his friends, Viktor returned to his ministry of "helps" with unabated enthusiasm and Joy. Soon after, he received the signal he had been waiting for. After ten years of service to the flood of Russian-speaking Slavic immigrants, the Holy Spirit nudged him to organize an English-speaking Slavic church.

He chose six couples who pledged to meet regularly with him for a year as he taught them biblical principles on such things as Christian worship, evangelism, church organization, doctrine, spiritual gifts, prayer, and other issues that arose. They caught Viktor's vision and passion and were eager to become involved under his leadership. After a year, he knew it was time to speak to the Russian-speaking pastors about establishing an English-speaking Slavic church in the area. He was sure he would meet some heated opposition, and he was right.

Viktor prepared a carefully reasoned presentation for the six leading pastors who had come together to discuss the issue. First, the pastors explained why they thought it necessary to preserve their religious tradition in their native language. They feared American culture would pollute their own. They disapproved of the worship styles of American Pentecostal and Evangelical churches. Unspoken, but factual, none wanted to relinquish the power that retaining the Russian language afforded.

"I certainly agree with you that there are aspects of American culture that are corrupt," Viktor acknowledged. "Freedom is dangerous in that it gives people opportunities to make bad choices. Rather than withdraw from the culture, teach your children how to make good choices that will elevate the whole culture. Jeremiah told the Jewish exiles in Babylon, *'Also, seek the peace and prosperity of the city to which I have carried you into exile. Pray to the Lord for it, because if it prospers you too will prosper.'*

"Another reality is this: you are going to lose many of your young people regardless of what I or anyone else does. Would it not be better to have them in an English-speaking church that understands our culture and traditions? Our Slavic traditions are not all good, you know. Some are carry-overs from decades of communist teaching and indoctrination and result from growing up in a totalitarian regime. I can help our youth combine the best of both cultures because I have lived years in each."

The pastors recognized that Viktor spoke to a reality they could no longer ignore. Reluctantly, they gave their approval with one abstention. He thanked them for their trust and asked they undergird him with their prayers. One pastor responded.

"We thank you, Brother Viktor, for your years of service to our Slavic community. You have been a blessing to us all. How will we possibly replace you in this helping ministry?"

"Elina, our secretary, will remain in the office," Viktor responded. "She is now able to converse in English reasonably well. I knew this day was coming, so I have trained her to do what she has seen me do. She can handle most situations that arise and will still be able to call me if need be."

The meeting ended with the pastors gathering around Viktor and praying for God's blessing upon him and his new ministry. Viktor was tremendously encouraged by the amicable outcome. He was now free to do what he knew God had called him to do. He already had a name in mind for the new church taken from Acts 2:1, which describes the first Christian congregation celebrating the feast of Pentecost. The church would simply be called Christians Together.

CHAPTER 31
"CHRISTIANS TOGETHER" IS LAUNCHED

V iktor enlisted his trained six couples to join him in four consecutive Sundays of fasting and praying for their new venture. God answered prayer in unexpected ways. They were able to rent a school auditorium for Sunday services for a nominal fee. A radio station announced the opening of "Brother Viktor's" English-speaking Slavic church as a community service. Most effective was the word-of-mouth gossip that spread the news that the popular and well-known "Brother Viktor" was establishing an English-speaking Slavic church. The opening service on a hot Sunday in May 2004 drew more than two hundred people. The church grew faster than anyone expected, including Viktor. By mid-2005, two Sunday services were necessary to accommodate the congregation. With a congregation approaching a thousand, the search committee began looking for larger accommodations.

Ivan Vostruk and Josef Kovarde, two of the men Viktor had discipled for a year, resigned from their secular jobs and were installed as associate pastors. Ivan's wife, Irina, became the church secretary. Josef's wife, Vera, became executive secretary to the pastor.

Viktor kept his friends back east abreast of what God was doing. They were pleased but not surprised and offered warm congratulations. Professor King offered sage counsel along with his congratulations.

"Viktor, allow me to make a suggestion. I believe God is going to continue to bless your ministry. After a few more years, you will not be able to rent a facility large enough to meet your needs. Now is the time to buy land upon which to eventually build. Don't wait until you are forced to buy or stagnate. Also, I suggest you obtain an architect experienced in church design and get a visible plan that your people can rally around."

"Thank you, Phillip. God blessed me immeasurably when he brought you into my life. I'll take your suggestions as counsel from the Lord."

Soon after he announced, "Brothers and sisters, if we continue our present growth rate, in a few years we will not be able to rent a facility large enough to meet our needs. What do you think we should do? Somebody suggested we rent satellite facilities for television viewing of our services. What do you think of that?"

"No way," "Too impersonal," "We can watch TV at home," voices rang forth from the crowd.

"What should we do?"

"Let's find land right away and build, Brother Viktor," a strong but obviously feminine voice called out.

The congregation looked to see who had spoken. A very attractive young woman with shoulder-length, blonde hair and classic Slavic features was standing, flanked by two young-sters. Viktor had not seen her before, but he was confident the Holy Spirit was nudging him to engage her in dialogue.

"Why do you say that, my sister?" Viktor asked.

"Because Christians Together needs a home that is ours and is associated with who we are and what we do. I want this to be the spiritual home for me and my children for many years to come. We need to cease wandering about looking for temporary rentals until we outgrow them. Let's rise up in faith, purchase property, and build our sanctuary, trusting God to direct us step by step. I pledge myself to pray toward that end, and I challenge this congregation to join together in prayer for divine direction."

The congregation sat for a moment as if stunned and then arose spontaneously and began clapping joyously and enthusi-astically. Shouts of "Amen" and "Praise God" came from scat-tered sections of the auditorium. Viktor waited a few moments for quiet to return before speaking.

"Brothers and sisters, I sense in my spirit that God has spoken to us through our sister. She has confirmed the godly counsel given by my friend, Professor Phillip King. Did not God say that in the last days his Spirit would be outpoured on women as well as men? We have heard. I believe we must now act. Our sister has challenged us to join together and pray for divine direction. I believe that is God's challenge to us this day, so I am going to curtail my usual thirty-minute sermon. But I believe the Lord wants me to prepare our hearts for prayer with three thoughts that will take about three minutes to present.

"First we must focus our prayer on our glorious Lord Jesus Christ and not on our desires. Pray to see Jesus Christ high and exalted in his omnipotence, seated on his throne. We must understand who it is we serve or we will grow weary in the battle. Don't focus on our needs but on the supplier of our needs.

"Second, pray that the Holy Spirit will help us to truly say, 'Not my will, but yours, Lord,' and mean it with all our hearts. There must be death to self-will before God's will can be manifested in resurrection power. I truly believe that it is God's will we purchase property and build. But what if God should clearly indicate that is not his plan for us? Are we willing to trust him and lay aside our plans and wait for his better plan to be revealed?

"Third, pray for holy boldness to do whatever the Lord directs. The Spirit called to my attention the Old Testament character, Gideon. Thirty-two thousand Israelites answered his call to fight the Midianites. God said, 'That's too many. Release all who are fearful. Twenty-two thousand went home.' God said, 'Still too many. Separate those who are eager to engage the enemy from those who are hoping the enemy won't attack.' Gideon lost another 9,700 soldiers.

"Think of it. Less than 1 percent of his troops remained. If our congregation of one thousand was so reduced, there would be ten us. Would I be one of the ten? Would you?

"Friends, Jesus Christ is not impressed by large numbers. Don't pray for more people just for the sake of a crowd. Pray for a burning love for our majestic Lord, for a will committed to do his will, and for a fearless passion to obey his commands.

The strongholds of hell will crumble if we attack them with this loving, bold assault. Cry out to God, Church. Seek him with all your heart as we pray."

An awesome sense of God's presence settled over the auditorium. People began standing, first in the front rows and then spreading across the congregation all the way to the extra chairs placed in the rear. Some stood with hands raised, and others were unashamedly weeping. Viktor moved back toward the microphone stand.

"God's presence has stirred the water of our complacency. His Spirit is speaking to you now and calling you to surrender to his love. God is good. He wants nothing but the best for you. Jesus died for you. Trust him with your life. Fellow Christians, we need the power of the Holy Spirit to flow through us. Ask the Spirit to fill you. Call out to him now, whatever your need. Seek him with all your heart. Jesus is walking through these aisles in the person of his Spirit. Reach out and touch him. He wants to minister to you."

The Holy Spirit did minister mightily. Sins were confessed, and hearts were cleansed. Sick bodies experienced the touch of the great physician. Discouraged parents saw their wayward children crying out to God and raced to be by their sides. Crumbling marriage relationships received hope for the future as the Spirit probed deeply into the hearts of discouraged husbands and wives. Viktor saw prayer as the key to victory in spiritual combat. Before dismissing the rejoicing congregation, he felt prompted by the Holy Spirit to share another brief word.

"God has dramatically demonstrated to us today the effect of earnest prayer by his people. I love to preach. Proclaiming the truth of God's word is my passion. However, at this stage of our church life, I believe prayer is more important than my preaching," Viktor said. "I want the Spirit to interrupt my sermon anytime he chooses. Don't be surprised if I pause sometimes in midsermon and invite people to come forward for prayer. It may be for salvation, it may be for healing, it may be for a fresh infilling of the Holy Spirit. And when they come, we will all join with Jesus and the Holy Spirit to intercede on their behalf."

Viktor was aware that God had used a young woman unknown to him to spark a prayer emphasis that had brought a fresh wave of spiritual vitality to the congregation. She had also challenged him to exert leadership regarding a permanent church home. He must discover her identity and thank her. But first, he must act on what she and Phillip King had recommended.

He called his staff together to consider their course of action. He asked his associates to form search committees to locate and recommend a building site and an architect. The secretaries were assigned a more immediate task.

CHAPTER 32
ANNA

"Vera and Irina, please find out who the lady was that the Lord sent to us Sunday to stir us to action with her challenge to build and pray. She disappeared before I had a chance to meet her. I want to thank her."

The next day, Vera called Viktor.

"Brother Viktor, the name of the woman you wanted to thank is Anna Melnik. She is a single mother with a seven-year-old son and a daughter who is four. I didn't inquire as to why she is a single mother, nor did she volunteer any information. I told her you wanted to thank her for speaking up last Sunday and she could expect a call soon. If you would like to do that now, I'll place the call."

"Thank you, Vera. Anna Melnik? That last name is vaguely familiar, but I can't place where I might have heard it. Don't place the call now. Give me her phone number, and I'll call her myself when it is convenient. I want to arrange a meeting with her sometime in the near future."

"I think she will appreciate that," Vera replied. "She is a very attractive woman, Brother Viktor. Or did you notice?"

"I barely caught a glimpse of her," Viktor said. "But yes, I did notice. She certainly is a lovely young lady. Even a glimpse revealed that. But don't get any ideas about my motivation to see her. I am looking for Spirit-led people, male or female, that have gifts that God can use to do his work in our congregation. I saw in Anna a confident, gifted woman able to express truth with grace and love. She analyzed our situation and proposed a solution. It was a solution I had already reached, but it needed to be offered by someone in the congregation. She didn't hesitate to offer it. You saw how God used that to spark a powerful time of prayer."

"I understand," said Vera. "Now let me speak as your friend and not as your executive secretary. You are thirty-nine years old, soon to be forty. You need a wife. Didn't God say 'It is not good for man to be alone'? You have no idea how many single women in this church are dreaming about becoming Mrs. Viktor Gorgachuk. You may not realize it, but in addition to being a brilliant scholar and powerful preacher, you are a very attractive man."

"I have been extremely careful never to give anyone the slightest encouragement that would feed a fantasy about a romantic attachment," Viktor said.

"I know that," Vera said. "Every sane person knows that. What you may not realize is that in a congregation this size, there are emotionally unbalanced, young women who confuse fantasy and reality. They can make accusations as a result of their fantasies that sound very convincing. You need a wife to protect you."

"Thank you, Vera, for sharing," Viktor said. "I need to hear a woman's perspective. I am not opposed to getting married, but it will never be just to protect myself against the danger of marauding women. I believe God wants to be involved in every Christian marriage, and I certainly want him involved in mine. I'm simpleminded enough to believe the Holy Spirit will lead me to the right person at the right time and that she will recognize that God has brought us together."

Viktor called Anna that evening after returning to his small bachelor apartment. "Hello, is this Anna?"

"Yes, it is. Who's calling, please?"

"This is Viktor Gorgachuk, pastor of the Christians Together congregation. You blessed us yesterday with your encouraging and challenging words. I thank you for daring to speak up."

"Thank you, Brother Viktor. I hesitated to say anything, but I genuinely sensed the Holy Spirit was urging me to speak as I did. The way people responded convinced me it was indeed the Spirit that prompted me."

"Sister Anna, I believe being open and honest are preferred to being veiled and evasive," Viktor said. "Our church is experiencing rapid growth beyond anything I expected. It's a pastor's dream but sometimes a nightmare. We have many converts that need to be discipled. We need more leaders that can help conserve the harvest. I have observed in you qualities that are essential for spiritual leadership. I am being presumptuous, I know, but if the Holy Spirit has placed this possibility in your heart and you are interested at all in pursuing this further, I ask your permission to have my secretary schedule a meeting with our pastor/elder leadership team so we can get to know each other."

"Brother Viktor, I am honored that you have presented me even the possibility of becoming involved in the spiritual leadership of this great church. You know very little about me. How could you speak to me about a leadership role when you don't know my spiritual gifts or qualifications?"

"It's because you ask those kinds of questions that I want you in a leadership role. But to be more specific, I have learned to be very sensitive to the inner voice of the Holy Spirit. I call them nudges. When you challenged Christians Together to build and pray, the Spirit nudged me to reach out to you. I don't know what the result will be, but I am reaching out."

"I understand nudges by the Holy Spirit. I refer to them as promptings, and I've learned to take them seriously," Anna said. "Therefore I will agree to meet with the leadership team at an agreed upon time and place. I'll await the call."

"Thank you, Anna. I don't know what the Spirit has in mind, but if we keep responding to his nudges, I'm sure we will be pleased with the result. Vera, my secretary, should contact you soon. I'm glad you agreed to meet with us. Good-bye for now."

Viktor immediately contacted his secretary. "Vera, I just called Anna Melnik and asked her to consider meeting with our leadership team concerning ministering in some position. She responded with what I considered the ideal response."

"She agreed to meet with the leadership team, and you want me to arrange the time and place. Right?" Vera said.

"Wrong, at least half wrong. Her initial response was to ask me how I could even consider asking her to assume some leadership role without knowing anything about her spiritual gifts and qualifications for ministry. For me, that was the ideal response, and it reassured me that it was the Holy Spirit that had moved me to reach out to her. After I explained further, she agreed to meet with us, so please arrange the time and place."

After her boss hung up, Vera called the church secretary. "Irina, sniff the air. Do you sense a delightful fragrance?"

"Hi, Vera. I'm sniffing, but all I smell is the usual stale office odor. Why? Did Brother Viktor get a big check for the building fund?" Irina asked.

"What I whiff smells even better than money," Vera said. "It's so slight you'll never guess, so I'll tell you. I detect the faint fragrance of romance in the air. I don't think Brother Viktor has detected it yet, but he will. I am sure he will. It's about time, don't you think?"

"I've been praying that he would recognize his need of a wife and start looking. Who's igniting this tiny flame? Anyone I know?" Irina said.

"No, I don't think so. But I am sure you will if my hunch is right. I don't even know if the young lady is free to marry. I'm referring to Anna Melnik. I doubt if she realizes what is brewing."

"Upon what objective data do you base your theory?" Irina probed.

"None. Brother Viktor has what he calls nudges from the Holy Spirit that help direct him in his actions and decisions. I have hunches from my woman's intuition. Maybe not as accurate as Brother Viktor's nudges, but usually right on."

"So how is this romance going to develop? Do you have a hunch about the timeline?" Irina asked.

"I'm not a prophetess," Vera said. "If this is of the Lord, as I believe it is, the Holy Spirit will oversee the process. I'll pray earnestly that he will. Brother Viktor wants the leadership team meeting with Anna as soon as possible, so I must get busy. Bye."

Two days later, the leadership team assembled for the vetting interview with Anna Melnik. The team consisted of Brother Viktor, Associate Pastors Ivan Vostruk and Josef Korvade, Elders Yuri Arminska and Elina Hamakrik, and Executive Secretary Vera Kovarde. After a bit of small talk and introductions around, Brother Viktor prayed and opened the meeting.

"We are here tonight primarily to get acquainted with Mrs. Anna Melnik. Anna is here because I was nudged by the Holy Spirit to invite her. As you all know, I take those nudges seriously. I believe Anna has leadership gifts that God wants to use in our church. Sister Anna, I am delighted that you agreed to meet with us. However, before I turn our meeting over to you, I think it only fair that we take a few minutes to introduce ourselves to you. I want each of my leadership team to take no more than two minutes to give you a thumbnail sketch of who he or she is. That should take no more than fifteen minutes. I'll begin."

Viktor chose to begin so he could illustrate what he meant by a thumbnail sketch. His sketch took thirty-five seconds. Within ten minutes, all sketches were completed. Viktor then addressed Anna.

"Anna, you will have plenty of time to get to know us. We are here primarily to get to know you. Take your time and share as much about yourself as you think appropriate for us to know. Then members of the team will ask questions to clarify issues if necessary," Viktor said.

"Thank you, Brother Viktor. I came tonight because I take as seriously as you do the promptings of the Holy Spirit. The Spirit prompted you to invite me, and he prompted me to come. But I have no idea where the Spirit is going with this. First, some personal information. I am a single mom with a son, Andrew, almost seven, and a daughter, Shana Dawn, three and a half. I was married for eight years to Stephen Melnik. He died three years ago, the victim of a head-on collision with a speeding driver illegally passing. The blood-alcohol test indicated he was almost three times over the legal limit and had four previous DUIs."

The get-acquainted session continued for another two hours. Anna covered her own family history as well as that of her late husband. They were all fascinated by Anna's personal background. She was born on August 15, 1974, in Uzhhorod, Ukraine, the only child of Vasil and Maria Genady. Her parents were Baptist believers. For administrative purposes, the USSR placed Baptists and Pentecostals together as one organization, so she experienced the influence of both as she was growing up. A Baptist tourist, with a small group visiting Uzhhorod in 1981, brought with her a Russian/English dictionary. When she departed, she left it with the Genady family. Anna began to spend hours studying the dictionary and developed a remarkable English vocabulary with proper pronunciation.

The first ten years of Anna's life were lived under the repressive regime of Leonid Brezhnev, who made a deliberate attempt to eliminate belief in God by flooding the public schools with atheistic propaganda in textbooks, lectures, and films. Confused as a child between home instruction and school indoctrination, she desperately wanted to know if there was really a God like the Bible described. As a twelve-year-old, she prayed with all her heart for God to make himself known if he really existed. God answered, and she had a powerful, transforming encounter with Jesus Christ. God's dramatic answer to her prayer created within her a hunger and passion for prayer that had undergirded her life ever since.

Under the regime of Gorbachev, openness with the West increased. The Genadys were permitted to immigrate to America in 1990 just as the USSR was beginning to disintegrate. The lady tourist had left her address and phone number in the dictionary, and Anna was able to correspond with her in 1989 when emigration looked like a possibility. The lady, named Martha Agnew, wrote back commending Anna on her use of English Language. She lived in Charlotte, North Carolina, and urged the Genadys to settle there. They did so and became part of a small Slavic community in Charlotte.

Martha Agnew, a wealthy widow whose husband had made a fortune in tobacco, was thrilled to discover that the dictionary she had left had helped Anna get a head start on mastering English. She was enthralled by Anna's intelligence and beauty and adopted her as a "mission project." She used her money and influence to get Anna enrolled in Davidson College, an elite, purposely small, superb school steeped in Presbyterian tradition. Despite Martha Agnew's sponsorship, Anna had to invest a solid year of hard work and earnest prayer before she could pass the required entrance exams. She passed all required exams, including the English fluency test, with flying colors. She was admitted to the Davidson freshman class in the fall of 1992.

Stephen Melnik was born in Taipei, Taiwan, in 1970 and lived there much of his youth. His father was a prosperous Presbyterian businessman with various shipping interests. His mother taught English part-time at one of the private colleges in Taipei. Both spoke fluent Mandarin, as did Stephen. James Melnik, Stephen's father, was an alumnus of Davidson and an ardent supporter. Although not demanding compliance, he strongly encouraged Stephen to enroll in Davidson when he was eighteen. Stephen did so and was a senior there in the fall of 1992.

Anna and Stephen met at the Intervarsity Christian Fellowship chapter on campus. They formed a bond quickly because of their international heritage and their strong Christian convictions. Both sensed God had some form of full-time ministry for them after their education was completed.

They began dating when Anna was a freshman and Stephen a senior. They continued dating through the next three years and were married on June 26, 1996. Anna had just graduated with honors from college, and Stephen had graduated from the seminary in nearby Charlotte a week earlier. They both believed God had called them to minister to international students on American college campuses. They joined a large para-church organization that effectively evangelized on hundreds of campuses. After receiving further specialized training, they were assigned an area in Northern California, rich in both colleges and international students. Anna focused on Russian-speaking students. Stephen reached out primarily to Asians who spoke Mandarin. God blessed, and many students were led to consider faith in Jesus.

In May 1998, Andrew was born. Three years later, Anna gave birth to Shana Dawn. Shana was a babe in arms when her father was killed in the auto collision. Left alone with the responsibility of caring for a four-year-old son and a six-month-old baby, Anna was forced to curtail her student ministry. Andrew was now entering second grade, and Shana Dawn was entering kindergarten. She concluded her personal family history with the following statement.

"My parents live nearby, and they dote on the children. Consequently, Andy and Shana love to have their grandparents tend them. I don't normally minister on campuses now, but sometimes I have students come to my home on weekends and spend a night or two. The children stay with Mom and Dad, and I don't know who is most pleased, the grandparents or the kids. Sometimes they will ask me if it isn't time to invite some students again. I sense the Holy Spirit is prompting me to consider resuming an active ministry. So that's where I am at the present. I'll be happy to respond to any questions."

"Sister Anna, I was on a rollercoaster of emotions as you shared how God has brought you to this place in your life. I personally know it takes time to heal when recovering from the severe emotional trauma caused by the death of a beloved mate. Can you tell us where you are in the process or would that be too painful?" Elder Elina Hamakrik asked.

"Thank you, Elina, for a very legitimate question. A year after Stephen's death, or perhaps almost two years after, I would not have been able to give an objective response to your question. The initial shock was emotionally numbing. I had difficulty accepting the reality of what had happened. Family and friends reached out to me, and their love enfolded me. The Holy Spirit, the comforter, ministered to me. He affirmed to me that I must grieve if I were to heal. He brought to my mind the picture of Jesus weeping with mourners just before he raised Lazarus.

"I enrolled in a grief management class. With other class members, I went through the deep pain of searing grief. I experienced hot anger when I heard who had caused the accident, intermingled with a variety of other emotions, including depression and loneliness. I shared all of these emotions with the Lord, and I knew he was walking through them with me. I cried out for his help to enable me to meet the various needs of Andrew and Shana, and he answered.

"I can remember vividly when the Holy Spirit told me I had grieved enough. Just over a year ago, the cloud of sadness lifted, and I began to look forward to the future rather than mourning the past. Instead of wanting to stay in bed, I couldn't wait to arise and enter a new day. I literally lived the reality of Psalm 30:5, 'Weeping may remain for a night, but rejoicing comes in the morning.' The sadness I knew will always be in my memory bank, but it is no longer a present reality. I am eager to fulfill God's will for my future, whatever it may be."

Several moments of silence indicated there were no more questions. Viktor sensed it was time to conclude the session.

"Anna, I will not attempt to gild the lily. Your journey has touched me deeply with a reminder of past sorrows in my own life. I believe only those who have suffered much can rejoice much, even as those who have been forgiven much are more likely to love much. I have not the slightest doubt that God has sent you to us. My only question is which of your ministry gifts would most fulfill you and best minister to our people?

"I have already prayed much and given this a great deal of thought. I am going to write on this pad where I think God could best use you to bless this church. Anna, if God has laid on your heart a ministry at Christians Together, please jot it on a piece of paper. Likewise, each of you record your conclusion after further prayer and reflection. Put it in an envelope later and seal it and give it to Vera. We will open the envelopes when we gather in my office Friday evening.

"Some may think this process I've introduced is strange, and it is certainly unusual," Viktor said. "Let me share with you what prompted me to do this. When the apostles had a key leadership position to fill, they made sure the Holy Spirit was given an objective means of indicating his choice. Instead of choosing by majority vote, they cast lots. That's much like flipping a coin or rolling dice. Humanly speaking, it's sheer chance, but when preceded by earnest prayer for divine guidance, the Holy Spirit enters the picture. May our procedure tonight be a constant reminder that we must operate under the guidance and power of the Holy Spirit."

Friday evening, the leadership team met again with Anna Melnik. A reverent hush settled over the group as the envelopes began to be opened. Viktor opened Vera's first. She had written:

Anna's call to congregational prayer this past Sunday and her testimony to the centrality of prayer in her own life, which she shared Wednesday, has whetted a desire in my heart to be more consistent and steadfast in prayer. I believe God wants to use her to stir up a passion for prayer throughout Christians Together.

Next, Elina's note was read: *Anna, God has graced you with a variety of gifts. You could have a powerful ministry to single mothers, an important but small part of our congregation. You could powerfully impact college youth and young married couples, say age eighteen to thirty-five. That is a larger group but still less than half. One ministry that God has gifted you mightily for is the ministry of prayer. That would impact everybody in Christians Together. I believe God wants you to be a leader in developing this ministry.*

Yuri's note followed: *Sister Anna, I was powerfully moved by your call to prayer last Sunday. As I listened to your spiritual journey Wednesday, I was convicted by my own anemic prayer life. I need someone like you to teach me biblical principles of prayer to guide me and motivate me to pray as I should. Leadership in that area would be most helpful to me and I think to many others.*

Josef had written: *Every ministry gift in this leadership team will be strengthened and enhanced if undergirded with prayer. This is equally true for every ministry gift in the body of Christ at Christians Together. I believe God wants to use you to lead us deeper into the undergirding ministry of prayer.*

Ivan was very brief: *Open, honest communication is the key to develop good, close, personal relationships. We need you to help us develop this kind of prayer life. I long for a closer, personal relationship with Jesus.*

Viktor opened his envelope slowly and then read: *Last Sunday, I sensed in the depths of my spirit that the Holy Spirit had selected Anna to lead our ministry of prayer.*

All eyes were on Anna as she arose to open her envelope. She read, *"I don't know what I shall do if your vision for me is different from what God has laid on my heart … except pray. I want to lead this exciting, growing congregation into discovering what it means to obey the biblical command, 'Pray without ceasing.' I want to go with them into the 'Holy of Holies' of intimate prayer."*

Tears glistened in Anna's eyes as she concluded reading her brief statement. She softly spoke: "I am humbled beyond words to be called by God and confirmed by you to this ministry he has placed upon my heart. Thank you for being obedient to the voice of the Spirit. Pray earnestly that God will enable me to be and do what he has called me to."

Viktor concluded, "The Spirit has spoken to us as surely as he spoke when he chose Matthias to be a leader in the early church. We too must obey his voice and install Sister Anna Melnik to our leadership team as minister of prayer. Let us gather around her and pray that she will be anointed with wisdom and power from on high to direct this vital ministry. Each member, please lead in prayer as the Spirit directs you."

The next Sunday, Sister Anna was introduced to Christians Together as the newest member of the spiritual leadership team. There were acclamations of approval from the congregation as they stood and enthusiastically clapped and praised God.

CHAPTER 33
GOD'S WILL OR MINE

T he committee appointed to find suitable property for lo-
    cating the new facility did their work well. A twelve-acre
retired almond farm southeast of the city limits was recommended. It was approved and purchased in September 2005.
The other committee found an architect experienced in
church design. They liked his work and highly recommended
him. He was commissioned to design and create a model of
the new facility.

The expanding congregation of Christians Together continued to grow, and the building fund increased accordingly.
In November 2005, the architectural plans were approved,
and a general contractor was selected to oversee construction.
Shortly after, a ground-breaking ceremony was conducted following the Sunday service, with a throng of two thousand excited, happy people in attendance. The *Sacramento Bee* covered

the event with a photographer and reporter. The next day, heavy equipment began to move mountains of dirt.

Prayer became a central focus of Christians Together. Attendance at the Wednesday prayer service increased to over a thousand. Sister Anna not only organized large congregational prayer meetings but also inspired small home groups to seek God earnestly. God was moving in miraculous ways. Serious diseases were being healed and confirmed by reputable doctors. Word-of-mouth reports were spreading beyond the Slavic community to the general population. Across the congregation were smatterings of African Americans, Latinos, and Asians, as well as various brands of Caucasians. They were welcomed warmly.

Teens and young adults were flocking to Christians Together, and many were surrendering their lives to Jesus Christ. Families were being transformed, addicts were being delivered, love and enthusiasm pervaded the congregation, and a spirit of liberality resulted in generous offerings. Sunday after Sunday. Viktor's ten years of servant seed-sowing, watered by prayer, was producing an overflowing harvest.

People were hungry for the Holy Spirit to flood their lives with his presence and power. There were tears of repentance as God's word cut through the façade of religious observances to reveal the hidden core of self-centered living. Collapsing marriages were being restored. Fractured relationships were being mended. There was an undercurrent of genuine joy and love spreading throughout Christians Together. The Holy Spirit was creating a body through which Christ could manifest himself.

As Viktor assessed all that was going on, he realized it was not the result of his preaching, although he was recognized as a superb preacher. Nor was it the result of his pastoral leadership, although he excelled in that area as well. He recognized it was a sovereign work of God that followed ten years of servant ministry preparing the soil. The prepared soil readily received the seed of the Word of God. It was then watered profusely with prayer, and now God was producing growth.

As he pondered the power of prayer, he thought of Anna. Where would they be if she had not galvanized Christians Together into a dynamic body of prayer warriors? What a gifted, lovely, and spiritually mature young woman she was. How could they possibly replace her if she should leave them? He pictured her flashing smile, her shoulder-length, blonde hair framing her lovely face, the sparkle of her blue eyes when she was amused … or angry. Why did his thoughts keep returning to Anna? Was he falling in love with this woman?

Viktor had never thought about pursuing a wife before. His experience with women had been trying to evade designing females pursuing him. He did know that infatuation is not love. It is primarily based on external sexual attractiveness and centers in the emotions. If someone more physically attractive comes along, the emotional attachment may shift. Infatuation provides no foundation for a lasting marriage. Viktor recognized this and knew he must not mistake infatuation for genuine love. He was in unfamiliar territory and needed guidance.

Should he try to pursue a relationship that would lead to marriage? He needed to hear from the Lord. Why was he so confused? He felt as if he were in a spiritual battle. He must have prayer support from someone, but who should he turn to? Who better than the minister of prayer? He would buzz Anna.

"Hello, Viktor."

"Anna, I am facing an urgent issue, and I really need to hear from the Lord regarding my decision. Will you pray that the Holy Spirit will direct me?"

"You know I will. Is there anything more specific you want to say about this issue?"

"Later, perhaps, but not now. Just pray."

Since Viktor had never gone through the process of falling in love before, he was trying to rationally analyze what was taking place. He listed the facts regarding his relationship with Anna:

(1) He had been initially drawn to her because of her spiritual maturity and sensitivity to the leadership of the Holy Spirit.

(2) He was convinced the Holy Spirit had prompted him to have her considered for a ministry assignment on the church leadership team.

(3) Since assuming her role of leadership, she had proved to be an invaluable asset. Viktor could not visualize ministering without her support and presence.

(4) He had become very much aware of her physical beauty and was powerfully attracted by what he saw.

(5) He wanted to protect her and her children from any harm.

(6) He could not tolerate thoughts of her becoming the wife of someone else.

Being the rational creature that he was, he concluded that he was not yet prepared to propose marriage. However, he had sufficient reasons for courting this delightful, attractive, spiritually gifted woman that had come into his life. What resulted from courtship was in the hands of the Lord. Once that decision was made, he felt wonderfully at peace. The storm within was quieted. He must tell Anna that her prayer had been answered.

"Good morning, Viktor."

"Anna, I know you have been praying concerning the request I talked to you about last week. God has answered, and now I can share more specifically about the issue I faced. Do you have any plans for lunch today?"

"None, so far. Did you have something in mind?"

"Yes, I do. Let's meet at Alvin's at 11:30 to avoid the noon rush. Does that fit your schedule?"

"I can make it fit," Anna said. "I have an eleven o'clock appointment with Jan Rivers, but I know what it is about, so I can easily reschedule."

"Great. I need to meet the architect and general contractor at the building site at one o'clock, so can we drive separately?" Viktor asked.

"Sure. I'll meet you in the parking lot at 11:25," said Anna.

They met and walked in together. Viktor wanted to hold her hand but refrained. The hostess greeted them.

"Good morning, Pastor Viktor and Anna. You are earlier than usual."

"Good morning, Alice. We have some important business to discuss and wanted to avoid the noon rush. Where is your most secluded table located?" Viktor asked.

"That small one in the far left corner is out of the traffic flow, and you should have privacy there."

After being seated, they each ordered a chef's salad, Viktor a regular, and Anna a small.

"I want to thank you for your joining me in prayer, Anna. God has helped clarify the issue in my mind for which I asked you to pray, and I want to give you more details. Months ago, I told you I want to be open and honest in sharing with you. Do you remember that?"

"Of course I do, Viktor. It was when you approached me about being considered for becoming a member of the leadership team," Anna replied.

"God led you to our church. I have come to believe he may have led us to each other. This is not a proposal of marriage … yet. But it is a proposal, a proposal that we spend time together and develop a solid, trust relationship. I want to get to know your children and have them get to know and trust me. I have never been in love before, and I don't know exactly how I should feel. But I want this feeling of tenderness and deep affection that I have for you to grow and develop until I can pledge my undying love for you with no qualms or questions. I don't know how long that will take, days, weeks, or months. You have known that kind of love. If you accept this proposal, I want you to set the time limit for this interim courtship period, if I may call it that."

"Viktor, you are a unique person, and that is what has drawn me to you. I cannot take the responsibility of telling you how long this courtship period should be. Your heart will tell you. It may be tomorrow or it may be next year, but however long it takes, I'll be waiting with open heart and open arms. I already know what my heart has told me. For your information, Andrew and Shawna have told me they wish they could have you for a new daddy," Anna said, smiling.

They finished their salads quickly and exited. Viktor took her hand in his as he walked her to her car.

"Viktor, thanks for continuing to be open and honest in sharing where you're coming from. Rest assured that I will accept whatever decision the Lord leads you to as his decision for our lives whether together or apart. The Lord's will is always best in the long run."

"Yes, I know," said Viktor. "But the best is not always easy."

As he drove away, Viktor mentally reviewed what had just happened. He was glad he had shared as he had. He was greatly encouraged by the response of Anna. She welcomed his courtship and seemed assured that the end result would bring them together. He wished he had that assurance. Why hadn't he heard definitively from the Holy Spirit?

"Lord, I do love this woman. I want her to be my wife. Why can't you release me to propose marriage?" Viktor cried out. "What do you want from me?"

He knew what the Lord wanted but was afraid to verbalize it. He realized he could ignore it no longer. He had heard the question days ago, but he had pushed it out of his consciousness.

"If I ask you to be willing to surrender your hopes and dreams about Anna, will you trust me with her future and yours?"

The Lord had spoken clearly. He knew this was his Gethsemane experience. Why couldn't he freely say, "Not my will but yours be done, my Lord?" He didn't like the answer to that question because of what it revealed about himself. Did he really think that he was more capable of caring for Anna and her children than the loving creator God who had come among men in the person of Jesus Christ and died to redeem them from self-centered bondage?

Suddenly Viktor saw the issue clearly. He had more faith in himself than in God. He trusted his ability more than God's ability. How could he have fallen into this trap after experiencing God's grace and protection throughout his life?

"Oh Lord, forgive me. I do trust you with Anna and Andrew and Shana. They are yours, not mine. I surrender them to you. Surround them with your love, mercy, and protection. Bring peace to Anna. Now heal my broken heart and keep me steadfast in my service to you. I do love you and trust you."

The inner battle was over. He was deeply wounded, but his relationship with Jesus Christ was restored. His deepest concern now was for Anna. He was sure that she loved him. Had she not indicated as much? He must intercede for her that she be spared the searing pain he had endured when he faced his lack of faith head-on.

"Oh, Jesus, I praise you for who you are and what you have done for us. I thank you for your compassion and your concern for each of us. I am deeply concerned about Anna. I fear her heart will be broken when I tell her our dream of life together is not to be. Send the Holy Spirit, the blessed Comforter of the distressed, to flood her heart with your peace that is beyond human explanation. Thank you, Lord Jesus, for hearing my prayer. Amen."

CHAPTER 34

LOVE AND MARRIAGE

Immediately he was aware of God's presence. He heard the voice of the Spirit that he knew so well speak to his heart, "Son, I didn't tell you to surrender your dream. I asked you to be willing to surrender it. You passed the test. Now go fulfill the dream that I placed in both your hearts."

Viktor had clearly understood the inner voice, but he could scarcely comprehend what he had heard. God had granted approval for pursuing marriage with Anna. He was so over-come with emotion that he had to stop the car.

"Thank you, Jesus! Thank you, Lord. I praise you! I worship you. How could I have ever not trusted you? Praise be to God."

Viktor could scarcely come down to earth he was flying so high, but he knew he must. There was work to be done in the valley. He looked at his watch. He had left the restaurant only forty-five minutes ago? It seemed like an eternity. Maybe his watch had stopped. No, it was ticking away. He could almost make his appointment. He arrived at the site ten minutes after one.

"I apologize, gentlemen. I had another meeting that was absolutely essential that I not miss. Maybe I'll tell you about it sometime. Now, what is it that you wanted input from me on before continuing?"

Within a half hour, the issue was resolved. Viktor rejoiced at what God was enabling them to do as he viewed the activity taking place.

"Are we meeting our scheduled completion dates for the first phases of the project?" Viktor asked the general contractor.

"As you can see, the concrete has been poured for the basement walls and support bases. We were delayed about a week with the concrete work because of our unusually wet January, but we will make that up as the weather improves. We can begin the steel skeleton next week," the contractor replied.

"It is nearly April 2007. Are you reasonably optimistic about being ready for occupancy by February 2010?" Viktor asked.

"Yes, or maybe by Christmas 2009."

"I'll remember that. I must go. I have an extremely important phone call to make. Keep up the good work and remember who you are working for," Viktor said, pointing skyward.

Viktor was in a hurry to get back in his office so he could call Anna. He had not yet invested in a cell phone but decided it was time to do so. As soon as he arrived at his office, he buzzed Anna.

"Viktor, you're back so soon. What's up?"

"Everything is up, Anna. I want to see you as quickly as I can. Do you have anyone in your office?"

"No, and no one scheduled for another half hour. Shall I expect you?"

"Yes, I'll be there in two minutes. I can't wait to tell you what happened."

Viktor buzzed his secretary. "Vera, I'm back, but I am leaving now for Anna's office and will be there maybe twenty minutes. Talk to you later."

Viktor strode rapidly down the hall to Anna's office. He quickly summarized what had happened after leaving the restaurant, concluding with this confession: "I saw that I had tried to supplant God as your ultimate lover and protector. When I acknowledged that and repented and relinquished you to God, he gave you back to me or at least gave me permission to ask you to marry me. You said our courtship period should last until my heart told me my love was genuine and undying with no qualms or questions. You said that may be tomorrow or next year, but you would wait however long it took. My heart told me today that I love you with all my being. I'm a day early, but I'm asking right now, Anna, my dearest, beautiful sweetheart, will you marry me?"

"Of course I will, silly man. I would have proposed to you, except I knew the Lord had to lead you through the process you just described. He had already led me through the same process, and I had to struggle before I was willing to put you on the altar as my sacrificial offering to God. Once I was willing to let go of you, God gave you back to me."

"Your appointment will be here soon. We have much to talk about. May I come to your place tonight? One more thing. May I announce our engagement to the staff?"

"Yes to both. It's treat night for Andrew and Shana, so we are having pizza and chocolate milk. Join us at six if that strikes your fancy."

"Sounds wonderful. Can I bring the pizza?" Viktor asked.

"By all means," said Anna. "Then we will be sure to have enough for you."

That night the children were let in on the engagement. They were ecstatic and wanted to know when the wedding would take place.

"That's what we need to decide tonight," Viktor said. "Your mother will have a lot to say about that. What do you think, Anna?"

"I prefer not to have a long engagement period. God has wonderfully guided us into this relationship, and we have already been through his testing period. How do you feel?"

"I concur completely, and I already have a date in mind," Viktor said.

"Tell us! Tell us!" begged Andrew and Shana.

"How about the Fourth of July. It's my birthdate and the birthdate of our adopted country. And there will be two added dividends. I'll never forget our wedding anniversary, and we will have a big fireworks display to mark our celebration. It's just over four months away. What do you think, Anna? Can you plan the wedding in that length of time?" Viktor asked.

"Oh, you dear innocent man. I've had our wedding planned for two months. Let me tell you what I would like. I've checked with Harmon, our general contractor, and he can have a roof over the new gymnasium as long as he has two months' advance notice. The new sanctuary has a more complex roofline, and it is not feasible to attempt to get a roof completed quickly," Anna said.

"Anna, what do roofs on buildings have to do with our wedding plans?"

"I want our wedding to be the first conducted at our new worship and education center. None of the buildings will be near completion, but by July they can have the roof on the gym. Of course there will just be a bare concrete floor, no windows or doors or electricity. But a roof will give us protection from July sun or an unlikely shower. We should be able to get a thousand chairs set up with a center aisle between them. I want to walk down that aisle flanked by those dear people that love us," Anna said. "Well, what do you think?"

"It's unique. People will never forget it. There must be a few sermon illustrations in there somewhere that I can extract. Yeah, I like it. How about the traditional reception after the wedding? Even a modest menu for invited guests, which includes all in our congregation, would cost thousands of dollars. Have you planned for that?"

"As a matter of fact, I have. We will have a big church potluck dinner like we used to have in North Carolina. We can get some of the talented musicians in our congregation to provide appropriate music. After the wedding service is completed, folding tables will be set up on the gym floor and food displayed on the tables. The only expense connected with the meal will be the cost of the paper plates and cups and plastic tableware."

"I love it," Viktor said. "It's simple. It gets everyone involved and doesn't cost a ton of money. I believe it will honor God."

The next day, Viktor assembled the senior staff and leadership team members together, and he and Anna announced their engagement and wedding plans. None were surprised, but most were stunned at how quickly it had happened. They were all deeply moved when Viktor shared his struggle as he worked through to surrender and peace. They rejoiced at

God's gracious response. They laughed uproariously when Anna confessed she had made wedding plans two months previously. Staff assignments were made to organize committees that would bring her plans to fulfillment.

Tuesday, July 4, 2007 was a great day of celebration for Christians Together as they gathered to watch their beloved Brother Viktor take their equally loved Sister Anna as his bride. Friends had come from far and wide to help them celebrate. Three members of the Vashchenko family were present. Martha Agnew from Charlotte had flown out and was seated with Maria Genady. Professor Phillip King proudly served as Viktor's best man. George McGinnis stood next to Phillip as a proud groomsman. Kathleen beamed from the front row reserved for family, alongside the Vashchenkos. Shari Melnik Anderson, Stephen's sister, was Anna's matron of honor. Vera and Irina were also bride's attendants. Andrew served as stately ring bearer, and Shana as glowing flower girl. The Reverend William Ballard, popular pastor of Sundale Community Church, officiated. In the past year, he and Viktor had become very close friends.

At the appointed time, Anna appeared clad in a simple, tasteful summer frock. She proceeded down the concrete walkway at the side of her father, Vasil Genady, her eyes fixed on the man awaiting her. The audience stood watching, marveling at her radiant beauty. The traditional vows were repeated with fervor but dignity. The nuptial embrace and kiss were greeted with thunderous applause.

After the ceremony, Viktor and Anna stood in line for over an hour shaking hands, exchanging hugs, and receiving congratulations. Finally, with Andrew and Shana in tow by their grandparents, the newlyweds were able to leave for an unannounced honeymoon location.

The potluck reception was a huge success. People filled their plates and gathered in small groups on grassy areas surrounding the construction site or in chairs in the gym. Professor King and the McGinnises along with Pastor Bill Ballard and his wife, Jennifer, joined the Genadys and Mrs. Agnew and shared favorite stories about the bride and groom. All agreed it was a never-to-be-forgotten wedding of two special people.

CHAPTER 35
RAPID CONGREGATIONAL GROWTH

Viktor and Anna marveled at the way Christians Together continued to grow after their marriage. Anna's teaching of persistent pursuit of God in prayer was producing a growing hunger for his manifested presence in worship. Viktor's ministry of expounding scripture powerfully presented the lordship of Jesus and challenged people to conform to his will. His emphasis upon developing Christ-likeness by the power of the Holy Spirit was producing mature, consistent Christians reflecting the character traits of their Lord. New believers were quickly enrolled in a discipleship class. The aim of the church was not to gain converts but to train disciples eager to serve Jesus. Many young people were responding to the challenge.

Despite growth numerically, spiritually and financially there were signs of an undercurrent of dissension from a small segment of the congregation. Most of this minority were old-er members who had been members of a Pentecostal Union in East Europe before coming to the United States. A typical conversation went like this:

"Brother Viktor, I believe the Lord has placed something on my heart that I want to bring to your attention. God is bless-ing Christians Together greatly, but I haven't heard a sermon for a long time on Spirit baptism and speaking in tongues. I am concerned about that since these are so central to our Pentecostal tradition. I think it very important that these doc-trines be preached regularly, and I encourage you to do so."

"Thank you, my brother, for your concern," Brother Viktor replied. "I am conducting a thorough examination of scrip-ture concerning these very matters. When I conclude, I will present what scripture reveals to the whole church. In the meantime, I would remind you that our Lord Jesus is the sov-ereign baptizer and pours out his Spirit on whom he chooses in accordance with his criteria. Keep your eyes fixed on Jesus and follow him."

The auditorium at the rented school seated fifteen hun-dred. Before Easter 2009, two services were necessary. On March 23, Easter Sunday, three services were provided. As at-tendance increased, Viktor and Anna watched with great in-terest the construction progress on the new church. Already they realized the four-thousand-seat sanctuary would be too small and rejoiced at the problem this presented. They were confident that the Holy Spirit would direct them as how best to minister to the people he was sending their way.

In early December 2009, Viktor visited the construction site and talked to Harmon Wixam, the general contractor. He was eager to get the latest estimated completion date.

"Harmon, I'm thrilled at the progress you are making," Viktor said. "What's our timetable look like for the final inspection authorizing occupancy?"

"Well, it won't be by Christmas as I had hoped," Harmon replied. "But even allowing for some inevitable problems, we should have it ready for occupancy by the end of February."

"So if we plan our official dedication service for Palm Sunday, March 28, 2010, we can be reasonably certain our sanctuary will be accessible on that date."

"Absolutely, Brother Viktor," Harmon affirmed. "Unless there is some cataclysmic earthquake, or other unexpected disaster, all phases of the construction will be completed."

"And that includes the parking area?"

"Yes, sir," Harmon replied. "Everything except some landscape plantings will be finished."

Viktor left the site rejoicing. In his mind, he was already picturing a glorious service in which this great church plant would be dedicated to Jesus Christ for the proclamation of the gospel and the advancement of the kingdom of God. The presence of Jesus Christ suddenly pervaded the car as he drove, flooding his soul. Seeing a roadside picnic area, he turned off and parked. He had to express the deep sense of gratitude that was welling up within him.

"Jesus, my Lord, my Savior, my God! How can I thank you for all you have done in my life? Who am I that you should so bless me? For my parents, for those who protected me at great risk, for my new life in America, for wonderful friends and colleagues, for my beloved Anna and children, and for this great church and its people, I praise and thank you. I love you, Jesus. I worship you and dedicate my life to serve you until you call me home."

The sense of the holy presence receded as Viktor continued to sit in the car and ponder what he had experienced. Many times he had sensed the presence of Jesus, but there was something especially intimate and personal about this encounter. It reminded him of one other time when he had similarly experienced Jesus's presence. He smiled as he recalled the occasion. It had been on this same road over a year ago when he had surrendered his dream pertaining to Anna to the Lord. Jesus had given him back more than a dream. He had received Anna herself to be his beloved lifetime friend, wife, lover, and intimate companion in ministry.

A stray thought entered his mind as he remembered the fierce struggle that he had endured before he could embrace God's will rather than his own. Would he ever again be confronted with a similar struggle? He couldn't conceive how that would be possible, but the thought persisted. He prayed earnestly that he would always be able to say from his heart, "Not my will but yours be done, Lord." He was grateful that Anna would be by his side if he ever faced such a situation.

When Viktor returned to his office, he asked Vera to arrange a time for a meeting with his senior staff the next morning. That evening, he shared with Anna the information he had received from the general contractor. Later, when the children were in bed, he told her about being inexplicably overwhelmed with a sense of God's presence as he was driving home. He shared how he had stopped the car and poured out his heart to God in love and gratitude for all the blessings he had received.

"Viktor, I am so pleased and grateful that you shared all this with me," Anna said. "I think God is preparing us for something that may come as a surprise to both of us. I have no idea as to what, where, or when. I believe God wants to reassure you of his love and his abiding presence regardless of what happens in the future."

"I hope his surprise produces as much joy as when he gave me permission to pursue you," said Viktor with a smile.

The next morning, Viktor joined his senior staff assembled in the conference room. Anna invited everyone to join her in praise to God. They did so with enthusiasm and hands raised heavenward. A spirit of joy pervaded the room. As a holy hush settled over the room, Brother Viktor arose and spoke quietly.

"God has led us to this moment. I am happy and grateful to announce that we must begin planning the dedication service for our new sanctuary and Christian education center. The date is Palm Sunday, March 28, 2010. We have just over three months to pray, plan, and prepare a service that will exalt Jesus Christ, honor the Holy Spirit, and display the love of God our heavenly father."

Viktor proceeded to assign areas of responsibility to help assure the kind of service he envisioned. He and Anna sent personal invitations to friends and family members. Viktor penned notes to his friend and mentor, Professor Phillip King, to his beloved sponsors, George and Kathleen McGinnis, and to members of the Vashchenko family. Anna did likewise to Vasil and Maria Genady, her parents who lived nearby, to Shari Melnik Anderson, her sister-in-law, and to Martha Agnew, her warm friend and advocate.

The Palm Sunday dedication service was covered by the *Sacramento Bee* and several religious periodicals. The four-thousand-seat sanctuary was filled to capacity, and two thousand more watched on closed-circuit TV in the gymnasium and fellowship hall. Additional thousands watched on their home TVs via coverage from a local TV station.

The service was all that the spiritual leaders of Christians Together had hoped and prayed for. The music led the congregation into the presence of God. There was a spirit of worship, praise, and joy that extended into the overflow areas. The choir's a cappella rendition of "How Great Thou Art," one verse sung in Russian, moved many to tears. Brother Viktor's sermon depicted Jesus as Lord of the universe and was powerfully anointed by the Holy Spirit. At the conclusion, he challenged listeners to commit themselves wholeheartedly to the lordship of Jesus. The Holy Spirit moved many to come forward spontaneously to accept Jesus as Lord or to renew their commitment to him. Viktor and Anna watched in amazement and gratitude as the wonder of God's grace unfolded before them.

CHAPTER 36
THE BONDING OF PASTOR BILL AND BROTHER VIKTOR

The remarkable close relationship that developed between Pastor Bill Ballard and Pastor Viktor Gorgachuk was a surprise to all who knew them. How could two Christian leaders, with very divergent theological viewpoints, develop such close friendship and mutual admiration? In retrospect, they both agreed that the Holy Spirit was surely involved in the process. The meetings, conversations and personal disclosures that cemented their relationship took place mostly from mid-2006 to mid-2009. As a result of their deep commitment to each other and to the trustworthiness of scripture the Truth Seekers pact was birthed. A summary of this personal bonding process is described in the pargraphs below.

The rapid early growth of Christians Together got the attention of the Sacramento religious community. In June 2006, William Ballard, well-known pastor of the large, influential Sundale Community Church, saw an article in the *Sacramento Bee* about the burgeoning Slavic church. It revived a dormant memory about Viktor Gorgachuk and the stories he had heard from Augustina and Vera Vashchenko. This was a man he had wanted to meet for a long time. He buzzed his secretary.

"Jan, please see if you can reach Pastor Viktor Gorgachuk at that amazing new Pentecostal church they call Christians Together. I have been fascinated by what little I know about this man, and I hope to discover more. I want to talk to him if he is available."

I'll find the church office number and call right away, Pastor Bill. It should only take a few minutes," Jan said.A few minutes later, his buzzer sounded. "Pastor Bill, Pastor Gorgachuk's personal secretary said Brother Viktor, her title, should be available in about ten minutes. She will call as soon as he is able to take a call."

"Jan, I don't think I ever told you about my interest in Viktor Gorgachuk," pastor Bill said. "I first heard about him as a result of meeting Augustina Vashchenko a number of years ago. She is one of the Russian Pentecostals, popularly known as the Siberian Seven, who was provided five years of sanctuary in the American Embassy in Moscow from 1978 to 1983. When she and other members of her family came to America they settled near Seattle not too far from where my Aunt Tina lived. The Vashchenkos became good friends of the Gorgachuks when both lived in southern Siberia. When Viktor's parents were killed the Vashchenkos took him into their family. He lived with their children while the parents were finding refuge in the American Embassy. Viktor has an intriguing history, and I am looking forward to meeting him for the first time."

"Thanks, Pastor Bill, for the background info. I hope I also can meet him sometime," Jan said.

Five minutes later, Jan buzzed the pastor's study. "Brother Viktor is available now. Shall I place the call?"

"Please do, Jan. I'll hold," said Pastor Bill.

"Brother Viktor speaking, may I help you?"

"Brother Viktor, this is Bill Ballard over at Sundale Community Church. I just wanted to call and let you know how excited and pleased I am to hear how God is blessing your ministry. You and your church are a great asset, not only to the Slavic community but to our entire city."

"Pastor Bill, thank you very much for your warm, loving spirit. I so appreciate your call. You and your church have blessed this city for many years. I hope we can emulate you in the years to come."

"I must tell you, Brother Viktor, I first heard of you quite a few years ago. I have been wanting to meet you ever since Augustina and Vera Vashchenko shared some of your history with me. Any chance that we might get together sometime soon?" Pastor Bill asked.

"You know the Vashchenkos! Of course we must get together," Viktor responded. "The sooner the better. You suggest a place and time, and I will make it a priority to be there. This may sound strange to you, but I have an inner witness in my spirit that God truly wants us to develop a trust relationship with each other. Does that sound far out to you?"

"Not at all. Sheep are expected to know and trust the voice of the shepherd," Bill replied. "You said name a place and time for a meeting. How about a late lunch at Alvin's at one o'clock tomorrow? That's near your place, and I will be meeting a family at the hospital near there at noon. I'm excited about finally getting a chance to meet you, plus I want to get your take on the awesome things I hear God is doing in your congregation."

"I admire your decisiveness, Pastor Bill," said Viktor. "I have a feeling that this will be the first of many meetings we will have together."

"I say amen to that. Let's dispense with the titles. How about just Bill and Viktor? Are you okay with that? "

"Yeah, I like that. Bill and Viktor it is."

The lunch at Alvin's was indeed the first of many meetings. Bill and Viktor established rapport quickly, and this soon developed into warm friendship. Sometimes Anna Melnik was included in their lunch dates, as was Bill's wife, Jennifer. Jennifer was an attractive, buxom brunette with a buoyant, fun-loving personality. She immediately was drawn to Anna's more sedate external demeanor. Their contrasting personalities complemented each other, but at the core of each was a deep devotion to Jesus Christ and the truth of scripture.

Anna developed deep admiration and warm affection not only for Jennifer but also for her husband, Viktor's close friend. When Viktor and Anna became engaged, they agreed privately they wanted Pastor Bill to engage them in pre-marital counseling and lead them in their exchange of vows. Anna revealed she planned to invite Jennifer to be her matron of honor.

A few weeks later, Viktor and Bill were together again for lunch. Bill greeted his friend heartily.

"Viktor, I want to congratulate you on your engagement and upcoming marriage to your lovely Anna. I wondered why you remained a bachelor so long. Now I know. God was preparing someone very special for you."

"Thank you very much," Viktor said. "She is very special and that is one reason we want someone very special to officiate at our wedding on July the Fourth. Bill, will you bless us by officiating at our exchange of vows?"

"Viktor, do you mean that? Of course I will," Bill said. "I can't think of anything that I would rather do. What an unexpected honor you have bestowed on me."

"I would like to share how Anna and I came to the place we're sure our marriage is part of God's plan for both of us. Is that okay?" Viktor asked.

"Viktor, don't expend time asking. Just do it. I can't wait to hear about your God-ordained romance," Bill replied.

Viktor shared the story of how God had tested them and then placed his imprimatur on his and Anna's love for each other and led them into marriage plans.

"You know, Bill, there was a point in which I think each of us must have felt much like Abraham when he escorted Isaak up Mt. Moriah," Viktor reflected.

"I think I understand what you mean," Bill said. "Your hopes and dreams of a life together had to be laid on the altar of surrender to God's will before those dreams could experience a resurrection more glorious than before."

"Yes, yes! That's it. I will never forget the thrill and exhilaration that flooded my soul when God communicated his approval of my pursuit of life with Anna," Viktor said. "Nor," Viktor continued, "will I ever forget the battle that preceded or the amazing peace that swept through my being when I surrendered my dream to his will with faith that his will was best for us both. I understand more fully what Paul meant by 'the peace of God, which transcends all understanding.'"

"Viktor, I feel like I have been on holy ground as you have related the wondrous way God has led you and Anna. I thank you with all my heart for trusting me with these precious, intimate glimpses into your personal life," Bill said.

⇒+⇐

After Viktor and Anna were married, the two pastors continued meeting together regularly. Their friendship had bonded into a deep trust relationship that enabled them to share secret struggles, doubts, and fears they would not dare reveal to any others except, perhaps, their wives. It was out of this trust relationship the following conversation took place at one of their lunch meetings.

"Bill, you have been involved in the pastorate much longer than I. In your view, what is the major problem challenging the evangelical church, particularly in America?"

"That's a tough question, Viktor. My longevity in the pastorate doesn't give me an edge in assessing problems within the evangelical church. It may just mean I have been part of the problem longer than you. I haven't given that question much thought, but you apparently have. What do you think the major problem is?"

"Bill, to me, a problem is not a challenge unless there is a possibility of resolving it. If it is impossible to remedy, then attempts to do so are useless. One major problem that I think we can do something about is lack of unity within the body of

Christ. Jesus was passionate about unity among his followers as his prayer in John 17 demonstrates."

"That is certainly a problem that presents a huge challenge to the church," Bill said. "How do you suggest we go about trying to remedy that malady?"

"There is much that we evangelicals agree on, but there is only one doctrine that we agree on that will help us resolve the disunity problem. To my knowledge, we all agree that scripture is inspired of God and is the authoritative rule of faith and practice. In other words, if a doctrine has no scriptural basis, then it should be discarded, particularly so if it is divisive," Viktor said.

"I agree wholeheartedly," Bill replied. "But what can we do to eliminate unscriptural, divisive doctrines from the Church? It would be like trying to drain the ocean with a thimble."

"I have thought and prayed earnestly about that issue. I have come to the conviction we must start in that part of the Church where we have influence and can make a difference," Viktor said.

"Do you mean what I think you mean?" Bill asked.

"I mean I must start in my church, and you must start in yours," Viktor said. "There is something in my church tradition that is a barrier to unity between our churches. There is something in your church tradition that precludes unity between us. We know it is there, but political correctness prevents honest discussion of the issues. We must surmount that wall."

"What do you suggest we do?" Bill asked.

"Here's what I propose," Viktor answered. "You tell me what is the most divisive aspect of our Pentecostal tradition that prevents unity between our churches. I'll do the same in respect to your tradition. Then you analyze and exegete pertinent scripture that supports your rejection of our tradition. I will follow the same process. Each of us will have a chance to critique each other's exegesis. Does that sound reasonable?"

"That's brilliant, Viktor. It makes conformity to the context of scripture the measuring stick for sound doctrine."

"Absolutely. Any tradition that has no firm foundation in scripture should be rejected. We are not defenders of the status quo but seekers after scriptural truth, wherever it may lead. Please go ahead, Bill, and tell me what you find most divisive in our tradition."

"Viktor, our times together have become treasured oases to me. We share so much in common regarding our Christian faith. But there is one area in which our traditions are at odds. Your tradition teaches that there is no valid baptism in the Holy Spirit unless it is accompanied by the physical evidence of speaking in tongues. I find no scriptural basis for that doctrine. But like you, I seek truth with all my heart. If there is solid biblical support for your position, I will support it wholeheartedly. Now, what is your bone of contention?"

"Bill, I have learned to love and respect you sincerely and deeply," Viktor said. "One of the things I most admire is your utter devotion to the pursuit of truth. I share your passion. Many clergy are more concerned with protecting their tradition from any negative connotations than discovering truth. But we have pledged to be truth seekers. Your church contends that the miraculous gifts of the Spirit were terminated either at the end of the Apostolic Age or when the canon of scripture was completed. I don't believe the Bible or church history supports this tradition. However, should I discover this position is biblically and historically confirmed, I will adhere to it with all my heart."

"We certainly have our work cut out for us, but it's the kind of work I revel in," Bill said. "When should we meet again to present what we have discovered thus far?"

"I think we should have a regularly scheduled time for bimonthly meetings," Viktor suggested. "An open-ended evening time would give us freedom to go as long as we wished."

"That's a good idea. With our busy schedules, I suggest a quarterly meeting rather than bimonthly. Let's meet at seven o'clock on the second Tuesday evening of every first month of each quarter," Bill said. "Something else occurred to me. I know practically nothing of the roots of the modern Pentecostal movement. I need to do some serious historical research before I do a critique from scripture. I suggest we give ourselves four months for this exploration before we begin our quarterly Tuesday meetings."

"I'm delighted to hear you say that," Viktor said. "I have barely scratched the surface of my own research into the cessationist position. I agree that we allow four months for more research. We will have our first scheduled Truth Seekers meeting on the second Tuesday of October at 7:00 p.m. My calendar indicates that would be October 14, 2008. And if you don't mind, may we have the first meeting at your place? Anna and I may be involved in moving into our new house if our offer is accepted. Do you think that will be all right with Jennifer?"

"I am sure it will be," Bill responded. "Invite Anna to come with you. Jenny wants to get better acquainted with her, and they can have some social time together while we share the results of our biblical and historical research. I hear God is doing some great things in your church, Viktor. Before we return to our offices, please tell me about it."

"You are right, Bill," Viktor said, "God is doing it. No one is more surprised than I at what has occurred. I'm convinced that much of what is happening is the result of the prayer ministry that Anna has developed. Your extremely wise and pertinent pre-marriage counseling, relating to prioritizing our ministry responsibilities and marriage responsibilities, helped us get off to a good start. I can't thank you enough for that."

"Viktor, I am indebted to you," Bill said. "I would never have fully known what a remarkable wife you have if we had not spent those hours together. You are blessed beyond measure."

"I've known that all along. She continues to serve as our minister of prayer and has galvanized our people to join together in fervent intercession. It's not unusual to have the sanctuary filled with people crying out to God on Wednesday night. Intercessory prayer has changed the spiritual climate of our congregation. People come to church with expectant faith, anticipating that God will manifest his presence. He hasn't disappointed us."

"I have never heard of an associate pastor with Anna's title," Bill confessed. "What does she do?"

"It is not so much what she does. It's who she is," Viktor replied. "She is truly anointed by the Holy Spirit and has a deep love relationship with Jesus Christ. She radiates his love and presence. It's not that she promotes prayer. She promotes a positive relationship with Jesus. Prayer is the honest, ongoing communication with Jesus that grows out of the relationship."

"That sounds intriguing. I love her approach. Do you think you might allow her to come and conduct a prayer seminar for Sundale Community?" Bill asked.

"Anna would love that, and I know your people would profit from her ministry," Viktor responded. "I must get back to the office. I'll let Anna know that she may receive a call from you."

CHAPTER 37

THE "SEARCH FOR TRUTH" PACT INAUGURATED

October 2008

Viktor and Bill did serious research during the allotted four months. They met together again on the second Tuesday of October as scheduled.

"Welcome, Viktor and Anna," said Bill as he embraced them both.

"Anna, I am so glad you could come," Jennifer said. "Ever since you stirred our hearts with your challenge at the prayer seminar, I have wanted to get together with you. I have some questions about developing our prayer ministry that I must ask you. Follow me to my sewing nook while the men seclude themselves in Bill's study."

"Jennifer, I'm delighted I have this private time with you," said Anna as she settled into a comfortable chair. "I have something exciting to share. It will soon become public knowledge, but I want you to be one of the first to know. Viktor has been such a wonderful dad to Andrew and Shana. They adore him, and he loves them both deeply. However, I wanted to give Viktor a son or daughter that would carry his DNA and name into the next generation. When I explained this to him, he assured me that he could love no natural child of his more that he loves the two he inherited when he married me. I believe that, but I explained that was not the issue. I wanted to have a child that was the result of our love and commitment to each other. And now is an ideal time. I am thirty-four, a good age for child bearing. To make a long story short, I am two months pregnant."

"My dear Anna, I understand as only a woman can," Jennifer said. "Of course you and Viktor must have a child, or more. Thank you for sharing this wonderful news with me. How excited Andrew and Shana will be. Have you told them?"

"Not yet," Anna said. "Viktor and I will do it together sometime soon. Now that I have shared my secret with you, I am ready to give my full attention to your questions."

After Jennifer and Anna went their way, Bill led Viktor into his inner sanctum and requested that he lead them in prayer. He did so, briefly thanking Jesus for his presence and petitioning the Holy Spirit to guide them into truth.

"Bill, I'm excited about this spiritual journey we have agreed to take together," Viktor said. "I have been immersing myself in the words of Jesus to his disciples at the Passover meal just prior to his betrayal and crucifixion. I am challenged by his promise concerning the ministry of the Holy Spirit. *When he, the Spirit of truth comes, he will lead you into all truth.* He has come, and we claim our Lord's promise. I am eager to hear the results of your search for scriptural truth about tongues as required evidence of Spirit baptism."

"This idea of subjecting divisive doctrines to the light of scripture was your idea, Viktor. If you don't mind, I yield opening honors to you," Bill replied.

"I'm happy to do so," said Viktor, "The research I have been able to do these past four months has opened my eyes to the complexity of the issue I have raised. I supposed that the doctrine of Cessationism would be easy to refute, but I discovered there are at least four different groups of cessationists. Perhaps the best known group, and certainly the one I am most familiar with, is called classical Cessationism. This group believes that *the sign* gifts, such as prophecy, speaking in other tongues, interpretation of tongues (languages), and healing, all ended with the completion of the canon and/or the Apostolic Age. Their purpose during the life of the apostles was to affirm the truth of the gospel by manifestations of supernatural divine signs that accompanied its proclamation. Once the Church was established by the apostles, these supernatural manifestations were no longer necessary and were thus withdrawn. Some classical cessationists do recognize that sometimes miracles of healing and divine guidance occur if they do not claim to support new doctrine or add to the canon."

"I recognize this doctrine," Bill said. "I was thoroughly indoctrinated in it by my seminary professors. I am eager to see how you deal with it. What are the other three cessationist groups?"

"Concentric cessationists believe miracles may be restored in areas where the gospel has not been previously proclaimed. Luther and Calvin acknowledged this as a possibility but were not always consistent in their support," Viktor said. "In essence, this group acknowledges that the supernatural gifts have not been removed from the Church, so I will not report further on them."

"I have a vague recollection that this was mentioned but not emphasized," said Bill. "It seemed reasonable to me at the time."

"Full cessationists insist that not only are the spiritual gifts not in operation today, but also miracles ceased after the Apostolic Age," Viktor continued. "Dr. Benjamin Warfield, renowned professor of theology at Princeton Seminary a century ago, championed this position. I consider him the godfather of modern Cessationism. It was his book *Counterfeit Miracles* that produced a great deal of scholarly discussion concerning miracles and the supernatural gifts of the Holy Spirit. Because of his wide influence, I will deal with his position separately at a later time."

"Yes, I remember Dr. Warfield. He was the author of one of my textbooks," Bill remarked. "He stands as a giant among evangelical Presbyterians."

"Consistent cessationists, the fourth group, insist that not only did miracles cease after the apostles got the church established, but that the five-fold ministries of apostles, prophets, pastors, teachers, and evangelists named in Ephesians 4 ceased to be operational after the transition period following the death of the apostles. I know you don't agree with this position. It has had little influence, and I won't deal with it any further if that suits you."

"That's fine with me. The one that has influenced me the most is classical Cessationism. I believe it is very likely the best known due to its ardent defense by well-known preachers and theologians," Bill said.

"The best defense I found for classical Cessationism was from a professor from your seminary," Viktor said. "He committed his life to Jesus during the turbulent youth revival of the 1970s and became involved in a popular arm of the Charismatic movement that was sweeping across the nation at that time. He was devoted to the Lord and wanted to serve him with all his heart. He ardently sought to be filled with the Holy Spirit in Charismatic fashion but never spoke in tongues. His mentor in the movement belittled him for not receiving the sign gift and questioned his salvation. As a result, he withdrew from the Charismatics but continued his devotion and service to Christ. Eventually he went to seminary, became an ardent cessationist, and is now a seminary professor advancing Cessationism."

"I think I know the professor you are referring to, although there are actually multiple cessationist professors at Dallas Seminary," said Bill.

"I admire him very much and have no doubt that he has been filled with the Holy Spirit without tongues," Viktor continued. "However, his argument for Cessationism is in error. He asserts that no one has the gift of healing today as did the apostles. He acknowledges that on occasion supernatural healing does take place in answer to prayer. However, he insists this doesn't correspond to the gift being resident in a person as it was in Peter and Paul, in which everyone ministered to was healed. I accept this as far as it pertains to the West. Interviews with well-known healing evangelists indicate they admit only a small percentage of those prayed for are actually healed. One of the best known reckoned no more than 10 percent. There is evidence the Holy Spirit has gifted some in other cultures with a phenomenal rate of healing. The gifts of healing may not have been restored to individuals, but they have certainly been restored to the Church. In China, Indonesia, Africa, Latin America, and India, few churches are established apart from response to miracles of healing and/or exorcism of evil spirits. But this begs the question. The professor admits there is no biblical basis for his stance. If God has withheld a gift that he promised, that does not mean that he has withdrawn it. He can still give all his gifts to whom he pleases, whenever he pleases, and where he pleases. To say otherwise is to challenge the authority of our sovereign Lord. I believe the doctrine of Cessationism is an affront to the Holy Spirit's sovereignty. This alone would hinder me from accepting this tradition."

"I have a strong suspicion you have other reasons, as well," said Bill.

"You are right, my friend," said Viktor. "Despite what the Dallas Seminary professor had said, I could scarcely believe there was not a single text of scripture that could serve as a sure foundation for this doctrine. I searched diligently to find one. To my surprise, there was not even one valid proof text that could be offered," Viktor said. "One of the most outspoken advocates of Cessationism is the president of a seminary, pastor of a mega church, and acerbic critic of Pentecostal theology. I'll call him Jacob. I am sure he is a devoted Christian, and there is much to admire in his ministry. But Jake's defense of this doctrine is neither admirable nor believable."

"I think you may be referring to a friend of mine," said Bill. "Where does he go wrong?"

"His whole argument rests upon his erroneous interpretation of 1 Corinthians 13:8–10," Viktor said.

"Are you sure there is no chance that his interpretation is correct?" Bill asked.

"Absolutely," said Viktor. "But you be the judge. Consider verse eight. The NIV translates it this way: *Love never fails. But where there are prophecies, they will cease; where there are tongues, they will be stilled* (Greek, *pausontai;* English, cease)*; where there is knowledge, it will pass away.* Jacob dogmatically asserts that the Greek verb that follows tongues and is translated *will cease* or *will be stilled* means to cease permanently. Jake is desperately trying to prove from scripture that the gift of tongues has been permanently withdrawn from the Church. He errs significantly in two of his conclusions, which he states as facts. If you will follow along with me in your New Testament Greek text, I will point them out."

"This is what I revel in. I love to carefully examine scripture to determine spiritual truth," Bill said. "Go ahead with your exegesis."

"First, his dogmatic assertion that the meaning of the pertinent Greek verb means 'to cease permanently' is simply not true. This verb is used twelve times in the New Testament, first in Luke 5:4 where Jesus is teaching from a boat occupied by Simon Peter and other fishermen. Luke records, *When he had finished (pauo, ceased) speaking, he said to Simon ...* Did Jesus cease speaking permanently? No, of course not. Another typical episode is found in Luke 11:1. Jesus has been praying, and Luke writes, *When he finished (pauo) ...* Did Jesus cease praying permanently? How absurd. Do you agree so far, Bill?"

"I can do nothing else but agree, Viktor," Bill said. "Jacob has given me no ammunition to fire in opposition."

"The second error of Jake is his assumption that the coming perfection in verse ten refers to the completion of the New Testament canon," Viktor said. "Then, he assumes, the gifts of the Spirit are withdrawn since they are no longer needed. There is not an iota of scripture to support this theory.

"It is true that tongues will eventually cease permanently just as gifts of prophecy and knowledge will pass away," Viktor continued. "But that will happen only *when perfection comes.* And when does perfection come? It is obvious from the context that Paul is looking forward to the grand fulfillment of human history when we see our Lord face to face. As Lutheran theologian R.C.H. Lenski aptly said, 'Paul is speaking regarding the consummation when Christ shall return in glory, when the kingdom of grace shall merge into the kingdom of glory.'"

"You allowed the force of the original language and the context to determine the conclusion of your exegesis," Bill said. "Jake is obviously way off base with his conclusions. So far off, I suspect he had already assumed a position and is desperately trying to latch on to a proof text to support it."

"I couldn't have said it better, but you know him much better than I. Anyway, that's the beginning of my search for a biblical foundation for the doctrine that the gifts of the Spirit were withdrawn at the conclusion of the Apostolic Age," said Viktor. "There may be more astute defenders of that position than your friend Jake, so I have more work to do. But now it's your turn, Bill. I'm eager to hear what you have discovered concerning the scriptural foundation for the Pentecostal doctrine that there is no valid baptism in the Holy Spirit unless initially physically evidenced by speaking in tongues. I have wrestled with this myself and have come to some conclusions. But I want to hear the results of your search for biblical truth untainted by my ideas."

CHAPTER 38

BILL'S FIRST REPORT ON TONGUES AS EVIDENCE OF SPIRIT BAPTISM

"Thank you, Viktor," said Bill. "I have been fascinated by my research into the history of modern Pentecostalism. But rather than get caught up in peripheral matters, I have decided to go immediately to the pertinent scriptures that Pentecostals use to support their tradition of speaking in tongues as required evidence of valid Spirit baptism. The primary passage is Acts 2:4: *All of them were filled with the Holy Spirit and began to speak in other tongues as the Spirit enabled them.*

"Tell me, Viktor, what does this verse prove?" Bill asked.

"It proves what happened at the feast of Pentecost following the outpouring of the Holy Spirit upon the 120," Viktor said.

"Yes, it affirms *what* happened, but does it tell us *why* it happened? *Why* did God ordain that they speak in other tongues after they were baptized in the Holy Spirit?" Bill asked. "The question asked by the astonished multitude of pilgrims celebrating the feast of Pentecost was, '*What does this mean?*' They knew *what* had happened. They wanted to know *why* these unschooled Galileans had been supernaturally enabled to speak all the languages represented in the Roman Empire."

"Pentecostals assume that it was evidence of being baptized in the Holy Spirit," Viktor said.

"But that is merely an assumption. What in this passage would lead to that conclusion?" Bill asked.

"There is nothing in this passage, but Acts 8:17 declares the Samaritans next received the Holy Spirit and something dramatic followed. It is commonly assumed that what happened is they spoke in tongues. Then Acts 10:45–46 describes the outpouring of the Holy Spirit upon the Gentile military garrison in Caesarea," Viktor said. "When the Spirit came upon them, they spoke in tongues and praised God just as the disciples did at Pentecost. When Paul met disciples at Ephesus, who had no knowledge of the Holy Spirit, he had them baptized in water in the name of Jesus. As he laid hands on them, the Holy Spirit came on them, and *they spoke in tongues and prophesied.* Don't you think that provides a biblical basis for declaring that every valid Spirit baptism must be accompanied by speaking in tongues?"

"Not at all, Viktor," Bill said. "There is not one shred of biblical evidence upon which to draw this conclusion. On three occasions (Jerusalem, Caesarea, Ephesus), the outpouring of the Spirit was accompanied by speaking in tongues. From this fact, Pentecostals have assumed that Jesus will not baptize in the Spirit without initially authenticating with tongues. They assume that the Samaritans and Saul also spoke in tongues and conclude that this further assumption establishes the validity of their previous assumption. One assumption piled upon another assumption does not establish a scriptural foundation for a doctrine that divides the body of Christ."

"But it is no assumption that a pattern does develop when the Holy Spirit is poured out upon these three people groups. They do all speak in other tongues. Do you acknowledge this pattern?"

"Yes, I certainly do," Bill replied. "But I see an explanation that is truly biblical and one that unites the Church rather than brings division. The pattern I see emerging is that the sign of tongues accompanying the Holy Spirit being poured out upon different people groups is following the concentric circles of humanity that Jesus spoke of in Acts 1:8. First on Jews in Jerusalem at Pentecost; next throughout Judea following the persecution led by Saul; then to Samaria as the persecution spread; next to 'the ends of the earth' as the Spirit was poured out on Roman Gentiles in Caesarea and Asian Gentiles in Ephesus. All of these groups were thought to be unclean and unacceptable by the racist Jewish disciples. If that isn't true, why doesn't Luke say the three thousand converts at Pentecost all spoke in tongues when they received *the gift of the Holy Spirit* as promised by Peter? The original disciples, all Jews, had to be convinced that non-Jewish people groups could be accepted into the Christian community as equals. But since the converts at Pentecost were all Jews or proselytes, they were readily accepted into the church without the imprimatur of tongues."

"Surely the Apostle Paul didn't think the Gentiles in Ephesus were unclean," Viktor said. "Why did tongues accompany their reception of the Holy Spirit?"

"I asked myself that question and prayerfully sought insight from scripture," Bill replied. "I am not sure I found an answer that will satisfy you, but I think it has merit. You will recall that when Paul departed on his second missionary tour, he planned to evangelize the province of Asia of which Ephesus was the capital. The Holy Spirit would not permit him to do so, and Paul and his party circled back to the port city of Troas. There the Lord directed him to go to Europe.

"When Paul completed his European ministry, he sailed from Corinth to Syria. His ship made a port call in Ephesus, and Paul debarked while the ship unloaded cargo and passengers. He visited the local synagogue and dialogued with the Jews. They wanted him to stay longer, but he refused. However, he promised, '*I will come back if it is God's will.*' I believe this last phrase is more than a pious addendum. Paul was still restrained by the command of the Holy Spirit not to do missionary evangelism in the province of Asia.

"After reporting to his home church in Antioch, Paul spent some days there before being assured it was God's will he return to Ephesus. He took a long overland journey back to Ephesus, not evangelizing but 'strengthening the disciples.' He arrives in the city and meets twelve men whom Luke calls *disciples.* Paul questions them and discovers they have no knowledge of Christian baptism, in water or in the Spirit. This is an opportunity for Paul to determine if the ban to evangelize in Asia has been lifted. He teaches them basic truths about Jesus and the Holy Spirit. After they experienced water baptism, Paul lays hands upon them. The Holy Spirit *came on them,* and they *spoke in tongues and prophesied.* I believe this was the Spirit's sign to Paul that he was now free to evangelize Gentiles in Asia. He lost no time fulfilling the desire that had been in his heart for a long time. Luke records that his ministry to Asians in Ephesus went on for two years, *so that all the Jews and Greeks who lived in the province of Asia heard the word of the Lord*. Paul did not have to go from town to town or from village to village to evangelize. The people met him in this teeming commercial center. Paul at last understood why he had been turned away from Asia years previously."

"Bill, that's an exciting concept I had never considered," Viktor acknowledged. "But why do you call the original disciples racists? Isn't that an overly harsh term?"

"It is harsh but true, as scripture clearly depicts," Bill said. "Under the Mosaic law, racism was not only condoned, it was commanded. For several years after Pentecost, the disciples continued living under the Old Covenant and proclaimed that Gentiles must submit to Mosaic rites in order to be saved. Remember Peter's experience at Joppa, about eight years after Pentecost? There God began to break his traditional religious bondage to racism with a dramatic vision that shook Peter to the core of his being."

"My friend, you have certainly done some serious research," said Viktor. "I had never considered the length of time that Peter and the other disciples had remained under the powerful influence of Judaism. Apparently, even Jesus's own example and teaching had not liberated them."

"That's what is so insidious about religious tradition that is not solidly based on scriptural truth," Bill said. "Now let me read Peter's confession of his bondage to racism as he addresses the Gentiles at Cornelius's house: '*You are well aware that it is against our law for a Jew to associate with a Gentile or visit him. But God has shown me that I should not call any man impure or unclean.*' (Acts 10:28) Peter then went on to acknowledge his recent conversion to racial equality: *'I now realize how true it is that God does not show favoritism but accepts men from every nation who fear him and do what is right.'* (Acts 10:35).

"Peter had his eyes opened to his own religious prejudices by the vision of the great sheet lowered from heaven. He publicly confessed to the Gentiles his former superior attitude. But God has one more arrow in his quiver to fire at Peter's arrogance. When the Holy Spirit was poured out unexpectedly on the Gentiles as at Pentecost, God administered the coup de grâce to Peter's bigotry. He surrendered gracefully and opened the door of the church to the Gentiles."

"Bill, I think our search for biblical truth is off to a good start," said Viktor. "I know you have given me a lot to consider concerning our Pentecostal tradition regarding tongues. Let's call it a night."

"I agree," said Bill. "In three months at your place."

CHAPTER 39

VIKTOR'S SECOND REPORT ON CESSATIONISM

January 13, 2009

"Hello, Bill. I can scarcely believe how the months have flown by since we had our first Truth Seekers report," Viktor said.

"Viktor, before we do anything else, let me offer congratulations and say how pleased and excited I am to hear that you and Anna are expecting a child," Bill said. "Jennifer asked a couple of months ago if you had told me about an exciting event that would be celebrated by Christians Together sometime this spring. I had no idea what she was talking about. She asked me again this morning, and I gave the same answer. She said 'Well, if the father isn't going to share the good news, the best friend of the mother will. Viktor and Anna are expecting a baby in early spring.' I was blown away with joy, as I know you must be."

"Bill, I'm sorry I didn't say anything." Viktor said. "I knew Anna had shared the news with Jennifer months ago, and I just assumed she had told you. Yes, I am very excited but don't want to make it too obvious. What's worse than a boastful expectant father. I'm just overwhelmed with gratitude to my heavenly father who invented families. Thanks for your great encouragement and support.

"Let's go ahead get right into our biblical search for truth regarding the topics we designated. Since Dr. Benjamin Warfield seems to be the fountainhead of much of Cessationism, I decided to focus my research on the biblical support he has for his position. Warfield clearly stated his position in the Thomas Smyth lectures entitled *Counterfeit Miracles* he delivered at Columbia Theological Seminary in 1917. These were published as a book in 1918. The first lecture, called "The Cessation of the Charismata," contains his thesis. Briefly stated, it is this: The purpose for which the supernatural gifts were given was solely to authenticate the ministry of the apostles. Thus, when that was accomplished, miracles were no longer needed, and they were withdrawn."

"You are correct about the highly respected Dr. Warfield," Bill said. "He has been the champion for many evangelical cessationists, including some in my congregation. However, my cessationist seminary professors saw the weaknesses of his position and pointed them out, as I am sure you will."

"Although Warfield insisted that the inerrant scriptures were the foundation of his theology, he scarcely referred to any at all to bolster his position," Viktor said. "Since there was no solid biblical basis, he attempted to enlist history on his

side. However, numerous scholarly examinations of histori-
cal records since Warfield show that miracles and gifts of the
Spirit were not universally withdrawn following the end of the
Apostolic Age. Furthermore, Warfield completely discounts
the testimony of Church fathers such as Origen, Tertullian,
Gregory of Nyssa, Chrysostom, Ambrose, and Augustine.
Their association with the Roman Catholic Church annuls
their testimony in his mind."

"I agree that Professor Warfield failed to demonstrate that
the supernatural gifts of the Spirit ceased to operate after the
end of the Apostolic Age. He did have a bias against reported
Catholic miracles," Bill said. "I believe some of it is justified."

"Not only is Dr. Warfield amiss historically, he also distorts
scripture by insisting the only purpose of miracles in the early
church was to authenticate apostolic ministry," Viktor continued. "He accurately and colorfully describes the worship
experience in the Corinthian Church and acknowledges that
this was undoubtedly the pattern of all Christian assemblies
gathered for worship. The gifts of the Spirit were welcomed
and freely exercised. Warfield emphatically declares, 'The
Apostolic Church was characteristically a miracle working
church.' But then he goes on to immediately say, 'These gifts
were not the possession of the primitive Christian as such; nor
for that matter of the Apostolic Church or the Apostolic Age
for themselves; They were distinctively the authentication of
the Apostles ... Their function thus confined them distinctively to the Apostolic Church, and they necessarily passed away
with it.' He makes this grandiose affirmation with no support
from the context of pertinent scripture. He uses Ephesians
2:19–20 as a proof text: *Consequently, you are no longer foreigners
and aliens, but fellow citizens with God's people and members of God's*

household, built on the foundation of the apostles and prophets, with Jesus Christ himself as the chief cornerstone."

"How could this passage cause Warfield to conclude that the gifts passed away at the end of the Apostolic Age?" Bill asked. "Is there something in this verse I've overlooked?"

"Warfield's reasoning went like this," Viktor said. "Apostolic teaching, confirmed by miracles, provided the foundation for the emerging church. Once the church was established on the truth proclaimed by authenticated apostles, there was no longer any need for miracles, and the supernatural gifts were withdrawn. Warfield assumed these gifts had no further function within the church."

"Since there is no scripture to support his assumption, have you discovered scripture that negates it?" Bill asked.

"He does not take into account the following scripture: *I always thank God for you because of his grace given you in Christ Jesus. For in him you have been enriched in every way—in all your speaking and in all your knowledge—because our testimony about Christ was confirmed in you. Therefore you do not lack any spiritual gift as you eagerly wait for our Lord Jesus Christ to be revealed. He will keep you strong until the end, so that you will be blameless on the day of our Lord Jesus Christ.* I Corinthians 1:4–8.

"This Corinthian passage supports the view that the spiritual gifts will continue to minister to the Church until Jesus returns. There is no hint they are to be removed or annulled at the end of the Apostolic Age. Nor does Warfield deal with this Ephesian passage: *But to each one of us grace has been given as Christ apportioned it … It was he who gave some to be apostles, some to be prophets, some to be evangelists, and some to be pastors and teachers, to prepare God's people for works of service, so that the body of Christ may be built up until we all reach unity in the faith and in the knowledge of the Son of God and become mature, attaining the full measure of perfection found in Christ.* Ephesians 4: 7, 11–13.

"These are ministry gifts given by the Holy Spirit to build up the Church," Viktor said. "How long will these gifts continue? *Until we all reach unity in the faith … attaining the full measure of perfection found in Christ.* Has the body of Christ reached unity in the faith or attained Christ's full measure of perfection? Not in my church. Probably not in yours. Certainly they have not been attained in the church at large. That is why we are seeking truth concerning important issues that divide us. Unity is one of the goals our Lord assigned when he called us to be pastors. I'm glad we are working on it together, Bill."

"I know of no one I'd rather be in spiritual unity with than you, Viktor," Bill said.

"I thank God daily for you," Viktor responded. "I relish these opportunities to work together to find a common basis in scripture for an even closer relationship. Let me conclude my investigation of Professor Warfield's scriptural basis for Cessationism. The most detailed teaching on the gifts of the Spirit is in 1 Corinthians 12–14. Dr. Warfield acknowledges that the gifts of the Holy Spirit listed there were quite likely manifested throughout all the churches during the Apostolic Age. He insists their sole purpose was to authenticate the ministry of the apostles, and once that was accomplished, their mission was completed. Warfield advances this grand assumption without the slightest hint from the Apostle Paul that he expected the gifts of the Spirit to be temporary. Dr. Warfield offers no biblical evidence for his full Cessationism.

"That concludes my presentation on Dr. Warfield's stance. I am eager to hear the result of your study of the scriptural basis for the doctrine of evidential tongues in connection with the infilling of the Spirit. Do you have any questions or comments before you begin?"

"I do have a question about the Ephesian passage. Does the gift of apostles end with those commissioned by Jesus or are apostles being apportioned to the church today?"

"As you may know, Bill, there is disagreement about this among some Charismatics," Viktor said. "A few Charismatic groups have spiritual leaders designated as apostles, but their teaching is not authoritative or foundational as is that of those called and commissioned by Jesus. In this one ministry gift, I agree with Professor Warfield. I am a 'limited cessationist' in the sense I believe that the gift of apostles ceased with those Jesus called. In fact, all evangelical believers, including Pentecostals, are cessationists when it comes to this core doctrine. We don't believe that any teaching that adds to or takes away from the New Testament canon is from God. All doctrine is to be measured by its adherence to scripture."

"It is encouraging to hear you say that," Bill replied. "I have heard that some Pentecostals teach that unless one has been baptized in the Holy Spirit, with the evidence of speaking in tongues, he is not a Christian. They claim this is a new truth the Holy Spirit has revealed to them by inspired prophecy."

"Not true," Viktor said. "To my knowledge, no Pentecostal or Charismatic group makes such a claim. It is possible that some small splinter groups have alleged this heresy, but none that I know of."

"Thank you, Viktor. I suspected it was not true concerning salvation, and I'm glad you confirmed it," Bill said.

CHAPTER 40

BILL'S SECOND REPORT ON EVIDENTIAL TONGUES

"These have been exciting months of exploration of scripture," Bill began. "I wrestled with where I might find a solid biblical answer concerning the purpose of speaking in tongues. I was not satisfied with assumptions or prooftexts contrary to the total context of scripture. Where would I look for an answer to the question asked at Pentecost, *What does this mean?* It is crystal clear that tongues did accompany Spirit baptism at Pentecost, Caesarea, and Ephesus. The Bible leaves no doubt about that. But why? What was the purpose of the accompanying tongues? As I pondered this question, I realized this is exactly the question the Apostle Peter had to wrestle with following the Spirit's outpouring in Jerusalem. The thousands of Jewish pilgrims who had come from all over the Roman Empire were thoroughly perplexed by the unexpected sound of their native languages being spoken by unschooled Galileans. They cried out for an explanation to this supernatural phenomenon. Upon hearing their demand for an explanation, Peter knew he must reply."

"Bill, I admire the way you visualize the biblical setting," said Viktor. "You make exegesis come alive. I feel like I am involved in the process."

"That's what I intend," said Bill. "Put yourself in the apostle's shoes. He along with all the other 120 disciples had just been baptized in the Holy Spirit. It had happened just as John the Baptist had predicted and as Jesus had promised. Nothing in the Baptist's prediction or in Jesus's instruction had covered the topic of supernaturally speaking in other languages. Peter certainly was no expert. He was a rank beginner on the subject. After all, the Holy Spirit had been outpoured only minutes before. Peter didn't have a clue as to the meaning of tongues. I believe he breathed an earnest, desperate prayer: "Jesus, you promised that when the Holy Spirit arrived, he would lead us into all truth. He is here, and I claim your promise. What shall I tell these thousands of perplexed people? I am also perplexed. Help me, Holy Spirit."

"I have been in situations like that," Viktor said. "I can sympathize with Peter."

"Jesus kept his word, and the Spirit led Peter to a glorious truth. The apostle was inspired to quote a passage from the prophet Joel. The Old Testament was the authoritative religious "road map" for Jews. Peter's quote from Joel clearly depicts God's purpose for tongues that accompany Spirit baptism. I have no doubt that this text came to Peter by the direct inspiration of the Holy Spirit. The question, "What does this mean?" asked by the amazed and perplexed multitude was prophetically answered by Joel centuries previously. This prophecy is revolutionary and strikes at the heart of traditional Judaism."

"I have never considered Joel's prophecy as revolutionary. What have I missed?" Viktor asked.

"Look carefully at Joel's prophecy the Holy Spirit prompted Peter to quote. *This is what was spoken by the prophet Joel: 'In the last days, God says, I will pour out my Spirit on all people … Everyone who calls on the name of the Lord will be saved.'* These brief statements summarize the essence of the larger quote. It may not seem revolutionary to us, but the implications of this prophecy turned Peter's world upside down. If you examine the text carefully, you will notice that Peter never did comment on or try to explain Joel's words. Joel certainly provides a clear answer to the purpose of tongues, so why did Peter ignore this text? There is a good reason Peter didn't preach from the Joel text. Peter did not explain the text from Joel because he did not believe it, nor was he willing to practice its implications."

"How can you say Peter didn't believe the text?" Viktor asked.

"If you read Luke's account carefully, it is obvious that Peter missed entirely the implications of Joel's prophecy. He was still living under the Old Covenant, although Joel indicated that tongues symbolized the 'last days' had come. The 'last days' was prophetic language for the final era before the Messianic kingdom was established. In other words, tongues marked the transition from the Old Covenant to the New Covenant. Peter was still in bondage to his ancient religious tradition that demanded subjection to Mosaic rites for all candidates seeking salvation. The tenth chapter of Acts dramatically describes how God eventually broke the chains of tradition that bound Peter. Historians estimate the Joppa episode was approximately eight years after Pentecost. Haley's Bible Handbook indicates it could have been as long as ten years. During this interval, the gospel was never taken to the Gentile world."

"Bill, you are opening up biblical truths I have never considered before," Viktor said. "Am I as bound by religious tradition as Peter was? Please continue."

"You of course know that down through the course of Old Testament history prior to Pentecost, the Spirit of God had been active. At various times, he had anointed different individuals with gifts for specific service and ministry, primarily prophets within Israel. However, never had there been an outpouring of the Spirit upon all humanity. At last the fulfillment of Joel's prophecy was at hand. What the inspired prophet had predicted would signal the beginning of the final age (last days) was actually happening in Jerusalem. Thousands watched and listened in wonder and bewilderment."

"I'm beginning to see where you're your exegesis is leading, but I'm not there yet," said Viktor. "Please go on."

"What were the signs that Joel predicted would announce the inauguration of the 'last days'? They are summed up in the first and last statements quoted by Peter. First, instead of selective outpourings of the Spirit upon a few Israelites, there would now be an outpouring on all humanity. There would be no gender barriers, no social, racial, or language barriers that would disqualify a person from being eligible to receive the Holy Spirit. Second, national origin no longer had a bearing upon salvation. It was no longer limited to Jews or Gentiles that converted to Judaism. It depended upon each person's response to God. *Everyone who calls on the name of the Lord will be saved."*

"Are you saying that Joel's 'last days' is the prophetic terminology for what we term the Church Age?" Viktor asked. "So the Holy Spirit at Pentecost ushered in the grace of the New Testament that replaced the law of the Old Testament?"

"Absolutely. The line of demarcation between the Old Covenant and the New Covenant was the outpouring of the Holy Spirit at the feast of Pentecost. Joel indicates the numerous national languages, supernaturally spoken at Pentecost, were the dramatic sign that all language groups were now equally welcome into God's kingdom. From our perspective, we can scarcely imagine how revolutionary this concept was for Peter and the other disciples. They completely failed to grasp what Joel said."

"I think I may be able to imagine it," Viktor said, "but I confess I don't understand it. How do you explain their blindness?"

"The sign of 'other tongues,' pointing to the universality of the gospel, was obliterated by their bondage to their old, outmoded tradition," Bill said. "Peter couldn't explain Joel's prophecy because he was still emotionally, mentally, and spiritually blinded by his biased religious tradition. At this time in his life, despite spending three years under the teaching of Jesus, he was still convinced that only Jews or Gentile converts to Judaism could be saved. His release years later began with a divine 'show and tell' display on a house top in Joppa and culminated in the home of a Roman army officer in Caesarea."

"I'm astonished at the binding, blinding power of religious tradition," Viktor said. "Bill, your search for truth concerning our Pentecostal doctrine relating to evidential tongues has made me realize I may be a victim of religious tradition. I've pledged to follow biblical truth wherever it leads, and I will do so. I know it's truth that sets one free."

"I believe the Holy Spirit had been dealing with Peter's heart over the years since he quoted Joel at Pentecost," Bill said. "When his heart was ready to receive the truth that contradicted his tradition, Jesus sovereignly poured out his Spirit upon the crude, despised soldiers of the Roman occupation army. At last, Peter's fetters were loosened. Without apostolic sanction, without any previous instruction, without any preconceived ideas relating to baptism in the Holy Spirit, these despised Gentiles began to praise God in languages supernaturally uttered. The tongues were not a sign to the Gentiles that they had been baptized in the Holy Spirit. They were a sign to Peter and his Jewish friends that Jesus welcomed Gentiles without Jewish rites. Bound by their tradition, they did not believe Gentiles were eligible to receive the Holy Spirit or be part of God's kingdom without first converting to Judaism.

"The significance of Joel's prophecy, the relevance of the house-top visions in Joppa, and now the surprising outpouring of the Spirit in Caesarea upon Gentiles convinced Peter of the true purpose of tongues. They were the divine sign that no language group, no race, and no nationality is unclean or unacceptable. Having at last gotten the message tongues were meant to convey, Peter ordered that these new Spirit-filled believers be baptized in water and welcomed into the infant church."

"Tell me, Bill, how is it that Peter had such an outstanding ministry in the years leading up to Caesarea despite his faulty theology?" Viktor asked. "Multitudes were won to Christ, and miracles were abundant. How could God so wonderfully bless him?"

"I have come to see that everyone whom God uses has areas of human weakness and is blind to some area of spiritual truth. We have acknowledged that to be so in our own lives, and that is why we are engaged in this dialogue and search for truth. We have determined not to stagnate in a tradition that foments disunity but to earnestly search scripture to see if there is an overlooked biblical truth that can bring us closer together."

"Well stated, Bill," Viktor replied. "I guess I look upon the apostles as spiritual supermen not subject to human foibles and failures like the rest of us mortals."

"There's something else I believe the Lord showed me as I wrestled with this issue," Bill said. "Jesus promised power to those filled with the Holy Spirit. At Pentecost, Peter was anointed with great power by the Spirit. Jesus also promised the Spirit would guide or lead into all truth. Guidance into truth is a process dependent upon following where the Spirit leads. At Pentecost, following his empowering experience, Peter needed guidance to understand the meaning or purpose of the supernaturally uttered languages. The Spirit led Peter to the quotation from Joel that explained their significance. But Peter refused to accept the implications of Joel. To do so would have been, in his mind, sacrilegious. Thus, for approximately eight years, the Gentiles never had the gospel proclaimed to them. If I may say so, Viktor, Peter reminds me of some outstanding Pentecostal preachers I have known."

"Tell me about them," Viktor said. "I have thick skin."

"Like many Pentecostal leaders today, Peter had been baptized in the Holy Spirit and spoke in tongues," Bill said. "He was a powerful and successful preacher. He was anointed with multiple gifts of the Spirit, including discernment, healing, and miracles. Nevertheless, he was absolutely blind to the purpose of tongues although his quote from Joel had clearly revealed it. The tentacles of his outmoded religious tradition still clung tenaciously to his mind and heart. As a result, the growth of the church was crippled, and the great commission was in jeopardy. It took a series of divine interventions as described in Acts 10 to free Peter from his obsessive bondage."

"I must confess that for years I have been aware that there is no solid biblical foundation for our doctrine of tongues," Viktor said. "But I had no explanation for why they accompanied the outpouring of the Spirit at Pentecost and subsequently. Consequently, I never made an issue of it. I'm reluctant to be against something unless I can point to a positive alternative. You certainly have offered a positive alternative strongly supported by scripture. It is a truth that will lead to unity within the body of Christ rather than division. I thank you."

"From our perspective, we can see the future of the church depended on Joel being taken seriously," Bill said. "Otherwise the Christian community would never have been anything other than a small segment of Judaism. Satan gains a foothold when revealed biblical truth is neglected or rejected or misused. Let me say something with which you may not agree. I believe that many of the abuses and aberrations connected with Pentecostalism are the direct result of misidentifying the purpose of tongues."

"How so?" Viktor asked.

"I think it sets a dangerous precedent that encourages more error," said Bill. "Since the doctrine was founded on religious experience and subjective assumptions with no solid basis in scripture, it sets a pattern for similar doctrinal distortions within the Pentecostal orbit," Bill Said. "We have talked

previously about some of the more egregious ones. You have
told me yourself that some Pentecostals are reluctant to confront unbiblical behavior or bad theology lest they 'quench
the Spirit.' It opens the door to some dangerous aberrations."

"Such as?"

"You are going to insist I be specific, aren't you?" Bill said.
"Okay. The most obvious is that branch of Pentecostalism
that denies the Trinity, popularly known as Jesus Only. In my
research, I discovered that the founders of this doctrine declared that their teaching must be true because Jesus Only followers spoke in tongues more than Trinitarian Pentecostals.

"Another aberration we both find deplorable is the 'super
faith' doctrine that leads people to trust in the amount of
faith they demonstrate rather than trust in God. This has led
to needless death when people refused medical help because
it would indicate lack of sufficient faith. It is particularly tragic when parents deprive minor children of medical treatment
that would save their young lives. As a result, the scriptural
truth about faith and healing is contaminated and warped
into something unseemly. If healing is not obtained, it is because of insufficient faith by the one seeking healing. Thus
guilt is added to the suffering.

"Another result of the unscriptural emphasis upon
tongues as evidence of Spirit baptism is a caste system of spiri-
tuality within the local church. Those who haven't had the
experience are relegated to a secondary position. It may not
be intended, but how can it help being otherwise?

"Speaking in tongues has become so important as a sign
of spiritual attainment that it has sometimes degenerated into
a mechanical process. I personally know of a Pentecostal evangelist who specialized in coaching candidates how to speak in

other tongues by manipulating their tongue and lips to help them provide the evidence that proved they were baptized in the Holy Spirit. In my historical resource, I discovered this was a problem a century ago shortly after Azusa Street."

"Unfortunately, pockets of these and other distortions of biblical truth do exist in some churches," Viktor conceded. "These groups are often very vocal and difficult for some pastors to administer biblical discipline or teaching to."

"Which makes my point all the more valid," Bill replied. "If a key doctrine is based on unscriptural assumptions flowing from a religious experience, it is difficult to control other aberrations flowing from unbiblical assumptions proceeding from a religious experience."

"Bill, I think we have given each other enough to think and pray about for a while," Viktor said. "I suggest we conclude our session for tonight."

"I wholeheartedly agree," Bill said. "Your place then next time?"

"Yes indeed," Viktor replied. "Let's see … that will be Tuesday, April 14."

CHAPTER 41

VIKTOR'S THIRD REPORT ON CESSATIONISM

April 14, 2009

"Bill, come in," Viktor said as he answered the door-bell. "I have really been looking forward to this time together."

"I too," said Bill. "At our Truth Seekers meeting in January, I had belatedly learned that you were an expectant father. And now the blessed event has taken place. Again, warmest congratulations to you and Anna on the birth of your son. Before we start sharing the results of our latest search for truth, tell me all about how Anna and the baby are doing and the responses of his big brother and sister."

"Bill, God has blessed me beyond my fondest dreams. Anna is recovering quickly, and the baby is the picture of health.

Incidentally, we have settled on a name, Peter Ivan. Ivan is the Cyrillic spelling for John, so we have named him after two great apostles. The timing of Peter's arrival couldn't have been better. He was born on Friday before Palm Sunday, which was also the Sunday we dedicated our new building. Family and friends from near and far had gathered for the dedication service and were here to welcome little Peter. Andrew and Shana couldn't be more excited or proud. I asked the children to announce the birth of their brother to the throng gathered for the dedication service. Eleven-year-old Andrew read the announcement with eight-year-old Shana at his side. You should have heard the thunderous applause that greeted them. We are going to dedicate Peter to the Lord some Sunday soon, and Anna and I want you to pray the dedicatory prayer. Do you think you could fit that in your schedule?"

"Viktor, I would be so honored to hold that little guy in my arms and dedicate him to the Lord Jesus Christ. Just name the Sunday," Bill replied.

"No," said Viktor. "You check your schedule and choose a Sunday that will be best for you. We will be delighted to accommodate our schedule to yours."

"I will do it," Bill said. "I think one of my associate pastors is scheduled to preach in June. I'll check and get back to you soon. Now we had better get down to business with our agenda for the evening. Are you ready?"

"Yes indeed. We have come a long way in our research and scriptural exegesis relating to two doctrines that produce disunity between our churches," Viktor began. "I believe I have demonstrated Cessationism has no support in scripture. Also, there is ample evidence that spiritual gifts continued in the church centuries after the death of the apostles. Now I want to shift gears and share what I have discovered about the supernatural gifts of the Spirit manifested in the Church today."

"I think the evidence is overwhelming concerning these gifts being operative in the early Church centuries after the death of the apostles," Bill conceded. "They may very well have been manifested in the great revival movements of the eighteenth and nineteenth centuries here in America. I am eager to hear what you have discovered about the supernatural gifts being poured out upon the Church in the twentieth and twenty-first centuries."

"First, let me acknowledge that you have shown convincingly from scripture that we Pentecostals misidentified the purpose of tongues poured out at Pentecost and subsequently, including at Azusa Street," Viktor said. "However, Pentecostals correctly proclaimed that the supernatural gifts of the Spirit were once again manifested among believers with signs and wonders affirming the truth of the gospel. On the other hand, faithful, diligent, and trained biblical scholars clearly saw that the doctrine of tongues as the necessary initial evidence of valid Spirit baptism was birthed by the union of a valid religious experience coupled with invalid assumptions as to its purpose."

"Are you saying the experience of speaking in tongues at Azusa Street was a genuine, supernatural gift of the Holy Spirit?" Bill asked.

"I am. I'm absolutely sure of that on the basis of scripture confirmed by personal experience," Viktor said.

"What is the scripture passage that supports your conviction?" Bill inquired.

"Paul states that tongues will cease when the perfect comes," Viktor said. "We can agree that the perfect has not arrived, ergo the gift of tongues continues. This gift is featured prominently in 1 Corinthians 12–14, and there is no indication it is to be withdrawn or cease to function. The apostle warns against its misuse or abuse but recommends it as a helpful spiritual gift for edifying oneself. He expressly commands that no one forbid tongues."

"Why then was the gift of tongues so vigorously opposed by many reputable Evangelicals?" Bill asked.

"For two reasons," Viktor replied. "The first you have already pointed out by showing we assigned a false and unscriptural purpose to tongues that accompanied the outpouring of the Spirit. Because the assigned purpose was invalid, they assumed the tongues were invalid. Notice how invalid assumptions are multiplied on both sides. The second reason for opposition is based on another assumption as grievous as that of the Pentecostals. Since it was assumed the tongues were invalid, then the supernatural gifts that accompanied the tongues (at Azusa) must be invalid as well. Forgive an overused cliché: you threw away the baby with the bath water."

"Viktor, something just came into focus for me," Bill exclaimed. "May I interrupt and run it by you for your evaluation?"

"By all means, Bill," Viktor replied. "Remember, this is a dialogue not a lecture."

"If the Pentecostals and the cessationists had both listened to scripture concerning the validity of the gift of tongues and then searched diligently for the scriptural purposes assigned this gift, we wouldn't be searching for truth that should have been discovered a century ago," Bill said.

"I think you are right, Bill," Viktor replied. "And there is something else worth a comment. The Pentecostal assumptions led to ascribing an unscriptural, divisive purpose for a valid supernatural experience. The cessationist assumptions led to denying valid supernatural gifts of the Spirit because they had not experienced such gifts. 'If I haven't experienced it, then it must not exist' seems to be their attitude."

"So the purpose for a valid supernatural experience wrongly interpreted can be as dangerous as a lack of supernatural experiences wrongly interpreted," said Bill.

"That's true," Viktor said. "In my research regarding Cessationism, I came across an ironic historic account of the Korean Presbyterian Church. About the same time that Dr. Warfield was publishing the defense of his thesis that supernatural gifts of the Spirit were withdrawn at the end of the Apostolic Age, Korean Presbyterians were experiencing a supernatural outpouring of the Holy Spirit in multitudes of healings a century ago. Presbyterian preacher Ik Doo Kim was a tremendously popular proclaimer of the gospel, which included the good news that Jesus still heals today. It is reported that as many as ten thousand experienced healing as a result of his ministry.

"The Presbyterian missionaries had brought their cessation doctrine with them from America and couldn't believe the reports of supernatural healing. A commission was appointed to evaluate the healing claims. The missionaries were surprised when the commission's report confirmed that genuine miracles of healing had occurred. The Korean Presbyterian Church in 1923 officially rejected the cessationist doctrine that miracles had ceased as proclaimed by the missionaries."

"I wonder how Professor Warfield would have responded to that?" Bill questioned.

"If he were alive today, he would have to respond to a surge of the Holy Spirit's supernatural activity that is reminiscent of first-century Christianity," said Viktor. "For one example, in multiple countries in Africa, supernatural manifestations of the Holy Spirit abound. This was true in the mainline churches as well as among the Pentecostals. The spiritual gifts of healing and discernment of spirits with power to exorcise evil spirits were the most common. The former presiding bishop of the Methodist Church in Ghana was approved as a traveling healing evangelist. Methodists and Presbyterians have cooperated in healing crusades resulting in many testimonies of healings and exorcisms. Much of their church growth was the result of these displays of the power of the Holy Spirit."

"Can you give me information as to how the mainline churches in Africa transitioned from Cessationism to affirming the gifts of the Spirit?" Bill inquired.

"I have information relating to the Methodist and Presbyterian churches in Ghana," Viktor said. "First, let me tell you why these churches and others decided to forsake the cessation doctrine taught by the founding missionaries. Simply put, it was a matter of survival. Members were leaving and joining the Pentecostal or Independent churches in droves. The missionaries had brought the western natural world view to Ghana, and the African's world view proclaimed the supernatural. Africans felt at home in the New Testament world of widespread disease and demonic activity. They looked for churches that had the power to overcome these twin evils."

"As a pastor, I can understand the concern over loss of members. So what steps did the leaders take to stop the bleeding?"

"The Methodists first looked inward and found Methodism was rooted in the supernatural," Viktor replied. "John Wesley's journal relates that demons were cast out and the sick were miraculously healed in his ministry. He writes of supernatural visions and dreams and people falling prostrate under the power of the Holy Spirit while he preached. Next, they established a committee of Ghanaian laymen to look at the strengths of the Charismatic movement and recommend how these could be incorporated into their church in Ghana in keeping with the African worldview and their own history. The Methodist Church began to emphasize healing and deliverance from evil spirits as Wesley had. As a result, the Church started to grow again, particularly in urban areas.

"The Presbyterian Church joined the Methodists and likewise began to minister in supernatural power without speaking in tongues. The lack of tongues made no difference to the Holy Spirit as multitudes were healed and delivered from evil spirits. The huge Ugandan Anglican Church often reported remarkable healings."

"I must admit, I'm intrigued," said Bill. "What else did you discover?"

"China was an interesting study," said Viktor. "The nineteenth and early twentieth centuries produced an influx of Western missionaries. In addition to Christianity with a cessationist bent, they brought with them much of their middle-class culture and biases. In their arrogance, too many demonstrated disdain for Chinese and their culture and refused to give native Christians places of power in the indigenous church. Resentment festered among the Chinese.

"Despite this weakness, they introduced much worthwhile. It was good social welfare but little if any supernatural intervention. This included modern medicine with hospitals and caring doctors and nurses and education and professional training for females. It also included opposition to these cultural evils: foot binding of girls, opium trade, infanticide, child marriage, and sale of children by poor families. Nevertheless, the festering resentment resulted in the Communist government ordering all missionaries to depart in 1953."

"What happened when the missionaries were expelled?" Bill asked.

"Many thought the Chinese Church would die, but it didn't. However, due to the intense persecution and opposition of the Communist government, it did go underground. Believers met secretly as families or in small groups of trusted friends. Bibles were treasured and hidden to prevent confiscation. They began to see scriptural truths the missionaries had never taught them. They were intrigued by the accounts of healings and demonic deliverances and wondered if these were only for the ancients or were available to believers now."

"I have heard that not long after the missionaries left, an explosive growth of the Church took place. Is this not true?" Bill asked.

"It is not true according to a reliable Chinese source," Viktor said. "There was slight growth but far from 'explosive.' The growth surge came after the mid-1980s when the government ceased its fierce opposition to Christianity. The Christians came out of hiding and began to practice what they saw portrayed in the Bible. Dramatic and verifiable healings began to sweep across the countryside. Church after church in village after village came into existence as a result of serious diseases healed in the name of Jesus or evil spirits expelled or both. I want to conclude my report for tonight at this

R Glenn Brown

point. Let me just add, around the world, in Latin America, India, among Muslims in various areas, wherever the Church is experiencing unusual growth, the supernatural ministry of the Holy Spirit is reminiscent of New Testament days. There has been no withdrawal of miracles from the Church."

"The reports from Africa, Asia, and Latin America lead me to agree with you that the gifts of the Spirit are still active today," Bill began. "I am tremendously encouraged to hear that the supernatural gifts are being displayed among main-line churches that reject the Pentecostal tradition regarding tongues. Now that my spiritual eyes have been opened to the biblical purposes for tongues that accompanied the outpour-ing of the Holy Spirit in Jerusalem, Samaria, Caesarea, and Ephesus, I am open to everything God has for me regarding supernatural spiritual gifts."

"That's a big step for you, Bill," Viktor said. "Are you sure? This could have some significant ramifications within your church."

"Viktor, for a long time, I have had a hunger for more of God's supernatural power in my life," Bill said. "But I knew of so much abuse connected with claimed manifestation of the gifts, including gross exaggerations and even counterfeit manifestations. These were all connected with some form of Pentecostalism. I was certain there was no scriptural basis for the doctrine that every valid Spirit baptism must be evidenced by speaking in tongues. It was formulated by Charles Parham and others solely on the basis of religious experience and a series of assumptions concerning the purpose of tongues. I have come to see speaking in tongues can be a valid spiritual gift even when sought for the wrong reason."

"That's beyond big, that's a huge step for you," Viktor said.

"Yes it is," Bill acknowledged "However, I also saw making tongues the sine qua non for validating Spirit baptism is unbiblical and needlessly divisive. Unfortunately, American Pentecostalism clings to its assumed purpose of tongues with utter tenacity. I associated the unbiblical assigned purpose of tongues with the biblical gift of tongues and presumed they were both false. As you said before, I discarded the baby with the bath water.

"Now that God has demonstrated around the world that the acquisition of spiritual gifts and the fullness of the Spirit have nothing to do with tongues, I am open to both tongues and all the gifts of the Spirit. I believe many evangelicals share my hunger for supernatural spiritual gifts, but we want the genuine, not some mechanical or emotionally induced imitation."

"Bill, I believe we are at the point where we can assess the results of our search for truth regarding the two divisive doctrines we have put under the microscope of scripture," Viktor said.

"I agree," Bill replied. "I suggest we also consider actions that we might or should take as a result of our conclusions."

"By all means," Viktor responded. "Our final meeting of this series then will be at your house on July 14. I am sure you will be praying much, as I will, that the Holy Spirit will direct us as we conclude this phase of our search for truth."

CHAPTER 42
THE SEARCH CULMINATES
JULY 14, 2009

"Welcome, Viktor and Anna," Bill greeted his friends. "Yes, welcome and do come in," Jennifer said. "I'm so glad you men decided to include Anna and me in this important final session. I am grateful that Anna's mother could watch the children tonight. I envy her opportunity to hold little Peter. Please come on into our gathering place, as we call it."

"Anna, I can't tell you how pleased I am that Viktor suggested he bring you with him tonight," Bill said. "We need a minister of prayer to intercede for us as we wrestle with important issues. Before Viktor continues with our program, will you please pray for us?"

"Gladly," Anna said. "While we are standing, let's join hands as a symbol of our unity in Jesus Christ."

Anna began to pray with her eyes open as if she were talking to a beloved friend. "Jesus, we welcome you to our meeting tonight. Thank you for sending the Holy Spirit to inspire our thinking and to lead us into your truth. And give us the grace to follow joyfully where you lead. Amen."

"Bill has asked me to suggest how we should proceed tonight," Viktor began. "Over a year ago, we faced issues in our church traditions that prevented us from having the kind of unity in Christ that we both desired. I was convinced that his doctrine declaring that miracles and supernatural gifts of the Holy Spirit were withdrawn at the end of the Apostolic Age was false and without any biblical support. Bill was equally sure that my doctrine that there is no valid baptism in the Holy Spirit unless accompanied by speaking in tongues was not true and had no support within the context of scripture. Using scripture as our ultimate standard of theological truth, we agreed to investigate each other's divisive doctrines.

"Tonight Bill and I will share the results of our biblical and historical research and seek to determine where we go from here. Since we have shared with our wives much of what we have discussed in our search for scriptural truth, we want Jennifer and Anna to participate in this session. We invite them to ask questions or make comments as they desire. I have asked Bill to first share his response to my critique of Cessationism, which is the doctrine that the supernatural gifts of the Spirit have ceased to be active in the Church today as they were in the primitive Church."

"When Viktor and I first talked about the lack of unity within the Evangelical community of churches, I agreed it was a major problem," Bill said. "When he suggested we do something about it, I thought he was dreaming the impossible dream. However, when he further suggested that we begin with our own churches and suggested a feasible plan to make it happen, I knew I had to put up or shut up. I decided to accept the challenge Viktor has already described."

"I remember when Bill came home after making this 'search for truth' agreement with Viktor," Jennifer said. "He was excited because he had found someone who had the same passion for truth that he did. He was eager to begin the search with Viktor."

"In one sense, I knew Viktor had the easier task," said Bill. "Even one of my professors in seminary, an ardent proponent of Cessationism, admitted there was no coherent basis in scripture for this position, and attempts to provide a proof text were exegetically inept. He based his defense, much like Warfield, on the absence of recorded miracles in Church history after the early Church era. However, as Viktor pointed out and I verified, pertinent literature does not support this premise. There are various good books by reputable scholars which show that miracles and supernatural spiritual gifts have occurred at periods throughout the centuries of church history.

"Another effort to deny supernatural gifts was to point out the abuses, exaggerations, and sham representations that characterized some Pentecostals. Viktor acknowledged these existed and deplored them. But he cautioned against discarding the genuine because of the counterfeit. Nevertheless, I was disturbed by these characterizations and didn't want to associate myself with something weird masquerading as a supernatural manifestation of the Holy Spirit. I knew that Paul had warned the Corinthians that there were false apostles who would invade the church influenced by Satan himself who 'masquerades as an angel of light.'

"At this point, I recognized the lack of biblical support for Cessationism, but I didn't want to trade one unscriptural belief for another. I was firmly convinced that the Pentecostal tradition on evidential tongues was false and without biblical support. It was based solely on assumptions and a spiritual experience wrongly interpreted. Nothing I had heard from Viktor up to this time had changed my view."

"As you know, I was not reared as a Pentecostal," Anna interjected. "I always understood that the Pentecostal tradition concerning tongues as required evidence of Spirit baptism was unscriptural and invalid. For me it was always an assumed purpose without merit or biblical basis. However, I knew that the gift of speaking in tongues was scriptural and valid. I also was sure that empowering experiences by the Holy Spirit following faith in Jesus were biblical. In fact, it is a biblical command. Paul enjoined the Christians in Ephesus to keep being filled with the Holy Spirit. Bill, I know you changed your view on Cessationism, but I haven't heard what caused you to do so. Can you share that?"

"I recognized my adherence to Cessationism was ended during Viktor's third report. My heart raced as he described the miracles and supernatural gifts of the Spirit being displayed in developing nations in Africa, Asia, South America, and elsewhere. What really caught my attention was that this was happening among mainline evangelical churches as well as Pentecostals. The fullness of the Holy Spirit was being received in power without any required evidence of speaking in tongues. I was delighted to know this was happening around the world except, sadly, in my own country."

"Bill, can you explain why this isn't happening in mainline churches in America?" Anna asked.

"In my opinion, for the same reason that I hesitated to seek an empowering experience by the Holy Spirit," Bill replied. "Even before I met Viktor, I had concluded the Pentecostal teaching regarding tongues as required evidence of Spirit baptism had no scriptural basis but was based on a series of assumptions coupled to a religious experience. Because the purpose Pentecostals assigned tongues was false, I assumed the whole experience was false. I assumed wrongly. Speaking in tongues is a valid gift of the Spirit, but Pentecostals poisoned the gift by misidentifying its purpose into something that divides the body of Christ and creates a spiritual caste system among Pentecostals themselves. When mainline pastors understand this, I believe many will discard the wrong purpose but retain and value the true spiritual gift. There are actually a few beginning to do this."

"Thank you, Bill. Viktor has told me how insightful and helpful your exegesis of scripture has been. It has helped him immensely to see the error of his tradition. I would love to particularly hear you exegete the pertinent Old Testament scriptures relating to tongues," Anna said.

"First, I want to acknowledge what a great spiritual experience it has been for me to go through this search for biblical truth with Viktor. I have engaged in discussions and even arguments about these divisive issues before but never in a serious search where each was willing to change his view if scripture demanded it."

"Pardon me," Jennifer interrupted. "I thought you had shared everything that you have discussed with Viktor, but I never heard about this. You mean you men agreed to actually adopt the other's view if the Bible supported it?"

"Why, yes," Bill answered. "What else could we do and remain true to our calling? We understood the risk and were willing to take it. We are serious about following scriptural truth wherever it leads. I thought and prayed about how to proceed in my search of scripture concerning the Pentecostal doctrine with which I differed. It suddenly occurred to me the only Bible the first disciples had was the Old Testament. It was there they must look if they were to find an explanation for tongues that accompanied the outpouring of the Holy Spirit at Pentecost and subsequently, and it was there I must look."

"Of course," Anna said. "The New Testament hadn't yet been written. How obvious, and yet I must confess I never considered the Old Testament as the source for truth about tongues."

"When thousands of Jewish pilgrims from across the Roman Empire heard their national languages being spoken at Pentecost by ignorant Galileans, they cried out for an explanation of this supernatural event. The Holy Spirit inspired Peter to quote the prophet Joel. Joel's prophecy clearly and unequivocally explains the purpose of tongues at Pentecost. Joel essentially said that tongues were a sign that the New Covenant had been ushered in. 'The last days' is prophetic language for the final era before the inauguration of the Messianic kingdom. This era will be marked by a radical, revolutionary change in the way God deals with humanity, according to Joel. No longer will Judaism be the channel by which the Holy Spirit speaks to men. The Spirit will now be poured out on every people group, every language, every nation, and every culture around the world. This universality of the Holy Spirit is what the languages at Pentecost clearly symbolized. Joel goes on to say that salvation is no longer limited to Jews and converts to Judaism. Rather, 'everyone who calls on the name of the Lord will be saved.' The supernatural tongues spoken at Pentecost symbolized all the languages of the world where people could call out to the Lord for salvation. I am going to ask Viktor now to respond to this part of my report," Bill said.

"My first reaction to Bill's report was disconcerting," said Viktor. "I was surprised that Bill realized so quickly what I had overlooked for years. I wasn't yet convinced that the purpose we Pentecostals assigned to tongues was unscriptural, but a big question mark had been raised in my mind. I asked Bill about the pattern that followed after Pentecost at Caesarea and Ephesus where tongues followed the outpouring of the Spirit. I said surely that supports the conclusion that speaking in tongues was the evidence of valid Spirit baptism. Bill, do you remember your response?"

"Yes, indeed. I said there is a much better explanation for the pattern of tongues accompanying these outpourings of the Holy Spirit. It is not based on assumptions but on the words of Jesus and the prophet Joel. The Holy Spirit is being poured out in keeping with the concentric circles of humanity Jesus spoke of in Acts 1:8: First on Jews in Jerusalem. Then on Jews throughout Judea as persecution scattered the church; then to Samaria as the persecution spread; then to the 'ends of the earth' as the Spirit fell upon Roman Gentiles in Caesarea and Asian Gentiles in Ephesus.

"The tongues that accompanied Spirit baptism at Pentecost symbolized the languages of all nations, people groups, and cultures around the world who were now eligible to be part of God's kingdom apart from Judaism. Tongues were a symbol of the universality of the Church and promoted unity within the body of Christ. They were a sign to the racist Jewish disciples that Judaism was no longer the door giving access to the kingdom of God. Christ is the door, and all people groups are welcome to enter through him. Requiring tongues as the evidence of valid Spirit baptism is based on invalid assumptions with no scriptural support and leads to needless division within the body of Christ."

"We Pentecostals have always used Acts 2:4 as the basis for our doctrine," said Viktor. *"All of them were filled with the Holy Spirit and began to speak in other tongues as the Spirit enabled them.* Your explanation of that text undermined my confidence in it and clearly showed our assigned purpose was assumed with no biblical support. Please summarize it again for Anna and Jennifer."

"As I explained in our first meeting, this tells what happened at Pentecost, but it doesn't tell why it happened," Bill replied. "It doesn't give a clue as to the purpose for tongues. The thousands of bewildered Jewish pilgrims heard uneducated peasants from Galilee speaking all the languages represented in the Roman Empire. They knew something supernatural was happening, and they sought an explanation. 'What does this mean?' was their cry. Peter's quote from Joel was the Spirit's answer to that question. I thought it strange that Peter never expounded on the quote from Joel. Why not? As I studied the historical context, I was startled by the answer Luke provides. Peter couldn't expound on the text because he didn't believe it. At this time in his life, to declare that Gentiles were welcome into the Church, without first converting to Judaism, would have been sacrilegious."

"That's astounding to hear you say that," Anna said. "I can't remember ever hearing that before. Are you sure?"

"I'll say something you may think even more astounding," Bill replied. "None of the other disciples believed Joel either.

They would have been offended if Peter had believed and declared the truth of Joel's prophecy. From today's perspective, Peter and the other disciples would be called racists. They considered all Gentiles unclean. None could be saved unless they converted to Judaism. Let me show you how scripture led me to these conclusions. One of the reasons I believe the Bible is inspired is because of its utter honesty in revealing the truth about renowned leaders. Several years went by after the events at Pentecost to the events described later in Acts. Historians estimate up to ten, although seven or eight is considered more likely. During all of these years, the disciples declared the gospel only to Jews or converts to Judaism called proselytes. We know this from what is described in Acts 10 and 11, as you will see if you read the account carefully. It took a dramatic 'show and tell' display in Joppa and the unexpected outpouring of the Holy Spirit in Caesarea to get Peter's attention and free him from his bondage to an errant religious tradition."

"Aren't you overly harsh when you label Peter and the other disciples racists?" Jennifer asked.

"You may be right if I had called them that before the New Covenant had been ushered in by the Holy Spirit at Pentecost," Bill replied. "But the covenant of law had served its purpose and had been superseded by the covenant of grace. Years passed before the disciples were able to accept the implications of the New Covenant. It is a striking illustration of how difficult it is to break free from an erroneous religious tradition. I have found that true in my own life."

"By this time, Bill had convinced me from scripture that our Pentecostal tradition concerning the purpose of tongues at Pentecost was invalid," said Viktor. "A great weight was lifted as I saw a vastly superior purpose that would unify the Church and motivate her to take the gospel in the power of the Holy Spirit to all languages in every nation. Now that I understand tongues are not the problem, but the purpose we assigned tongues, I can discuss this spiritual gift without creating an argument or bringing division. I rejoice in my new freedom. Also, an area of disagreement between Anna and me has been resolved, and we thank you with all our hearts."

"I knew that Viktor's Pentecostal tradition was based on assumptions and a wrongly interpreted proof text," Anna broke in. "And I told Viktor this. But he always answered, 'Tell me, then, what is the purpose of tongues that accompanied the outpouring of the Spirit at Pentecost?' I didn't have an answer, but I knew there must be one somewhere in scripture. I see it so clearly now in the Old Testament prophecies of Joel and Isaiah as quoted by Peter and Paul. Joel indicates all the languages supernaturally spoken at Pentecost symbolized all the languages of the world where the Spirit would be outpoured and the gospel would be proclaimed. Paul depicts Isaiah's prophecy concerning tongues at Pentecost as a supernatural sign to unbelievers, not to believers. I believe this marvelous symbol of the universality of the gospel is depicted in the prophetic vision of John: *After this, I looked, and there before me was a great multitude that no one could count, from every nation, tribe, people and language, standing before the throne and in front of the lamb. They were wearing white robes and were holding palm branches in their hands. And they cried out in a loud voice: 'Salvation belongs to our God, who sits on the throne, and to the Lamb.'*"

"Jesus said the Holy Spirit would lead us into truth," Bill said. "Viktor and I have experienced the reality of this promise. We didn't know our destination when we pledged to follow wherever the Spirit directed. As you know, the light of scripture has revealed error in both our traditions. Now we must determine how we are going to respond to the truth we have seen."

"I have given this prayerful thought," said Viktor. "I long to see our congregations experience the unity in Christ that Bill and I now enjoy. Here is a starting point for discussion. What if we get our congregations together and Bill and I share our journey with them?"

"At some point, this will be necessary," Bill said. "But I am not sure we should do this immediately. Why not start with our key leaders and get their responses? We will then be better prepared to share our search for scriptural truth with our congregations. Anna and Jennifer, please join the discussion. I know each of you has given this some thought."

"We have thought and prayed about it together," Anna said. "The dark powers will try to destroy the unity that the Holy Spirit has provided you. We are going to mount a prayer assault against the forces of evil that plot the destruction of everything wholesome and good in this city. These devilish forces will particularly try to thwart unity within the body of Christ and to promote everything that fosters division between churches and disunity within churches. Jennifer and I have agreed to lead a small prayer group of individuals carefully selected from each congregation. They will dedicate themselves to intercede earnestly for God to guide you in all your deliberations and decisions. So press forward in the power of the Holy Spirit. We have your back," Anna concluded with a smile.

An awesome sense of God's presence suddenly filled the room. All four dropped to their knees in worship, acknowledging the presence of the almighty Creator in their midst. They waited in hallowed silence, filled with an indescribable joy and peace. After a few moments, each began to audibly worship. With hands raised, they expressed a willingness to trust and follow Jesus Christ wherever he led them. Enthralled by the experience of his presence, they arose and embraced each other. They knew they had experienced a fresh infilling of the Holy Spirit.

"Our Lord is gloriously alive," Viktor said softly. "Sometimes I think he sends a bit of heaven's atmosphere down just to make us homesick. But we can't bask here. The Holy Spirit has filled and empowered us for the tasks that lie ahead. Let's be about our Father's business."

"Amen, my friend, amen," Bill responded. "Many of my people have never known the intimacy with Jesus that we experienced tonight. God helping me, that will change."

The couples bid each other goodnight and parted, rejoicing in spirit.

CHAPTER 43
ADDENDUM
BY PASTOR BILL BALLARD

July 15, 2014

I am sitting in my study reminiscing. I can hear Jennifer stirring around in the kitchen preparing dinner. It scarcely seems possible that only eight years have passed since I first met my close friend and confidant, Viktor Gorgachuk. I feel like I have known him all my life. In these intervening years, we have poured our hearts out to each other and developed an unbreakable trust relationship. I once said, "Of all the people I have known, none has impressed me as much nor influenced me more than a Russian immigrant by the name of Viktor Gorgachuk." That statement is just as true today, or more so, than when I wrote it years ago.

Viktor asked me to draw some loose ends together before we conclude. Viktor and I shared our truth journeys with our congregations. Both of our churches lost a few members initially, but soon new arrivals more than compensated. There was a wonderful spirit of unity that prevailed throughout the congregations and between Sundale Community Church and Christians Together. It was as if the Holy Spirit had replicated within the congregations the unity between the pastors. The presence of God was evident in every service. At times, an awesome sense of conviction of sin settled over the people, and many knelt at their seats and wept tears of repentance.

Not only were people repenting and committing their lives to Jesus Christ, but people were experiencing supernatural deliverance from various diseases and addictions. Following the example of Jesus, those healed were told not to broadcast what had happened and thereby draw attention to themselves. Rather, they were counseled to continue to live and work as they were accustomed to among those who knew of their bondage to disease and/or addiction. When their close associates began to question them about the dramatic change they saw, then they should share what Jesus had done for them. Thus, the testimony was given in response to questions initiated by friends and family members. This accomplished two things. First, the deliverance was observed over a period of time, lending credibility. Further, the testimony targeted a given circle of acquaintances and multiplied its influence. The curiosity of many was aroused, prompting them to visit the church where their friend or family member was healed. This resulted in more conversions and further expansion.

The years 2010 through 2012 were years of tremendous growth. Christians Together's new sanctuary was obviously going to be outgrown after a few years. The gymnasium accommodated the overflow with closed-circuit TV for more than a year. By the end of 2012, two services on Sunday were necessary in both churches. Viktor and I knew we must do something that would permit growth to continue outside the confines of our buildings. We got together with our associate pastors and elders for a day of bouncing ideas off one another.

Somebody suggested we consider satellite gathering places rather than enlarging present facilities. That struck a chord, and we discussed the various possibilities. We ended up deciding that we should concentrate on four satellite locations in different areas of the city. Pastors would be selected by a joint pastoral search team from candidates on our pastoral staffs as well as from other candidate applicants. Volunteers from the mother churches who lived near a satellite would comprise the initial congregations of the satellite churches.

We presented the vision to our congregations, and their positive response encouraged us to proceed full speed ahead. We were able to rent Seventh Day Adventist churches for three satellite areas. A private college auditorium was rented for the other. The joint pastoral search team for satellite congregations selected two pastors from outside candidates. Two were selected from candidates within our pastoral staffs, one from each church. Our people responded enthusiastically and selflessly to this new arrangement. We announced on the fifth Sunday of each quarter everyone from both mother churches and the four satellite churches would come together for a massive fellowship rally in a designated college sports arena. The announcement was roundly applauded, and the rallies have proved to be all we hoped for.

We didn't seek outside attention, but eventually the media got involved in reporting how two mega evangelical churches, formerly opposed in significant doctrines, became so united and supportive of each other. A local independent TV station interviewed Viktor and me, and we were able to share our search for biblical truth that brought about our unity. The *Bee* sent a reporter to interview us, and not long after, a national religious periodical featured our story. Inquiries began to pour in from across the state and then the nation. Viktor suggested we jointly sponsor a symposium for interested pastors to come and dialogue with us. I readily agreed.

Three hundred pastors registered for the symposium conducted November 8–9, 2013. It was a cross section of evangelical preachers ranging from traditional Pentecostals to ardent cessationists. Viktor and I shared the stories of our search for biblical truth about opposing and divisive doctrines. Questions or comments were then invited.

"I am pastor of a large Pentecostal church in the Midwest," a pastor spoke up. "I believe my denomination has inherited a tradition that clearly misidentifies the purpose of tongues that accompanied the outpouring of the Spirit at Pentecost. If I preach or teach that the denominational position is not supported by scripture, I will be dismissed, and it will create havoc in my church. I am in a quandary as to what I should do. Any suggestions?"

"I have talked to many pastors associated with your denomination," Viktor answered. "Several are struggling with the same issue, and there is no easy solution. All are good men who love God and the people in their congregations.

Speaking in tongues is not the issue. It is the purpose assigned to evidential tongues that is erroneous and divisive, as I discovered from Pastor Bill's insightful exegesis. The biblical purpose given tongues is far greater than that bequeathed by Charles Parham and his devotees a century ago. The ideal solution would be for the denomination to modify its doctrinal statement to correspond to the purpose for tongues expressed by Joel and quoted by Peter at Pentecost. I'm convinced that many more people would then welcome the infilling of the Holy Spirit and the supernatural manifestation of his spiritual gifts."

"I agree, that would be the ideal solution," the pastor responded. "That has been tried, but it has never succeeded in coming to the floor for debate. I don't see this as a solution in the near future. Any other suggestions?"

"All I can do is affirm truth you already know and then share my own experience," Viktor said. "The truth you know is this: If you are willing to follow wherever he leads, the Holy Spirit will direct your steps and lead you aright. You will never regret responding positively to truth quickened by the Spirit. When I committed myself along with Pastor Bill to follow the truth of scripture wherever it led, I had no idea this would lead me to a significant doctrinal shift. In my journey, I discovered that I could no longer affirm the Pentecostal tradition that valid Spirit baptism must have the initial evidence of speaking in tongues. I knew I must share this with the church leadership and let the chips fall where they may. Almost all of my associate pastors and elders were traditional Pentecostals.

"When I shared the process that led to my change of doctrine, three of the nine elders resigned. They were not even willing to research scripture with me. My associate pastors and the other elders enthusiastically saw and affirmed the truth of what I presented. When we shared with the congregation, only a smattering left. In a matter of weeks, we had gained many more than we lost. I realize that being pastor of a church tied to a loosely organized fellowship is much different from being part of a tightly controlled denomination. I was at peace through the process because I knew my security rested in God's hands and not in the church … as does yours. Find trusted brothers to pray with and for you. When you genuinely surrender to follow the Spirit's guidance wherever he leads, you will be at peace, although the answer may not come immediately. I will be praying for you."

"Thank you, Brother Viktor. If I may, I have a follow-up question?"

"Please continue," Viktor replied.

"How did the traditional Pentecostal pastors of immigrant churches respond to your search for truth?"

"I was hoping you wouldn't ask that," Viktor said. "It's a painful subject. Many of the older pastors accuse me of betraying them and refuse further fellowship. The younger pastors, by and large, are open to Bill's solid exegesis of scripture and an interpretation that leads to unity in the body of Christ. Several of them have requested to meet with us for dialogue. We will see where the Spirit leads us."

"I have a question for Bill," said another pastor. "What caused you to change your mind about the manifestation of supernatural gifts of the Spirit in the church today?"

"For years, I assumed that the miraculous was withdrawn from the Church when the New Testament canon was completed and the church established," Bill said. "I had been taught this by respected seminary professors. A sliver of doubt began to creep in when I got acquainted with Viktor and heard his miracle stories. On the other hand, I had observed exaggerations, false claims, TV quackery, and misuse of proof texts among some Pentecostals, which lent support to my assumption. Of course, I overlooked the multitudes of Pentecostal believers who genuinely loved the Lord and served him well despite their divisive doctrinal error. I made the mistake of discarding the valid supernatural gifts of the Spirit along with the invalid purpose of tongues. Or, as the old cliché goes, I threw out the baby with the bath water. Deep in my heart, I wished I was wrong about the spiritual gifts. I thirsted for more of God's power.

"As Viktor pointed out to me, nowhere in scripture is there a hint that the gifts were ever withdrawn by God. More than that, missionaries visiting my church spoke of dramatic miracles taking place regularly on the mission fields of China, Africa, or India. I falsely assumed these reports were from Pentecostals and figured they were unreliable. To my surprise, I discovered that mainline missionaries were being filled with the Spirit without any evidence of tongues. Gifts of healing and casting out of evil spirits were abundantly evident in their ministry, and many converts resulted after this evidence of God's supernatural presence. Also I discovered there were multitudes within the worldwide Pentecostal/ Charismatic community who did not insist Spirit baptism must be validated by tongues.

"This made me realize I could be filled and empowered by the Holy Spirit without becoming entangled in an unbiblical doctrine subject to multiple abuses. This gloriously freed me to open my heart to the fullness of the Holy Spirit. As a result, my ministry and my church have been revolutionized.

We expect and experience supernatural expressions of God's presence with physical healings, deliverance from various addictions, and exorcism of demonic powers. We neither believe nor teach that tongues must validate Spirit baptism. We do believe and teach that speaking in tongues is one of the gifts bestowed by the Spirit. As a result, numerous former cessationists now welcome this gift as a prayer language they can exercise for personal edification."

"God blessed the Pentecostals despite their unbiblical teaching about the purpose of tongues," said another pastor. "Don't you think that strange?"

"Not at all," Bill replied. "He blessed Peter with multiple supernatural gifts following Pentecost despite the fact that Peter was still racially biased and would continue ministering under Old Testament legalism for most of another decade. God doesn't limit his blessings to those who have purity of doctrine but to those who have purity of heart. But if Peter had not chosen to eventually reject his erroneous doctrine, it would have been disastrous for the future of Christianity. Fortunately, God got his attention in a Roman army garrison at Caesarea following a dramatic rooftop revelation in Joppa. He belatedly accepted the truth of Joel's prophecy, which he had quoted years previously ... but then rejected. At last he saw tongues at Pentecost signified all the languages of the world where the gospel was to be freely proclaimed in the power of the Holy Spirit. I believe Pentecostals will eventually follow Peter's example and align themselves with sound biblical doctrine and bring healing to a major division in the Church."

"I have a comment and a question for Viktor," said a lady participant. "It seems to me there are legitimate differences of opinion about certain issues or doctrines. How do you determine whether a tradition or doctrine should be rejected?"

"You are certainly correct," Viktor said. "There are numerous issues on which Christians can differ and still have spiritual unity. For example, the interpretation of end-time events, the mode of serving communion, regulations pertaining to food and drink (Paul faced this one, Romans 14–15). In our church, we have people with differing convictions in all these areas as well as others. Nevertheless, we have marvelous unity and love throughout the congregation.

"Within scripture, I see two tiers of issues that should not be countenanced. The first tier is a belief system that denies a cardinal scriptural truth. Examples of such truths would include one God revealed in three persons, Father, Son, and Holy Spirit; the incarnation of God by the Holy Spirit via the virgin Mary; the price of human redemption paid by Jesus on the cross; the resurrection of Jesus from the dead; spiritual rebirth by faith in what Jesus Christ accomplished through his death and resurrection. These are not all the cardinal truths but illustrate what I mean by the first tier.

"The second tier of issues that produces disunity and needs to be discarded is based on ignorance of scripture and/or human pride and egoism. It is found within different Christian denominations in which one secondary issue has been made a primary issue for fellowship. Some may even make it the key issue. Adhering to the secondary issue exalts one to a place of spiritual superiority that other 'mere Christians' have not attained to. The church then becomes a religious system bent on promoting the secondary issue no matter how divisive. This is how I see it. Hope that clarifies it some?"

"It does, and I thank you."

"I have another question for Brother Viktor," said a man who was waving his hand vigorously.

"Yes sir," Viktor said. "We will take time to respond to this last one. Please state your name and church followed by your question."

"I am Jess Jones and I pastor a growing Baptist church in the great state of Alabama. You and Pastor Bill have seen a remarkable explosion of new converts flooding your churches. If I understand scripture we are commanded to make disciples, not just converts. How do you bring these new Christians into maturity so that they are genuinely committed disciples of Jesus Christ?"

"A great question, Pastor Jones," Viktor said. "Bill and I have spent hours praying about and discussing that very thing. I must confess, I have not done very well making disciples out of converts. Just this past week I believe God brought a book to my attention by a visiting missionary from a Middle Eastern Muslim country. He recommended a book **called MIRACULOUS MOVEMENTS. You can order the book from Amazon. I ordered a dozen copies immediately for myself and staff and for Bill and his staff. Bill, please share with Jess your response to this book.**"

"With pleasure," said Bill. "Jess, the concepts about making disciples shared in this book are so revolutionary and 'out of the box' that I was astounded. It turned my thinking upside down on my approach to this subject. Perhaps I should say, 'right side up'. I am open to some serious experimentation on the approach it presents."

"Thanks, Bill. I believe the principles presented in this book can revolutionize our traditional way of making disciples.

Starting next week, Bill and I are going to analyze the process that MIRACULOUS MOVEMENTS presents to see if there is a biblical foundation or precedent for each step. If so, we have agreed to experiment by applying what is called the DISCOVERY BIBLE STUDY method in each of our churches.

"If we have whetted your appetite for more information I suggest you first read MIRACULOUS MOVEMENTS. Consider forming a partnership with a trusted pastor friend to pray about and discuss the ideas presented in the book. Whatever you do undergird it with much prayer. Go slowly and lay a good foundation for whatever course of action you take. Perhaps in a year or so we will want to come together and share what God is doing to help us make disciples that are involved in growing the kingdom of God. In the meantime we can pray, study and work together as brothers and sister to learn and apply what God wants to teach us.

"It is time to stop," said Viktor glancing at his watch. "But I believe the Holy Spirit wants us to conclude in prayer. Will three of our visiting pastors lead in prayer as the Spirit directs. Then pastor Bill will dismiss us with God's blessing. Let us pray."

Three pastors, obviously moved upon by the Holy Spirit, prayed with fervor and conviction. Before the third prayer was concluded some men and women had dropped to their knees. A spirit of worship and an awesome sense of God's presence saturated the very atmosphere. Pastor Bill stepped to the microphone to lead in the dismissal blessing.

"We are on holy ground, my friends. The God of the universe whom we dare call our Father through the merits of his Son, has placed his imprimatur upon our gathering. His Spirit has ignited our hearts with fresh love for Him and

for one another. Now go serve Him who is able to keep you from falling and to present you before his glorious presence without fault and with great joy---to the only God our Savior be glory, majesty, power and authority, through Jesus Christ our Lord, before all ages, now and forevermore! Amen."

Viktor and I were blessed by the interaction and dialogue in the November symposium. We are earnestly pursuing the goal we set for ourselves to develop an effective, scriptural method of making disciples. The Lord used the book **'MIRACULOUS MOVEMENTS'** to open our eyes to an "out of the box" method of growing disciples. I think it will be sometime in 2015 before we are ready to have another symposium and share what God has taught us about making disciples and producing unity in the body of Christ.

I don't know what the Lord has in store for us or his Church. Viktor sees the present efforts of secularism to stifle historical American freedom of religion as the first step toward the introduction of an anti-Christian, socialistic society. He views a united Church, committed totally to the lordship of Jesus Christ and to fellow believers, as the only realistic defense against this slide into moral chaos. He loves America but sees the seeds of her deterioration being broadcast by propagators of humanistic materialism and moral relativism, ideologies that have chipped away at our moral foundation. That's what drives him to vigorously promote Christian unity. He is even more zealous since the birth of his son.

Viktor remembers vividly the same socialistic propaganda that constantly flooded the society in which he was reared. He doesn't want his children subjected to the pressures that intimidated many in his native land. He is confident that a praying church, united in love to Jesus Christ and one another, can ignite the fires of spiritual renewal. Anna stays at home more now that she has an infant to care for. Nevertheless, she squeezes out time to help organize and train leaders for intercessory prayer teams in churches throughout the city. She is passionate about the necessity of persistent prayer as a prerequisite for revival accompanied by moral transformation. She is heavily engaged in prayer for her native land of Ukraine as it is threatened by encroachment from Russia.

Viktor assures me the Father will eventually answer his Son's "deathbed" request for unity. He thinks it may take an onslaught of persecution by a depraved world system to separate the wheat from the chaff. He has lived through that very thing, and he is not intimidated by the prospects. Divisive and unscriptural religious traditions will be abandoned as the attacked Church coalesces around the core of Christian truth. The dark depravity produced by a God-defying society will result in an opportunity for the light of the gospel to shine forth with increased brilliance. The eternal truths of the incarnation, the cross, the resurrection, the outpouring of the Holy Spirit, and the anticipation of God's everlasting kingdom will provide beacons of hope emerging from the humanistic morass of despair.

Jennifer and I face the future unafraid, regardless of world conditions. We know that God will have the last word and his kingdom will eventually be established. Sundale Community Church is vigorously alive in the power and presence of the Holy Spirit. The Spirit has enriched our lives and ministry more than we once thought possible. Viktor and Anna continue to inspire us by their devotion to Jesus Christ, to his church, and to one another. Our lives are entwined with theirs in a spirit of love and unity, and we will be forever grateful to our Lord for bringing us together. We are humbled to learn that the story of our search for biblical truth leading to unity has challenged others to follow our example. We pray with Jesus, *"That all of them may be one, Father."* Amen.

Made in the USA
San Bernardino, CA
11 October 2014